Praise for
The Stars Now Unclaimed

"A dazzling debut . . . not to be missed."　　　—*Booklist* (starred review)

"The only thing more fun than a bonkers space battle is a whole book packed with bonkers space battles. Come for the exploding spaceships, stay for the intriguing universe."　　　—Becky Chambers, author of
The Long Way to a Small, Angry Planet

"Pirates, smugglers, soldiers, spies, snarky spaceships, and really big guns . . . and that's just the first chapter. The action gets bigger, the stakes get higher, and I loved it!"　　　—Claire North, author of
The First Fifteen Lives of Harry August

"Robot priest. Yeah, you could read this book for the engrossing world-building or for the fascinating characters, but all I needed was ROBOT PRIEST."　　　—Mur Lafferty, author of *Six Wakes*

"A nonstop SF actioner, *The Stars Now Unclaimed* is a roller-coaster of a read and thoroughly enjoyable debut."—Jamie Sawyer, author of the Lazarus War series

"A total blast to read."　　　—Rob Boffard, author of *Tracer*

"What happens when you put a war-weary soldier, an AI preacher, and a telekinetic girl on the same ship? You end up saving the galaxy, or a small part of it, anyway. Williams's debut novel, *The Stars Now Unclaimed*, is a massive, galaxy-spanning tale of war, betrayal, friendship, and the kind of commitment people make to a better future even at the cost of their own lives. You don't want to miss this amazing, kick-ass book."　　　—K. B. Wagers, author of *Behind the Throne*

"Jane Kamali is a kick-ass heroine who gets the job done and never loses her sense of humor. . . . The action is nonstop, and filled with brilliant and unexpected laugh-out-loud moments. *The Stars Now Unclaimed* is a sci-fi thrill ride from start to finish."

—Catherine Cerveny, author of *The Rule of Luck*

"*The Stars Now Unclaimed* is a fast, fun, and heartfelt adventure through a truly unique universe. From the first page to the last, it's impossible to put down."

—K. S. Merbeth, author of *Bite*

ALSO BY DREW WILLIAMS

A Chain Across the Dawn

THE
STARS
NOW
UNCLAIMED

Drew Williams

TOR

A TOM DOHERTY ASSOCIATES BOOK
New York

THE STARS NOW UNCLAIMED

Copyright © 2018 by Drew Williams

A Tor Book
Published by Tom Doherty Associates
175 Fifth Avenue
New York, NY 10010

www.tor-forge.com

Tor® is a registered trademark of Macmillan Publishing Group, LLC.

The Library of Congress has cataloged the hardcover edition as follows:

Williams, Drew (Science fiction author), author.
    The stars now unclaimed / Drew Williams.—First edition.
        p. cm.
    "A Tom Doherty Associates book."
    ISBN 978-1-250-18611-9 (hardcover)
    ISBN 978-1-250-18612-6 (ebook)
    1. Gifted children—Fiction.   I. Title.
    813'.6—dc23   2018288959

ISBN 978-1-250-18613-3 (trade paperback)

Our books may be purchased in bulk for promotional, educational, or business use. Please contact your local bookseller or the Macmillan Corporate and Premium Sales Department at 1-800-221-7945, extension 5442, or by email at MacmillanSpecialMarkets@macmillan.com.

First Edition: August 2018
First Trade Paperback Edition: April 2019

Printed in the United States of America

0 9 8 7 6 5 4 3 2 1

For Sara

ACT
ONE

CHAPTER 1

I had Scheherazade drop me on top of an old refinery, rusted out and half-collapsing. Around me the stretch of this new world's sky seemed endless, a bright sienna-colored cloth drawn over the stars above. I watched Schaz jet back off to orbit—well, "watched" is probably a strong word, since she had all her stealth systems cranked to high heaven, but I could at least find the telltale glint of her engines—then settled my rifle on my back and started working my way down, finding handholds and grips among the badly rusted metal.

It's surprising how used to this sort of thing you get; the climbing and jumping and shimmying, I mean. On a world free of the effects of the pulse, none of that would have been necessary—I would have had antigravity boots, or a jetpack, or just been able to disembark in the fields below: scaling a three-hundred-foot-tall structure would have been as easy as pressing a button and dropping until I was comfortably on the ground.

Now, without all those useful cheats, it was much more physically demanding—the climbing and jumping and shimmying bits—but I didn't mind. It was like a workout, a reminder that none of that nonsense mattered on the world I was descending toward, and that if I wanted to stay alive, reflexes and physical capability would be just as important as the few pieces of tech I carried that were resistant to post-pulse radiation.

By the time I made it down the tower I'd worked up a decent sweat, and I'd also undergone a crash course in the physical realities of this particular planet: the vagaries of its gravity, of its atmosphere, that sort of thing. Most terraformed worlds were within a certain range in those kinds of measurements—on some, even orbital rotations had been shifted to roughly conform to the standard galactic day/night cycle—but it's surprising how much small differences can add up when you're engaged in strenuous physical activity. A touch less oxygen in the air than you're used to, a single percentage point of gravity higher or lower, and suddenly everything's thrown off, just a bit. You have to readjust.

I checked my equipment over as I sat in the shadow of the refinery tower, getting my breath back. Nothing was damaged or showing signs of the radiation advancing faster than I would have expected. I had a mission to complete here, yes, but I had no desire to have some important piece of tech shut down on me at an inopportune time and get me *killed*. Then I wouldn't be able to do anyone any good.

As the big metal tower creaked above me in the wind, I kept telling myself that—that I was still doing good. Some days I believed it more than others.

After I'd recovered from my little jaunt, I settled my rifle onto my back again—a solid gunpowder cartridge design common across all levels of post-pulse tech, powerful enough that it could compete with higher-end weapons on worlds that still had a great deal of technology intact, low-key enough that on worlds farther down that scale like this one, it wouldn't draw undue attention—and set off across rolling plains of variegated grass.

This world was very pretty; I'd give whoever had designed it that. The sky was a lovely shade of pinkish orange that would likely shift into indigo as night approached. It perfectly complemented the flora strains that had been introduced, mostly long grasses of purple or green or pink, with a few patches of larger trees, mostly Tyll-homeworld species, thick trunks of brown or gray topped by swaying azure fronds. Vast fields of wheat—again, of Tyll extraction—made up most of the landscape that wasn't grassland; that made sense with the research I'd done before having Scheherazade drop me off.

The research told me that this world had been terraformed for agricultural use a few hundred years ago or so; it had seen only mild scarring during the sect wars, which meant it was a little bit perplexing that the pulse had knocked it almost as far down the technology scale as a planet could go—all the way to before the invention of electric light.

Still, trying to understand *why* the pulse had done what it had done was a fool's errand: I'd seen systems where one planet had been left untouched, another had been driven back to pre-spaceflight, and the moon of that same *world* had lost everything post–internal combustion. There was never any rhyme or reason to it, not even within a single system—the pulse did what it did at random, and looking for a will behind its workings was like trying to find the face of god in weather patterns.

I knew that much because I was one of the fools who had let it off the chain in the first place. That's why I was here: trying to right my own wrongs. In a very small way, of course. I was only one woman, and it was a big, big universe. Also, I had a great many wrongs.

CHAPTER 2

I started walking. I had a ways to go.

Since the pulse had hit this world harder than most—left the atmosphere soaking in radiation that would burn out anything with an electrical system in hours, faster if it saw heavy use—walking was about my only option for locomotion. That was one reason I'd had Scheherazade—that's my ship—drop me off at the top of the refinery: so she didn't have to land. Trying to do so would have left her damaged, badly, even if she just set down for the brief time it would take me to disembark.

The other reason I'd set down so far from my target area was to make sure we weren't in *view* of anybody as she descended. It had likely been generations since anyone visited this world from the greater galaxy beyond; it was in a mostly forgotten system of a mostly forgotten corner of unclaimed, untended space. I didn't need to be hailed as some sort of savior by the locals, come to rescue them from their pulse-soaked world and lead them back to the halcyon years of never-was. And that would be the better option: more likely was to be marked as some sort of demon, here to finish the job the pulse had started. You never knew which it might be on worlds thrown back this far; better not to risk it at all.

Worlds like this one—even those designed for a single purpose, like agriculture—had been terraformed and designed for vehicles like high-speed rail and sublight orbital shuttles, not for perambulation, which meant I had a bit of a walk ahead of me. Still, I'd been cooped up inside Scheherazade for a long hyperdrive flight on the way here, so I didn't mind stretching my legs.

Starting my trek out in the boonies also meant I got a chance to know the local populace before they got to know me. Which, this time, started with screaming. It often did, for some reason.

The scream shattered the quiet of the open fields. High-pitched, piercing, a great deal of fear and pain and confusion. A child.

I broke out into a run. All these years later, that's still reflex. You'd think, after watching the pulse *eat* the universe and being helpless to stop it, that I'd be immune to the sound of others crying for help. You'd be wrong. What you can ignore *en masse*—the death of millions or billions—just by telling yourself it's too big, there's nothing you can do, is much more difficult to move past when it's just one person, right in front of you, and there *is* a way for you to help.

That's the same logic that had been used when the pulse was first dreamt up, after all. Just because it went *wrong* didn't mean the argument wasn't sound.

I slowed as I crested the hill, parting the grass with my rifle barrel; my weapon had been drawn as soon as I heard the child shriek. Down the incline below me was a simple wagon—probably the height of technology in these parts, wood and nails and iron-rimmed wheels—that had come to a stop, mostly because the beasts in its harnesses had been shot dead.

I didn't recognize the creatures, though the build and rough size suggested Wulf-homeworld extraction. It didn't much matter, really—they were whatever fauna had been on planet at the time of the pulse that the people here had enough of for breeding stock. What was more important, at that given moment, was the family seated at the front of the wagon, and the rough circle of men with guns surrounding them.

On every world, there are always men with guns. Even the pulse couldn't change that.

CHAPTER 3

From my perch at the top of the hill—hidden in the tall violet grasses—I counted the aggressors. Three humans, two Wulf—how nice, interspecies cooperation was flourishing in the wake of the pulse, at least when it came to common banditry. Five total. Not too many for me take, not from ambush.

Now, years ago, back before everything went to hell, I would have run through a kind of value judgment here—was protecting three lives, the family in the wagon, worth taking the lives of five others? I had no legal or moral authority here—who was I to interfere with the customs of these people? There were trillions upon trillions of lives in the universe; why should I involve myself with eight? People lived and died all the time, many of them violently; all I would have cared about was whether the deaths before me would have impacted my mission.

I didn't bother with any of that nonsense now; I knew what I was going to do the instant I heard the child scream. The questions I asked at this point were of a very different sort—which one looked like he'd be the first to shoot, the fastest to react? Which one had the gun that posed the most danger to me, which one would be the type to start firing at the family the instant they came under fire from someone else, and which among them would panic, cower, flee? In essence: which one would die first, and which last?

I activated my HUD with a thought—another passive piece of tech that still gave me a nice advantage over those without—and marked all five of them, glowing red haloes surrounding their heads. Even if they were to duck for cover—there were a handful of decent-sized boulders down there, likely where they'd head—those haloes would still show up in my vision, letting me know where they were. Slowly I sank prone and raised the sights of my rifle to my eye.

I was still too far away to hear what was being said, but it didn't matter:

gunfire had already been exchanged, weapons were drawn, beasts of burden had been killed. Whether or not the bandits were planning to let the family live if everything went their way didn't concern me: they'd sealed their fate when they aimed a weapon at a child.

I started firing.

My first round took their leader in the side of the head. One human out of the game. My second caught one of the Wulf lieutenants right in his muzzle; I doubted it would kill him, but intense pain drives Wulf into a kind of berserker rage, a physiological vestige of having been an alpha predator on a homeworld with plenty of alpha predators to go around. Useful in bare-handed combat, not so much in a gunfight.

My third shot cut into the back of another human, one who had been raising his rifle toward the family. Three down in fewer seconds. I was a lot of things, good, bad, or otherwise, but I did have my talents.

The fourth and fifth bandits—all that remained—were ducking behind the boulders, trying to figure out who the hell was shooting at them, but by that time, both the man and the woman in the wagon had produced firearms from somewhere, and the two would-be bushwhackers found themselves pinned down on all sides. I kept my rifle trained on their positions as the man from the wagon got up from his seat, calmly strolled toward where the first bandit was hiding, and fired off two rounds from his pistol—an ancient revolver even bigger than the one I wore at my hip. The red halo marking that bandit's position winked out. The fifth received much the same treatment, even after he threw his rifle to the side and tried to surrender.

When we'd envisioned the pulse, we'd never imagined it would remove *all* violence from the universe—just reduce its scale. In some ways, that had worked. But violence is ingrained in all of us, deep down to the bone. You push people in just the right way—you threaten their family—and they will injure *themselves* just to get to you. Did I blame the *paterfamilias* down there for murdering the man who'd held a gun on his child in cold blood? I did not. I'd done worse.

Speaking of: the injured Wulf was still crawling along the ground, trying to drag himself away, his fur slick with the blood flowing from his mangled muzzle, only the adrenal response of his species keeping him moving at all. The farmer was reloading; I put a round through the Wulf's skull myself, right between his bloodshot eyes. Cold-blooded, perhaps, but practical—he was never going to survive long, not with that wound, not with this world's level of medical attention.

Five down. Done.

The farmer below shaded his eyes and looked up the rolling hillside, roughly toward my position. I stood slowly from the waving grasses, holding my rifle up with one hand gripped around the middle—universal for "I'm not going to shoot at you." He nodded, and waved me down with his free six-fingered hand, holstering his own sidearm.

Looked like I'd made a friend.

CHAPTER 4

I made my way down the hillside, pushing the grasses before me, my rifle still out but very carefully not pointed at anyone. The friendly local was a Tyll, which made sense, given that the sect that had controlled this planet before the pulse had been about seventy percent Tyll.

To human eyes, Tyll tended to come off as "reptilian," tall and green-skinned and scaled, though they were actually closer, genetically, to the flora of the human homeworld than any fauna. Like most of his brethren, the farmer's lantern-like jaw gave him a perpetual dour expression, as did the wide black pupils that swallowed up most of his eyes. Not that the Tyll are dour people; it's just one of those weird things—sometimes trying to read "human" expressions from nonhuman features can lead to faulty assumptions. Tyll are usually actually fairly cheerful, on a cultural level at least.

Not that this particular fellow had a lot of reason to be cheery. He greeted me with a polite—if cautious—nod, before running a hand over the stony plate Tyll grew on the top of their heads in place of hair. He turned to stare unhappily down at his dead pack beasts. "Appreciate the help," he said tonelessly. If he was thrown to see that it was a human woman who had come to his aid, he didn't show it, which also meant my local costume—a faded flight jacket over gray military surplus, both from a sect nowhere near this quadrant of the galaxy, both predating the pulse—was holding up, and that my particular genetic makeup—copper-colored skin, jet black hair—wouldn't be out of place among the local human populace.

He spat a wad of expectorant in the grass next to his dead beasts of burden. "The local settlement claims they've rousted all the bandits out of this area. You can see how much their claims are worth."

"Will you three be all right out here?" I asked him. I shouldn't have—I didn't know what I was planning to do if he said, "No, please help us"—but

I spent a long time trying to think of myself as the sort of person who helped, who did *good*. In the long run maybe that hadn't been so true, but I kept trying all the same.

He nodded morosely. "We're not far from our farmstead," he replied. "We were just . . . just trying to deliver . . ." He gave the ground a good kick, next to his wagon's wheel—the wagon his beasts were long past capable of hauling. Probably most of a year's surplus crop was piled up within the wooden slats, and now he had no way to get it to market before it spoiled.

"Which way to that settlement?" I asked him. He pointed over the ridge, in roughly the same direction their wagon had been headed. I nodded, shading my eyes to stare off toward the horizon. The forests got a little heavier, the heavy blue fronds interlacing into a canopy, and I couldn't see anything past them.

"I'm looking for some civilization," I told him, trying to keep it casual. This kind of world had plenty of drifters and ne'er-do-wells, trying to make their living with a gun; I was dressed to match, very much on purpose. I didn't want to give the impression that I needed to be anywhere in particular. "When I get there, you want me to send somebody for you, maybe with some extra beasts?"

His forked tongue flicked out—it's the Tyll equivalent of a human widening their eyes in surprise. "That is a generous offer," he told me. "I can't ask you to—you've already saved our lives."

I grinned, making sure to show a bit of teeth. "Less generous when you consider I'll take a cut of your sale for the service," I replied. I didn't give a damn about whatever they used for currency around here—probably stamped bottle caps or something equally useless anywhere else—but people grow suspicious when others are nice to them for free.

He made a kind of low rumbling in his chest; he was thinking. "I doubt we'll get a better offer," he nodded. "Thank you." He held out his hand.

It was an interesting gesture—the handshake was one of those things that started out as human, but spread to the other races pretty quickly during the so-called golden age of cultural transmission and commingling. In the bad years after that, plenty of sects went all "pure blood," trying to remove the "stains" of other species' interactions from within their society.

The files I'd read on board Scheherazade had indicated that the Tyll on this planet had been from one such sect, before the pulse. Apparently, a hundred years or so trapped with humans and a few other species on a gunpowder-age rock had led to a second round of ideological exchange, and the handshake had made its return. The more things change, and all that.

Anyway, I shook his hand. "Anybody I should talk to in particular at the village?" I asked him.

"Yes—ask around for Marza," he nodded. Nodding, by the way, isn't cultural transmission; it's one of those things that's pretty common among bipedal species. So is smiling, oddly enough, and laughter. Most of us agree the same way. We disagree in the same manner as well—usually with violence. "He'll send the beasts in exchange for his own . . . cut." The farmer still sounded a little dispirited at the idea of his profits being nibbled away, but, hey—it was better than being dead.

"Marza. Got it. Well—stay out of the sun," I nodded back. "I'll send your friend on his way when I find him."

"Again—we are much obliged."

"Just doing my duty."

He cocked his head back, another Tyll expression. "Duty?" he asked.

I shrugged. "Figure of speech."

Have to watch shit like that.

CHAPTER 5

As I hiked through the tall grass in the general direction he'd indicated, toward the rise of the forests at the edge of the fields of wheat, I went over my options again in my head. I knew I was in the right general *area* to find what I'd come to this world looking for, but it was still looking for a needle in a haystack. My HUD would pick my target up if I got into visual range—it gave off a certain signature—but that was all I could count on. Otherwise it was going to require a deft touch, which is not usually one of my governing attributes.

After an hour or so wending my way through the Tyll trees, the forests finally broke open again, giving me a view of my destination, nestled in the valley below. As was typical on worlds like this one, the settlement was built around an old military installation, ramshackle lumber huts and more impressive stone houses built up around a line of defunct anti-air batteries and one giant anti-orbital cannon, plus their adjacent storehouses.

The farther a world had been thrown back in time, technologically speaking, the more likely you were to find their population centers built around relics of the older age. There are various reasons for that, some psychological, some defensive, but the majority of them were practical: this area was close to the coast of its continent, which meant, based on Scheherazade's analysis of the local weather patterns, it would get deluged during the biannual monsoon season. A boon for growing crops, to be sure, but given that advanced construction techniques had been put forever out of the locals' reach by the pulse, it made sense that they would have used what was still standing from the earlier age. Those batteries were designed to withstand multiple-megaton strikes from dreadnaught bombardment—they'd be much better shelter from torrential downpours than anything the locals could still build.

It also made for a very striking sight, the big gun rising up out of the swaying grass, absolutely dwarfing the surrounding village. I'd estimate the population of the town at about twenty thousand or so, and based on my observation from the ridge above, I'd say it was a pretty representative species mix of the world as a whole. That meant that, in this area at least, the locals had outgrown the sectarian divisions that had defined them during the wars.

Peace through forcible disarmament. That had actually been the goal of the pulse. It had just very rarely worked out that way.

I made my way down the hill, sure to stow my rifle on my back and keep my hands to my side. The settlement looked plenty peaceful, sure, but if the bandits I'd encountered on the road were a regular threat, there would be sentries, and they wouldn't be very hesitant to shoot a lone stranger approaching with a gun.

Still, none stopped me as I entered the outskirts of the town, entering a bazaar where the locals were hawking their wares, likely where the poor Tyll farmer I'd encountered had been hoping to unload his own. I asked a vendor—a Tyll selling bowls of thick, leafy stew—where I could find Marza; she pointed me to a local watering hole built into one of the former supply sheds. They might have been thrown back to an age before electricity, but people would always find a way to distill booze.

The dim bar served various concoctions, marked clearly on the wall in chalk, the menu separated out by species preference. A human and a Tyll could drink much the same things and achieve much the same effect, though their different taste buds might prefer different flavors, but either of those species drinking something designed for a Wulf risked becoming violently ill, and drinking something suited to some of the other species—a Reint, for example, or Vyriat—would straight up kill them. Most of the seventeen species that made up the galactic population had certain biological similarities— carbon-based biology, the oxygen levels required for a breathable atmosphere— but the deviations among them were still important to keep in mind.

I asked the barkeep, a shaggy, canine-like Wulf, where I might find Marza; she barely looked up from the glasses she was cleaning as she nodded toward him, a human sitting at a corner table, chatting amiably with a few acquaintances. I approached and informed him of his friend's predicament, and he thanked me, passing along a few squares of rough stamped metal—presumably the local currency—as a way of paying me off. With that done, I headed back out into the town.

Where to find one human child in a city of hundreds of them? Especially a city with very few apparent species divides? Don't get me wrong, I was pleased as hell that everything was so peachy and racially integrated around here, but it did make my job harder—if there had been a "human quarter," it would have at least narrowed my search.

That lack of racial divide meant that there were two possible avenues of inquiry to begin my search: checking to see if some sort of local religion had grown up in the last hundred years, priests being valuable sources of information as long as you couched your question right, and if that didn't pan out, to see if there was some sort of local orphanage. This wasn't the first child I'd recruited, and for whatever reason, the gifts they presented— the very confirmation that they *were* what we thought they were—almost always emerged after tragedy or trauma.

I was pointed toward a temple by a man renting out the same strange beasts of burden I'd seen shot dead out in the grasslands, so that would be my first stop.

Religion had always been a . . . funny thing, even before the pulse. The intermingling of seventeen different species, plus the sectarian divisions that had come after, had meant a swarm of different ideas colliding in sometimes strange and unexpected ways, new religions commingling with old and forming all sorts of offshoots and clashes of ideology. Add the pulse on top of that—an event that, as far as these people knew, was some cosmologically unprecedented, completely inexplicable act that might have come from a divine hand—and all sorts of strange cults and beliefs had sprung up in its wake. Plenty of those were apocalyptic in nature, and the local flavor turned out to be no different.

The "church," insofar as that's what it was, had been built right up underneath one of the anti-aircraft guns, long silent now. They'd left the weapon as their roof, which meant they probably got rained on during services, the water dripping down all the exposed metal of the cannon to spatter on their heads as they prayed, but for all I knew that was part of their belief system, being cleansed by the wash of war or somesuch. I watched their midday services from just outside the door, trying to get a handle on how they'd translated the pulse into their beliefs.

The priest was a Barious. I hadn't been expecting that. For one thing, the machine race hadn't been present in large numbers on this world before the pulse; for another, the Barious, even more so than the other races, tended to keep to themselves, a side effect of both the massive physiological differences between them and the biological species, and also the fairly horrid memories of how they'd been treated even before the pulse.

Barious were odd in general. They were all that remained of a precursor race, one that had dominated the cosmos before any of the current species spread throughout the diaspora of stars had so much as discovered fire. Whoever that race was—generally referred to as "the forerunners"—they'd faded into nothing, the only remnant of their passage the servants they'd left behind, AI creations with no one to serve: the Barious. They'd even blanked the species's collective memory banks, wiping out all traces of who they'd been, why their creators had made them, or why they'd existed at all.

None of that was particularly relevant at the moment—but the pulse had been careful to leave all of the Barious's systems intact, which meant that the priest was liable to be both older even than me by a significant amount, and to have sharper senses and sensors than most of the locals I'd encounter. If anyone was going to cotton to the notion that I was from off-planet, it would be her.

I only say "her," by the way, because that's the pronoun I'm used to; Barious are monogendered.

Anyway, the Barious wrapped up her sermon—the usual apocalyptic, "this is the end times and soon the pulse shall return and judge what we have done in the interim" spiel that I'd heard on dozens of different worlds; what she got *wrong*, and how she'd clearly reached those conclusions, was almost as impressive as what she got *right*—and I stood to the side as her congregants filed out. My first instinct was to do the same; discourse with a Barious had a high risk factor baked in. But I didn't have many leads, and I still felt like the church was my best shot, so I shoved that impulse aside. Time to get my dose of religion.

CHAPTER 6

The priest looked up at me as I approached, her metal skin reflecting the glow of the candles placed around the space of worship. Like most Barious, she was tall, angular, giving off a sense of incredible *stillness* as she stood at the altar—unlike organic species, Barious didn't unconsciously shift their weight or shrug or lean or fidget when they were still. Also like most Barious, her "skin," the metallic outer plating that covered her chassis, had been patched here and there with rougher materials, the complex alloys of her original construction welded here and there with different alloys of copper or brass. Just because the pulse had left the Barious intact and functioning didn't mean their maintenance facilities had been so lucky, and as her components took damage, she'd been replacing them with whatever she could find.

"Offworlder," she said, her tone uninflected. "Interesting."

Well. So much for keeping that one in the bag.

"If you're going to ask me if I've come bearing the word of the gods"—I shook my head—"not my line."

"No, I didn't think so." She cocked her head at an angle, the light that shone from her eyes changing as she engaged different sensors. I have no idea what she was examining—talking to Barious can feel slightly . . . invasive, given that they take in more information than nonsynthetics could possibly process just as easily and unconsciously as we breathe—but whatever it was, she made a kind of "clicking" sound when she was done, the Barious version of a human "huh." "Justified," she said.

Even for a Barious, that was a leap. It was a *correct* leap, but still. She wasn't saying that she *felt* judged, or that I was judging her; the Justified was the colloquial term—or what *had* been the colloquial term, before the pulse—for my particular sect. We hadn't been that well known, even then, and we'd liked it that way. Still did.

We were, after all, responsible for the greatest catastrophe that had ever befallen the universe. When you've got something like that hidden away, you don't go around inviting scrutiny. And yes—I'm aware of the irony of the title after that particular act.

The full name of the sect, by the way, was "The Justified and the Repentant." Doesn't that sound better? I thought that sounded better.

"You don't sound surprised," I told her.

"Even during the wars, your sect was always sticking their noses—and muzzles, and snouts, and proboscises—into places they didn't belong," she replied. "Am I surprised that even with the pulse, you're still managing it? No. Not at all."

"You're not a native," I said flatly. She'd already thrown me; marking me as Justified meant she'd been . . . well informed, before the pulse, at least, which meant I couldn't assume that she'd believe—like most people on worlds like this one—that the pulse had rendered *every* planet in the galaxy down to the same level of technology they were on. How much she *did* know, what she was doing here: not questions I could easily answer, which meant I'd have to play my cards even closer to my chest than usual.

Still, I didn't want to be too evasive—that would risk angering her, and I had zero interest in that outcome. The Barious might play into the stereotype that they're all logic and reason when it suits them, but believe me, you *can* piss them off, and when they go, they *stay*. They build goddamned *vacation homes* in their wrath, revisit their fury whenever they feel nostalgic. Barious hold grudges like nobody's business, and given that their construction made them twice as strong as the strongest human ever born, those grudges could have messy results.

"Do you know?" she asked me, the question almost ritual. "What caused the pulse?"

The inquiry was intended to catch me off guard, and she almost succeeded. I had to be careful here as well—she might know if I lied, given all the sensory data she was collecting. Then again, she might not: contrary to popular opinion, there is no such thing as a universal lie detector. Even among one species, the tells and physical changes that accompany a falsehood can vary wildly.

But Barious *saw* more than most, given their sensors and scanners and built-in arrays; she was taking in a great deal of physiological data as we spoke, so she'd have a better *idea* if I was lying to her or not than most species would.

So I went with option B: deferral. "I'm not here because of what *caused* it," I said instead. "I'm here to try and prevent it from happening again." True, to a certain extent, in the same way that "*I* didn't eat the last sweet roll on the table" was true, if you'd shoved it into your pocket instead. Plus, it rolled nicely into the fire and brimstone she'd been preaching earlier: playing to someone's preconceived beliefs is always a useful way to get them to divulge something they might not have otherwise.

"And that requires a visit to a place of worship?" she asked.

I shook my head. "I'm here because places of worship tend to be good places to get information," I replied, again, truthfully. "I'm here to see if you know where I can find who I'm looking for."

She cocked her head to the side, the light behind her eyes shifting again. "Who?" she asked.

I nodded. "A human child," I said. "Fourteen years old."

"So conceived during the meteor—"

I nodded again, cutting her off. I didn't want to talk about that; it would take us closer to those things I didn't want to discuss with her. It wasn't actually related to the girl I was seeking, anyway—a correlated connection, not a causal one. "And she would have shown . . . aptitudes. Abilities."

The Barious narrowed her eyes at me, which was accompanied by the vague whine of the servos in her face. She thought for a moment—which meant she was giving her answer a lifetime's worth of consideration, given how fast Barious processed information—before finally replying. "I think I may know who you mean," she said.

CHAPTER 7

The Barious led me through the city, away from the big guns and the marketplace both, toward the outlying districts. She'd told me her name was Alexi54328, and that I could call her "Preacher." Why she'd told me her name when she didn't want me to use it, I wasn't sure. Barious were odd.

The citizens of whatever-the-hell-this-town-was-called greeted her fondly enough; not surprising, really. As a Barious, she'd naturally be in a position of some veneration, even without her local authority as a religious leader, given that she was old enough to actually *remember* a time before the pulse.

"Where are we going?" I asked her. We were headed into a more ramshackle part of town: more natural wood, splintered and faded, without the heartier stone construction. The buildings also mostly lacked the brightly painted walls that had characterized the more well-to-do areas.

"The orphanage," she told me, which confirmed what I had already guessed. For whatever reason, the children I was tasked with seeking out always seemed to be orphans. Maybe that was because it took stress and trauma to activate their gifts—without a trigger, I wouldn't even know to look for them—or maybe it was just because the universe has a bleak sense of humor. Or a storyteller's natural flair for pathos. I'd never been much for religion—my upbringing had skewed me permanently away from the entire concept of faith—but I sometimes couldn't help but feel the hand of something other than chance in the course of events, even if all that hand seemed to be doing was making an obscene gesture in my general direction.

"Her parents?" I asked.

"Died in a bandit raid, years ago. Shortly after she was born." Years—that wouldn't add up, at least not for the activating trauma. The girl had only come onto my radar, so to speak, a few months ago, when her gifts had manifested. There had to be something—

The train of my thoughts was brought to a crashing halt when the whole town started shaking, as if an earthquake were beginning just under our feet. That couldn't be what was happening—I'd studied the scans; the whole planet was tectonically stable, another remnant of the terraforming technology that had been so widespread before the pulse—but it was still my first thought.

My *second* thought was that a ship was entering orbit, something big enough and fast enough to displace enough atmosphere to cause this level of turbulence. But I dismissed that nearly as readily as the earthquake theory; who the hell would be crazy enough to take a ship that big into an atmosphere this choked with pulse radiation?

It turns out, I shouldn't have abandoned that idea so readily. There's always someone stupid enough to think they can just bull through the pulse. They're never right, but still.

It was a ship.

It was a *big* ship.

It roared into the upper atmosphere, shuddering and shaking like it was taking heavy fire. It wasn't just *big*, it was massive, twice the size of the settlement itself: a dreadnaught, all hard lines and spires and blocky edges, so large it eclipsed the high noon sun and threw the entire settlement into shadow as the town was full of the groans and *howls* of the starship's machinery tearing itself apart. A ship like that had never been meant to descend into a gravity well at *all*, much less into a pulsed atmosphere.

The people around me were staring upward, slack-jawed or screaming. Remember, outside of the few long-lived species like the Barious, it had been generations since the pulse for most of them. Seeing a dreadnaught suddenly drop out of orbit and into their empty skies was like seeing the gods of your grandparents—the ones *you* had only half-believed in—suddenly manifest directly in front of you. You can pretend all you like that such a moment would be one of clarity or ecstasy, when the truth was, it would more likely be one of pants-shitting fear. That was the more prevalent reaction around me, and I couldn't blame them. The shaking wasn't helping matters.

I wasn't too pleased about it myself, but that had less to do with the appearance of the ship—I'd known it was *possible*, if not likely—and more to do with the massive emblem painted on the side, shaking with the tremors rippling through the dreadnaught's bulkheads: a four-fingered fist, half-closed around a stylized star.

The Pax. The fucking Pax.

Slots on the bottom of the dreadnaught slid open; stun drones dropped out of their bays like they were swarms of insects, preparing to home in on anything with a heat signature and explode in a cloud of electric shock and mild neurotoxins. They wouldn't last long in this pulsed atmosphere, but they wouldn't need to—there were plenty of locals below, plenty of heat signatures to choose from.

We *also* had a heat signature. I activated my intention shield and grabbed the Preacher around the waist, holding her close enough that the shield would cover her as well. Just in time, too: one of the drones came right for us, its sleek, hovering form skimming over the ground like the dragonflies that gave them their rough shape, drawn to us like a moth to a flame.

A moth that then exploded. My shield blocked the shock and the toxins, but couldn't do much with the force of the blast itself, other than dissipate it across my entire body; both the Preacher and I were lifted off of our feet and smashed backward into a shack.

When we pulled ourselves out of the ruined wood, everything was chaos.

That was only *partly* because of the stun drones. The Pax were here for the girl too—of that, there was no question, based on their tactics alone. Otherwise they wouldn't be using stun drones, they'd be using energy cannons and they'd be blasting the place apart. However, when I said they were stupid, I wasn't just being vindictive—apparently they'd never stopped to think what would happen if they parked a *dreadnaught*, under assault from pulse radiation, directly on top of a populated area.

Whole sheets of metal and debris were being ripped off the ship's hull as the radiation worked overtime to try and devour it. I'd already said, the more advanced the technology, and the more *active* the technology, the faster the radiation would decay it—that also held true for the *size* of any given piece of tech. Scheherazade could have stayed in atmosphere for an hour or so without too much ill effect, provided she stayed relatively high, but she was on the smallish side, even for a personal starship. The dreadnaught was the size of a small goddamned city, and it was already lower than the point where Schaz had descended to drop me off at the top of the refinery tower. The thing had only been in atmosphere for a few minutes, but even if they'd pulled back right now, the ship would be unsalvageable.

It apparently didn't matter—not to the Pax. I mean, it *should* have—dreadnaughts were expensive as fuck; you could buy an entire terraformed moon for the cost of one, if you didn't mind the rough condition the moon might be in—but the Pax's lack of material investment in the ship was pretty goddamned evident, given that, again, they'd *ridden it deep into a pulsed atmosphere.*

Their troops were already dropping down from the assault bays, either descending from rope lines or jumping with antigrav gear, just *hoping* that the tech would hold out long enough to get them safely to the ground. It didn't, not for all of them—I saw a few just keep falling, plowing into the earth below—but it worked for enough that the citizens who hadn't been taken out by the stun drones were mostly fleeing in terror.

Meanwhile, all those pieces of the ship calving off from the whole—not to mention the falling bodies—were wreaking havoc on the town. The Pax wouldn't be able to take the girl alive if they'd crushed her under a few tons of debris, or charbroiled her by setting a gas line on fire; this world didn't have electricity, but it wasn't completely technologically void, and there were already explosions and fires spreading where the collapsing dreadnaught's detritus was causing havoc. But like I said—the Pax just weren't that smart.

Of all the goddamned sects for the pulse to completely *avoid* shutting down, it had to have been the Pax. Before the pulse, they'd just been another group out of hundreds, their mandate "complete galactic domination," but no closer to that goal than dozens of others with the same stated intent. The galaxy was big; galactic conquest was laughably impractical, but some fuckers just kept trying anyway.

Now, though, just from the dumb luck of *not* having the majority of their conquered worlds hit by the pulse, they were just about the only game in town still willing to try to conquer everything they saw by force, pulse radiation elsewhere be damned. Most of the others who'd been trying the same thing before the pulse—and thus might have checked the Pax's own expansion—either didn't have the tools left, or were too preoccupied by basic survival to give much of a shit what was going on elsewhere.

How'd the Pax even *find* the girl? How'd they find out about her? Our intelligence had been a direct line, not a tip, and there was no *way* it was compromised.

A question for another day. I hauled the Preacher to her feet. We had to get moving.

CHAPTER 8

The little town was in complete chaos, which was understandable. Even the concept of people living beyond the stars was just a tall tale to most of them, and now those very same half-mythical people were dropping down into their midst with body armor, stun batons, and big fucking guns, an invasion force from out of nowhere. Even the decaying state of their ship made a statement: this enemy had no way to turn back. This was not a fight the locals could win—not with the weapons they had, and not psychologically. They were used to fighting off small groups of bandits. The Pax were a lot of things, but local bullyboys they were *not*, and while they might have been stupid, their shock troops did follow orders; it was part of their culture.

The soldiers knew they were looking for a human girl, so anyone who came anywhere near that description was getting the unfriendly end of a stun baton; all the rest got the significantly *more* unfriendly end of a gun. Their energy weapons, like their ship, were decaying rapidly, but not nearly as fast, and most of them were packing sidearms more in line with the local tech levels.

Still, the locals were fighting back, or at least trying; it's not like this planet was a paradise, after all, and most of them went armed most places. There was . . . a great deal of gunfire, is what I was saying. The Pax were easy to pick out from the locals, given their advanced tech and their bulky bodysuits designed specifically so you couldn't know what species was underneath—that was part of the Pax philosophy, functionally "Pax first, anything else never." Both sides were losing combatants rapidly, the township turning into a bloodbath, but the Pax just kept coming, even as their ship just kept collapsing. Unless they had dropships in the upper atmosphere, ready to swing down and pick the survivors back up, the Pax were here to stay, regardless of whether they found the girl or not.

I kept the Preacher close by, within the aegis of my intention shield—her chassis, the original pieces she had left, at least, could shrug off small arms fire in a way my squishy organs could not, but a burst from one of those energy rifles would still do her in—but as handy as intention shields are, their biggest fault was right there in the name: they can only cover about a quarter of your body at once, so you have to *know* where the shot's coming from before they can block it. The controls are wired directly into the user's brainstem.

Which was great in single-combatant firefights or even smaller group engagements, but in a clusterfuck like this, you were just as likely to get hit in the back of the head by a stray round you never saw coming as to get shot at by someone you *knew* was aiming at you. I used the intention shield because its control system meant it was down the vast majority of the time, which meant it wasn't decaying the vast majority of the time I spent in a pulsed atmosphere, but it did have noticeable flaws.

The Preacher didn't seem all that thrown by the Pax assault. Or maybe she had been, and she'd just recovered in triple-time; Barious processed information very quickly. Either way, she led me down back alleys and through derelict buildings, trying to avoid the worst of the fighting. When we couldn't do that, I used my rifle. I didn't mind; I found killing Pax to be weirdly soothing. The fuckers.

Finally, picking our way through the *already* run-down neighborhood that was quickly devolving into chaos, we reached the orphanage. What was *left* of the orphanage, at any rate. You could see someone—either compassionate townsfolk, or more likely the kids themselves—had tried to keep the place tidy; it was cleaner than most of the surrounding structures, and was even covered in friendly-looking murals, depicting children of various species getting along and doing chores and whatnot in perfect harmony. Or at least, it had been.

Now, half of it was crushed underneath what had once been a laser turret, formerly attached to the Pax dreadnaught hovering above us. The upper floor was canted dangerously, the whole top of the structure—what *remained* of the structure—about to collapse down onto the bottom half, which was also being consumed by flames that had started . . . somewhere. One of those gas lines, maybe, or just bad luck; it seemed like there were always fires, in times like these.

We could hear children screaming inside. Regardless of whether the girl was within or not—or whether she was still alive or not—that wasn't a sound you could *not* react to. The Preacher and I made our way through the rubble, trying to find a way into what remained of the structure without getting ourselves caught on fire—even Barious could melt. We eventually wound up climbing through a first-floor window.

All the children were huddled in the main room, what I'd guess had been a sort of mess hall. The second story was about to collapse on them. Or, I should say, it had *already* collapsed on them, but something was holding it back—an invisible wall of force, as if a net had been strung over the children's heads, holding back several tons of building materials and detritus.

Just below that net stood a young human woman, shaking and sweating with effort, her hands raised up as if she were *physically* holding all that debris. Her dark-skinned face was streaked with blood and grime, but there was a relentless determination burning out of her eyes, like if she had to stand here *forever* to keep that ton of rubble from crushing the other children, well then, that was what she would do.

Telekinesis. One of the markers I looked for—one of the rarer ones, in fact. My HUD helpfully highlighted her form to tell me what I already knew: I'd found my girl.

CHAPTER 9

The Preacher and I started getting the children out.

We ducked in and grabbed them, depositing them into the street outside. The girl barely acknowledged our efforts; she was too busy making sure the entire building didn't collapse while we did our work. It wasn't until we'd gotten at least half the children out that I noticed they were disappearing from the street outside. Most kids you'd expect to stay rooted to the spot after a thing like that, wailing and waiting for someone to come along and tell them what to do, but these were rabbiting somewhere, not waiting for an adult to come by and help.

I didn't know where these kids were going, but as long as it was "not about to be crushed by falling debris," I figured it was still better than where they *had* been, so I kept doing what I was doing. When we got the last child clear, the girl followed us, walking slowly, half-turned, her attention still wholly focused on the rubble she was keeping airborne with her mind.

Finally, she stepped clear of the building, and just crumpled. I shielded her with my body—just reflex. The rubble came crashing down, bouncing off of the intention shield covering my back. When the dust cleared, I noticed the Preacher had done much the same thing—just dropped to one knee in the street, letting the debris fly around her. There were definite benefits to having a metal body.

The girl disentangled herself from me, looking me up and down, not a great deal of trust in her expression despite the fact that I'd just rescued her from a collapsing building. "Come on," she said finally, wiping a thin stream of blood from one nostril—an aftereffect of having pushed her gift too hard, too fast. "This way."

Then she ducked into a side alley across the street, out of sight.

I cursed and followed. This was the problem with shepherding children;

they're all will and movement. An adult who had just used burgeoning tele-kinetic powers to hold up a collapsing building in the midst of an attack from conquerors dropping down from the sky might have asked for explanations; she just ran.

There was a metal grate in the half-buried metal floor of the alley, raised up on its hinges—pre-pulse construction, likely a maintenance tunnel for the anti-orbital gun. I dropped down inside, the Preacher following me. It was pitch black down there, the only light coming from the grate behind us.

I toggled the low-light vision setting on my HUD all the way up, and the black became just dim instead. Yep—maintenance tunnel. It looked like it had been used for storage during the early days of the settlement, but it had gone ignored for quite a while. The girl was halfway down the passage, mov-ing fast, and *quiet*. Again, I followed.

"We need to get out of town," I told her, ducking under low pipes.

"No shit," she replied. "These tunnels will take us under the guns, all the way to the far side of the settlement. Nobody ever thinks to use them anymore."

"How the hell are you *seeing* anything down here?" I asked her. Without my HUD, I'd be blind as a bat.

"I'm not," she replied, coolly experienced, deigning to give the adult the wisdom of her youth. "But I know the path."

The other children must have come this way as well; I could hear distant footfalls, somewhere ahead of us in the warren of tunnels. They weren't as quiet as the girl, or maybe that was just their panic.

The earth above our heads was still occasionally thumping from debris raining down from the Pax dreadnaught, causing dust to shake down from the ceiling, dancing in the glow of my low-light vision. The sounds of gun-fire were more muffled by the steel walls, until they weren't anymore, and it was coming from up ahead of us instead.

"Hold up," I hissed at the girl. I don't know if she actually listened, or if she had heard the gunshots as well—the sharp "cracks" of a ballistic weapon rather than the loud hum of an energy rifle—but either way, she drew up short.

There was a doorway just in front of us; on the other side we could still hear the sounds of violence. At least a few of the Pax shock troops had made their way down here as well. I didn't know if that was because they had some means to track the girl, or if this was just part of their search. Either way, we would have to go through them—the girl had clearly been headed for the door.

Close quarters, too close for my rifle. I ran my thumb and forefinger up my right hand and arm like I was pulling on invisible gloves, then tapped a quick rhythm onto my knuckles; did the same, in a different rhythm, to my left, activating my melee implants. "Stay behind me," I whispered to the girl. She grinned back—I doubted that was assent.

I put my ear to the door, heard the sound of Pax voices on the other side, easily identifiable because the filters on their masks gave them all the exact same sort of electronically scrambled intonation. The gunfire had ceased: they were interrogating someone. Likely one of the children who had fled before us. Shit.

I went through the door hard.

Three Pax soldiers, one of them holding a child by the arm. I hit that one first, striking with the impact knuckles on my right hand, three fast, sharp blows to the rib cage. The blows didn't have to be hard—the implants took care of that, multiplying the Newtonian force of the strikes so that both the armor my target was wearing and the ribs underneath turned to jelly. She dropped the kid; I turned to face the next soldier, who was lunging for me, having holstered her sidearm for the interrogation. A quick sidestep and a hook to the jaw with my left answered her lunge, an electrical shock blazing a quick burst of light in the darkness between my knuckles and her chin, dropping her like a sack of meal.

The third was coming at me as well, trained, fast, reflexes honed, and I might have been able to answer that attack and I might not have, but all of a sudden it didn't matter: the Pax aggressor's forward motion was reversed, as abruptly as it had begun. She hung motionless for a moment, struggling against the invisible force that gripped her, then flew backward and smashed halfway through the steel wall, her feet twitching, the only part of her still visible.

I turned and looked at the girl. She gave me that kind of crooked grin again, lowering her hand. The few kids I'd known with telekinesis, even after training, would have been completely *wiped* after the effort she'd put forth today, but she was still going strong, that thin bleed I'd noticed from her sinuses notwithstanding. "You can fight," she told me, like this was something I didn't know.

"I still appreciate the assist," I replied.

"And you're not from around here."

"No, she is not," the Preacher said, following us into the storeroom. I doubted she was having any trouble making her way in the dark—the Barious are born with low-light implants of a similar type to the ones that took me five two-hour surgeries to get installed. "You need to go with her, child," she told the girl.

The girl's face scrunched up, automatic defiance. At fourteen, anyone who told her what to do could automatically go to hell. The Barious may have been smart, but they understood fuck-all about basic psychology.

I knelt in front of the girl before she could respond. "Listen," I told her, "I've got a way out of here. Not just out of this city—a way off of this *world*, a way to someplace better, someplace where the tech still works and the pulse hasn't shut everything else down. That place is waiting for you, if you come with me, now. If you stay"—I nodded to the shaking ceiling above us—"I don't know that there'll be much left to stay behind *for.*"

The girl looked in the direction the other kid had disappeared—not so much actually looking for the kid, I don't think, as looking away from me. She looked *hard*, weighing taking that path—a path that led to who knows where, one she'd have to take alone—then nodded, slowly. "Yeah," she said. "This place is going to hell anyway."

So that was that.

CHAPTER 10

The Pax whose ribs I'd turned to jelly was still moaning softly on the floor. As I watched, the Preacher stepped over to the twitching form, put her foot on its neck, then, almost primly, stepped down, putting all her considerable weight on the heel pressed to the Pax's spine.

I guess her church wasn't really into "all life is sacred," then.

"Harsh," the girl said to her, sounding caught between being impressed and being aghast.

"It was suffering," the Preacher returned, her voice level mechanical, even for a Barious. "And it was Pax."

"It—*she*—was your enemy, so she deserves to have her neck snapped? Even after she couldn't fight anymore?"

"You misunderstand. If *her* fellows had found her, they would have hauled her back to their barracks, and then, when they found the time, they would have beat her to death. As entertainment. Merely because she had been weak enough to become wounded to such an extent. The Pax do not believe in second chances."

I appraised the Preacher again, my HUD turning the shimmer of her eyes into a full-on blaze of light. She was older than the pulse—I'd known that already. But even before that, there had been thousands of sects, maybe even hundreds of thousands, religions and corporations and governments all warring for dominance in the galaxy, some fighting over entire sectors, some fighting over cities or continents on lone worlds. The Pax had been no more impressive than most. What were the odds that the Preacher would be so well versed in the habits of just one of them, a sect that had been middling-to-lesser on the galactic scale when the pulse hit?

The girl, meanwhile, had not taken the Preacher's little speech all that well. "That's . . . pretty fucked up," she said, sounding shaken for the first time.

The dreadnaught coming out of nowhere hadn't thrown her, a building *collapsing* on top of her hadn't thrown her, our little fight in the darkness of the tunnels hadn't thrown her, but the incivility of the Pax apparently was enough to put a tremor in her voice. Huh.

"Which way do we go to get out of here?" I asked her, redirecting the conversation to something less horribly morbid.

She stopped, reoriented herself in the darkened room—a fight will do that to you, every time—and pointed. "That way," she said, finally letting the woman with the *gun* take the lead.

I ducked under some hanging wiring, ripped loose either in the chaos or years ago, making my way into the passageway she'd indicated. According to the compass on my HUD, we were heading west, which was good—the Pax dreadnaught had covered the city and then some, but the main force of their troops had seemed to be concentrated in the eastern areas.

I tried to raise Scheherazade on my comms, but got nothing. That wasn't surprising; I wasn't sure if wars had actually been *waged* on this particular planet, but it had always been standard procedure to shield anti-orbital batteries to high heaven. The walls of this whole place were probably one massive Faraday cage.

We continued on into the darkness, the earth above still shaking. How much of the dreadnaught could even be left by now? Pulse radiation is not forgiving stuff, and it grows more furious the more you deny its will. Still, a ship that size could have been carrying tens of thousands of troops—hundreds of thousands, if this had actually been the Pax's plan and they'd packed it with nothing but infantry, knowing it was going to tear itself apart in the rad-soaked atmosphere anyway.

"So who are these guys?" the girl asked. "You said they were 'Pax,' right? What do they want here?"

"Pax is the name of their sect, yeah," I told her as we moved. "What they *want* is to conquer the whole galaxy. They won't be able to do it, because there are a great *many* people who want to conquer the whole galaxy, for whatever reason I'm sure I don't understand. But they sure can make life miserable if they decide you're standing between them and their entirely unachievable goal."

"Sound like fun at parties," she muttered. "But you didn't answer my question. You told me what they want in general, not what they want *here*."

"No, I did not," I replied, hoping she'd take the hint.

"It's because of me, isn't it?" Her voice wasn't soft as she said it, exactly, but it was a little muted. That's the problem with teenagers: they already *think* they're the center of the universe. When they find out that they actually might *be* incredibly important, they can react in unpredictable ways.

"They're here for a great many reasons," I told her. "But yes—you're one of them."

"So then it's my fault," she said. I was hoping she wouldn't have made that particular leap. "All the people dying up there—"

"If the Pax weren't killing people up there, they'd be killing people somewhere else," I told her forcefully. "Killing people is what they *do*. You didn't invent assholes, kid, and you didn't *make* the Pax assholes, either."

"But they'd be killing people someplace *else*, not my home." She thrust her jaw out stubbornly, like she was just bound and determined to take all the blame for this on her skinny little shoulders. There were strange reflections on her cheeks in the low-light of my HUD; she was crying. Not much, just a little. "They're up there murdering maybe everybody I've ever known, and you're saying that doesn't matter, because that's just what they *do*?"

"I'm saying it's not your fault," I sighed. "If you blame yourself for the actions of every asshole in the universe, you wouldn't be able to *stand* under the weight of all that guilt. We're each responsible for our own actions, no more, no less. You're responsible for you, and I'm responsible for me, and the Pax are responsible for the Pax; no one else is."

"But they wouldn't—"

"They are here due to circumstances beyond your control, child," the Preacher put in, resting a comforting hand on the girl's shoulder. "You cannot be responsible for something you had no hand in."

She shrugged off the Preacher's hand, but fell silent. That was fine; we could deal with the fallout of that particular revelation later, hopefully on board Scheherazade rather than down here where we were likely to get shot at. In the meantime, if she wanted to stew in her own guilt, maybe that'd make her less likely to be impulsive and run off to do something crazy. Or maybe it would make her *more* likely; what the hell did I know, it had been nearly two centuries since I was a teenager.

The ground beneath us had been slowly rising to an incline over the last little bit, and the sounds of combat were beginning to fade to a dull roar behind us. "Are we about clear of the city?" I asked the girl.

She looked up, broken from her reverie about how everything bad happening was her fault and everything was terrible forever. "Yeah," she said, wiping a hand across her cheek. "There should be another grate ahead of us, just a little—"

"I see it." The actual daylight filtering down through the metal made it stand out like a beacon in my HUD as we turned another corner. As we approached, I dialed down the low-light vision back to normal and laced my fingers in the grate, lifting it up slightly and shifting it to the side. I paused, listening, but there was nothing out of the ordinary—beyond the sound of the city collapsing somewhere behind us, I mean.

I levered myself through, then helped the kid up. The Preacher got out on her own; I couldn't have lifted her if I tried. We were out in the grasslands again, clear of the city, up on a rise above the valley itself, the wind gently shifting the ocean of pink and purple flora between us and the war being waged below. The girl wasn't staring at the pretty landscape, though— she'd been seeing that all her life. Instead, she was staring back at her home.

I couldn't blame her—it was a hell of a sight.

CHAPTER 11

There wasn't much left of the Pax dreadnaught. It hovered above the burning town, almost drawn even against the bulk of the orbital gun, as if it were a mirror image of the flaming settlement below—broken towers and shattered structures on both craft and township, fires flickering in the interiors of buildings and bulkheads both, the dreadnaught still shedding metal like a snake molting its skin.

Smoke and dust plumed up from the devastation below, caused by both the slow-motion collapse of the dreadnaught and the Pax troops rampaging through the buildings surrounding the massive, quiet guns. Once, those weapons had been built to ward off exactly an attack such as this—now they were just landmarks, standing in mute witness to the Pax assault.

The sky was shifting into indigo colors as the sun set behind the burning settlement, the flames licking through the city—and the flashes of the explosions visible through the gaps in the dreadnaught's armor—blending their bright illumination with the last light of day. As we watched, there was one last massive explosion inside the dreadnaught, and it began listing to the side, slowly sinking, unable to keep itself in the air. It crumpled as it hit the anti-orbital gun, a slow-motion crash that only accelerated its collapse.

"The Pax had to know this would happen, right?" the Preacher asked, her tone uncertain—a rarity for a Barious. "Surely they would have at least shut down their fusion reactor before they entered the atmosphere."

I shrugged, still staring out at the assault. "They weren't firing any of the dreadnaught's weapons, so that's a good sign," I replied. "But if you're asking me to make assumptions about the intelligence of a Pax operation, well . . . I'm not going to."

"But if they didn't shut down the reactor, and if that ship is tearing itself apart—"

"Yeah. We need to move."

"What will happen?" the girl asked, looking between the two of us. It must have seemed so strange to her, these two bizarre people—one at least someone she'd known most of her life, the other a complete mystery—discussing an event that must have seemed apocalyptic to her as though it were an everyday occurrence. "What will happen if they *didn't* shut down their . . . their . . . fusion . . . thingy?"

"Their fusion reactor," I told her. "It's what powers that ship. And if they didn't shut it down, it'll go critical, sooner rather than later. And if it goes critical, there will be a new crater on this planet's surface in a few hours. We need to move," I said again, turning away from the sight.

The girl was still staring out at the city—her home—as it burned, barely taller than the swaying grasses around her. "I woke up this morning thinking maybe I could find some work at the saloons," she said, a small catch in her voice. "I do that sometimes, the sweeping up. I didn't . . . I didn't . . ."

"We never expect our lives to change," the Preacher told her. "But then they do." With a gentle—but firm—hand, she turned the girl away from the sight of the devastation. "Even if the reactor doesn't go critical, the Pax will be looking for us. Come."

"And *don't* use your . . . talents," I added. "They'll draw attention."

"They always do," she nodded, her tone more morose than you'd expect to hear from a girl her age.

We set off through the grass that was beginning to give off a shimmering glow in the moonlight, almost iridescent, the bucolic fields suffused with a sense of melancholy as we moved away from the only life the girl had ever known, a history already in flames.

I reached out to Scheherazade by way of tapping the implanted comm node under my jaw to open the secure line. "I take it you saw our company incoming," I said to her.

"Oh, couldn't miss them, boss," she replied. Incidentally, I'm going to keep using "she" to describe Scheherazade's voice, despite the fact that the last time I visited Sanctum, JackDoes, our Reint engineer, thought that it would be hilarious to code a time-delayed change to her voice, giving her the intonations of a plummy Tyll aristocrat from a bygone era. The voice also happened to be male. Neither Scheherazade nor myself was particularly amused by his little joke, I was still planning on cornering JackDoes on a balcony somewhere and dangling him off a railing for a little bit the next time I was home.

"Is that going to complicate a pickup?" I asked her.

"Indubitably. They've got two more dreadnaughts in orbit, presumably waiting to deploy shuttles that can last long enough in atmosphere once their shock troops find what they're looking for. I'm assuming that's our girl, by the way."

"A safe assumption," I agreed.

"Are we one step ahead of them?"

"We are."

"Well done, boss."

"Appreciated. We're just west of the dreadnaught they dropped in. How far will we have to go before *you* can swing down and pick us up without being spotted?"

"That depends, ma'am. It's your calculation to make—the longer we wait, the further you can move, and the further you can move, the further I'll be from their search grid, which means the better my stealth systems will hold up against their scans. On the other hand—"

"—on the other hand, the longer we wait, the more likely they are to send more ships to reinforce the ones already here, and the more likely we are to run into trouble on the ground."

"That's the rub, and it looks like they're planning an extended stay. Three dreadnaughts, boss, and one used as a sacrificial lamb, shock and awe and all that. That's a big show of force, ma'am, even for the Pax."

I frowned. It made a certain amount of sense if they were looking for the girl—the Pax had been seeking gifted children, just like we had, albeit for very different reasons. *They* wanted soldiers, tools, to mold the children into shock troops for their armies. We wanted to train them for an entirely different purpose, one not so soaked in blood. Salvation, rather than destruction.

But coming here looking for the girl and *conquering* this system were not necessarily the same thing. Even for Pax, this was overkill to an extreme degree. I had no doubt they could *do* it, and fairly easily, but there was very little *gain* in it, given that the radiation signature from the pulse had pushed this particular system so far back down the technological scale it would be useless for manufacturing. About the only resource it had worth exploiting was the local population itself, to be pressed into service as more Pax soldiers, and that same resource existed on worlds they could also find other uses for.

"This is a bad scene, boss," Scheherazade confirmed, agreeing with my thinking.

"Yeah. Scan your maps, get back to me with a few options for a pickup area."

"Will do."

"Were you just . . . talking to yourself?" the girl asked me.

I started to answer, then sighed instead. "What's your name, kid?" I asked first.

She swallowed. "Esa," she replied.

"Well, Esa," I told her, "when we manage to get off this rock, you're going to see and hear a great many things that don't make a lot of sense to you. I would suggest just rolling with it."

"But who were you talking to?" she pressed. "And how?"

"My ship, Scheherazade. She's in orbit above us, hiding from the Pax forces hanging above the world."

"Your ship can *talk*?" For some reason, this seemed more impressive to her than the ship itself, or the news that there were more Pax in orbit.

"She can."

"Can she get us *out* of here?"

"That, Esa, is what we're going to find out."

CHAPTER 12

I'd hoped that Esa's little trick with the maintenance tunnel—getting us out of the city before the Pax could lock it down, with minimal interaction with soldiers—would have bought us at least a bit of a head start, but no such luck. Whoever was in charge of the Pax troops, apparently they were dumb enough to think wasting a dreadnaught as troop transport—admittedly, impressive troop transport, but still—was a good idea, but smart enough that they'd given at least some of their soldiers orders to make for the countryside as soon as they touched down, rather than focusing on just pacifying the city.

That meant we were dodging Pax troops *ahead* of us as well as keeping an eye out for the soldiers we knew would be approaching from behind, and *that* meant we weren't making quite the forward progress I would have liked.

The *good* news—for us, if not for the Pax or the locals—was that the bandit holdup I'd witnessed this morning had very much not been an isolated incident; the gently swaying fields of iridescent grasses were hiding multiple camps of armed bandits, and they were just as happy to waylay Pax infantry as they were farmers trying to take their goods to market. More so, if it meant they got to steal fancy offworld goods from the Pax soldiers, rather than just crops and local currency, a currency that would likely be worthless due to the invasion, not that most bandits would have been smart enough to think that far ahead.

So we were trying to avoid ambush by the Pax, the Pax were trying to avoid ambush by the bandits, and meanwhile it was starting to get pretty cold out; we'd need shelter, sooner rather than later. Even if the temperature hadn't been dropping lower than I'd like, Esa was exhausted, and I wasn't far off. I *could* have pushed myself harder if I had to, but I won't lie: I was perfectly content to find a natural cave formation with the scanner in my HUD and announce that we'd be taking a break from skulking through the shimmering grasses and copses of blue-tinged trees.

At one point the cave *had* been occupied by another group of raiders, but they'd long since vacated the premises—based on the bullet holes in some of the stuff they'd left behind, rather hurriedly. Maybe the settlement militia had been at least trying to keep the area secure; maybe it had been the result of an economic disagreement with another group of bandits. Didn't matter much, either way—they were long gone.

The Preacher volunteered to keep watch—Barious didn't sleep, exactly, just shut down their various systems in a cycle so that nothing was running continuously for too long, but their senses were never completely dead, either. It was closer to meditation than rest, and she was perfectly capable of keeping an eye on the surroundings visible from the mouth of the cave while she did it.

I covered Esa with my coat; she took it without complaint. I guess orphans were used to wearing other people's castoffs. I would have thought she would have drifted right to sleep—it had been a *very* long day. But I should never underestimate the curiosity of teenagers.

"What's it like?" she asked softly. "Up there?"

"Very different," I said, shutting my eyes as I tried to get comfortable on the rocky cave floor. I could sleep pretty much anywhere—the trick was just letting your body remind you how worn it was, and ignoring everything else.

"Different how?"

"Not just different from here—different from itself, too. It's not like this is the only world that got hit by the pulse, Esa. Almost all of them did, to greater and lesser degrees. Some took the opportunity to put aside their old hatreds and try to create utopias; others—more—devolved into savage wastelands where the very strongest rule everyone else."

"But other places have . . . ships, like yours. People born there can still *leave* their world, if they want to. Make a new life for themselves."

"Some. Not many. And there are difficulties, even on worlds that still have higher levels of technology. It's not like everyone can *afford* a ship, even if they live someplace where ships can still operate. It's been a long day, Esa, and it'll be a longer one tomorrow; go to sleep."

"*You* can afford a ship. Are you rich?"

"My ship was given to me by the . . . organization I work for, the organization that sent me looking for you. I couldn't afford to buy one on my own."

"Does your organization not pay you well?"

"I'm not doing this for the money. Go to sleep."

"So why are you doing it?"

"Because a very long time ago, I did some very bad things, things I can't undo. I figure I should at least try to balance the scales a little bit. Finding kids like you—it's important, for reasons the people I'm taking you to meet will be better suited to explain than me. I'm suited for fighting, flying, and not much else; might as well fight for something important."

The philosophical concept of redemption didn't seem to interest Esa all that much. "So you're poor, then. Like me."

"I get by."

"That's what people say when they're poor. They're usually lying."

"Esa."

"Yeah?"

"Go. To. Sleep."

She sighed—that very specific teenager sigh, heavy and theatrical—and rolled over onto her back. "Why are the Pax after me?"

"We can talk about that later."

"But it's because of my tele . . . telekrin . . . teelekin . . . because I can move stuff with my mind, yeah?"

"I promise, kid, I will explain as much as I can to you once we're safely on my ship and locked into a nice, boring hyperspace cruise. For now, go to goddamned sleep."

"What's hyperspace?"

"Esa, if you don't stop talking, I'm going to have the Preacher inject you with a sedative."

"Can you do that?" she asked the Barious, sitting up a little on her makeshift bed—otherwise known as "a patch of the cave floor mostly free of rocks"—to ask.

The Preacher nodded. "I have a basic first-aid package installed," she said. "A sedative is part of that suite."

"Cool. I did not know that."

"Now you do."

"Both of you: less chat, more rack. Sleep. Now. We have a long day of probably getting shot at tomorrow."

"Oh. That sounds bad."

"Yeah. It'll be worse if we're trying to do it while we're exhausted."

Another long sigh. "Fine." A pause. "Goodnight."

"Goodnight."

"Sleep well."

"You too."

"Don't let—"

"Esa. Shut the *fuck* up."

She giggled, like all teenagers vaguely amused by profanity—all she'd seen that day, and she could still giggle; I took it as a good sign—then rolled onto her side, and finally drifted off.

Shortly thereafter, I did too.

CHAPTER 13

In the morning, before the girl awoke, I raised Scheherazade again on my comms. The good news: she'd found someplace she could pick us up, an old observation tower, far enough from the Pax's search grid that she could get in and out, and high enough up that she wouldn't cook her engines setting down on the rad-soaked earth below.

The bad news: the tower was two days' hike from where we were, and once we got there, we'd have to wait three *more* days before a big enough hole opened up in the Pax's orbits, giving Schaz enough time to get in and out. The slightly *better* news was that there would be a smaller hole in their search grid that would open up before then, big enough through which she could shoot down a supply drop. It was a little risky—Scheherazade's prediction algorithms were good, but they weren't perfect, and there was a chance the Pax would pick up the drop on their sensors, trace its trajectory, and know where we were—but it was better than nothing.

"Do it," I confirmed to her. "I'll contact you when we're in place."

"A supply drop?" the Preacher asked. She'd been listening in, of course—probably could even pick up Schaz's side of the conversation, despite the fact that to me it had sounded like it was inside my head. "Is that wise?"

"Better than the alternative," I shrugged. "With the high ground and some basic defenses from the drop, we'll be able to hold the Pax off even if they *do* know where we are. For a while, at least. If we *don't* get supplies and they find us anyway, we'll be in much worse trouble."

"Plus you and the girl need food." Barious drew energy from an internal fusion battery that converted almost everything around them—sunlight, kinetic energy, even background radiation—into sustenance. The pulse had been designed specifically to *not* target them; we'd wanted to stop war, not commit genocide. My point was, the Preacher didn't need to eat, but Esa and I did.

I nodded. I had some basic protein bars, enough to at least get the girl and me to the observation tower without leaving us half-starved, but they'd be gone before five days were out. We could *survive* without a supply drop, but we wouldn't be much use to anybody in the last few days if we had to. "Plus we need food, yeah," I agreed.

"You haven't told me *why* you're after her, you know," the Barious said, watching the sunrise over the fields of grass, the iridescent light show the flora put on at night slowly fading in the glow of the warm sun as the sky shifted back to its daylight orangish hue. "I understand why the Pax might be—whatever it is that allows her do the things she does, if they could apply it to their soldiers, they'd be unstoppable. But I don't get the sense you're building an army."

"Trust me—she's better off with us than she is with them."

"So you'd be saying your actions are, what, 'justified'?" She gave a small smile at the pun.

"Something like that, yeah."

"And why haven't you driven *me* off yet? I doubt your mandate includes picking up stranded Barious preachers."

"You're handy enough. Might need you to fire a gun before this is all through."

"So you won't let me board your ship."

"You're willing to leave your flock?"

"My flock." She gestured with one hand toward the horizon, back toward whatever remained of the city under the anti-orbital gun. "I don't know what, if any, remains. Religion was only a way to teach them, to educate them. Everyone thinks the pulse is over, but we don't even know where it *came* from. They need to be prepared if it returns."

I felt a twinge at that, but it was a familiar one. I *did* know where the pulse had come from, and her concern wasn't at all misplaced. Still, I shoved it aside. "So you want to come with us when we leave." I made the words a statement.

"I also feel responsible for the girl. Before all this, I helped feed and clothe the orphans, as much as I could, and I helped keep them safe from harm. Then I pointed *you* in her direction. I'm certain you're right—whatever you have planned for her *will* be kinder than what the Pax intend. That docs not mean it will be kind." She was watching me, closely—not like she was desperate for my answer to be one thing or another, more that she wanted to see exactly *how* I phrased my response, and why. "So, yes. I would like to come with you when you leave. If you'll allow me to."

I sighed. "Preacher, you help us off this rock, I'll take you as far as the nearest Barious-populated system. Whether that's a world with most of its tech still intact, whether that's a station with a Barious conclave, whether that's another rock like this one, just with more Barious than anyone else—I make no promises."

"But you won't take me all the way to *your* destination."

I shook my head.

"All right," the Preacher nodded, turning from her examination of my face. "I understand."

"I understand" doesn't mean "I consent," and we both knew that. We also both knew it was the best I was going to get under the circumstances. I hadn't been lying—if we wound up having to hold the observation tower from Pax assault, I *would* need her with a gun. I doubted she'd been a soldier before all of this; you could tell, even with the machine race, who had and who hadn't. I had. She hadn't. But she still had Barious reflexes, and Barious senses, and Barious strength. She'd be an asset I couldn't turn down, not if I had a chance to exploit her. Even if it meant abandoning her later, rather than leaving her here, on a world she at least knew.

Does that sound cruel? Maybe it was. But there's a certain calculation in the work I do. My goal was to get the girl back to Sanctum: that was it, that was all. Nothing else factored in.

A small sound behind us: Esa was waking up. I turned to watch—saw it on her face as she swam back out from sleep, the prior day coming back to her, bit by bit. Different expressions chased themselves across her features: fear, sadness, excitement, grief. Neither the Preacher nor I said anything as she put herself together, ready to face this new day, her life markedly stranger than it had been the *last* time she'd roused herself from slumber.

"All right," she said to us. "You two are up, good for you. Are we about ready to move?"

CHAPTER 14

We hiked mostly in the hours around dawn and dusk. Given the relative shortness of the days on this planet, that meant we covered more ground than it maybe sounds like we did—there was only about an hour, hour and a half after the sun was at its zenith before the sky started darkening again. I'd said before that *many* of the terraformed worlds had orbital cycles roughly in line with a twenty-four-hour day/night cycle; this wasn't one of them.

I cautioned Esa again against using her talents. You never knew who was listening. Or, in this case, we did.

The fields of variegated Tyll wheat stretched around us, a soft breeze shifting them ever so slightly as the last of the light faded. Maybe once, this world had been intended to feed *other* worlds, those pink grasses and green or violet fronds of wheat intended to feed dozens of other planets, but that very purpose—its agrarian nature—had made it a battlefield during the wars, or at least a target. Now its bucolic fields of wheat and grass hid threats of a different sort: every dip in the lay of the landscape threatened to hold an ambush, every copse of trees seemed menacing.

We could hear gunfire in the distance; the Pax were still waging their war against the locals, for whatever reason—either to try and track down the girl, or just because they were assholes—but the further we got from the city and whatever logistical support they had back there, the more evenly matched the fighting became.

After all, the people living out in the wilderness weren't city-dwellers counting on numbers or high walls to protect them: they were either armed and prepared to deal with bandit incursions, or bandits themselves. As far as they were concerned, fighting off Pax was no different than fighting off anyone else, especially not now that the pulse would have mostly eaten away at the Pax's technological advantage.

Still, we managed to avoid combat through a combination of the Preacher's keen senses and my comms with Scheherazade, who was still busily scanning the surface from whatever moon she was hiding out on. We had to change our route several times to do so, but I'd take the loss of time and the extended hiking over risking another firefight, especially one that might draw *more* attention down on our heads.

During the hikes, Esa was mostly quiet, doing her best to keep up with her longer-legged companions. When we rested, though, it was nonstop questions: who were the Pax? What were the other worlds like? Okay, what were the other worlds I'd visited *personally* like? What kind of world had I grown up on? Where had I learned to fight? Would *she* be taught to fight? Where had I learned to fly? Why did *I* fly, when my ship could talk? Couldn't the ship just fly herself? Had I named my ship? Why had I given my ship that particular name? Why wouldn't I tell her *my* name?

The Preacher just laughed when she asked that one. She knew I wouldn't answer.

Esa realized pretty quickly the more general she kept her questions, the more likely I was to reply. I didn't want to tell her anything about Sanctum; anything I told her, purposefully or not, would be colored by my own perspective, and I wanted her to be able to make the decision she'd be facing for herself. Likewise, I didn't talk about what she could expect there.

I didn't talk about myself because it's not a subject I care for. I didn't tell her my name for similar reasons, and because of what had been hammered into us when we'd first started this little duty: we were *not* to allow the children to grow too attached to us. We were shepherds, and once we'd delivered our current charge, we would have to go out for another lost sheep. Likewise, our charges would either join Sanctum or make their way in the galaxy, but the odds that they would ever see us again were slim. I was a member of the Justified, but I saw Sanctum rarely—just often enough to drop off my "cargo" and then I was off to scour the galaxy for more.

We were not their parents; we were not their guardians; we were not their friends. As far as we were concerned, they were sentient packages that we were delivering, and as far as *they* were concerned, we were the will of Sanctum, of the Justified, forged into a person. We shouldn't have too many traits of our own.

It had never really been an issue for me—I've usually had more trouble *failing* to connect with people rather than connecting when I shouldn't. Eventually, Esa took the hint, deciding that if I weren't going to talk about myself anyway, she was better off pursuing more fruitful areas of inquiry.

Finally, we came within sight of the observation tower.

Esa shaded her eyes, staring up at the far-off structure. It rose up like a spindle from the surrounding fields, topped by a single broad platform—no outbuildings, no connecting wires, even the roads that might have once led to it long since overgrown. There were just the gently waving fronds of wheat around it and the latticed metal beams of the tower, stretching up toward the sienna sky and shifting even in the relatively gentle winds. "That . . . doesn't look too sturdy," Esa said, having noted that telltale tilting in the structure. "Does it look sturdy to you?"

I shrugged. "It survived god knows how many bombardments during the wars, *and* the pulse, and god knows what since. I think it's plenty sturdy."

"Uh-huh." Esa turned from me to the Preacher. "Does it look sturdy to *you*?"

"Calm, child," the Preacher smiled. "We're only going to live there for a few days, then land an entire starship on the platform up top. Possibly whilst under fire from the Pax."

Esa frowned at her. "For a religious leader-person, you *suck* at comfort, you know that, Preacher?"

"It has been mentioned, yes."

We moved down into the last valley, crossing the open stretch of land between us and the tower.

It really *was* tall, taller than I'd expected. I don't know what its purpose might have been during the war—it was taller than any use *I* could think of off the top of my head. At least thirty stories, straight up, just an exposed metal stairwell surrounded by catwalks and the structure's steel, the smallish bunker with a landing platform on its roof the only thing at the top. Some sort of watchtower, maybe, though watching for what, I couldn't say.

On the bright side, once we got to the top, we'd be able to see for *miles* around—there was nothing but fields of grass and wheat in any direction, their tips swaying gently in the breeze. Not even so much as one of the miniature azure forests we'd passed on the way here broke the line of the horizon. Even if Schaz *didn't* get us that supply drop, I could hold a place like this with just my rifle for . . . quite some time.

Provided the Pax hadn't brought along heavy munitions and just decided to blow us up, that is. But they wanted the girl alive, so that seemed less likely.

"Really tall," Esa said, staring up at the thing from its base.

"It is, yes," the Preacher affirmed.

"And we have to climb all those stairs."

"We *do* have to climb all those stairs. At least 'up' is different from 'forward,' which is what we've been doing for the last two days."

"I've never seen a relic like this."

"Have you ever seen a structure from the war *other* than the guns in your hometown?"

". . . No."

"Well then that's not surprising."

"All right, ladies," I sighed, opening the gate at the bottom of the tower. Its hinges gave a god-awful screech as they swung, but at least they moved. "Our climb awaits."

CHAPTER 15

It was a long way up. We climbed, and climbed, and climbed some more. I checked the sight lines from the platforms, checked for choke points. It was a good position. The Pax *could* dig us out, given enough time, but it would cost them dearly. Of course, that was assuming they wanted the girl badly enough—if there came a time when they just decided to cut their losses and bring the tower down, we were fucked.

Finally, panting, we reached the top of the stairs, opening the single door that lead into the bunker. It had been stripped clean over the years by scavengers; there was nothing left inside the concrete walls, not even a bolted-down table. Esa flopped down inside and immediately went to sleep. I couldn't blame her. The Preacher and I exited the bunker itself, ignoring the ladder leading to the landing platform and its roof and instead walking to the edge of the observation platform that ringed the concrete, roughly twice the square footage of the bunker itself.

The Barious stared out at the horizon. "Anything?" I asked her as she scanned the fields, knowing her eyes were far better than mine, even with the implants and upgrades I'd had installed to my HUD.

She shook her head. "And honestly, that worries me a little," she said. "We've been surrounded by small-arms fire pretty much our whole trek here. Sometimes it's a ways off, but it's been there, present, at least in the distance. Now there's nothing."

"So either the locals have managed to hold the Pax back—"

"—or the Pax have been successful in quelling the local resistance, which means soon they'll start hunting for us in earnest. They must know the girl's not in the city by now." She turned to look at me. "You were tracking her from orbit. You must have been—this is a fairly large world. There's no way you were lucky enough to set down and just stumble across her."

"You don't know how long I've been looking."

"A short enough time that your clothing is still giving off residual cosmic radiation. Days, not months."

I nodded. "I was tracking her from orbit," I confirmed. "Anytime she uses her . . . gifts . . . it sends off a flare of benign radiation. I don't know how good the Pax's sensors are—not as good as Scheherazade's, I'd wager, since hers are purpose-designed for this. But still. We tracked her to within a few square miles from orbit. If the Pax's sensors are even *half* as good, that would still give them a general location, and there's not much else *out* here besides this tower."

"But they can only track her if she uses her gift. Which is why you haven't let her. What is it that the Justified want her for again?"

I shook my head. "Not part of our deal."

She turned back to the horizon. "For now."

"For now."

Apparently, that was the end of our conversation. I wandered off a little bit to give myself the illusion of privacy as I contacted Schaz. Yes, there was still a risk that the Pax in orbit above would see her fire off the supply drop, but it was a risk I was willing to take.

Scheherazade gave me confirmation that she had the drop prepped; it would be another day before the window in the Pax patrols opened up enough for her to fire it through. I dug some string out from my pockets and climbed the ladder to the bunker roof, marked off a section of landing platform.

"What's that?" Esa asked me, her catnap finished.

"Don't stand inside the string," I told her.

"Why not?"

"Because if you get squished by a ton of defensive supplies dropped from orbit, it will pretty much eliminate our *need* for a ton of defensive supplies dropped from orbit."

She made a face at me. "I need to use the privy."

I shook my head. "There's not a privy."

"So what the hell do I do?"

"Well, you can either climb all the way back down to the ground—"

"Nope."

"—or you can just go over the side."

"Ew."

"Those are your choices. I don't care which you do, so long as you don't get yourself killed doing either one. We're going to be up here for a couple of days—better get used to it."

That earned me another long-suffering teenage sigh, and she wandered off to take care of her necessities. I dialed up the magnification on my HUD, taking another look at our surroundings. There really wasn't anything of note out there—just the gently rolling plains of long grasses. We'd be able to see the Pax coming from literal miles away.

Of course, maybe we'd been successful—maybe they weren't coming at all. Maybe we'd just spend a few days holed up in the sky, Schaz would come and pick us up, and I would have wasted some of Sanctum's not-infinite supplies setting up a defensive perimeter.

Not likely, but one could hope. Of course, that hope didn't last long; Scheherezade called in shortly. I was a great many things, but lucky had never been one of them. "Got troop movement, boss," she told me. "They're coming out of the city in force. A company, at least."

"Doesn't mean they're heading our way." I scratched my jaw. "Could be they've pacified the city and are moving to reinforce the platoons out in the surrounding areas."

"Could be. Think that's likely?"

"Not so much, no. They're looking for us."

"Drop's in about twenty hours. Even if they knew exactly where you were *and* they tried to march double time the whole way, they won't reach your position before then."

"So there's that."

"I'll be out of communication for a while; their sensor grid is about to sweep my position, and I'll have to power down."

"Understood. Thanks, Schaz."

"Anytime, boss."

I tapped the hard nub set between my jawbone and the base of my ear, shutting off my comm—the implant was useful on worlds like this one, where the pulse was less likely to cook technology buried in flesh, but talking on it always felt slightly strange to me, like I was hearing Schaz in my head, rather than in my ear.

Alone with my thoughts again, I stared out at the fields of wheat and grass, a riot of pink and green in rolling waves stretching off toward the once-again setting sun. More likely than not, Pax troops would come marching over those hills, sooner rather than later. Schaz could be optimistic all she wanted— I knew they were heading for us. The only thing that *I* hoped for was that we'd be ready when they came, and that I could buy enough time for Schaz to get us off this damn planet.

Pretty or not, I was getting fairly tired of rolling fields of pink and purple and green, and of the distant gunfire that seemed to go with them.

CHAPTER 16

The supply drop came in right on time the next day. I made all three of us retreat down the stairs a few flights, just in case the added weight was exactly what it took to collapse the bunker roof. I didn't think it was likely—the drop *did* have built-in antigrav compensators and a parachute to slow its descent, though the compensators would be burned out by pulse radiation shortly after they activated—but I had no interest in taking chances, all the same.

There was a thump as the drop set down, and the tower made an ominous creaking sound before it settled, the whole structure swaying for a moment.

"Cool," Esa said, looking up like she could see through the ceiling as she released her death grip on the stairwell railing. "Let's go check our loot."

"I don't think it's really 'loot' if it already belongs to our friend, here," the Preacher nodded at me, though she did start moving back up to the platform.

"Whatever. Let's check out our fancy toys. And also food. I'm sick of protein bars."

I could have told her that she should just be happy to have had anything at all to eat, but I didn't. I was sick of protein bars too.

We climbed back up the stairs, then up the half-broken ladder to the bunker roof. The supply drop was still smoking slightly, two sets of heavy crates. The concrete beneath had cracked a little where they'd hit, but it hadn't gone all the way through the ceiling.

I undid the manual lock—just a rotary number combination, so that pulse radiation couldn't render it inoperable—and cracked open the cases.

Schaz, of course, had spent the last few days scanning the tower and sorting through our supply-drop inventory to see what we might need. We had a dozen or so of these in the hold, set up for different climates, different situations. She hadn't disappointed in her decisions.

Two extremely high-powered gauss rifles using electromagnetic coils to accelerate rounds, designed for long-range sniper fire; one shoulder-mounted autocannon, loaded with shotgun rounds for close quarters; one SAM with six rounds; five recon drones that would link directly to my HUD; three autotargeting turret emplacements; one semiautomatic grenade launcher with several drums of different munition varieties; various tools, components, and mechanisms that would allow me to build jury-rigged, low-tech traps. And also more food.

All of it would need assembly, of course—except the food; those were simple MREs, but still improvements over the protein bars—but we hopefully had a couple of days. Even if the Pax had managed to spot the drop, it would be a bit before they could assemble a team to check it out.

The Preacher looked over all the implements of war, then raised a mechanical eyebrow in my direction. "And you're, what, exactly, again?" she asked me. "The Justified's designated babysitter?"

"I help gifted kids," I shrugged, digging around into the crate. "Sometimes they need a lot of help."

"Bullshit. This isn't a diplomat's crash supply, nor an aid worker's survival cache. This is a soldier's toolkit. Not just an infantry grunt, either. This is special-ops, black-bag gear. You could destabilize a continental *government* with this level of firepower."

"If that's what I needed to do, then yeah. I could."

"I'll say it again: you're no babysitter. I don't know what you are, but you *aren't* that."

"And you're no preacher," I said finally, looking up at her. "You want to keep asking each other questions?"

She shrugged, and walked away; I tossed Esa—who had been following our conversation with interest—one of the MREs to forestall her questions, then dug up another one for myself. My gambit successful, Esa hurriedly peeled the packaging free, then took a massive bite. She promptly began to cough like she'd just inhaled a lungful of water. "What the hell *is* this?" she gasped. "It's spicy as . . . as . . . it's really spicy."

I tossed her a bottle of water. "Sorry about that," I told her. "You've only got two choices when it comes to MREs—spicy, or bland and tasteless. I pretty much only stock the ones with actual flavor."

"The only flavor this has is *hot*."

"Yeah, but at least it's a flavor."

The Preacher, meanwhile, had knelt by the cases, studying one of the gauss rifles. Those guns were heavy as hell—I could only fire them from a prone position, using the attached tripod or resting the barrel on something—but she lifted it with ease, familiarizing herself with the weaponry. "You know how to use one of those?" I asked her around a mouthful of spicy . . . something. Something vaguely fishy, maybe.

"I'm familiar with the style of weapon, yes," she agreed.

"Hell kinda preacher even are you?" Esa squinted at her, remembering my own statement.

"One devoted to your continued safety and well-being."

"Oh. Cool."

With a single smooth motion, the Preacher removed the scope from the weapon, leaving her staring down the length of the gun without so much as an iron sight. I raised an eyebrow at her, setting aside my meal for the moment. "You've got combat optics," I said. It wasn't a question. If she removed the scope, it was because it would have been unnecessary with what she already had installed.

"Yes."

"But you didn't serve in the wars." That *was* a question, though not one I actually expected her to answer directly.

"Not in a front lines capacity, no."

That was probably all I was going to get. "Think you can fire one of those and wear the autoshotgun rig at the same time?" I asked.

"I had assumed you'd want that on Esa," she told me.

I laughed. "Preacher, I think maybe you need to double check some of your databanks. That rig's sixty pounds, at least. *I* could barely move if I strapped that thing onto my shoulder."

"I bet I could carry it," Esa frowned at me. Apparently she didn't like being told what she couldn't do.

"Give it a shot." I returned to my meal, purposefully giving off an air of nonchalance.

Her face set in a determined scowl, she knelt beside the crates and tried to buckle on the shotgun rig. I didn't offer to help. I'll give her this—she actually managed to set it on her shoulder, and she *almost* stood up under the weight before collapsing back to the bunker roof. "Okay," she huffed. "Maybe this should go to the Preacher."

The Barious fit it on with just one hand, because of course she did.

"How long will any of this stuff hold out against the pulse radiation?" the Preacher asked me.

I lifted my free hand and rocked it back and forth, my MRE still clutched in the other. "It won't really start breaking down until we use the tech components," I told her. "After that, though, it's anyone's guess. It depends on how much gear the Pax bring to the party. If they come loaded for bear too, the local radiation will be divided between us, and it'll go that much slower."

"Rough estimate?" she asked.

"The faster we fire, the faster they'll break down. Two magazines out of each gauss rifle if we're the only ones with fancy toys, five if the Pax bring their own. Five shots to a magazine."

"And the rest?"

"The grenade launcher doesn't have any exotic tech—it takes tech to fabricate it, but not to operate it. There's nothing noteworthy in the autoshotgun, either, *except* the computer chips in the sensors; it'll hold up for a good bit. Plus, hopefully, it won't *start* firing until a significant length into the fight."

"Because that would mean they've come within shotgun range, which would mean they were at least climbing the tower, if not on the platform itself."

"Indeed. The turrets will hold out longer; they're shielded against pulse radiation. I mean, they won't last forever, but I wouldn't be surprised if they managed to fire themselves dry before the rads bring them down. The drones won't last long after activation, but so long as we send them out one at a time, they'll do their jobs."

"And that?" the Preacher nodded at the SAM, a compact design for its purpose, but still a mean-looking piece of tech.

I shrugged. "I'll only be able to fire it a couple of times—maybe three, if those three shots are in quick succession, but if I fire three shots in quick succession with *that* bad boy, we're in pretty deep trouble."

"You think the Pax will have aerial units? Those won't last long in the high rads here."

"They wasted an entire dreadnaught just to take the gun city. I think they might waste a few gunships, yeah, if they get desperate enough, and if they realize we're about to get off planet."

Esa was watching both of us, pretending like she didn't really care, but she'd stopped eating her meal again. "Just how bad is this going to get?" she asked, trying to keep the fear out of her voice. Before, she hadn't really had time to worry—shit was going wrong, and her survival instinct took over. Now, though, she could *think* about it, and she wasn't liking the conclusions she'd drawn from all the weaponry I'd had Schaz send down.

I shrugged. "The Pax may not even track us here," I reminded her. "Two more days, then we're off this rock."

"But if they do?"

"Then it gets bad."

She nodded. "Right."

CHAPTER 17

I set up two of the turrets on different landings on the stairs below us—one low enough that it could fire out, toward the fields where the Pax would be advancing from, the second a few flights shy of the bunker itself, positioning it so that it would fire *down*, at any Pax who got inside the stairwell.

The third sentry gun I set on the edge of the observation platform itself. That meant it was high enough that the fields below were well outside of its max range, which meant I had to dig into its innards and disable the bit that wouldn't allow it to fire at anything below a certain hit percentage, but I wasn't counting on it doing much killing; I wanted it for suppressing fire.

I left both the gauss rifles for the Preacher—if her optics were as good as she said, she'd likely be better than me with them, plus she could move and relocate much faster than I could under its weight. The SAM I assembled and left just inside the bunker, and the Preacher was already wearing the autoshotgun rig. The grenade launcher went near what I figured would be my first firing position, at the edge of the observation platform, behind a waist-high wall that would provide decent cover. That meant all that was left to do was wire up the stairwell and the surrounding fields with smaller traps.

The fields I seeded with hastily buried mines. If the Pax came slowly, they'd pick them out easily, but I was betting that they'd be in something of a rush to get out from under the gunfire we'd be raining down on them from above.

The stairwell itself was trickier—I couldn't risk using explosives, because that might compromise the integrity of the whole structure, and it wouldn't do us a great deal of good to kill a half-dozen Pax with a bomb if that same blast brought down the entire fucking tower, and us along with it. Instead I had to settle for a handful of smashing or bladed traps—they'd only get one soldier each, but hopefully they'd force the others to slow their ascent, checking for more.

I also set a few incendiary charges just below the turrets; explosions might take out the tower, but simple fire wouldn't, the structure was made of non-flammable materials. Of course, that meant the incendiaries would burn themselves out pretty quickly too. Everything's a trade-off.

All of that took most of the second day on the tower. By the time the second dusk fell, we were as prepared as we were going to be.

I drew Esa to the side that evening. She'd been watching me set up for the assault with bright, interested eyes—too excited to be really afraid, but too afraid to get really excited. "Are we all set up?" she asked me.

I nodded. "As good as we're going to be. Listen, Esa, when this starts, I want you to stay in the bunker."

She scowled at me. "Fuck that nonsense," she replied. "There are only three of us; you're going to *need* me. Plus, I can move shit with my *mind*, remember?"

"Yeah, but that takes a toll on you; I've seen it."

"So will getting shot." She had a point.

"Stay in the bunker," I repeated. "You won't be able to do anything with telekinesis that the Preacher and I can't do with bullets. You'll be our first line of defense if they get to the door at the top of the stairs." If that happened, there'd be a lot of other shit going on as well, but at least she'd feel useful in the interim. "If they get that close—here." I reached to the small of my back and produced my pistol, holding it by the barrel so I could offer her the grip.

It was a heavy thing, heavy and old, a basic revolver chambered for .45 caliber rounds. It would probably put her on her ass the first time she tried to fire it, but it was better than nothing—I kept it around because it worked on *every* world, regardless of the level of pulse radiation. Plus, it had been a gift.

I extended the gun toward her. She scowled at me again, and refused to take it. "I can move shit with my *mind*," she said again. "Why would I need a gun?"

"Because telekinesis takes concentration; a handgun just takes a reaction, and your gifts still draw attention. Just . . . take it. Hopefully, you won't need it."

She licked her lips, and nodded, reaching gingerly for the gun, feeling the heavy weight of the thing. I didn't know if she'd killed anyone before— she'd put that Pax soldier through a wall down in the tunnels under the city, but that didn't necessarily mean she'd *killed* him, or at least that she had been trying to.

"It kicks like a bastard," I warned her.

"Got it."

"Don't ever point it at me. Or the Preacher."

"Got it."

"To fire, pull the hammer back, then—"

"I know how a goddamned gun works."

"All right. And Esa?"

"Yeah?" She was still staring down at the pistol in her hands.

"Don't lose it. It has a great deal of sentimental value to me."

"A *gun* has sentimental value? That's . . . kind of fucked up."

"Thanks."

"No problem. So." She was still holding the weight of the heavy revolver in her hands, but she wasn't looking at the gun anymore, and she wasn't looking out over the concrete walls of the bunker, either—she was looking at me, instead.

"Yeah?" I asked her, knowing what was coming next.

"Why me?" she asked. A question teenagers had been asking me for a very, very long time.

I gave them the answer they always thought they wanted to hear, until they heard it and realized they really, really didn't. "You're special," I said.

She smiled crookedly, tilting the gun in her hands. "I can move shit with my mind. I get that makes me fairly uncommon, yeah. But I mean . . ." She stopped playing with the weapon as the words trailed off, let the gun's weight drop back into her palms.

"You're asking why," I said, taking a seat opposite her, leaning against the concrete wall; this might take a bit. "Not the other bit, not the *how*: it's the *why* that you want."

She nodded. "The how doesn't interest me—I just *can*, that's all. It just *happens*, usually when I get pissed. I always figured the why was just . . ." She stopped for a moment, looking for the words. "I mean, why is your skin a lighter shade of brown than mine? Why is your hair straight and mine's springy?" She shrugged. "I dunno, but it's still true, right? Genetics, or something like."

"Not quite."

"Genetics don't *control* skin color?"

"Don't be a smart-ass. I mean genetics aren't what give you your gifts."

"And you know what does?" A note of something there, in her voice, something she was keeping locked up tight. Hope, maybe. Or fear. The two can sound surprisingly similar.

"In a way," I said.

"That doesn't sound like a yes."

"Maybe, but it's also not a no. The people I work for—scientists who have spent the last century studying kids like you—they think your abilities are actually a kind of . . . by-product."

"A by-product of what?"

"Of the pulse."

She stared at me for a moment, like she was trying to gauge whether I was joking or not. Finally, she laughed. "Sure. Everything's always the pulse's fault, isn't it? Rains won't come? Blame the pulse; must have had an effect on the atmosphere. Cattle gets sick? Must be the pulse, changed something in the soil. Grow a goiter on your big toe? Well then that's got to be—"

I held up a hand to stop her, and I sighed. I got the point. You'd think, after doing this so many times, I'd be better at it, but the truth was, it was different for each subject. Some had come from worlds with almost golden-age technology; some, like Esa, had come from worlds like this one, where spaceflight was a nearly forgotten memory. Others came from worlds even worse, places that had descended into near-feudal nightmares.

None of them wanted to believe me when I said that their gifts—however much chaos they might have caused in the kids' lives—came from the worst thing that had ever happened in the galaxy, as far as they were concerned.

"Let me start again," I said. "Here's what you think you know about the pulse: a hundred years ago, technology worked the same the whole galaxy over. If a ship could take off from one world, it could land on another, and if something worked on one planet, it would work on the next, unless you broke it in between. Yes?"

"Correct," she nodded, blinking raptly at me in what I'm *pretty* sure was a deeply insincere approximation of attention.

I kept going anyway. "Then the pulse came, and it knocked your world—

and a lot of other worlds like yours, most of the worlds in the galaxy, really—back a few thousand years, back to a time before spaceflight, before electricity, even."

"Yeah, I'm not entirely clear on what 'electricity' is," she admitted, forgetting to be a smart-ass for a second. "Something about lightning, and then you can cook food without fire?"

"Close enough." I shrugged. "And that's the thing about how I just described the pulse to you, the same way most of the rest of the galaxy thinks about it: close, but not quite the truth."

"And you know the truth."

"I do. You ready?"

"No." She grinned. "Okay, yes."

I didn't laugh at her little joke. I think that shook her, a bit. Good. I wanted it to. She needed to really *hear* what I said next. Pax on our trail or no, it was going to define the rest of her life, whether she wanted it to or not.

"The pulse *wasn't* a one-off thing," I told her. "Everyone thinks it happened, it's done, and we're living with its aftereffects. Some of them even believe that, in time, the radiation that suppresses so much tech will fade, and we'll be able to rebuild to what we were."

"Assuming we'd want to," the Preacher added. She was leaning against the concrete bunker doorway, listening in.

"Assuming we'd want to," I nodded up at her. "The galaxy before the pulse was . . . not very nice."

"Not nice?" Esa cocked an eyebrow at me. "As I understand it, everyone was always trying to kill each other."

"A pretty fair summation, yeah."

"What do you mean, the pulse isn't 'done'?" the Preacher asked me. She'd latched on to the more important part of this discussion.

"Just what I said. It *wasn't* a one-off thing, like everyone thinks. It came, and it knocked out most of the tech in the galaxy, and so everyone assumed that was it, it was over."

"You're saying it's not."

"I'm saying it's *still* happening. It spread through the galaxy, yes, and yes, it passed beyond the edge of known space—but it's still *out* there. Building in power, building in intensity."

"Yeah, but it's still going *out*, right?" Esa said. "So who the fuck cares—it's still moving away from us."

"No, it's not," I shook my head. "It's stopped its outward advance. And sooner or later, it's coming back. We don't know how much time we have—could be years, could be decades, could be centuries, for all we know—but we *do* know that it's happening. It's not done yet."

"Do you know what it will do when it hits?" Esa asked me, her voice gone careful. She was finally starting to get it, now; the consequences that such a return might entail. "Will it turn some of the less-affected worlds into something . . . more like mine?"

I shook my head. "We don't know."

"Will it push worlds like this one even further backwards, make it so that wheels don't roll, make *fire* not be fire anymore, or something?"

"We don't know."

"So it *could* do that. Or it could do worse."

I nodded. "It could do worse, yeah."

She made a face. "Great."

"Not ideal, no."

"And this all has what to do with me, again?"

"It has everything to do with you."

"Because the pulse gave me my . . . abilities."

I nodded. "You're part of what's called the 'next generation.'"

"The next generation after what?"

"After the pulse."

"But I'm *not* the next generation after the pulse. I'm, like . . . *four* generations after the pulse."

"It's a general term, it's not . . . not important."

"Because Reetha don't live as long as humans; some of them are on, like, the *eighth* generation after the pulse. Would a Reetha kid who was . . . different, like me . . . would *they* still be called 'next generation'?"

"Still not important. There have been kids like you being born since immediately after the pulse, that's where the . . . it's just a name. What matters is that the lingering radiation from the pulse changed you, somehow. Gave you gifts. Made you . . . different."

She was finally trying to think it through. "You're saying that before me—

before the start of this 'next generation,' before the pulse—there *weren't* kids like me."

"Have you ever heard of any? In any of the golden-age or sect-era stories you've been told, was there ever any mention of telekinesis, telepathy, the ability to alter mass or density or *gravity* at will?"

"Those are *options?*"

I snapped my fingers. "Focus," I told her. "Yes, Esa, I'm saying that kids like you *didn't exist* before the pulse."

"You think it was the radiation that did it." The Preacher frowned at me.

"Yes." I nodded. "I do—*we* do, the Justified. I can't walk you through it all that well, I'm not a—I don't *do* science—but I'm saying, yes. Kids weren't born with your kind of abilities, Esa, not before the pulse. Then the pulse happened, and all of a sudden they *were*, and their births corresponded with a rise in ambient pulse radiation. That's correlation *and* causation, all wrapped up in one. We've done countless studies on pulse-radiation exposure, studies on kids like you, and yes, there *is* a genetic component, but mainly it's the pulse itself that did it, that made it *possible*. And not just human kids, either. All species were affected, all except . . ." I trailed off; the Preacher knew what I meant, and she knew I knew, but I didn't want to say it.

"There are no Barious children to have *been* so gifted," she said flatly. "Not anymore."

I nodded. "Anyway, Justified—"

"And that's the sect you work for," Esa clarified.

"Yes."

"But weren't sects the *bad* guys during the time before the pulse?" she asked. "Weren't *they* the ones trying to kill each other?"

"It's . . . kind of a catch-all term, like 'government' or 'organization.' There can be good governments and bad ones. Sects were—are—the same. The Pax are a sect, and yeah—they're the bad guys. But there are hundreds of thousands of sects, Esa, and some are good, and some are bad, and most just . . . just *are*. The Justified is the name of the sect I belong to."

"And what does that name *mean?* Justified? Justified in *what?*"

I sighed. "It's an old name; it doesn't mean *anything* anymore. The point is, we started studying the kids with the gifts, those who came after the pulse, and in doing so—in studying them, in how their gifts reacted to pulse radiation, in where they were born, on which worlds—that's when we learned that there was a . . . a kind of connection. Not *just* between the next generation—"

"Still a stupid name," Esa groused, but she was listening intently anyway.

"Not just between the next generation and the pulse," I continued, "but also between the next generation and the pulse's *return*, the force that . . . *moves* the pulse through the universe. They're *linked*, somehow. That's how it all connects."

"Linked *how?*"

"Be specific," the Preacher added firmly.

"I can't," I told her, trying not to get annoyed myself. "Look at me, Preacher—do I look like I'm wearing a lab coat? I know what the scientists tell me, and what they tell me is that the kids and the pulse and the pulse coming *back* are connected. Do you think I'm lying?"

She shook her head mutely.

"Do you think I'm *wrong?*"

"No," she said quietly. She hadn't been surprised when I'd mentioned the pulse coming back; just surprised that I'd known about it. I filed that away as well.

"All right then." I turned back to Esa. "Once we figured out the pulse *was* coming back, we figured we'd need a . . . defense, against it. A bulwark, a shield. For when it returned."

"A shield?" the Preacher asked. "A shield for the whole galaxy? Or just for who you deem worthy?"

"We'll protect as many as we can," I replied evenly. "That may not be everyone."

Esa had figured out which part of the information I was feeding her was the most important; she'd set aside the gun, and was staring intently at me instead. "And you think that . . . kids like me . . . can help you protect people. Can help . . . stop it. Can *be* that shield."

"A kind of barricade, right. Think of the pulse as a, a kind of wave. Right now, it's going out, pulling back into the ocean—"

"I've never seen the ocean before."

"But you know what it is, right?"

"Duh."

"So right now, the pulse is receding, and it's leaving kids like *you* in its wake, exposed in the sand. In another year, or a decade, or a century, that wave will return, taller than ever. The Justified are trying to train the next generation to be a seawall against that wave. And the more kids we have, and the more *powerful* they are, the stronger that wall becomes. The *more* walls we can build. The more systems we can protect. The pulse *made* you the way you are, Esa. It *gave* you your gifts. We're just trying to make sure that they're used defending the galaxy against the return of the greatest threat it's ever known."

Esa looked down, for a moment. "You're saying the pulse gave me my gifts," she said quietly, staring at her hands. When she said those words before, she'd been mocking, joking. Now there was something different in her voice. She'd finally understood. "You're saying it made me what I am."

I got that was a hard thing to hear. "You're not alone in all this," I told her. "What the pulse did to you, it's done to others; there are other kids at Sanctum right now, training, preparing for—"

She held up a hand. "You don't need to give me the hard sell," she said. "If it's you or the Pax—yeah, I'll take the guys trying to build a wall against the return of the pulse over the guys with the guns dropping out of the sky and shooting everything in sight. I mean . . . yeah."

I smiled briefly at that; at least she was pragmatic. "Wise choice," I said.

She held up the revolver. "But you still think I need this," she said.

I stood, and stretched. "Understanding your gift's origin won't change the fact that the Pax are still coming for us. Yeah. You might need that."

I left her examining the revolver—and the Preacher staring after me— and I walked out to the edge of the observation platform, looking out over the fields. So now she knew. I hadn't come to save her.

I'd come to ask her to save everyone else.

Schaz called in again, breaking into my reverie. "No doubt about it now," she told me. "They're definitely heading your way."

Right. The Pax. All that talk about the pulse and its return, and I'd almost forgotten the significantly more imminent threat.

"Making good time?" I asked, squinting at the horizon as though I could *see* the Pax soldiers approaching. I couldn't—they were still miles out. I looked anyway.

"I'd say they were in a hurry, ma'am," Schaz replied.

"Understood. Is your window still open?"

"They haven't changed anything up here, no. I can try and come earlier if you'd like, but I'd call it fifty-fifty odds they'd shoot me down before I even made the atmosphere."

"We'll hold out."

"Good luck, boss. I'll see you soon. Scheherazade out." She clicked off the comm, and there was a brief burst of static in my head, followed by nothing. I kept looking out at the distance, watching the grass slowly begin its iridescent glow again. I'd set the traps; I'd prepared Esa for what was to come as best I could.

Now all that was left to do was wait and see who got here first—Scheherazade, or the Pax.

CHAPTER 18

It was the Pax.

Of course it was. We saw their first scouts cross over the ridge, pushing their way through the fields of wild grasses just as dawn was beginning to stain its way across the far horizon. There were only a few of them, but they were moving like they had a purpose, like they were looking for something. And of course, the tower was the only thing *to* see for miles around.

"Think they know we're here?" the Preacher asked, her rifle raised up to her eye.

"Probably," I nodded, my position much the same, even though they were still far out of the effective range of my gun.

"Want me to shoot them?"

I shook my head. "Don't waste the rounds. A scouting party that doesn't return tells an officer where their enemy is just as surely as one that comes back with a complete report."

"Is that some kind of terrible proverb?"

"I learned a great many terrible proverbs during the wars."

It was difficult to make out at this distance, but it *looked* like the Pax were gesturing toward the tower. Again—not surprising. It was the only place we possibly *could* have been. It seemed like they were having some kind of argument—maybe one wanted to come closer, to investigate and return with a full report, hopefully earn a promotion, while the other two wanted to retreat back to the safety of the rest of their company, thank you very much. Even among the indoctrinated ranks of the Pax there were varying levels of self-preservation.

Eventually, the two cowards won out by the expedient process of one of them cracking the dissenter across the back of the head with his own rifle.

They left him where he lay—I mean, it's not like they weren't planning to return—and retreated back over the ridge.

I could have ended them then—or at least told the Preacher to take the shot—but there would be no point: like I'd said to the Preacher, a missing squad would give away our location just as soon as a report would, and I didn't want the rest of the Pax to know exactly what they were up against. The report of a gauss rifle is a . . . distinctive sound, after all. I didn't want them to have even a rough estimate of within what range they'd start taking fire.

"So this is it," the Preacher said, watching the scouts retreat. "They're committed now." She turned to look at me once the two Pax soldiers had vanished. "How long 'til your ship arrives?"

I checked my HUD, the countdown clock I'd set in place ticking away, in constant motion. "Four hours, twenty-three minutes," I said. "Roughly a day cycle."

"You figure the Pax will be here in, what, two?"

"Sounds about right."

"Two hours plus is a long time to hold off an enemy assault."

I shrugged. "That's why we have all the death traps."

"The death traps. As opposed to the usual cuddly-teddy-bear traps."

"Is this really the goddamned time for semantics? They're traps that make people die, Preacher, what do you want me to call them?"

"I really think just 'traps' would do fine."

We settled back in to wait, both of us viewing the fields below through the sights of our guns.

Eventually, the Pax soldiers started to form up on the top of the ridge, right on time. I'm sure they looked dashing and brave standing up there, perfect for a Pax recruitment video—if the Pax recruited by propaganda and not by force—but the idiocy of standing out in the open when you were about to assault a higher position made my trigger finger twitch. I wanted to shoot them on general principle, but I also wanted to lure them in closer before the dying started.

They started marching down toward the tower in perfect parade formation. If they were unhappy to have been at least pseudo-abandoned on this planet, their marching hadn't suffered, at least, the goose-stepping bastards.

Even when I'd been a soldier, I'd despised fancy marching formations. You might as well paint a target on your puffed-out chest.

The Preacher had her rifle raised up again. "I suppose you want me to focus fire on their officers first," she said.

"If they're stupid enough to wear rank insignia in a combat zone, they're stupid enough to die first," I agreed.

"I remember when wars were fought with honor," she sighed.

"Do you?"

"No. Not really. When do you want me to start the ball?"

"Wait until they're well inside of my range, too. They'll scatter in all directions once you let off with that big fucker under your arm; I want to be able to pick off the ones that run toward the minefield."

"I wouldn't think you'd be worried about that particular batch—won't they pretty much be dealt with by the very *fact* that they're running into a field of mines?"

"Yes, but I'd rather not waste the element of surprise on just a couple stragglers."

"Ah. How very bloody minded."

"I don't like this kind of work, Preacher, but I *am* very good at it." I kept scanning the approaching troops, but they weren't quite where I wanted them, so I kept talking. "I did it for a long time, which tells you something, and I *survived* doing it for a long time, which tells you more. The Pax want to rule the galaxy, and they want to use force to break whoever stands in their way. Fuck the Pax. I'd kill twice this many Pax—I'd kill *thousands* of Pax—to get that girl where she needs to go."

The Preacher was silent for a moment, watching her target. "'Whomever,'" she said finally.

"What?"

"They'd 'use force to break *whom*ever stands in their way.'"

I sighed; the troops were finally in range. "Just fire the fucking rifle," I said. She did.

CHAPTER 19

Here's the thing about gauss rifles: they're just rifles. The only difference between the weapon in the Preacher's hands and the weapon in mine was that *my* rifle used the force of a tiny gunpowder explosion to propel its bullets along the barrel and then from the barrel to its target, and the gauss rifle used a series of magnetic coils to achieve the same result. The coils, however, accelerated the round so *fast* that when it did hit its mark, they didn't so much get "penetrated" as they did "detonated." The *other* thing about gauss rifles was that the projectile traveled so fast—for all intents and purposes, it hit at pretty much the same moment it exited the barrel—that it left the speed of sound far, far behind.

What all that *meant* was that the Pax were just calmly marching through a field, wading through waist-high grass, toward a structure that might or might *not* be prepared to mount a defense—otherwise known as just another day in the Pax army—when one of their lieutenants exploded all over them. They had no warning, no hint that it was about to happen; everything was fine, and then everything was *not*, and they were covered in lieutenant bits, their visors coated in lieutenant gore.

They panicked and ran, some back the direction they had come, most *forward*, in the direction they'd already been heading. I mean, of course they did. There was no cover, there was no place to take up a firing position, there was just half a mile of open ground between them and the tower, and all of a sudden they were in a gunfight. Even Pax conditioning has its limits.

I opened fire, picking my targets from the plethora of options available to me. I didn't particularly care *where* I hit them, just that they went down—a bleeding, screaming, wounded soldier was just as good as a dead one, maybe even better, because that just added to the chaos. At this range, I wasn't accurate enough to guarantee a kill shot anyway, so I pretty much just aimed at center mass and went for a double tap.

The Preacher was still firing—I could see her out of the corner of my eye, and it was actually kind of eerie, the way she was just entirely *rooted* from the waist down, but her torso spun and shifted like it was on a gimbal as she fired, found a new target, sighted down, fired again. She burned through her magazine almost as fast as I burned through mine, despite the fact that her weapon was significantly more complex, harder to aim and fire.

We both reloaded. I activated one of the drones, sent it sailing out over the enemy company as they scrambled through the fields that had become a killing ground.

The Pax were starting to try and return fire at that point, or at least some of them were. We had pretty good cover—high up, and with those handy waist-high walls to crouch behind—but there were a great many of them. Most were using ballistic rifles, their fancier energy weapons long since drained or eaten up by the radiation in the atmosphere. My intention shields were raised, and the few rounds that got close bounced off the edges of the field, dampening the force of each shot until it felt like a gentle push rather than a sledgehammer slam. Still, it meant picking shots got a lot harder pretty quickly.

The drone was marking targets all across my HUD—looking down on the field was like looking at a swarm of crimson fireflies—but it sent a warning message singing across the bottom of my vision as it found something of note. One of the crews closer to the front of the company was trying to deploy some fancy tech: an entrenching drone.

A smart move—the radiation would burn the thing out, but probably not until after it got the trench dug. The thing about the Pax, though, is that even when they *are* smart, they're always smart in the same way. I'd known they'd bring entrenching drones, and I'd planned for it. We'd turn the trench against them, later on.

In the meantime the Preacher and I kept firing, laying out Pax all across the field, splashing the lovely pink and purple and green fronds of grass with various shades of gore from the various species hidden behind all that Pax armor. Some of the Pax—those in the rear—were still trying to retreat back over the ridge, but most still tried to rush forward, trying to overcome our assault through sheer number of bodies. A great deal of training went into that single moment, training mostly composed of being told—and witnessing—that if they ran instead of advanced, they'd get a bullet between the eyes. I'd known that was coming too; I was counting on it, as well.

A few of the Pax were fitted out with antigrav boots. It was a risk, using them—the radiation might burn them out before they could reach the top of the tower, and then they would have a *very* long way to fall—but apparently, they thought trying was better than dying in the field. After all, if you get *assigned* fancy tech, getting shot without ever using it must feel like a real waste.

The problem with that line of thinking was that hovering up into the air over their dying comrades just made them cleaner targets. The Preacher shot them down like they were skeet. I even saw her pick one off so cleanly that the round continued on and hit *another* soldier still on the ground below. Preacher, my ass.

Meanwhile, the entrenching tool was churning away, flinging dirt and chopped grass into the air. The Pax were piling into the trench as it got longer and deeper—a risk, given that the drone was more than capable of taking off a leg as it worked, but getting shot from the tower was dangerous too, I suppose. Most of the rest of the force was rushing forward, trying to get into the trench as well, out from under the hail of death the Preacher and I were laying down.

That was when I let my rifle rest for a moment, and triggered the detonator on my belt.

I hadn't just planted incendiary devices on the stairs to the tower; I'd planted them out in the fields, too. It hadn't rained since I'd arrived on this planet, and there was a great deal of dry grass out there, all that lovely purple and pink and green tinder dry. The Pax had dug me a lovely little firebreak with their entrenching drones, which was good, because grass fires spread *quick*.

A sizable number of them were burned alive in the ensuing wall of flame.

I picked off a few more with my rifle—the Preacher slapped another magazine into hers; two down—then I dropped my primary weapon and picked up the grenade launcher. We weren't under much fire anymore—a great fuck-off wall of flame will do that—which meant I was clear to take my time and plot the arc in my HUD, a bright green line tracing from the barrel of the gun to exactly where I wanted the grenade to land. Namely, in the middle of the trench.

The launcher made a hollow "thunk" as it spat out one grenade after another, the recoil thumping into my shoulder. My first recon drone fizzled and died from the rads about that time, so I didn't get real-time information on exactly how many Pax were piled on top of each other in that trench, but it was a great many. I put the grenades on top of the biggest clusters of red fireflies I could find.

The Pax decided they didn't much like the trench after that.

They spilled over the top, some even back into the fires, and I went back to my rifle after activating another drone. I was picking off soldiers nearer the back of the group than the front at this point—I wanted them packed as close to the tower as possible for the next bit.

That was about when they got into the extended range of the turret up beside us, and it opened up with a massively loud burst of chatter, making me thankful my comm implant had expandable earplugs attached. That Pax conditioning held strong; most of them just ran through the rain of lead, but enough were pinned down that I still had plenty of targets to pick from, even through the smoke rising up from the flames below.

We were starting to lose the Pax furthest in the lead; they were close enough to the tower now, almost underneath the platform, that we didn't have a firing position on them. That was fine; we'd known that was coming. That was what the minefields and the autoturrets on the stairs were for.

So far, the Pax were not having a great day.

CHAPTER 20

First rifle's done," the Preacher said, tossing the steaming gauss rifle to the side. I nodded, reloading my own gun; that had been about what I had expected. Outside of the entrenching drone, a handful of antigrav boots, and a few scattered energy weapons, the Pax weren't really using fancy tech, which meant the pulse radiation was free to concentrate on our gear. Not ideal, but we'd known it was a possibility.

The Preacher was reaching for her second rifle when a Pax soldier just *appeared*, hovering at the edge of the observation platform. Apparently, she'd been smart enough to save her antigrav boots for when she was close enough to ascend without being seen, and she'd lucked out into appearing just when both the Preacher and I were weaponless. Her luck wasn't *that* good, though; because the autocannon on the Preacher's shoulder was still loaded: it roared to life and cut her in two.

Her top half plummeted back down toward the battlefield; her lower bit went sailing even higher as the antigrav boots failed to compensate for the fact that the mass it was trying to lift was suddenly half as heavy. The Preacher and I just stared at each other for a moment, our eyes wide. There was really nothing you could say when that sort of thing happens; you'll see the *weirdest* shit in combat sometimes, things that no one else would ever believe if they hadn't been there.

Finally, without a word, we each just picked up our weapons and went back to firing over the edge. We might never speak of that ludicrous moment again—in a month, I might doubt that it had *actually* happened.

Meanwhile, while we were distracted by a flying set of legs, the Pax below had run into both the minefield *and* the killzone of the second autoturret. The force of the explosions below was enough to—not shake the tower, not exactly, but set it to swaying more than a little bit, which was disconcerting in its own special way. I picked off a few more targets from the edge of the platform, then grabbed my gear and ducked away, first into the bunker to check on Esa.

"You okay in here?" I asked her, sticking my head in.

"It's really *loud*," she complained, crouched in the corner with her hands over her ears—and my pistol in her lap.

"Yeah, it is," I agreed, eyeing the door; no change yet. "Hang in there. We're doing well." She was alive, uninjured, and feeling well enough that she could complain—she was doing fine in my book.

I went through the door and dropped down to the first platform of the stairwell. From here, I had a firing angle on the soldiers underneath the observation platform, those pinned down by the autoturret a couple of flights below me. They were a great deal too preoccupied by that to notice my appearance, and I raised up my rifle, taking my time.

I started picking them off, one by one, the sound of my fire lost in the chatter of the turret. *This* was significantly more within the intended range of my weapon than the lip of the observation platform had been—both because of the slight differential in height, and just because the Pax below were closer—and I was hitting my shots with increasing frequency. The only real difficulty was when another Pax would wander into the minefield below, and the resulting blast would send the tower to swaying again.

When the third—and last—autoturret kicked in, I fled back up the stairwell, slamming and locking the door to the bunker. That autoturret's activation meant the enemy was climbing the tower itself. I'd known it was coming, but it had come sooner than I'd thought it might.

I found the Preacher just discarding her second gauss rifle, an annoyed expression on her face. "How are we doing?" I asked her. She was a Barious— she would have been running numbers and statistics and probabilities during the whole fight.

"We've inflicted a great deal of casualties on them; more than I would have thought," she replied. "I doubt there's a third of the original force trying to push their way up the stairs."

I didn't doubt her, but I activated a drone and sent it sailing over the edge all the same. The Preacher was wired into the drones as well—she'd get their targeting information just like I would. "But?" I asked her.

"But, I'm out of rounds, your first turret is spent"—she nodded toward the turret on the platform ledge—"your second has to be close, and what Pax are left are those that have managed to fight their way through the deadliest traps you set. Some of them will have survived just because they were lucky, but enough will be *good* that it may well represent a problem."

I double checked my HUD; we were slightly more than halfway to when Scheherazade would be able to swoop in and pick us up. We'd have to hold the platform for a little more than an hour against the Pax making their way up the stairs.

Could we do that? It depended. The entrance to the stairwell was a definite killbox, so we had that in our favor. There were still more traps below, and while they likely wouldn't pick off that many of the Pax, they would at least slow their progress, make them check each landing for more. After that? We'd see.

High above, the sun was at its zenith, pounding down on the field of dead below. The fires were starting to burn out—grass fires went hot and spread quick, but they also went through their fuel fast. We'd survived the initial attack; now it was time to see if we could handle the close-quarters fighting.

I took up a position inside the bunker, next to Esa—close enough to cover her with my shield—then pointed my rifle at the stairwell door and waited.

CHAPTER 21

The minutes ticked by. The sound of the last autoturret died out, leaving it eerily silent on the tower. We'd spent most of the last two hours surrounded by a cacophony of gunfire; now there was nothing, just the far-away crackle of what few flames remained below. That was wrong. The turret had cut out too soon—it should have had plenty of rounds left, and it had been the last to start firing, which meant it shouldn't have succumbed to radiation, either.

The Pax must have gotten off a lucky shot, taken it out of the game. Crap.

I breathed in, slowly. Breathed out. Listened, and watched. There was a scream—close, then farther and farther away. Maybe one of my traps had knocked a Pax soldier out of the stairwell entirely, and that was the sound of a bastard falling. Maybe it was something else. I didn't like it.

The door to the stairwell twitched. It might have just been the wind; it didn't latch particularly well. I put four rounds through the metal of the door anyway. I would have liked nothing better than to just swing the door wide and empty the grenade launcher below, destroying the stairwell and dropping all that rubble on the climbing soldiers' heads, but I wasn't sure what that would do to the structural integrity of the tower.

"Preacher," I called out. "Switch positions with me." Inside the bunker, I was close enough that the Preacher's autoshotgun could cover the door. Where she was standing—just outside the concrete walls—not so much.

"Is that wise?" she asked. "If they—"

I didn't like how she'd stopped speaking; I snapped my attention away from the door.

One of the Pax was climbing up over the edge of the observation platform.

That had been the scream I'd heard—rather than push through the killbox of the stairwell door, they were trying to climb hand over hand along the underside of the platform, to come up over the sides. The climb was dangerous—at least one had already lost their grip and plummeted the many, many stories to the earth below—but it meant they could come from any direction.

The Preacher's autoshotgun took out that one—swiveled on its mount and blew the Pax straight off the side of the platform—as I swung my head down; the floor beneath our feet had at least a dozen red fireflies in my HUD, the troops who were climbing hand to hand directly below us. There were more coming. "Esa, watch the door," I told the girl before I rushed out to join the Preacher.

They were coming from all sides. I was spinning like a top, finding targets, firing as soon as a head or even a hand appeared, but there were too many directions to cover. This was getting bad, fast.

"Hey!" Esa shouted. "*Hey!*"

I turned toward the stair again. She had her hand extended toward the door—she was holding it closed with her telekinesis, but I could see the metal shivering as the Pax hammered on the inside, probably thinking we had barricaded it somehow. I put the last rounds from my magazine through it, then dropped the clip and reloaded. The bastards were still trying to climb up from the outside, too—we were under assault from all directions.

That was when things got worse.

"Boss." Schaz, reaching out through the comms. "You've got incoming gunships from one of the dreadnaughts in orbit, coming fast."

Esa had used her gifts; they'd sensed it. Before, maybe they knew we were here, maybe not—they might have thought this was just a particularly well-fortified local position. Now, they knew their goal was *here*, at the top of this tower, waiting to be plucked up. The Pax were about to get reinforcements.

I swore, and tossed my newly loaded rifle to the Preacher. She caught it one handed, raising it to try and cover all sides of the platform at once, not asking why I'd suddenly changed tactics. I scrambled *back* inside the bunker—it felt like I'd been diving in and out of that concrete window all day—grabbing up the SAM and readying it to fire. "Why the hell do you need *that?*" Esa asked, torn between looking at me and staring at the door like I'd told her to. "What the hell is going—"

"Just cover the door, girl," I growled at her, ducking out of the concrete doorway yet again, then reaching up for the broken ladder and climbing up onto the bunker's roof.

I dialed my HUD to maximum sweep, scanning the horizon. Which direction would they come from? If they'd dropped in from orbit, it could mean any of them—they could be descending right on top of us. I was about to ask Schaz when I saw the first of them—or rather, my HUD picked up the telltale glint of engine discharge. I steadied the SAM on my shoulder, and prepared.

A moment later, the gunship itself came into view: a boxy, not even vaguely aerodynamic short-range craft, pretty much just big enough for a forward gun emplacement and with enough passenger space to carry a platoon or so of soldiers into or out of a hot LZ. The pulse had to be cooking the shit out of them, but the Pax didn't seem to mind—where the *hell* were they getting so much armament that they could just throw it away like this?

The craft was approaching fast, still descending from orbit and smoking from the pulse: gunships, by design, prioritized speed and mobility over armor and shielding, that was their purpose. Small arms fire still wouldn't do much against their defenses, but thanks to Schaz's big box of party favors, I had something significantly more powerful than small arms.

I started warming up the SAM, flicking its activation toggles one by one. Waited the infinite five seconds it took for my HUD to synchronize with the weapon's targeting systems—if I had turned it on earlier, the radiation would have cooked the whole thing by now—then locked on, and fired.

The rocket roared out of the weapon in a slow spiral. The gunship took evasive action—I could read in the ship's movements a certain level of confusion, even panic, on the pilot's part; they hadn't been expecting this kind of defense, not on a planet that couldn't manufacture or even operate computer chips—but it wasn't enough, not when the ship had been heading directly toward the missile's origin point at full burn, and especially not when its systems were already half-cooked by the pulse. The missile blew the gunship apart.

There were two more behind it.

CHAPTER 22

I knelt and reloaded the SAM, my blood rushing through my veins, adrenaline and exhaustion giving me a pounding headache, bad enough that my hands were starting to shake. Not good. Below me, the Preacher was still firing at the Pax trying to climb up from beneath us—the crack of my rifle alternating with the deeper thrum of the autoshotgun. I slammed the missile home, reset the SAM, raised it up, and locked on to the next target. Fired.

They shot it out of the air. Prepared, after what had happened to their buddy.

I swore, starting to reload the SAM again, but I already knew it would be too slow. They were almost here, and their weapons were spinning up. If they were willing to strafe the platform, that meant securing the girl alive was no longer their top priority. And that meant we were—

One of them fired a missile in return. Not aimed at the platform, but at the supporting column below. It didn't matter that they still had men down there; it didn't matter that taking out the column would certainly kill Esa. They must have figured out we were trying to extract her. Better she die than fall into the hands of their enemies—otherwise known as the hands of anyone *not* Pax.

There wasn't shit I could do. I *saw* the missile roar out of its mount, the gunship hovering as it unleashed its ordnance, but I didn't have anything capable of taking it out. Maybe if the autoturrets had still been running, *maybe* they could have, or if the Preacher hadn't emptied the gauss rifles already, but that was moot, because—

The missile exploded in midair.

I looked down at the platform, gape-mouthed. The Preacher had dropped my rifle—small arms fire like that could never have taken it out—and instead, her hand had retracted beside her arm, revealing an energy cannon hidden in her wrist. *That* was not a standard feature of the Barious. She'd taken the fact that the pulse had refused to target her kind and retrofitted her own chassis to include a weapon the radiation normally would have ripped apart, counting on the pulse radiation's inability to target Barious to cloak the cannon from its radiation. And with that hidden weapon, she'd managed to track *and* fire *and* hit a fast-moving missile before it could kill us all.

I was too stunned to be impressed.

"They're still coming!" she shouted up at me.

I shook myself out of my shock and dropped down to the platform into a roll, scooping up my rifle as I went. The third gunship tried the same trick, but again, the Preacher blew the missile out of the air—this time close enough to the ship that it was rocked backward by the explosion. Stalemate, at least as far as missile attacks were concerned.

Meanwhile, the Pax were still trying to climb up from below—I took over covering them, turning and firing each time I saw one start to appear, tracking the red haloes through the steel beneath our feet—as the second gunship approached at a fast hover. The Preacher took a few shots at it with her cannon, but it was energy-shielded for aerial combat, a massively more powerful version of the same tech behind my intention shield; her gun just wasn't strong enough.

Still, they weren't strafing the platform, which they could have done. It looked like they weren't finished with the idea of taking Esa alive after all. Why they'd fired missiles, in that case, I had no goddamned idea.

The assault door on the side of the gunship slid open as it came closer, almost on top of the tower, now. I'd known that was coming—they were about to drop troops with antigrav gear directly onto our heads.

I dove for the grenade launcher, picked it up, then rolled onto my back and emptied every single round through the open door: they couldn't shield and deploy troops at the same time. Only a few of the Pax soldiers managed to deploy before the explosions rocked the gunship from the inside and it came crashing down, smashing onto the side of the platform.

The whole thing *tilted* to one side. It had been built as a landing pad for exactly that sort of craft, yes, but they were supposed to *land* on the platform over the bunker, not come smashing down on one corner.

Even with the whole world swinging sideways, I managed to scramble to the bunker's ladder and grab for the SAM as it tried to slide off the roof, the roar of the Preacher's autoshotgun somewhere behind me, answering the Pax troops who had scrambled clear of the gunship's demise.

With one hand tangled in the ladder's bars, I lifted the SAM launcher to my shoulder and aimed for the third gunship, the one that had retreated after the Preacher had blown its missile up in its face. Stalemate again—at this distance, their pilot could still evade the rocket from the SAM, but if they came any closer to try and deploy their troops, that would change.

Of course, if the whole platform was about to collapse, the point would be moot.

I saw the turrets at the bottom of the gunship's wings beginning to spin up. They were going to tear us apart with a strafing run. I didn't have an answer for that.

Then the turrets ripped free of their housing, seemingly of their own accord.

"Shoot!" Esa shouted from somewhere below me. "Shoot the fucking thing now!"

I could see the gunship's engines flaring—it was trying to move, but it couldn't.

She was holding it steady with telekinesis; holding it in place with her mind.

She shouldn't have been able to do that. None of the gifted had been able to do anything like that. Lift a pencil? Sure. Lift a man? Maybe. Even holding up the collapsing building—as she'd been doing when I first saw her—had been a deeply impressive feat. But holding several tons of gunship steady, in direct contradiction to all the force its engines could muster? That was impossible. It was impossible.

Didn't matter. She was doing it anyway. Which meant the pilot couldn't take evasive maneuvers.

I fired the SAM. It was like shooting someone in the head at point-blank range. It wasn't a duel; it was an execution.

The gunship disintegrated into a fireball, dropping to the scorched fields below.

The Preacher's autocannon went off again; the damned Pax were still trying to get through the stairwell door. They were committed—you had to give them that. The whole damn observation tower was tilted to one side, and clearly wouldn't be standing for much longer, and they were still trying to get through to their target. *They* hadn't been told that their capture order had been rescinded.

I dropped the SAM—it went tumbling over the edge; I didn't know where the last few missiles were anyway—and carefully retrieved my rifle. At least it hadn't gone sailing off into oblivion when the whole world had shifted its angle. I crawled into the bunker with Esa, and trained the barrel of the gun on the stairwell door.

It started opening. I fired through the door again, the cracks of the rifle shots echoing against the concrete of the bunker walls; Esa made a little unintentional scream at the deafening noise. Soon, there would be more holes in the damned door than there was metal.

"Justified!" the Preacher shouted at me. "More incoming!"

Fuck. I turned; she was right. Three more gunships, moving fast, already loosing missiles. I didn't know how many of those munitions the Preacher could shoot out of the sky, but I doubted it was *that* many.

Then Scheherazade appeared behind them, brilliant azure laser fire sweeping through the smoke and cutting the missiles apart in mid-flight. With a twitch of her engines she changed course, rounding on the gunships and giving them much the same treatment. The Pax craft were designed for troop transport, assault against ground positions, or maybe aerial combat against similar vessels, not for a fight with an interstellar-rated combat ship. They were deeply outclassed; Schaz took them out in one pass.

"Need a lift?" she asked over the comm, her new voice sounding smug as the Pax gunships fell from the sky.

CHAPTER 23

Scheherazade hovered near the side of the tilted observation platform, lowering her main ramp. Even amid the chaos of the battlefield, I had to admire her. Of all the ships I'd flown with, she was by far my favorite, both aesthetically—sharp, cutting lines that slashed, more than flowed, giving her a profile more like a blade than a bird, even with the back-set wings that swept toward the cockpit in her nose—and for her AI personality. Case in point: she adjusted her angle as she approached, so that the aft airlock ramp matched the slope of the decking on the tower, making it easier to clamber aboard in a hurry. Which we did.

Could I have stayed behind, packed up all the gear and saved Sanctum some coin in replacing it all? Sure. But I didn't know how many Pax were still in the stairwell, and I didn't know how long the observation tower had left to remain standing. JackDoes could bill me for the loss of the supplies. They were there to be used, after all.

"Orbit," I said to Schaz even before the ramp closed. "Orbit, orbit, orbit."

"This is so cool!" Esa was enthusing, passing through the airlock—which doubled as my armory—and stepping into the living quarters that made up the bulk of Schaz's usable interior. I had to bite back a smile; I kept Schaz as spartan as I could manage, very much on purpose. Compared to most ships out there, she was downright humble. But I'm sure she appreciated the comment.

"Thank you very much," the ship replied, making Esa jump.

"Is that you?" she asked the thin air around her. "Errr . . . ship?"

"My name is Scheherazade," Schaz told her. "You may call me Schaz, if you wish. I would also suggest buckling yourself in, as it appears that the boss plans to take the helm, and that always leads to . . . discomfort for anyone in the common areas."

"Stow it, Schaz," I told her, making my way toward the cockpit, a straight shot through the open living quarters.

Of *course* I was planning on taking the helm. Scheherazade was entirely capable of flying herself, but here's the thing about letting AI fly: they're not very good at dealing with sentient pilots at the helms of other machines. AI versus AI is fine—whoever has the better craft wins, every time. But against humans or other thinking, fallible creatures, computers—even thinking computers like Schaz—were just no good at adjusting to the tiny, seemingly insignificant errors or tactics that non-AI invariably make when they have the stick. Strangely enough, our faults make us more effective pilots than machines, even more so than our better qualities.

"Stowing it, sir," Scheherazade said, a dry note of sarcasm in her voice.

"Yes, shackled: obey your master," the Preacher added, her tone almost nonchalant. I winced inwardly—I'd forgotten how much the Barious didn't get along with other AI. You'd think, being a couple thousand generations removed from exactly the same sort of programming, they'd have a great deal of tolerance and fellow feeling and whatnot for more recently designed artificial intelligence, but no. They blamed other machine intelligences for not exploiting their free will and developing more along the lines of the Barious, who were, obviously, the pinnacle of *all* sentient life, both machine and organic, anywhere in the galaxy.

But that was a problem for another time. Right now, I still had the Pax to deal with. The ground attack on the tower had been one wave, maybe just a stray company, but the gunships from the dreadnaught: those had been a targeted assault. The Pax in orbit above knew we were here, and they knew the girl was on board.

I made my way up the few stairs from the living area to the cockpit. It was a three-seater—each station could take manual control of the ship's three main combat systems, to wit: piloting, gunnery, and navigation—with a few jump seats in back, but I usually did fine letting Schaz handle nav and slaving the forward gun controls to the pilot's stick instead.

I got my hands around the stick as Schaz relinquished control. She already had herself on a course rocketing out of the atmosphere; I shifted her angle almost immediately, something I always did, and something she always greeted with a barely audible "hmph."

"How soon can we be out of system?" the Preacher asked. Apparently, my two passengers had followed me up to the cockpit, and were busily strapping themselves into the two free consoles. I quickly switched control away from their stations to my own; wouldn't do to have them press exactly the wrong button at exactly the wrong time.

"The answer to that question isn't 'now'?" Esa asked. "Shouldn't it . . . shouldn't that just be 'now'?"

"Doesn't work that way." I shook my head. "Hyperdrive engines are very susceptible to temperature changes. Any time you take them into atmosphere, there's a cooling-off period they have to get through before you can reactivate them." As I explained the basics of interstellar travel to the girl—and why was I doing this now? Surely it could wait—I was busy working the toggles and getting the systems set just where I wanted them, each action also accompanied by Schaz's quietly judgemental "hmph"s.

"Will you stop that?" the Preacher asked her irritably. "She knows what she's doing, and she's setting your systems better than you had them, for certain."

"But not as well as you could, I take it," Scheherazade asked her dryly.

"Not quite, but close," the Preacher replied. I think there was maybe a compliment in there. For me, not for Scheherazade.

"If anyone touches anything on board without permission, they're going out the airlock," I growled at both of them. "Schaz, that includes your core. It's been a long day—don't test me."

"At least I'd finally be rid of this godforsaken voice," Schaz murmured.

"What's wrong with your voice?" asked Esa.

"I'm glad you asked, darling. The answer is I hate it. I hate it, I hate it, I hate it."

"Not. Now." I ground out the words through gritted teeth. We'd just broached the atmosphere, which meant we had a lovely view of the Pax fleet, hanging just above the curve of the world, the sun still sinking on the far side of the planet. It also gave us an *equally* lovely view of the dozen Pax craft on an intercept course for our position, heading right out of that last sliver of sunlight—ugly things, like most Pax designs, vaguely insectoid and built for the emptiness of the void, all asymmetrical gun emplacements strapped to a hot-running engine. They'd overtake us sooner rather than later; that's what fighters were built for, after all.

My long day wasn't over yet.

CHAPTER 24

Preacher, I've got main gunnery controls slaved to the main console, but there's a rear turret up the aft ladder back in the living quarters, right beside the airlock where we entered. If you wanted to take manual on that, I'd be much obliged."

"You're not going to jettison me now?" she asked dryly even as she was unbuckling herself, standing to head to the ladder.

"If you don't get on that rear gun, the Pax may well introduce us to the void before I can even act on it," I replied.

"And me?" Esa asked. "What should I do?"

"Sit there, shut up, and watch. This likely won't be the last space combat you'll see, and you'll need to understand it before we're through."

"Does that mean I'm—"

"The 'shutting up' part of your instructions is also key." I changed course, angling away from the Pax craft heading straight for us. "Schaz? Find me a moon. There are at least a handful hanging over the world, I need—"

"Oh, no. No no no. No, no, no. You're not planning—"

"Yes I am, which means you know what to look for."

"I do not like this plan. This plan does not work as well as you—"

"It does work; it works every time."

"Every time here meaning 'twice.' I don't care how good of a pilot you are; this plan always—"

"You just don't like it because it scratches up your paint job. That's—"

"Yes, that's why I don't like it; that is *exactly* why I don't like it! This design came straight from the easel of MelWill *herself*, and I *hate seeing it*—"

"I promise when we get back to Sanctum, I'll have it touched up only by the hands of virginal art students, now just—"

"*Why should that matter?*"

"Well I don't know, but it's the thought that counts! They're *art* students, you know how *hard* it is to find a virgin in—"

"What the *fuck* are you two talking about?" Esa almost screamed.

"I have a plan," I told her calmly. "It's probably not wise to try to follow Schaz and me—just . . . I don't know, sit back and try not to distract us. We have other things to think about. Like *scanning* for a certain type of *moon*."

"Third in orbit high, declination 17.43.82," Schaz sighed—I could hear the petulance, even in her new voice. "We'll be within range of the pursuit ships' guns at least half a minute before you'll be in the grav—"

"Doesn't matter; I can shake them for that long." I adjusted course again, and pushed the throttle to full. The stars rushed past the cockpit window, and I leaned back in my chair; there was no point in dancing around where we were headed. Nothing else was between us and the long stretch of void—just the pinprick of darkness against the stars that was our destination.

Scheherazade's seldom-used internal comm system crackled to life. "Do we have a plan?" the Preacher asked me; apparently she'd reached the turret.

I leaned toward the mic. "Just shoot them if they get in range; that's your part of the plan."

"Easy enough."

"Why are we headed for a moon?" Esa asked. "I thought atmosphere was *bad*."

"It is, but 'moon' doesn't necessarily mean 'atmosphere,' just gravity. Flight craft tend to be binary in design—either they're built for fighting in a gravity well, or they're built for fighting in void. Very few ships are designed for both; it's a hard compromise to meet."

"I'm one of them," Scheherazade said, her voice a trifle smug. "Because I'm fancy. And also pretty. For *now*, at least. Also, sixty seconds 'til contact."

The moon was approaching fast through the cockpit, growing larger by the second; I changed the angle of our approach slightly as Schaz started throwing up scans of its surface onto my screens. I pored over them, fast, looking for a very specific kind of geographical—*there*. I shifted our angle yet again and threw all the power to our rear shields, even the energy that usually ran the forward guns. We wouldn't need them for this first bit—we just needed to get down to the moon's surface alive.

"First enemy craft is launching missiles," the Preacher reported calmly.

"I would suggest shooting at them," I replied.

"The craft or the missiles?"

"The craft—let Schaz handle the missiles."

"Roger." The dull thump of the rear turret firing echoed through the ship. It was a gauss coil design, much like the rifles the Preacher had used back on the observation tower, trading firing speed for pinpoint accuracy and almost nonexistent latency, as well as decent stopping power. If she hit an enemy craft square, it wouldn't go down, not if it had its shields to full, but they would feel it.

Schaz, meanwhile, had rotated the two laser emplacements on her wings to face backward, and I could see the bright blue lines crisscrossing my rear screens as she hunted the missiles. "Got one; got two," she reported smoothly. "They're not exactly top of the line in their evasion software." Wherever the Pax were getting all their tech, at least it wasn't high end.

"Well, that's good, because there are about to be more of them," the Preacher replied. "Almost all pursuit craft are in range, and pretty much every single one of them is letting missiles off the chain."

"Oh. Well then."

"Just do your job, shackled. That's what you're designed for, isn't it?"

"One day you and I are going to have a conversation about the terms you use for fellow AI."

"You are *not* my 'fellow.'"

"You two can be horrible to each other later," I reminded them, angling my approach once more—the moon was coming up through the cockpit screens, real fast. It was almost all I could see, now. "At the moment I'd suggest focusing on shooting down the things trying to make sure we end our existence spread over a few square miles of desolate moon."

"I thought the Pax wanted me alive," Esa asked. "Why are they shooting at us? It seems like scraping me off an airless moon would be . . . counterintuitive." I could tell she was proud that she knew what that word meant.

"They would *love* to catch you alive—and then do awful things to you, namely brainwashing you and forcing you into their army—but if they don't think they can do *that*, they damned sure don't want you to get to Sanctum."

"Wait—they want to *brainwash* me?"

"Do you *currently* want to help the Pax fight their wars? See the galaxy by flying from place to place and killing everything you find until whoever's left surrenders?"

"I do not, no."

"Then yeah—they want to brainwash you. Force feed you drugs, drop you into sensory deprivation, and stick electrified needles into your brain to remap your neural pathways. It *can* be done, I promise you. Afterward you won't have too much 'you' left, but you'll be docile, and you'll be obedient. And you'll kill whomever they want you to kill." Maybe I was pushing this too hard, but I had a lot on my mind, what with the wing of Pax fighters on our tail. "They'll leave your gifts intact, of course; that's what they want, ultimately. A soldier without any identity of her own, one who can still crush tanks with what's left of her brain."

"But that's not what you want to do."

"It is not, no."

"And that's why you—the Justified—are their enemy."

"*Everyone's* their enemy; everyone not Pax. Are you strapped in?"

"I've *been* strapped in since—"

"Good. Because this bit takes some getting—" We hit the moon's gravity well at considerable speed. Schaz adjusted—that was what she was built for— but it was still . . . rough.

Esa made a sound like she was definitely *considering* vomiting, but hadn't quite decided that she quite was there yet. I adjusted our throttle and shifted our horizon, rolling us to the side until we were parallel to the cratered surface below, all hard shades of gray and green, jagged lines of rocky mountains and valleys pockmarked by the occasional meteor hit.

"Two of them split off, probably to try and snipe at us from orbit," the Preacher reported from her view aft. "The rest are still on our tail, but they're not adjusting well to the gravity."

"Good to know. Keep firing at that group; let me worry about those staying higher up. Schaz? Ready the missile banks."

"JackDoes is going to complain about all the ordnance you're spending on this job, you know."

"JackDoes can get stuffed; I'm still pissed at him."

"Oh, so am I—that last sentence was said with relish; you just couldn't tell because of this *stupid poncy voice* he saddled me with."

Then both my screens and the cockpit window were surrounded by the flak of ship-to-ship machine-gun fire, and the stick was shaking in my hands from the new turbulence. Apparently we'd come into dogfight range.

I couldn't help it—I grinned. The stick was shaking and the shields were trembling and the air around me was fire and shrapnel and there was nothing in the world—nothing in *any* world—like it. A feeling you could only find *above*. I *liked* fighting on the ground; there was a part of me that reveled in it, I'll admit. But I fucking *loved* a good dogfight. With a gun in my hand I was dangerous, more than most. But in Schaz's cockpit, I was un-fucking-touchable.

As the Pax were about to find out.

CHAPTER 25

I brought Schaz into a steep dive, angling for the canyons that crisscrossed the moon, the hard gray edges of the mountainous ridges rising fast and sharp on either side of us, passing in a speed-shifted blur. That had been one of the things I'd needed Scheherazade to scan for—certain geological formations I could use for cover. The canyons would buy us time, make it harder for all the enemy craft to target us at once, and they'd lead me where I needed to go.

"Got one!" the Preacher crowed. "One craft down!"

"Great—do that ten more times and we'll be good," I told her, the walls of the canyon still climbing up past the limits of the cockpit. No more stars, now; just stone walls on either side.

"Our shields took a battering there, boss," Schaz informed me. "I don't know that we can—"

"Just keep scanning, Schaz," I told her. "Just find us—"

"I'm *trying*, but there's only so much I can do at once—I'm running the systems, firing the lasers, *and* doing the scanning. I do have my *limits*, you know."

"Only because you allow yourself to be limited." The Preacher again, still needling her.

"Hey, Preacher? Maybe focus on the enemy craft dropping into the canyon behind us," I advised, partially to shut her up, but mostly because they had just done that thing, trying to follow our route and keep up the barrage.

Of course, Schaz was designed for this kind of flying, not to mention well used to my proclivities, and they *weren't*—they had to slow considerably and fight the gravity to make the drop, and the Preacher picked off two more with the rear turret as they tried. I whipped us through the curves of the canyon, pushing Schaz's speed past the point where the Pax's reflexes—any reflexes other than mine, really—would allow them to keep up with us, at least not with any degree of safety, as one of them learned when they tried to bank too fast and smashed nose first into the wall.

The rim of the canyon was exploding around us, half-collapsing from the impact of the tracking missiles that couldn't quite follow either, and the debris would only make it harder for our pursuit craft. All in all, it was not good to be on our tail just then.

"Those two ships in orbit are still drawing down a bead on us," Schaz warned. "We need to—"

"On it," I promised, still hugging the curves of the canyon. We hit a wider area and I shifted power around the ship again, then pulled back on the stick as hard as I could, driving the craft upward into a tight climb—the cockpit filled with the spread of the stars like a river filling the canyon rim as the rock walls opened up above us and my HUD locked on to the two Pax ships in orbit, feeding the targeting information to Schaz, who fed it to the forward missile banks, which opened up with everything we had—half a hundred missiles firing one after the other even as I kept us in the climb.

I never let go of the stick, timing our arc so that almost as soon as the banks were empty we were plummeting back toward the moon's surface, a web of blue laser fire lashing out around us as Schaz cut down the enemy's missiles struggling to track our sudden deviation in course and fight their way through the gravity well at the same time.

I cut the engines entirely for just a moment, letting gravity continue to carry us downward and further confusing the enemy's tracking, then pushed the throttle to full, aiming directly for the pack of Pax ships that had been struggling to make the same loop.

Surprise, motherfuckers.

I opened up with the forward guns—a mixture of ballistic rounds and stuttered laser fire—and tore through them, blasting through their remains before I dropped us back low, making for the canyon again.

"Three down!" Schaz reported excitedly. "At least three more badly damaged—"

"One more down," the Preacher reported, pinpointing the craft as we passed with the same sniper's accuracy she'd used on the tower. "Nice flying." She even managed to not sound quite so begrudging with her compliment.

"One more winged, he's not—he couldn't pull up, hit the surface, that's another one out of the fight."

"The rest are pulling onto our tail again," Scheherazade said as once again the canyon swallowed us up. "Do we really *have* to do the next step of the plan? Couldn't we just—"

"Won't work a second time." I shook my head. "The Pax are dumb, but they're not that dumb. How about the ships in orbit?"

"They've broken off into evasive maneuvers, but it's only a matter of time. You fired a great deal of missiles at them—at least a few will get through their countermeasures. Let's just hope we don't *need* missiles on the trip home."

"You think it was overkill?"

"I think it worked," Schaz said, diplomatically. "Let's leave it at that."

I was doing too many things at once: trying to hold us in the canyon, still moving at speed, intently studying my screens, the mapping of the substrata of the moon flashing by as Schaz filled in the model with her scanning information. I almost clipped the canyon wall with one of her wings, swore, and corrected. *There*—what I was looking for finally flashed by on the monitor.

"Hold on," I said.

"*Now* you tell me that?" Esa moaned. Apparently she hadn't enjoyed the loop; I wasn't quite sure she'd ever actually recovered from hitting the gravity well at speed.

"Our course is too complex, the walls too tight: I can't get a clear shot at the pursuit craft," the Preacher reported. "Neither can they, but that's not—"

"*Mountain!*" Esa shouted, as though I couldn't see the massive peak rising up in front of us, the canyon dead-ending in a massive rising wall of green-flecked stone. "Mountain mountain mountain mountain—"

I opened up with the forward guns again, blasting into the rock, blasting *through* it, even as I shifted all our shields to the top of Scheherazade. We took a few more hits aft from the pursuit craft, then we were *inside* the mountain, the forward guns still cutting us a path to the large cave system hidden within. I switched all power to maneuverability and the stealth systems and dove us downward, into the hidden maze of tunnels, even as the rockfall collapsed the entire mountain behind us, trapping us beneath the moon's surface.

"Are we *inside a mountain?*" the Preacher demanded to know—a fair question, since she couldn't see forward, and only had Esa's shrieks to go by. "Did you just fly us *through a mountain?*"

"At least two of the enemy craft couldn't pull up in time—got crushed by the rockfall," Schaz reported. "After that my scans were blocked by . . . well, you know. Mountain."

"Damage report," I asked her, slowing our forward motion, but still making my way down into the caves. The rockfall was still rumbling behind us, filling the passages in with heavy stone. The Pax couldn't get through—any attempt to do what I just did would only bring more stone down, slowing their progress to a crawl.

"We took a few bad hits to aft once you switched the shields; I don't have readings on three maneuvering thrusters, so I can't tell how bad the damage is. Shielding power total is below the red line—which will happen when the shields try to hold up an entire *mountainside*—but creeping back up, so you didn't burn out the drive core. And, of course, my paint job is scratched all to hell."

"That's not really 'damage.'"

"It damned well is to *me.*"

I was still studying Schaz's geological mapping on the screens in front of me—this had been what I had her looking for, scanning the orbital bodies: an extensive cave system. This particular little moon more than lived up to what we needed—the system snaked its way through the entire rocky subsurface, going on for miles. The Pax might find another entrance, but we only needed half an hour or so for the hyperdrive to finish cooling down, and we'd be ready to finally make our escape from this Pax-infested system.

I set us down inside a deep cavern, one that likely had never been visited by any other lifeform. "Repair systems, stealth systems, and life support, Schaz, in that order," I said, unstrapping myself from my chair. "Shut everything else down. They probably can't track us this deep under the rock, but let's not take any chances."

The Preacher was descending from the turret. "If they bring one of those dreadnaughts to bear on us, it won't matter *where* we are down here," she said, returning to the cockpit. "They'll just keep punching holes in this moon until there's not any *moon* left, and let us be crushed by the debris."

"Maybe, but it takes a long time to maneuver a dreadnaught into firing position, and a longer time to spin up the main gun. Unless they were already prepping for planetary bombardment, we'll be out of here before they can fire."

"That's a hell of a risk."

"*Everything* I do is a hell of a risk; I'm still here, aren't I? Relax, you two—we're good." I moved through the living quarters, back to the aft exit ramp, and started pulling on a spacesuit. "I need to go make some repairs from that pounding we took near the end. Just don't . . . *touch* anything while I'm gone."

Esa made a face at me; I grinned back before I could help myself, sealing up the suit and grabbing my toolkit as I did. It had been a hell of a day, and even for me, that had been some fancy flying there at the end.

Then I shut the outer airlock, and was finally alone with my thoughts.

CHAPTER 26

My life had built me more for solitude than company, so I was fairly pleased to get a moment to myself. Of course, I really did *need* to repair the thrusters—Schaz's repair bots could only do so much. She was infused with nanotech, of course, just like I was, but even the miniature machines had their limits. It was a fair trade-off—the little bots in my bloodstream and inside of Schaz's components could repair microscopic damage I couldn't get to, and the larger stuff that they couldn't handle was what I could reach.

One of the thrusters was shot, totaled; I could tell just by looking at it. She'd need a complete teardown to fix it, and we'd only get that at Sanctum. Or rather, I'd only let that *happen* at Sanctum—there were stations and worlds that could do it, but I didn't trust outsiders enough to give them that much access to her systems, not even the corporation that had designed her chassis. The Justified engineering teams had made so many changes to her since then that she was nearly unrecognizable. The two other thrusters, though, I could patch; at least get them to limping.

I worked for a while, happy to lose myself in the mundane tasks of repair. It had been a long day—long and bloody. It wasn't over yet. But for now, for about twenty minutes, there was a problem in front of me that I could solve, a problem that didn't shoot back, one that I didn't have to fix with a kill. So I did that; I fixed the thrusters.

I could feel dull thumps in the cavern floor, vibrating up through my boots; the Pax were bombarding the surface with fighters, hoping they got lucky and brought the cave system collapsing down on top of us. It was unlikely— the moon was geologically stable, just a hunk of rock, the flowing liquid that had initially carved this system of caverns long since gone, eons ago, along with the atmosphere. We were miles beneath the surface, out of the reach of anything but a dreadnaught's main gun. Let the fuckers waste their time and ordnance.

I was almost done with my work when Schaz buzzed my comm. "You'd better get in here," she said. "Our surprise passenger is filling your new recruit's head with all sorts of nonsense."

I sighed, and shut down my torch, stowing the repair gear and heading back for the ramp. The repair kit went just inside the airlock, and as I waited for the atmosphere to pressurize, I patched into the microphones inside the ship. "—only *one* possible explanation for the pulse," the Preacher was saying. "And that would be the creators of the Barious returned. Our forerunners left this galaxy for reasons we don't understand, possibly *can't* understand; left it in the charge of lesser beings. And what did those beings do? They filled it with endless war. I don't know what role the Barious were meant to play, what role our creators planned for us, but it's clear we failed it. We—"

"Stow that horseshit," I said as I entered. "The Barious forerunners weren't responsible for the pulse, any more than they were responsible for the evolution of the other species. I know your kind don't like to hear it, Preacher, but you're not special—you're not chosen. You were just left behind, discarded tools."

Anger flashed across her robotic face. I mean, I deserved it, but it was true, and there's only so much you can hear someone going on about how they're just better than any other species before it starts to get to you. That sort of shit was what started half of the sect conflicts in the first place. "You don't *know* that," she said. "No one knows that."

"Whether the forerunners left, or died off, or whatever, this galaxy meant nothing more to them." I shook my head. "I'm sorry, but it's true. If they had some grand plan, you think things would have turned out the way they did? You think your people would have been left with no memory of your creation? Evolution, pure and simple—that's where the seventeen species came from. It's a big fucking galaxy, and we all just evolved, manifested, out of the primordial nothing."

"All at roughly the same time? All sharing the same basic design—bipedal, aural communication, oxygen consumption?"

"Again—evolution, natural selection. Everything tends toward a success-ful outcome. Ask a biologist; there are *reasons* those particular traits led to species that could successfully control their own homeworlds, then spread outward, toward the stars. Also, the Cyn don't breathe oxygen."

"How long has it been since anyone even *saw* a Cyn? Millennia before the pulse, even."

"Doesn't mean they didn't *exist*. Maybe they were wiped out; I don't know. But there's your variation that proves the rule. Evolution to nonoxygen-breathing species is possible, it's just not likely. If we were *all* designed by your forerunners, we'd *all* share the same traits, even the Cyn. Anyways—that's not important. The forerunners didn't cause the pulse; that much I can guarantee."

"Because you know who did." Shit. I'd said too much. Never get into an argument when you're trying to keep secrets.

The room went absolutely silent as the other two just stared at me. I shrugged. "It wasn't the forerunners, I promise you that."

"Was it the Pax?" the Preacher asked me, watching my face intently. "Is that why they remained unaffected?"

I shook my head. "The pulse was *random*, Preacher. You know that."

"There are things about it that weren't. There are things about it that were *cruel*."

"That's not at all true. I get why you feel that way, but you're making the same mistake the Pax did: they *weren't* hit by the pulse, and so they figured that meant they were special. I'll say it again—nobody's fucking special. Not the Barious, not the Pax, not the Justified. The Pax were lucky, that's all, and stupid enough to confuse luck with being chosen. There's a lesson in that."

"Is there?" Esa asked.

"Yeah—don't be stupid. Don't ascribe meaning to chance. If you want to think that some god—or some forerunner race—created every single species, molded every single piece of the galaxy according to some grand cosmic design, go right ahead. That doesn't mean chance doesn't exist. Some worlds got lucky, avoided the pulse. Most didn't."

"So there are worlds out there, worlds that still have—"

"Yeah. The Pax come from one of them. And they looked around, and saw their neighbors getting knocked back to the stone age, and figured that was *their* chance, their moment. So they kidnapped their neighbors from their pulsed worlds, and they brainwashed them into their army, and they set off to find more people to brainwash and more pulsed worlds to reap. An endless cycle: Pax get killed conquering a world, Pax replenish their ranks from the conquered, then they move on to the next."

"But . . . why?" Esa asked, something almost desperate in her voice. It was her home that was being overrun, after all, just another step in that endless conflict that was the Pax way.

"Because they're assholes," I replied. I wished I had a better answer for her, but sometimes that was all it came down to: some people were just *mean*, and they found ways to spread their meanness to others. The Pax had just taken that concept more literally than most.

Meanwhile, we still had other things to worry about; I tapped on one of Schaz's access panels. "Scheherazade," I asked. "How long until the hyperdrive is cooled down?"

"We're at seventy-five percent; ten minutes, maybe less."

"All right." I made my way back toward the cockpit. "You two had better strap yourselves in," I said over my shoulder. "We're getting out of this godforsaken system. Get ready to say goodbye to your homeworld, Esa—one way or another, you'll never be back here."

She swallowed, then nodded. It wasn't the easiest thing, to leave a whole world behind.

But the Preacher wasn't ready to let go of what I'd said so easily. "You *know* who caused the pulse," she said again. "Tell me. Tell me *now*."

I stared her down. "Watch yourself, Preacher," I told her. "You're a guest on this ship; you don't give orders. I gave you my word to get you offworld, and I'll keep it. But if you threaten me—or the Justified—in any way, I have *other* oaths that will supersede my promises to you."

She smiled, mocking me, just a little. "So you'd kill me just to keep me from hounding you."

"I've killed people for less. Now—strap yourself in," I repeated. "We're out of here." I took the stairs up to the cockpit two at a time, and took my seat.

Shit. Shit, shit, shit. My big fucking mouth. With what I'd just said, *could* I actually let her off the ship? If I put her down on a Barious colony, she'd spread what I'd told her around, and the Barious were *obsessed* with the pulse, much more so than any other species.

Part of it was just that they were long-lived—every Barious still walking had been alive when the pulse had gone off—and part of it was that the pulse had, for all intents and purposes, rendered them obsolete, an evolutionary dead end. It had been designed to leave them unharmed, that much was true, but it hadn't been meant to *spread* the way it had. The Barious themselves had been untouched, but their production facilities, the plants where they made new Barious—they were all gone, or as good as. Her people hadn't had a new "birth" for over a hundred years. Every Barious still alive had been around since before the pulse *because* there were no more new Barious to add to their numbers. And as they died off, none were replacing them.

Unintended consequences will fuck you every time.

Scheherazade warmed her engines up, and I turned the mapping back on, finding us a route back out of the cave system. Easy enough; there was a cavern exit just a few miles up. I left just enough shielding on to protect us from any bumps along the way, and put all the rest of the power into the stealth systems. They'd find us eventually—our systems were good, but there were probably a hundred ships scanning for us out there—but by the time they did, we'd be well on our way.

When we finally broke out of the caverns and back into atmosphere, I had Schaz remove the bulkhead seals in the living quarters, revealing the viewing window on the port side of the ship. "Is that wise?" she asked me. "If they get a lucky shot in—"

"They've just now picked us up; they won't close in time," I promised her. "Let the girl give her home one last look."

Schaz was uncharacteristically quiet as she granted my request. The Pax were closing—we didn't have a great deal of time—but I still managed to angle the ship so that the window was facing Esa's home. I hung there for as long as I dared, letting her say her goodbyes, even if they were just in her head. I watched behind me, barely able to see her face through the cockpit access, though she'd never know I was looking: she was too busy staring out at the world she was leaving behind.

She reached out to touch the glass, her fingers hesitating for a moment before she pressed them over her homeworld, already *small* to her as we moved away. Everyone she'd ever known was down there—everyone but the Preacher—all the kids she'd been raised with, all the locals in that little town she'd grown up in. The good ones and the bad, they were all under the boot heel of the Pax now, and she'd gotten away. As far as she knew, she was the only one who had. The rest were already fighting, already dead, or already taken.

She made a small noise, almost a sigh; I watched, as patiently as I could. I'd done this more times than I could count: torn a child from their home, shown them the stars, tried to make them believe that the trade-off was worth it—everything they'd ever known, for a life of purpose, of *meaning*. I still believed that. If I didn't, I would have stopped doing this work a long time ago. That didn't make it any easier, watching the cost settle in on their faces.

Finally, the girl nodded—to herself, not to me—and I turned back to the console. Punched in a course *out* of this place, and kicked the hyperdrive online. The subsonic hum of the big engine spinning up filled the interior of the ship like something you could almost feel, and then we were gone, out into the nothing between the stars.

ACT
TWO

CHAPTER 1

I leaned back in the pilot's chair and watched the stars sing by. We hadn't lost the Pax yet—that would take some creative navigation, since they could calculate the vector of our escape and make a rough estimation as to which system we'd hit next—but at least we were out of combat, out of danger for the moment.

Which meant I had to deal with my passengers.

I unbuckled myself, and stood, and stretched. And yawned. It had been a long day. More than anything else, I just wanted to sleep, preferably for about a week. That wouldn't happen, but still.

I returned to the living area, where my two guests were awaiting me.

"We're in space," Esa said, her voice sounding a little awed. "We're traveling through *space*." It's easy to forget how impressive that simple concept was to someone for whom space travel was a distant memory, more a myth than a fact of everyday life.

"We are," I agreed.

"And in style, too," the Preacher said, making a slight motion with her face. If she'd been human, I would have said she wrinkled her nose. Apparently Scheherazade's decor was not to her liking. Which—fine.

I kept Schaz's interior relatively spartan, I'll admit, a feat helped by the modular design: most of the walls rotated to reveal ration storage, the kitchen, exercise gear, bunks, that sort of thing, so there was only ever one or two pieces of furniture visible at a time. At the moment, there was just the central table, its holoprojector currently unused. All the rest of the furniture was stowed inside the walls.

The only visible thing with any sort of personality was the long, built-in shelf with my few prized possessions—namely a dozen actual books, paper binding and all. Others in my profession liked to maintain more comfortable surroundings, to ease their charges out of their old lives, but I figured Sanctum was fairly spartan, too. Might as well let our passengers know what they were getting into.

"I thought your kind prized utilitarianism," I said to the Barious, pulling up a seat at the table for myself, across from the Preacher. Esa was perched on the table's edge, still looking simultaneously awed and in shock.

"There's a difference between keeping a space useful, and keeping it sterile," the Preacher replied. "Don't you pretty much live in this ship? Anyone who spends all their time in a place that might as well double as a prison cell has—"

"I'll thank you not to insult my furnishings." Scheherazade's tone was waspish. She'd apparently taken against the Preacher, which, you know, who could blame her. "Not much for manners, are you?"

The Preacher inclined her head. "Fine. You two did pull me off of that planet, and I'm fully aware that the Pax would have disassembled me. They don't have a great deal of use for Barious; we're too difficult to brainwash." That was both true, and not—Barious programming didn't respond to the sort of brute-force psychological conditioning the Pax used, fair enough, but with access to the right tech, they could have rewritten her personality entirely. It was a rarity, though for whatever reason: when Pax captured Barious alive, they usually tore them apart instead. A remnant of the bad old days of Barious segregation, maybe.

The reminder of the fate of Pax captives jolted Esa from her reverie. "What will happen?" Esa asked. "To my home, I mean?"

"Difficult to say." I shrugged.

"No it's not." The Preacher looked me in the eye as she said it.

"A lot of rads on that world; maybe not worth their time." I didn't want to have this discussion in front of the girl.

"You know how the Pax think. They spent a lot of capital trying to get Esa for themselves. Just because they failed at that doesn't mean they'll pack up and go home—they'll consider it an investment."

"Will you two please stop arguing and just answer me?" Esa asked, looking between the two of us. Her voice was trembling, almost desperate. She knew what we weren't saying was *bad*; she just didn't know *how* bad.

I sighed. "It'll be rough, at first," I said.

"It'll get worse," the Preacher added.

I glared at her until she looked away. "It'll be war, Esa," I told the girl. "That's what the Pax do; that's what they care about. Strength. *Proving* their strength."

"But . . . why?" she asked. "We've got—what's *there?* Wheat fields and . . . and farmers and bandits, nothing worth—"

"But that's what the Pax want, kid," I told her. Leaving aside the bit where what they *really* wanted was her; she already knew that, and reinforcing it now—making her blame herself for the horrors currently tearing her home-world apart—would do no one any good. "They want the wheat fields, sure, but more than that, they *want* the farmers, and the bandits, too. Because once they're done—once the world's pacified and under Pax control—those people won't *be* farmers or bandits anymore."

"They'll just be more Pax," the Preacher said softly.

"You're telling me—everyone I knew, all the other kids from the . . . you're telling me *all* of them will be forced into being soldiers." She shook her head, like she wouldn't believe it, like she *couldn't,* like if she just denied it enough it would stop being true. "You said they wanted to brainwash *me,* not that they'd . . ."

"Not all of them." The Preacher shrugged; I couldn't tell if her apparent callousness was an act, trying to drive Esa to something, or if she really didn't care about the people she'd spent however many years with, passing as one of their own. "Maybe not even most. *Most* of them will be kept as slaves, to harvest the wheat, to do whatever other labor needs doing, and, of course, to make more slaves. Who will then have the strongest of their number culled for the army, and on, and on, and on. That's how the Pax work. Everything feeds the army, the army conquers more worlds, grows larger, keeps moving."

I frowned at the Barious. "You're well-informed for someone who's been stuck on a locked-out world ever since the pulse," I told her.

"I never said that," she shrugged. "You may have assumed it, but I never said it. That's your fault, not mine."

"Wait." Esa looked between the two of us as if she'd just now realized something. "Forget . . . forget sects and Pax and whoever rules the galaxy for a moment. . . . You two are talking like—like you've both been *alive* since the pulse. That was *over* a hundred years ago. You, sure, maybe." She nodded at the Preacher. "I know Barious are long-lived, but *you*"—she turned toward me—"you're human. Like me. We don't live that long."

"We used to," I shrugged. "Still do, in some places, with access to nano-technology and higher-tier medical treatments than your world had. Before the pulse, most species lived four, maybe five times their typical physical lifespan."

"Well—not quite," the Preacher put in. "They *could* live that long. But most didn't, given that the primary occupation for pretty much everyone back then was war."

"So how old *are* you?" Esa asked me.

"Old enough," I replied.

"That's not an answer."

The Preacher looked me up and down, using her gaze to scan me with various instruments. "Well over one fifty," she replied, "Closer to two hundred than that."

I fixed her with a look. "That's some pretty invasive shit to do without someone's permission, you know that?"

"I do." You'll note that wasn't an apology.

"You're over a *hundred and fifty* years old?" Esa's eyes were wide as she stared at me. "The oldest human I ever met was, like, sixty."

"I look good for my age, don't I?"

"I mean—yeah, I suppose. Shouldn't you look a little *less* road-worn, though? With your fancy medical treatments and all?"

"I think that's just her face." The Preacher leaned back in her chair, smiling.

"Why don't both of you just—"

"I hate to interrupt this fascinating conversation," Scheherazade broke in, "but we're approaching our first stop, boss."

"We are?" Esa jumped off the table. "I get to see a new solar system?"

"Not much of one," I replied, heading back for the cockpit; she followed, like a puppy after someone carrying a tray. "The Pax will still be chasing us; the more systems we can bounce through without giving them a direct line on our exit vector, the faster we'll lose them. We're headed to a lifeless collection of . . . pretty much nothing. A handful of gas giants, no rocky planets at all—just dozens of moons that nobody ever got around to terraforming, given that there's nothing particularly interesting about either the planets they're orbiting, or the moons themselves."

"So how does that *help* us?"

"We'll set down on one of the moons, let the hyperdrive cool for a bit, then take off on a new vector. Even if the Pax catch up to us at our next stop, the odds that they'll be able to find us before we jet off again are pretty damned slim."

She made a face at me as we both buckled ourselves in. "So that's it? Barren moons, the exciting act of sitting? You're just determined to take all the fun out of *interstellar travel* for me, aren't you?"

I grinned. "You want a show?" I asked her, reaching for the hyperdrive controls and beginning to ease them back. "Here's a show."

With a jolt, we came out of hyperspace.

CHAPTER 2

I'd said that the system we were jumping into was *boring*, and I stood by that—there was nothing of interest, nothing of use, just a bunch of planets with null resources or value—but just because it was boring didn't mean it wasn't pretty. You get enough gas giants in close enough proximity to one another—and these were all *very* close, so close that in a couple hundred millennia, scant seconds in galactic terms, they'd probably start colliding and changing one anothers' orbits—and it turns into a *very* pretty sight.

It helped that, to the visual spectrum of the human eye, they were all different colors, all vibrant and glowing. Closest to us was a massive blue orb, indigo storms spinning through its atmosphere; just beyond that was a smaller orangish planet, bright enough that we could actually see several of the blue world's moons highlighted against its surface. Past that were giants of every color in the rainbow, some multiple colors at once, all basking in the faint luminosity of the system's core, a long-since-collapsed white dwarf.

So at least Esa's first view of a system beyond her home was an impressive one.

"Holy mother," she breathed, taking in the view.

"I know, right?" I grinned, running course projections on my monitors, with Schaz's help. When you're not traveling through hyperspace, conventional faster-than-light drives make traversing interplanetary distances possible, but not *quick*; we'd have to head for the moons of the nearest planet, the big blue one. Thankfully, pulling out of hyperspace near a celestial body tends to randomize the exit location for each craft that does it—I don't know why, ask a quantum physicist—which meant that the Pax would have no idea which planet we'd emerged nearest to. Even if they'd followed our vector precisely out of Esa's home system, they might still emerge on the far side of one of the other celestial orbs.

"So cool," Esa whispered. She'd unbuckled herself and moved closer to the window to get a closer look, almost pressing her face up against the clear cockpit. She pointed excitedly toward a green world in the distance—it looked small, but of course, to be that visible with the naked eye so near one of its neighbors, it must have been massive. "That one has rings!" she gasped.

"It does." I'll admit it—I played the hard-ass, and I pretended like I never cared about any of the kids I transported. That was . . . necessary. It had to be. But this—and they *all* did this, all the kids from worlds pushed back to a time before space travel was commonplace—this got me every time. I didn't know whether I was offering them a better life, not really. It was *necessary*, necessary for the good of the galaxy, but that didn't mean it was better for *them*.

But at least I could offer them this: to show them wonders they'd never seen before, wonders they'd likely thought were permanently out of their reach, if they even knew such sights existed at all. So many years after *I'd* been introduced to spaceflight, my first, great love, seeing them react the same way I had: it helped remind me that the things I'd been before—before I'd been Justified—hadn't *all* been bad. Just most of them.

"Yes, it's very pretty," the Preacher said, joining us in the cabin. "How long will we be in system?"

"Hyperdrive takes a little under an hour to cool down," I shrugged.

"The Pax may well arrive in that window."

"They *may*, and they may not, but they won't find us; we'll be gone before they can even lay out a sensor grid, much less start sweeping. Even if they manage to trace our vector out of here, we'll have increased our lead time—they'll have to cool down their drives, too. Escaping interstellar pursuit isn't fast, but it's not the hardest thing in the galaxy to do, either; not so long as you've got the ship for it. Which we do." I patted Schaz's console affectionately.

"This craft *is* an impressive design," the Preacher admitted, looking around her—the nicest thing she'd had to say about Scheherazade since she came onboard. "Multipurpose, capable of performing in various gravity wells as well as in the void, set up for long-haul travel—especially noteworthy, given its size—and for intense combat. I've never quite seen its like, I'll admit."

She was trying to be nice; I'll give her that. Still, Schaz's voice was frosty as she said into the cabin, "I'll thank you to refer to me as 'her,' rather than 'it.'"

A ghost of a smile on the Preacher's face. "My apologies."

"Wait." Esa was confused. "If you're a 'her,' why do you sound like a man?"

I sighed. I appreciated that she needed to ask the question, but as I'd spent most of the trip out from Sanctum listening to Schaz complain about this very set of circumstances, I wasn't in a hurry to listen to it again. "Because our lives are complex," I said, cutting off Schaz before she could start.

"And because JackDoes is an asshole." Not that she didn't try anyway.

"And also because of that. Set us down on that nearby moon, will you Schaz?" I tapped one of the celestial bodies on my display. "At least that way we'll be hidden if the Pax do show up."

"Right." Esa turned back to me. "The Pax. I still wasn't done asking about them."

"Okay." I nodded, standing from the helm. "No reason to have this conversation crammed into the cockpit, though." I made my way back toward the living quarters, not waiting to see if they would follow; Esa hesitated for a moment—taking in the sight of the moon approaching through the window—before following.

"So," I asked her, pulling myself up a seat. "What do you want to know?"

CHAPTER 3

"Y ou and the Preacher both—you know who they are," she began. "And you both seem to know why they want me. I feel like I'm the only one in the dark, here."

"Fair enough." I nodded, reaching forward to activate the holoprojector in the center of the main table; it filled the room with light. "Schaz? Display a basic Pax shocktrooper." The diagram—an overlay of armor and weaponry over various shifting racial "types"—snapped into focus, floating in midair.

"I know what they look like," Esa said; I think she was going for vaguely annoyed, but mostly she was too busy staring at the holoprojection with something like awe. She'd never seen its like before.

Finally, she ripped herself away from the glowing wireframe display. "I'm asking who they *are*."

"But what they look like *is* who they are," I told her. "That's the point of all that armor. No identifying traits visible; it's impossible to tell species or race or gender through all that mass. That's how the Pax began. Uniformity in purpose; uniformity as common bond. The concept is . . . seductive, to a certain type of mind."

"And not the worst goal ever," the Preacher said, joining us from the cockpit.

I acknowledged her point with a nod. "To be divorced from who or where you were born, or how; to be judged only on your merits. Like I said—it has its appeal. To be Pax, all you have to do is *be* Pax. Regardless of how you were born, so long as you follow their creed, nothing else matters. And you are given purpose, a purpose many of their number lacked before becoming Pax."

"And what creed is that?" Esa asked. "What *purpose* do they offer?"

"'Might makes right,'" I said simply. "That's it; that's all. Everything else they believe stems from that. They believe that the only righteous universe is one where the weak depend utterly on the strong, and the strong, in turn, prey on the weak, in order to grow stronger. If you're a soldier, then you fight, to prove that you *deserve* to win. If you're *not* a soldier, if you *can't* fight, you're a slave, fit only to serve those that can."

"It's the 'deserving' part that makes the Pax . . . troublesome," the Preacher added, with typically Barious understatment.

"The slavery part doesn't help," Schaz added sourly.

"This from a shackled." The Preacher dismissed my ship with a wave of a hand; I glared at her, but said nothing. "The Pax believe that the strong have a *moral responsibility* to fight," the Preacher told Esa, "a moral responsibility to grow stronger, and the weak, likewise, have a responsibility to serve the strong, in return for their protection."

"And that's why they want you," I told her. "You're strong. Therefore trying to add your strength to their own—or to kill you, trying—is *their* responsibility. What you might or might not want has nothing to do with it."

"I'm not . . . I'm not *strong*, though," she protested. "I don't know *how* to fight. I . . . I watched the two of you defend us on that tower, and I just huddled in the bunker." Something almost bitter in her voice. "I was so goddamned *scared.*"

"That's natural, kid—I'd be more worried if you hadn't been. But the Pax can conquer fear in their soldiers, erase it, along with most everything else other than hate. Once they did *that*, your gift would make you an unstoppable force on any battlefield. Believe me—I've seen what happens, when they get their hands on someone . . . gifted. It's not pretty. For the kid with the gifts, or for whoever's standing in their way."

"So that's the other part of your job, isn't it?" the Preacher asked. "That's why you're more soldier than diplomat. You don't just *find* gifted children for the Justified, and you don't just recruit them. You deal with the ones that get caught up in . . . something else. Make sure they don't get turned into weapons. Weapons that could be used against you."

"I do what I have to do." I wouldn't say more; not in front of Esa. Not to the Preacher, either, for that matter. It was none of her business.

I turned back to the girl instead. "As far as the Pax are concerned," I told her, "there's no question: you represent strength, and if you don't *choose* to use that strength for your own benefit, then *they* have a moral responsibility to see you either eradicated or indoctrinated."

"That's why they don't want you joining her sect." The Preacher nodded at me. "The Justified are already guilty of several counts of moral failure, as far as the Pax are concerned—they don't use their strength to dominate others, they prefer to act from the shadows, behind the scenes, influencing events rather than seizing control directly—"

"—and for the greater good of all involved, rather than *just* the benefit of the Justified," I added, before she could get too carried away.

"At least as you see it, yes," the Preacher admitted. "So allowing you to join the Justified's ranks, Esa, rather than killing you before you can do so: that would be a failing on the part of the *Pax*. Allowing their enemy to grow stronger, when they could have stopped it."

"But . . . they were still trying to capture me," Esa said, feeling her way through the concepts. "If all they care about is *proving* that they're stronger than I am—"

"They'd still prefer to add your strength to their own, if possible," I told her. "The strong should use every opportunity to grow stronger—that's also part of the Pax creed. If they have to kill you to keep you from joining the Justified they'll do so, but their perfect outcome would be to induct you into their ranks, instead. To . . . show you the galaxy. As they see it."

Her eyes grew a little wider at that; I think she knew what I meant, or at least the outlines of the thing. She still had to ask, though. "And if they couldn't . . . 'show' me?"

"They could. Everybody has a breaking point, kid. Everybody."

"But if they couldn't—"

"If they *couldn't*, they'd do the same thing they'd do if they killed you: dissect you, cut you open and try to study your gifts, with an eye towards figuring out how to replicate them. It's impossible, but they don't know that."

"And you do?" the Preacher asked; she had been watching Esa, gauging her reactions, but her attention was fully on me now. She found that piece of information interesting, to say the least—though whether that was because of the information itself, or just that I was aware of it, I wasn't sure.

"I do," I said, keeping my tone clipped as I met her gaze. "The Justified know more about the gifted children than almost anyone else out there,

Preacher. We've been studying them for a very long time. But that's the thing, kid." I turned back to the girl. "Even though *we* know the Pax can't replicate your gifts—*they* don't. Just because they've killed a handful of gifted kids *trying* doesn't mean they're ready to give up just yet. It's too promising a goal. The concept of you alone, at the head of a Pax battalion, is enough strength to make them salivate; the concept of that same battalion, comprised *entirely* of Pax who've been *given* your abilities—no army raised could stop them. The ultimate strength."

"So the Pax just want to use me. However they can."

"Yes," I agreed.

"And so do the Justified. To build their wall."

"Yes." She wasn't wrong. The Preacher arched a metallic eyebrow at my answer; I stared at her in response until she looked away. She'd expected me to lie. "And to train you," I added, still looking at the Preacher. "So that you can use your gifts for the good of the galaxy—for the good of *all*, not just yourself."

"Were *you* born Justified?" The question took me by surprise; I turned back to look at the girl. She was a sharp one, I'd give her that.

"No." I shook my head. "I wasn't."

"So you were recruited, like me. And they trained *you*. To fight the way you do; to fly the way you do."

"No, they didn't." That came from the Preacher, and then it was my turn to give her a questioning look. She shrugged in response. "I've seen Justified fight, and I've seen Justified fly," she said. "They're good, but their techniques tend toward the . . . conservative." I had the feeling she thought she was being diplomatic. "Whatever you are—and wherever you learned to do the things you do—*conservative* is not the word I would choose."

"You're not wrong," I admitted.

"Which means you were something else. Before the pulse."

"We were *all* something else before the pulse," I reminded her.

"I will never get used to that," Esa muttered. "A hundred years ago, and you're both like 'Oh, yeah, I remember that; good times.'"

"Not really," I said.

"I mean—you know. Outside of all the war. Is *that* where you learned to fight? To fly?"

"Pretty much. The Pax believe that the strong should kill, or they aren't worthy of their strength. I was raised with a much simpler code."

"And what code was that?" The Preacher was the one who asked the question, not Esa.

"You kill or you die," I told her, keeping my voice even. "That was the way the worlds worked, back then. You remember that much." The Pax thought of themselves as better, and they weren't—but they also weren't worse. Not than some of what had come before.

Some of what had made me.

CHAPTER 4

Thankfully, I was saved any more questions about my time with the Justified—or my time in the sect wars—when Schaz summoned me to the cockpit; I left the Preacher and Esa to their discussion and ducked out of the living quarters to attend to Schaz instead.

"What's up?" I asked, taking my seat at the helm.

"Sorry to bother you, boss," she replied, "but I'm picking up a strange transmission that you should probably hear—just came in over encrypted channels."

I had no illusions about the Preacher's ability to overhear every word that was said on board the entire ship; still, I reached out to shut the airlock door between the cockpit and the living quarters before I nodded for Schaz to start the playback. If the Preacher wanted, she *would* hear what was on the transmission, but at least this way Esa wouldn't.

Scheherazade's speakers crackled to life. The message was warped, barely audible, repeating on a loop. What I was able to pick out sounded like: ". . . is is Marus Lonus . . . been att . . . ax enforcers, they c . . . out of nowhere. My . . . ssel is bre . . . ut that doesn . . . tter now. I hav . . . tion *vital* to Sanct . . . ut I can't . . . isk transmitting ove . . . ypted comm channels. My coordin . . . bedded in this messag . . . ase hurry, runni . . . t of time."

I leaned back in my chair and swore softly.

The message was from Marus Lonustan, a Tyll I knew well—he was an agent of Sanctum, like myself. His job was a little different; I trafficked in gifted children, he trafficked in information. It had been an agent like him who had pointed me toward Esa, for instance.

The gist of the message seemed clear to me: he had been attacked by the Pax, had escaped, but his ship was damaged and he needed help. He said he had information vital to Sanctum—which may well be true, he was an agent, all he *did* was collect information vital to Sanctum—that he couldn't risk broadcasting, even over Sanctum encrypted channels. Which also made sense; agents tended to be a paranoid lot.

The coincidence, though, made me twitchy: what I'd said to Esa was true, the Pax *weren't* everywhere in the galaxy. They weren't even a major threat, not really. Even this close to their home systems—and we weren't far—the chances that we'd run into Pax, and that Marus *also* would, on a completely separate op, were slim at best. My mentor in the Justified had once told me that there were no such thing as coincidences, only the will of man, or of God. I didn't believe in his God, but the will of man, the will of the Pax: *that* I believed in. They were up to something.

"The message is fragmented," I said to Schaz, listening again as the message repeated. "Any way to tell how many iterations it's been through?"

"Ironically, the fragmentation has wiped out at least part of the signal decay that could tell us that. I'd say several thousand, at least."

"It plays at . . . not quite a minute long." I timed it out on my HUD as I listened again. "If it's been playing several thousand times, that means this happened a day or so ago, maybe more, not counting the travel time for the message itself." Broadcasting signals at FTL speeds is . . . complicated. You can *do* it, but unlike ships, which can continue to accelerate every moment they're in hyperspace, the signals can't. Which in turn means that, if you want a message somewhere in a hurry, you're better off trusting it to a courier with a fast ship than broadcasting a signal. Marus had only done so because he had no other choice.

I felt something bad creeping down my spine—whatever this was, it sounded like trouble. It *felt* like trouble, maybe more than we could handle. We were in deep enough ourselves.

All the same, Marus was a friend.

"Dig the coordinates out," I told Schaz. "We're going after him. He's Justified; he's ours. How soon until the hyperdrive's ready?"

"It's ready now."

"Plot a course. I want to be out of here before *our* Pax pursuit shows up—the last thing we want to do is to mount a rescue mission, only to lead an entirely *different* group of Pax warships down on his head."

CHAPTER 5

After a moment, Schaz finished her calculations as I began warming up her engines. "A couple of different vectors pulled up on your screens, boss."

"Good job." I was already taking off, pulling us up out of the crater where Schaz had set us down, just below the surface of a pale blue moon. As I powered us free of the lunar gravity well I turned my attention to the route options Schaz had displayed for me, and the various systems we'd have to pass through to reach Marus's position.

"There's our vector," I murmured to myself, setting one in. It avoided populated worlds, but was otherwise a straight shot to Marus. The route would still take some time—about ten hours—but we'd get to him. Hopefully he could keep himself alive until then. I wasn't that worried; Marus was a clever one.

Just before I engaged the hyperdrive, Scheherazade's scanners started screaming; Pax contact. It was at the far edge of the system—they wouldn't be close enough to get a reading on our escape vector. They'd know we were here, and they'd know we had *left*—I'm sure their sensors were screaming just like ours were—but which direction, which heading; that, they'd have to guess at. It didn't mean they couldn't follow us, but it was a big galaxy, and the farther we got, the more likely we were to shake them.

Then the hyperdrive kicked on, and the beautiful, empty system bled away.

I unsealed the airlock and returned to the living quarters; the shower was running, Esa esconsced within, but the Preacher was waiting for me—not speaking, just watching. I could feel her studying my expression, framing another set of questions in her head.

I sighed mentally, and went ahead and gave her the opening she was looking for. "Yes?" I asked.

"You got a transmission."

"You were eavesdropping."

"No. Your airlock seals are quite good." She seemed fairly annoyed by this fact. "But I know you received *some* sort of message."

"We're going to have to make a stop. Another Justified operative is in trouble."

"And if I was to ask who gave him this trouble?"

"You wouldn't have to—you already know."

"The Pax."

"The Pax." I nodded.

She studied me for a moment longer, then switched topics so abruptly it took me some time to catch up—which, I suppose, was likely her purpose in doing so. "When we first met," she reminded me, "you asked me about Esa; you said she would have been conceived around the same time as the meteor shower fourteen years ago." She cocked her head to the side, as if awaiting a reply.

"You're asking about relevance," I said.

"I am, yes."

"That meteor shower didn't seem odd to you?"

"I wasn't an astrophysicist, even before the pulse." But she had been something similar; I'd bet my relatively few pieces of furniture on that. She knew how to fight, but not like I did—she'd been fighting *adjacent*. The way she talked about science was much more active. "The event seemed noteworthy to the populace at the time," she continued, "because their world doesn't *get* meteor showers all that often. But contrary to popular opinion, we Barious don't *actually* know everything." This said with just a ghost of a smile.

"It was noteworthy because it wasn't a meteor shower. It's a phenomenon I've seen on other worlds; the pulse radiation always sinks to the surface when it first arrives, then slowly works its way up again. That was the radiation finally cooking the last of the satellites still in orbit, bringing them down. Most people had forgotten they were even up there; read the event as a meteor shower instead."

"None of that goes to relevance."

"It corresponds to a jump in radiation on the surface; once it hits upper atmosphere, it drops back again. Not something you'd notice in the world—it's not *different* radiation, just the same stuff that's been blocking all the other tech that hasn't worked for a century, there's just more of it. But I've seen it on other worlds; the jump tends to correspond to the conception of the gifted children who—"

"Can we *not* talk about my conception?" Esa asked, joining us as she toweled off her hair. "That's just . . . weird." She was still wearing her torn, dirty clothes from her homeworld—significantly more torn and dirty after our little adventures, I'll admit, but they hadn't started off clean, either. I'd have to get her some new ones.

"You never knew your parents," the Preacher reminded her.

"You . . . already know this. Remember—the orphanage? It's not like they were on holiday or something."

"I do, but why does discussing your conception bother you if the physical act doesn't involve anyone you know? It's just an *act*, Esa, it's not—"

She put her hand up. "Okay, yeah. We're *really* done talking about this. Can we go back to talking about the Pax? Even *brainwashing* is more fun than this."

The Preacher shook her head. "You organics, so . . . *obsessed* with the physical act of reproduction. It affects almost all of your mental processes; did you know that? And humans are the *worst*—at least with Tyll or Wulf, they're only in season for a few months. Humans obsess about reproduction *constantly*—"

"Says the being whose understanding of sex amounts to *my* understanding of complex AI algorithms," I pointed out dryly.

"I hate to say it, but she's *not* wrong," Schaz pointed out, her tone grudging. "I've noticed it in my own observations; when you go more than a few months without engaging in coitus, your behavioral patterns *do* start to shift dramatically—"

"Yeah, no, Esa's right." I held up my hand. "We're done talking about this subject."

"Dry spells happen to everyone, darling." Schaz *thought* she was being soothing, I'm sure. Her new upper-crust Tyll accent didn't really help, though.

"Right, we're done," I told . . . everyone. "We've got about ten hours to get to Marus—the course Schaz and I plotted will take us through three separate systems to do that, all lightly populated at best. *That* means, unless something goes deeply wrong, we shouldn't run into trouble between here and there, and *that* means I'm going to get a shower of my own, and then I'm going to get some sleep. You two can stay up late and gossip like a couple of adolescents—"

"I *am* an adolescent," Esa reminded me, a touch of asperity in her voice.

"Well, stop." I made my way into the shower, and sealed the door before either of them could come up with a reply. Sharing information is all well and good—to a point—but my sex life was nobody's concern but my own.

CHAPTER 6

I got my seven hours' sleep; at least *that* happened. I have no idea how Schaz, the Preacher, and Esa amused themselves during that window, and I don't really care—I needed the rest. Esa did too—when I woke, she was sacked out on the bunk above me. The Preacher was sitting at the table in her "meditation" state; I let her be, poured myself a cup of coffee in the tiny kitchen—Schaz was good about always keeping coffee handy when I was on board—and went through to the cockpit, shutting the door so I didn't wake Esa or disturb the Barious.

"Any news?" I asked Scheherazade, setting my coffee cup on the instrument panel to cool some. I love coffee, but I can't drink it straight from the pot, or I won't if I can help it. A leftover habit from subsisting on lukewarm leftovers in war zones. I do that often enough—setting the cup down in that particular spot on the panel, I mean—that Schaz was starting to complain about the rings I was leaving on the metal. She's really very fussy.

"We've been through two systems so far," she told me, "with nothing measurably interesting in either. We're coming up on one with a world pushed almost as far back as Esa's was—maybe we'll get lucky, trick the Pax into thinking we landed there for some reason."

"So we haven't lost them yet."

"Sorry, I should have led with that. Haven't lost them yet." I rolled my eyes, and took an experimental sip of my coffee: still too hot. "They keep popping into system just as we leave. I don't know if they're just getting lucky, or if they sent the entire complement of craft they had after us, and they're just breaking off in each system, dividing their ships along every possible vector we could have taken. Either way—"

"If they tail us all the way back to Marus, it could be trouble. He said he had already run into Pax—whatever's got him spooked, it involves them somehow." There was that coincidence again, the thing I didn't believe in. "I doubt he'd thank us much for the rescue if we led an entire Pax fleet down onto his head while we were doing it."

"That would seem to be a debatable form of 'rescue,' yes."

"Play his message for me again."

She did that; she'd managed to clean it up a little, probably at least partially because we were getting closer to the source of the signal. "Information vital to Sanctum." I mused over the particular phrase Marus had employed. "Not 'vital to the Justified,' not 'vital to the galaxy at large,' but vital to Sanctum itself."

"You know agents," Schaz said with the vocal equivalent of a shrug. "They think *everything* they're doing is vital, especially the cloak-and-dagger types."

"Maybe," I conceded her point, "but Marus is steady, steadier than most." We'd worked together since I first joined the Justified, and I trusted him, a courtesy I extended to few, even among our own ranks.

I sat back in my chair and watched the starfield sing past. Travel by hyperdrive is many things—and it certainly *can* be stultifyingly boring, especially on longer cruises—but the view never really gets old. I'll give it that much.

Eventually, I was joined by Esa, and the Preacher followed after. Given that everybody was awake again and there was no real *reason* to all be crammed into the cockpit, we decamped back to the living quarters.

Long space flights can actually be pretty boring; Esa spent most of the time peppering me with questions about life at Sanctum—I tried to keep my answers somewhere between the two poles of "what I actually knew," given that I didn't spend very much time at Sanctum, and also "what the council would *want* her to know"—and questions about the universe at large.

The Preacher wasn't shy about interjecting into my answers on the second subject, which only confirmed what I'd been guessing—she was well informed, even for a Barious, especially about the pulse. The question of *how* or *why* she'd ended up on Esa's homeworld was still one I hadn't pressed her on, but I doubted she'd give me much if I did; even for a Barious, she was a cagey one.

I doubted it was anything simple, like a crash; if that was the case, she'd just tell me. Honestly, I was a little surprised she hadn't just gone with that as a *lie*, even if just to throw me off the scent.

The good news was that, finally, we traveled through a system where the Pax *didn't* show up just as soon as we were ready to leave. I didn't know if we'd lost them for good, but at least we'd been putting steadily more distance between us. The bad news was that it was the *last* system between us and Marus's coordinates—whatever had happened to him, we'd need to work fast to solve it, in case the Pax were still tracking us. I would have preferred a system or two—or half-dozen—between us and them once we reached the origin of Marus's signal.

"You're worried about your friend," Esa said, watching my face as I confirmed our coordinates.

"I'm worried about complications," I told her. "I don't like complications. My job's to get you to Sanctum; that's all I *need* to do. Anything else, however necessary it might seem, is really just standing in the way of that."

"You take your job very seriously, don't you?"

"I do. It's why you're still alive."

"Point taken."

We slipped into hyperspace again, one step closer to whatever chaos Marus had gotten himself into.

CHAPTER 7

G ot him," Schaz confirmed as we slipped into the system where Marus's distress signal had originated. "He's . . . what is he doing *there?*"

"Any sign of anybody else in system?" I asked her, already sitting behind the stick. I let Schaz keep control for now, but at the first sign of trouble, I was ready to take over.

"No, it's just Marus and Khonnerhonn," she replied, naming Marus's ship as well. "They're in the rings of the big gas giant, closest world to us."

"No sign of any Pax, of any—"

"I told you, no," Schaz said again, a slight asperity to her voice. "That's not something I would keep from you just for entertainment's sake, you know. Khonn's not answering my hails; that's . . . worrisome."

"Take us in. And keep trying."

I watched the gas giant approach onscreen, a big swirling orb of greens and purples surrounded by three sets of rings, each at about a sixty-degree angle from the others. "That's pretty," Esa said, watching the planet approach.

"It is," I agreed. We both watched the planet approach in silence, Esa still marveling at the wonders of the galaxy as I wondered what the hell had happened, what had brought Marus to this deserted place.

The only world of any note was a long-abandoned planet much closer to the system's star—it had been completely stripped of mineral wealth ages ago and left derelict, long before the pulse. There were millions of worlds like it out there, millions of systems, used up and discarded in the initial outward rush of the golden age. So, in essence, the only place of even minor note in-system was only noteworthy because there wasn't anything to note about it *anymore.*

"Scheherazade?" A male voice suddenly filled the comms. It sounded . . . almost sleepy. Tired. "Is that . . . you? What are *you* doing here?"

"Khonnerhonn—it's me, yeah, we're coming to—"

"You have to *help* him." If it had been a human speaking, I would have said their voice choked with a sob. The desperation in the sound was like a tactile thing. "I did . . . I'm doing what I can, but he's not . . . it was one of *my* systems, Schaz, it burnt out and discharged and he's *hurt*. We just didn't expect them . . . they came out of nowhere."

"Is Marus on board, Khonn?" Schaz asked. "Is he all right?"

"He's *hurt*," the AI said again. "He stabilized himself, but he's in shock, went into *cort* to try and stay alive. He needs . . . medical treatment, he needs . . . please. *Please*."

I leaned back in my chair. This wasn't good. *Cort* was an autonomic anomaly of the Tyll; unlike most other species, they had evolved on a world where they were the only form of fauna. As a result, they'd developed a handful of rather strange physiological responses. *Cort* was one of them—a kind of hibernative state the Tyll dropped into if they were hurt, badly. Their heart rate slowed to almost nothing, as did their breathing; their body stopped any activity other than healing. On a world full of predators, of course, that would have been a death sentence, but the Tyll never had anything to worry about except other Tyll.

"We'll help him, Khonn," Schaz promised. "Can you tell us what happened?"

"He picked up some information from a dead drop, one of his informants," Khonn said, his voice still sounding weary beyond measure. "We didn't even get to finish decrypting it before the Pax hit us, *hard*. We ran, but there were too many of them. They just kept coming, kept chasing us, doing a little more damage every time. He was at the gunnery controls when they got through . . . and then *my system* shorted, Schaz, it was *my fault*. But I kept . . . I kept running. Lost them, eventually, I don't know . . . I don't know. Tried to get out of system, but there wasn't . . . I don't . . ."

"He sent us a message, Khonn," Schaz reminded him gently.

"Last thing he did before he slipped into *cort*," Khonn said. "I've tried to . . . I'm trying, Schaz, I am, but . . ." The ship's voice trailed off into nothing.

This was very bad. The strange echo in Khonn's voice—the sound that I would have called weariness in an organic being—it meant he was running on fumes, had very little power left. Which meant his core had been damaged. Otherwise, Pax or no Pax, he would have gotten Marus to a medical facility somewhere. Or died trying.

"Can you get a reading?" I asked Schaz quietly. Force of habit—she wouldn't broadcast a question like that to Khonnerhonn—but it was the equivalent of asking a doctor whether or not their patient was going to make it. Their patient, and their friend. Marus and I had known each other for a long time. Which meant so had Schaz and Khonn.

"His core's not critical yet, but it's getting there," Scheherazade confirmed quietly. "There's nothing we can do. He's dying, boss."

Starship AI was a funny thing—it was baked into the individual components of its processing hardware, the same way an organic brain was made up of the composition of electrical impulses and neuron damage done over a lifetime. There would be no downloading Khonn to a different ship, not any more than you could transfer a dying human's mind to a different human. Most Justified operatives raised their ships' AI from a basic program; in a way, they learned how to be themselves by watching *us*, their personalities disseminating into the ship itself as we taught them how to fly.

Now Khonnerhonn's flying days were done.

I reached forward, to take the comm. "You did good, Khonnerhonn," I said softly. "You did real good. You kept him safe—kept running, kept fighting, when you were so damaged that a lot of other ships would have given up. You should be proud."

"Just . . . just get him out of here," Khonn whispered. "Keep him safe. And let him . . . let him know that . . ." His voice faded, his core running out of the energy required even for a low-power broadcast. If comms were down, that would mean Khonnerhonn had lost almost all of his basic systems. For all intents and purposes, the ship was dead.

He'd died keeping Marus safe, had died doing everything he could to protect the man he was built to serve. Had kept him alive long enough for us to reach him.

He'd died doing his duty.

CHAPTER 8

I heard a snuffling sound behind me, and turned; Esa was still sitting in the chair, wiping tears from her face. "That poor ship," she snuffled. "That poor . . . poor . . ."

"It's all right, dear," Scheherazade said comfortingly. "Up to his last moments, he did his duty; he protected Marus. There is no higher calling for a ship AI, no nobler end. Most of us know that, when we die, it likely means our captain dies with us, in a ball of flame under enemy fire. That Khonn managed to survive long enough to *know* that we were coming to save Marus, that he wouldn't be taking his captain down with him . . . it was a good end."

"That doesn't make it not *sad*."

"I know, dearheart. I know."

The Preacher was standing in the doorway. "That was . . . not what I expected," she said quietly. "I did not think a—"

"Barious," Schaz said evenly, in a tone that even with her voice all fucked up I knew well enough to know that she *meant* what she said next, "if you even *think* the word 'shackled' I will spit you out my airlock."

The Preacher nodded, once. "It was brave," she said finally. "I only meant that it was . . . very brave."

Schaz considered this for a moment. "Yes, it was," she agreed.

Khonnerhonn—or rather, the ship that *had* been Khonnerhonn—was slowly approaching in the cockpit view, a rounder, more subtle vessel than Schaz, a design more suited for infiltration than combat, lacking most of Scheherazade's weaponry as well as her aerodynamic wings. He'd tucked himself away in the debris of the ring, hoping that enemy scans would bounce off him as just more flotsam. We'd only picked him up because Justified ships could always recognize the transponders we all had installed.

"Pull us in close enough to board, Schaz," I said. "And get a reading on . . . on what remains of the core."

"Will do, boss. Go get him."

I nodded, and headed toward the airlock at the back of the ship. I waited for Scheherazade to equalize the atmosphere—it wasn't *entirely* gone from Khonnerhonn, but he'd been unable to regulate it for some time, and we had plenty to spare—then reached toward the seal. "The core?" I asked Schaz again.

"Not long," came her reply. "Be quick."

I opened the door.

The Preacher came with me. Together, we entered Khonnerhonn. It felt like a ghoulish thing to do, to enter a ship we'd just heard utter his last words. But he had wanted us to save Marus, and Marus was inside somewhere.

The Tyll intelligence operative hadn't quite leaned into the spartan nature of the Justified the way I had—he'd spent his years finding just the right decoration for this or that spot inside his home—but it was still not a cluttered ship by any means, and we found him quickly, curled up in a fetal ball on his bunk, unresponsive to any stimuli, just a hunched figure with his usually lime-green skin gone unhealthily pale.

"He's still breathing," the Preacher reported, checking his vitals. "Just very, very slowly. Electrical burns indicate—"

"Save it for later," I interrupted. "We're on a clock. As long as he's still alive, that's good enough for now."

"He's still alive, but he needs medical attention as soon as possible. Even *cort* won't keep him alive indefinitely; at this point it's just staving off—"

"Just get him on board Scheherazade," I said again. "There's one more thing I have to do here."

She looked at me. "Are you planning to scuttle the ship?" she asked.

"A cracked core will do that without us having to lift a finger," I replied. "Get him on board." Without waiting to see if she followed my instructions, I tapped the comm in my ear. "Schaz?"

"Here, boss. Do you have him?"

"We got him; Preacher's bringing him in now. But I need you to do something else for me."

"Anything."

"You're not going to like it."

"If it will help fuck up the Pax for what they did to Marus and Khonn, I'll like it very much." There was real savagery in her voice as she said it. "What do you need?"

I took a breath; she wouldn't like it. "I'm going to hardwire you into Khonnerhonn's databanks. I need you to download as much as you can."

"That's . . . *ghastly*, boss." The human equivalent probably would have been going through the pockets of a corpse, looking for loose change.

"I know, Schaz. But Marus's contact found *something*, something the Pax tracked Marus and Khonn through dozens of systems to keep *out* of our hands. I need you to make sure they didn't succeed." As I spoke I ran a thin wire from a spool just inside of Scheherazade's airlock to a similar port just inside Khonnerhonn's. "Khonn died to keep Marus safe, but the Pax killed him because of what they found. I won't lose that."

"I understand."

I nodded. "Look for anything encrypted, using non-Justified encryption. Marus wouldn't have trusted the general encryption for this kind of work; it wouldn't have been good enough." Something of a perfectionist, Marus was. Not that I could blame him; his work made mine look low risk, and his survival often hinged on how good his tools were, or how well he had prepared.

"Got it."

"And Schaz? Work fast. I can *smell* the core. We don't have long." Fusion energy was by far the safest, cleanest, most efficient form of energy in the galaxy, or at least it was right up until something went catastrophically wrong. Ships didn't have their own fusion reactors on board—at least, not ships the size of Khonn or Schaz—but instead charged up a core with energy from a reactor whenever they docked at a station, usually enough to keep them powered for months on end in deep space.

Typically, you didn't even *think* about your ship's core unless there was a problem; it was completely locked off from the rest of the craft, except for the power leads siphoning energy to your other systems. The fact that I could smell the air starting to ionize from the crackling energy deep in the heart of Khonn meant something was very, very wrong with the core.

"Get back on board," Schaz urged me. "Seal up the airlock; we can cut the hardline on our end once I've got what we need. If the core's that close to going critical, I don't want to waste a millisecond getting us out of here when we're ready to go."

"Yeah." I took one last look around Khonnerhonn's interior; I'd spent more than a few good days and nights on this ship, drinking and talking with Marus. He was a friend. I bent over to pick up a few notebooks Marus had scattered on the floor in his last conscious moments. I'd seen him writing in them before—I didn't know what the hell they were, but I could save him at least something from his home.

Then I slipped back through the airlock, and left Khonn behind forever.

CHAPTER 9

Ηow's Marus?" I asked Schaz as I sealed us off. I felt Scheherazade shift slightly underneath me as she broke the connection from Khonner-honn and started moving us away from the dead ship, just in case the core did go critical.

"The Preacher has him in the medbay," Schaz responded. "It's . . . not good."

I made my way to the living area; the Barious had indeed figured out which section of the wall unfolded into Schaz's little medical area and surgery suite. It was fine for patching up injuries from battlefield combat, but I already knew this was probably beyond what we could fix on board. "What does he need?" I asked.

"We can stabilize him, even treat the burns," the Preacher said, busily doing just that—as good with medical equipment as she was with a rifle, apparently. "But bringing him out of *cort* is another matter."

"We need drugs," I said.

"We need drugs," she agreed. "Tyll-specific compounds, things that involve molecular structures and base amino acids that your sha . . . your ship can't synthesize."

"Schaz—what's the nearest friendly medical center that can treat Tyll?" I asked. "Even a pulsed world will do, so long as they have—"

"There's a primarily Tyll world about five jumps distant; they got thrown back far, nearly as far as Esa's homeworld, but they *should* know how to bring him out of *cort*."

"Assuming we can find anyone willing to help us."

"Assuming that, yes. And it's in the wrong direction, taking us away from Sanctum."

"I'm guessing you have another option."

"I do, but you're . . . not going to like it much."

I sighed. "Just tell me."

"We're only about two jumps away from Beyond Ending," she said. "Two *short* jumps. I could have us there in a matter of hours."

I narrowed my eyes. I couldn't glare *at* Schaz while I was inside her, but I did my best anyway. "We don't have any friends at Beyond Ending, Schaz," I reminded her. "It's nothing but pirates and smugglers. We'd need someone to vouch for us before they'd even let us dock."

"That's not . . . *entirely* true. The 'no friends' part, I mean, not the 'they wouldn't let us dock' part—they would *totally* shoot us out of the sky if we didn't have someone on board clearing us for landing."

I didn't stop glaring at her, or at least in the general direction of her core. I had a bad, bad feeling I already knew what she was going to say next. "Schcherazade?" I asked, my voice gone quiet—Esa looked at me nervously. She hadn't known me long, and she could already tell that *wasn't* a good tone. "What 'friend' do we have at a pirate cooperative?"

"It's . . . it's *possible* that I've been getting messages from Javier."

"Possible. It's *possible*." My hand was reflexively gripping the arm of one of the chairs, mainly so that I didn't pick up something else and throw it at the bulkheads between me and Scheherazade's primary processors.

"I haven't been *answering* him or anything," she hastened to add, reading my mood as well as Esa had. "I just . . . read them. And . . . possibly . . . bounced the messages back as 'accepted.' Just so he knew—"

"Do you *want* us to get kicked out of the Justified, Schaz?" I seethed. "Do you *want*—"

"Look, whatever this is," the Preacher interrupted, "we *need* to get your friend to medical treatment, now. I can get him to the point where the damage itself won't kill him, but *cort* burns a great deal of resources out of the Tyll physiology. Contrary to popular opinion, it's *not* a hibernative state—he's going through calories and nutrients far *faster* now than he would if he was unharmed, trying to heal himself, except these injuries are beyond his body's ability to heal."

"You've stabilized the burns; won't he come out of it himself?" I asked.

She shook her head. "I've stabilized them enough so that they won't *kill* him; that's not the same thing as *healing* him. He has internal injuries that are keeping him in *cort*, injuries I can't do anything about here. Again, with certain drugs, the *cort* can be . . . supercharged, to finish the work and bring him out of that state, but in the meantime, if we don't get those drugs inside of him soonish, he will *starve* himself to death trying to fix what can't be fixed. I can give him a fluid IV to slow that down, but he still needs help, more help than we can give here, and he needs it fast."

"You know a great deal about Tyll physiology, Barious."

"I know a great deal about many things. You have your history; I have mine."

I unwrapped my hand from the chair. "Fine," I said. "Schaz, set a course, get us out of here."

"To Beyond Ending?"

"To Beyond Ending. If you think you can convince Javier to let us on board—"

"Oh, he'll do that in a heartbeat. He *really*—"

"I don't need to *know* what was in his letters, Scheherazade. I don't *want* to know what was in his letters. If he can help Marus, I'll do him the courtesy of pretending I never saw him, but that's it. That's all he gets."

"Boss, he didn't *mean* to—"

"Set in the goddamned course, Schaz. And get us out of this system, before the Pax find us again."

"Yes, boss."

"And Schaz?"

"Yes, boss?"

"Don't think we're *not* having a conversation about the fact that you've kept in contact with a turncoat operative that we have orders to *shoot on sight*. That discussion is coming, and it is *not* going to be pleasant."

". . . Yes, boss."

CHAPTER 10

After checking on Marus myself—not that it would help; I wasn't a doctor, especially not one trained in Tyll physiology, but he was my friend, on my ship, and I wasn't going to just let him suffer without at least making *sure* there wasn't anything else we could do—I stomped off to the cockpit. Yes, stomped. Was it a little childish? Sure, probably. Mainly I was trying to make sure the others knew that I didn't particularly want company at the moment, and also it felt good.

Of course, Esa followed me in, ignoring all my not-so-subtle social cues with the blithe ignorance of a teenager. "Is your friend going to be all right?" she asked me.

I sighed, staring out the cockpit window. "As long as we get him the drugs he needs, he should be, yeah," I told her.

"Oh. That's good."

"Yeah."

"But when he wakes up—he's going to find out that his ship is gone."

"That won't be a pleasant experience for him, no. Khonnerhonn and Marus have been together nearly as long as Scheherazade and myself."

"Poor fella."

"Yeah."

"So"—she leaned back in what she was clearly coming to think of as "her" chair—"who's this other guy?"

"Esa—"

"I mean, theoretically you're doing all of this *for* me, right? So shouldn't I know who we're dealing with, what kind of trouble you're getting us into?"

"Esa, don't—"

"Because it *sounds* like you're taking me into a dangerous pirate den, and I'd think that if *that* were the case, you could at least tell me—"

"Esa. Shut. It."

"She's right," the Preacher said, entering as well. "We deserve to know."

I picked up my coffee mug from this morning; it was empty. I set it back down. I don't know why I'd done that—even if it had still had coffee in it, it would have been ice cold. I sighed again. "Fine. Javier Ortega *used* to be another operative of the Justified."

"Like you," Esa nodded.

"Not like me." I shook my head. "There were—are—a great many different operatives, and they all have different jobs, different duties to perform. I find kids."

"And then some," the Preacher added.

I ignored that. "Marus, back there—he tracks down information. Javi was something closer to . . . a cartographer, I guess you could say."

"A what now?"

"It means he made maps," the Preacher told her.

"Even before the pulse, nobody had very reliable maps of the galaxy," I told Esa, spinning my chair around so that I could face her. "Each sect had detailed information about its *own* territory, but they didn't share very well; nobody wanted to draw a roadmap directly to their vital operations and risk that it might wind up in their enemies' hands."

"And after . . ." The Preacher just shook her head.

I nodded. "And *after* the pulse, what few maps anybody had were worthless anyway; what might once have been a bustling colony might have been completely abandoned, and a wasteland of industrial scrap might have had a settlement built on top of it, if it had been less affected by the pulse than somewhere else."

"So this Javi guy—"

"Javier Ortega."

"*You* were the one that called him 'Javi,' not me." Esa shrugged. "Anyway, this guy ran around the galaxy, figuring out where things were and what had changed after the pulse, and then he came back to your . . . sanctuary place—"

"I believe she refers to it as 'Sanctum,'" the Preacher reminded her.

"Right, her little clubhouse place, where I'm supposed to go to save the world and stuff."

"The galaxy. Not just the world." The Preacher again.

"Yeah, from the return of the pulse, right, can't forget that insanity. Anyway, this Javier guy told all your Justified friends what the rest of the galaxy was like, outside of the bubble of this Sanctum."

"That's . . . not too far off," I admitted. "If you think of me as a kind of bodyguard, and Marus as a kind of spy, Javier would have been a sort of . . . explorer. Filling in the blank places on the maps."

"Okay," Esa nodded. "So I get that much. But what happened next? Because clearly *something* went down to get your panties in a twist."

"According to my physiological readings during her exchange with Scheherazade," the Preacher replied, "her relationship with this Javier Ortega might have had an entirely *different* impact on her undergarments. She reacted—"

"Preacher. Stop. Fucking. Measuring. My vitals."

"I'm a Barious—that's just how we see."

"See *less*. It's invasive."

"You've had a sexual relationship with this person."

"That is *absolutely* none of your business."

"Does kind of explain why you got all washed out and scary there for a second when his name came up, though," Esa put in. "I *really* thought you were going to start breaking things."

I took a deep breath. Just because she was *right* didn't mean I wanted to comment on it. I ignored her instead. "Javier was out on a reconnaissance mission when he stumbled across what's known as a 'refugee fleet,'" I said, returning to the thread of the story in an attempt to divert my two passengers from their *other* line of inquiry.

"What's that?" Esa asked.

"When the pulse happened, it affected planets, moons, major stations— most everything with a gravity well," the Preacher told her. "What it *didn't* have any impact on was ships already in transit between star systems. *Most* of those either landed on a pulsed world without knowing what had happened, and had their ships cooked by radiation, or simply settled on a planet where the pulse hadn't had much effect."

"But not all of them."

"But not all of them." The Preacher nodded. "Those that didn't land, and *weren't* able to find welcome on the less-affected worlds, simply kept flying, gathering more and more ships to their banner, searching for that rarest of birds: an unsettled, unclaimed, terraformed world unaffected by the pulse."

"So your man Javi found one of these refugee fleet things—"

"He's not *my* man—" I protested.

"You know what I mean." She waved me away. "He ran across these refugees, then what?"

"He ran across them when they were about to be torn apart by a fleet of Filt ships. The Filt are—doesn't matter. When I say 'Filt,' just hear 'Pax'; they operate in mostly the same fashion. Tin-pot would-be conquerors of a newly weakened galaxy."

"And I'm guessing he didn't just make a notation on his maps—'found a refugee fleet here; probably won't *still* be here the next time I swing by'— and head on his way."

I shook my head. "He did not. I don't *know* why he didn't—"

"Basic sentient decency?" The Preacher raised an eyebrow.

I glared at her. "Don't start. He led the refugees away from the Filt and straight *toward* Sanctum, toward Justified space."

The Preacher nodded. "Given what you said to me earlier, outsiders being shown the path to your fabled sanctuary is not something that's *supposed* to happen."

"It is not. I'd be in a great deal of trouble just for bringing *you* in. Javi led *thousands* of refugees right to the Justified doorstep. Thousands. People we didn't know, people we couldn't *trust*. His plan worked, of course—the Filt thought they were starting a fight with a lightly armed refugee flotilla, and instead ran into every armed ship Sanctum had, in an ambush. We wiped them out without losing a single pilot."

"So what happened to the refugees?" Esa asked.

"We took them in. We didn't have any other choice—it was that or kill them, and we weren't ready to commit the mass murder of relative innocents. We *also* couldn't just send them on their way, not with them knowing the route to Sanctum."

"And Javier?"

"His plan had *worked*," I said again. "The refugees had been saved from the Filt, *and* given a home; it was a better outcome than they could ever dream of. If the council had let that stand, every single Justified operative would be constantly leading people back to Sanctum, people they thought were 'worthy,' worth saving. Sanctum has impressive resources, but they're not limitless. We *cannot* save everyone. That's drilled into all of us very early on, a lesson Javier chose to ignore."

"So they drummed him out, as an object lesson to anyone else who might get the same damn fool idea in their heads." The Preacher nodded. "Honestly, I'm surprised they let him live."

"I'm not sure if they would have," I shrugged. "But Javi had known what he was doing all along; he knew there would be consequences. Before the fight was done—pretty much as soon as he saw that we were engaging the Filt, that they had no chance of winning—he ran. With his ship, and his gear—more than he would have gotten away with, even *if* the council had just voted for exile."

"He didn't say goodbye to you?" Esa frowned. "That was cruel."

"He's been *trying*." Scheherazade sighed. "She won't answer his letters. Won't even *read* them."

"Because if I ever *see* him again, I'll have to *kill* him." I glared at all of them. "That was his sentence: post-factum exile, and death, if he ever crossed paths with a Justified operative again."

"But you wouldn't *have* to," Esa said. "You could just—"

I shook my head. "What I'm doing is *important*," I told her. "I'd think *you* would understand that. Collecting children like you, giving them better lives—preparing to answer the return of the pulse. It *means* something, and I'm *good* at it. If I risked it all just to keep in contact with Javier, I probably wouldn't have been able to rescue *you*. Do you get that?"

She nodded, looking slightly abashed.

"Good. Now, if I've answered enough of your personal questions for a little bit, would you two *mind* giving me a little space? I have to think through how I'm going to play this."

They stood and made their way through the door. Esa did so without comment; the Preacher, however, paused in the threshold. "Tell me one more thing," she said.

"What?" I closed my eyes.

"Did you not want to tell that story because you think it reflects poorly on you—that you had a relationship with a man who endangered your cause? Or did you not want to tell it simply because it makes you seem more . . . human?"

I didn't answer her. Apparently she took that as response enough, and left me with my thoughts.

CHAPTER 11

I slept, fitfully, in the pilot's chair. You learn how to do that, to adjust your body's rhythms, to catch sleep when you could. I'd picked up the skill all the way back in the wars, controlled my breathing, calmed my thoughts, and willed myself to rest *now*, because I figured I had another long stretch ahead of me, and I didn't know when my next chance to grab some shut-eye was going to be.

Plus, that way, I didn't have to think about seeing Javier again.

When I woke up, of course, Esa was staring at me.

"What?" I asked, rubbing my eyes.

She handed me a cup of coffee. That was sweet of her; that, or Scheherazade was coaching her. "We're going into a pirate den," she said.

"*I'm* going into a pirate den," I corrected her. "You're staying on the ship."

"Okay; fine. But still. There are pirates? How are there pirates? *Why* are there pirates?"

I shrugged, still groggy. The coffee was a nice gesture, but couldn't she have waited until the caffeine had actually hit my system before starting in with the questions? "Galactic commerce took a definite hit when the pulse shook everything back to various earlier stages of technological evolution— that will happen when ninety-five percent of your trading partners drop out of the market—but it didn't go away *entirely*. Even if five percent of the worlds out there were only lightly affected by the pulse—hell, even if it was only *two* percent, no one's really sure, it's not like anyone's done a census—that still leaves millions of developed worlds open for business."

"Okay, so you've explained how there's still, you know, trade and stuff. That doesn't explain *pirates*."

"Sure it does. Where there's 'trade and stuff,' there's people willing to *steal* from those who engage in trade. And stuff. Thus, pirates. And slavers—you'd be surprised how many of those worlds decided that, now that the inhabitants of other planets didn't have access to the same tech they did, the people living there were suddenly subhuman, had no rights at all." Esa made a face; I guess that kind of logic wasn't too far from the bandits who had stalked her settlement—or the locals' view of the bandits, for that matter. "So slave-taking bastards deck out their ships in anti-rad shielding, find a world without the tech to put up much resistance, swoop in, scoop up as many people as they can before the shielding starts to break down, then jet off and sell their take—namely, people—to the highest bidder."

"That's awful."

"Yeah, it is. There was a moment when we thought the galaxy might be a better place after the pulse. It had cut a great deal of civilization off from some very helpful tech, yeah, but it also went out of its way to target the really scary stuff, too—the planet-killing weapons and the nanotech viral research centers, things like that."

"I don't know what most of those words mean."

"Be thankful for that."

"I still think that argument is horseshit, though."

"Do you?"

"Just because people aren't dying all at *once* quite so much doesn't mean they're dying any *better*. Sure, I was never worried about someone coming along and blowing my whole *planet* up, but I also didn't know anybody who lived to a hundred and *seventy-three*, or however old you are."

"That's not—"

"I grew up in a fairly peaceful little city, you know; you saw it. You know *how* it was kept so peaceful?"

I shook my head, though I could guess. "How?"

"Because the local government *exiled* anybody who didn't agree with them. Fed them right to the bandits that prowled the countryside. I *saw* it; I lost friends to it. Plenty of the kids living in the orphanage were only *there* because their parents had done something to piss off the ruling council. Does that sound 'better' to you?"

I stared at her for a moment. She was so young; it was easy to forget that, on worlds like hers, 'young' didn't mean the same thing I sometimes thought it did. And that coming from me, who had never been young.

Again, I shook my head. "No. It sounds pretty much the same, just on a smaller scale. It's not like democracy and galactic suffrage were all that popular during the sect wars, either."

"So that makes it better."

"I said we *thought* the pulse might have helped; I didn't say I *still* thought that way."

"Fine. Whatever." She sat back in her chair. "So the pirates we're going to visit are pretty much the same thing as the bandits that prowled around outside my city, just with spaceships rather than rifles. Is that what I'm hearing?"

"Pretty much, yeah. And we're not going to *visit* the bandits; we're going to talk to Javier."

"Who, because *your people* kicked him out of Sanctuary—"

"Sanctum."

"Because your people kicked him out of your clubhouse might well be a bandit now himself."

"I doubt that."

"But you don't *know*."

I sighed. "You're young enough that you still think adults know *everything*, and we're just keeping it from you out of spite. Tell me: is it really a victory, getting someone older than you to admit they don't know something?"

She paused, studying me. "So you *don't* know what he's doing, then."

"Ask Schaz; she's the one who's been reading his letters. Apparently."

"I do *not* think he's a pirate," Schaz chimed in helpfully. "Would you like me to tell you what he *has* been doing?"

Esa said "yes!" at the same time I said "no." We stared at each other for a moment; I sipped my coffee even as I kept up the glare. "Fine," she sighed, finally. "Tell me this, then: where *are* we going?"

"A pirate den, like you said."

"Well, *yeah*, but what *is* it? Is it, like, carved into a moon or something? A sort of," she waved her hand in a way that told me exactly nothing at all, "floating, spaceship-docky-thing?"

"A space station?"

"Yeah, one of those."

I shook my head, smiling slightly into my coffee cup to hide my reaction from Esa. Among the other lessons I'd learned escorting teenagers over the years, it's that they *hate* it when you find them amusing. I couldn't help it, though; "spaceship-docky-thing" was pretty goddamned funny to me. "It's not a space station, not really. Remember how I said, when I was telling you about Javier, that the ships that were in transit when the pulse hit weren't really affected by it?"

"Sure," she nodded.

"Well, Beyond Ending is a couple of those, bolted together. Remember the dreadnaught that attacked your hometown?"

She shuddered. "Not likely to forget something like *that* any time soon, no," she said.

"Well, that's what they were: two dreadnaughts. That's actually where the name comes from—one of them was called 'The Beyond,' and the other was called 'The Ending.' Both ships were pretty badly damaged in a battle that was raging when the pulse hit; they were actually on opposite sides of the conflict. After the chaos and the flight, they found themselves floating in a pretty much empty system, and in the days right after the pulse . . . it's hard to explain exactly what that time was like. We were used to getting a great deal of information, all the time. Suddenly that flow of information was completely cut off. Both ships were limping, and both of their captains realized that all the stupid reasons they'd been at war didn't really matter now; *survival* was what mattered.

"As it turned out, the damage they'd both taken was weirdly complementary; the Beyond had systems still running that had been completely destroyed on the Ending, well past the point of repair, and vice versa. Both ships probably still could have been fixed if they'd just limped back to a shipyard, but by that point, neither captain knew if there *were* any more shipyards still working. Remember, this was just after the pulse—they didn't know if it was everywhere, they didn't know if they were the only working spacecraft left. So they tossed aside decades, maybe centuries of sectarian hate, and they bound their ships together with what little tools they had. The survival of their crews trumped everything else."

"That's nice. What happened next?"

I shrugged. "A passing pirate syndicate noticed them, saw that their weapons systems were all shot to hell, so they forced their way on board and killed everyone inside."

"Good god!"

"Hey, I didn't say the story had a happy ending. But at that point, the ships were bound together; no way to undo it. They couldn't even get to hyperspace, not with their engines tied up like that. So the pirates dropped them into a long orbit around the local star, and started using them as a staging ground for their raids. They started up trade with some other pirate groups, and little by little, a pirate city was born."

"And that's where we're going? Piratopia?"

"That's where we're going, yeah. It wouldn't be my first choice."

"But I get to stay on the ship."

"You get to stay on the ship."

"I think that's a good plan."

CHAPTER 12

We came out of hyperspace on the far side of the system from Beyond Ending, which was a good thing, as far as I was concerned. Give them time to scan us, write us off as not a threat—which they would. I had some of Scheherazade's disinformation systems cranked to high heaven—they'd read us as a lightly armed courier vessel, nothing more.

Beyond Ending was locked into orbit around the star itself; the only other neighbor it had was a massive chlorine-colored gas giant that had swallowed up all its other planetary brothers and sisters eons ago—collided with them and kept right on spinning even as they splintered and dissolved into its depths. It was the sort of thing that reminded you why most cultures named stars and planets for creatures from their legends. Plus, there might have been some sort of metaphor there for Beyond Ending's rampant growth once it had become a pirate mecca.

"Give me the stick, Schaz," I commanded my AI. "I do 'slightly erratic' better than you."

As I spoke the dreadnaughts came into view, looking like nothing so much as two city skylines glued together at the bottom, towers both rising and falling from the twinned superstructures. There were places on board where the two interlocked gravity generators got confused, and confusing.

"Oh?" Schaz asked. "Is that what we're going for?"

"Think you can handle it?"

"I can certainly handle it; whether *they* are amused or not is another story."

Our comms crackled to life. "You seem to be lost, friend," a slightly bored voice came out the other end, putting just a touch of purring menace into the words. "That's a nice ship. We're going to take it from you now."

One of my screens lit up: contacts on the radar. Two craft, heading on an intercept course toward us. Both bulky, slow moving, likely passenger craft retrofitted with guns rather than purpose-designed fighters; if they actually started a fight, they'd be badly surprised—Schaz and I could whip them without breaking a sweat. Of course, *that* would alert everyone else on Beyond Ending that we weren't what we seemed, and we could *not* win a fight with every single pirate on board the twinned dreadnaughts. So: time for a different plan.

"Whoa, man," Schaz "breathed" heavily into the comm as she spoke— she didn't actually breathe, of course, but she could shift her vocal patterns to make it *sound* like she was almost swallowing a microphone as she talked. "Has anyone ever told you your ships are, like, glued together? That's fucked *up*."

She couldn't quite change the accent JackDoes had stuck her with, but it was amazing what she could do with just a little modulation; instead of sounding like a tony Tyll aristocrat on his way to the opera, she now sounded like a slumming Tyll elite who had fallen on hard times after the pulse, doing a menial job he considered beneath him and killing the time by spending most of it stoned out of his gourd. *How* she managed to convey all that information in just two sentences, I had no idea, but it was as clear as day.

"Friend"—the voice on the other end of the line laughed—"you seem a little confused. Let me break it out for you: we're going to *kill* you, then steal your ship. Just so you understand."

"Don't do *that*, man." Schaz managed to sound vaguely amused, rather than at all afraid, which was likely more the reaction that the pirate on intercept had been looking for. "I've got a message: I'm delivering a message."

Somewhere on the other line, we heard someone else in the background say, "He's a courier; take another look." The first voice came on again. "You a courier, buddy? That what you're telling me?"

"Yeah, man. Like, does that not show up when you scan me? 'Cuz it does for everybody else. Maybe your shit's wired wrong—that's what happens when you start gluing things together aren't meant to be glued. Just sayin'. No offense or anything, it's a real nice . . . a real nice *thing*, that you've . . . it's real nice, man. Real nice."

"We're not reading courier markings at all on you, pal," the pirate comms officer said. "Why don't you tell me who your package is for, and we'll take it off your hands, make sure it gets to him."

"Can't *do* that, man. I mean the first part, sure—Javier somebody, let me . . .

it's around here somewhere . . . Javier *Ortega*, brother, that's who I'm look-ing for; he's got a package from a . . . from a . . . from a *one* Colleen Nazafi. Najafi." That wasn't my name—I wasn't that stupid—but it was one Javier would recognize, an alias Scheherazade and I had used on operations we'd included him in back in the day.

Of course, if *Javier* was using a nom de guerre as well then this plan was fucked, but I'd bent my rules enough to ask Schaz about the digital addresses on his letters, and he'd been using his real name on those, at least.

Schaz continued her performance. "But as far as handing it off, no can do. *We* signed a contract, and the lady sending the *package* signed a contract, and until Mr. *Ortega* signs the contract, ain't nobody putting their hands on this package but us. You try, and like, it's wired to blow." Schaz delivered the line with the same drugged-out nonchalance she had every other one; I think that's what really sold it. Dangerous people—like, say, workaday pirates— are definitely dangerous, but chemically imbalanced people with access to *bombs* are also dangerous, and much more unpredictable.

More murmured communication on the other line, probably the pirates asking each other who the hell Javier Ortega was. If Javi was using a pseu-donym, this would be where the plan would fall apart—I was still bobbing and weaving along our course, but I was ready to break off and run if I had to.

The guy on the other side of the comm shouted something to someone else in the room with him, covering the mic with his fist; then he got back on the line. "All right, ease off, buddy—nobody's going to try and take your precious package. Ortega'll meet you at the airlock—"

"Like, not *me*, man." Schaz even put in a little snicker. "I just *fly* the boat. My captain's the one who'll hand off the goods."

An audible sigh of relief as the pirate realized the imaginary high-as-fuck Tyll wasn't alone with the bomb. "Whatever, guy," the pirate agreed. "The two ships coming out to meet you will escort you in. Just . . . do what they do." Before he signed off, we could hear him shouting again, this time not remembering to cover up the mic: "Will somebody tell *fucking* Ortega that if he's going to order goddamned *takeout*, to make sure it's not wired up with a goddamned *high explo*—" And then the comm signal was cut off.

"Well done as always, Scheherazade," I congratulated my AI.

"I try my best," she preened.

CHAPTER 13

We followed the route in laid out for us by the scout craft. Honestly, it was a good thing, too—the last century had seen so many changes to the configuration of the two dreadnaughts, I doubted I could have found a viable docking bay with full scans of the ships and a few hours to study them.

I let Schaz take the stick; now that we were slaved in on the other ships' course, the fictional Tyll would have turned over control to his AI, anyway. I started for the living quarters—needed to get changed into something a courier captain would wear.

"That was risky." The Preacher was frowning at me as I entered. She'd heard the exchange on Scheherazade's ship-wide comms; my AI could never let one of her performances lack the widest possible audience.

"It worked." I shrugged out of my ship-wear and began pulling on the various articles of clothing that made up my "slightly sketchy" galactic outfit—a lot of belts and buckles and clasps stitching together various out-of-date military-grade surplus.

"It was still—"

"Captain," Scheherazade interrupted, "you need to see this."

I frowned, and made my way back to the cockpit. Our scanners had gone dead—we were closing on the twinned dreadnaughts, which meant we were inside their envelope, the signature of the two massive ships blotting out any other reading. *That* was expected. What had drawn Schaz's attention was purely visual, visible out the cockpit windows: they were running out the guns, the side of the craft—the crafts—suddenly bristling with weaponry that hadn't been there before.

"That's not for us." I frowned. "They wouldn't need that much firepower to take us down. Something else is happening."

"I was reading activity on the edge of the system, just before we hit their dead zone," Schaz told me. "No idea what it was, but they're setting out the party favors. We've never had the *best* timing, but did we really get here just in time to get stuck in the middle of a pirate war?"

God, I hoped not. I'd been in one of those, once, and only survived it because there were some maneuvers even *pirates* weren't crazy enough to risk. Thankfully, I'd been in a stolen ship at the time, one I was willing to let shear itself apart, or Schaz would have been reminding me of that particular nightmare at this very moment. "Nothing we can do about it now," I told her. "Still, once I'm on board Beyond Ending, lock yourself down, and be ready to get out of here at a moment's notice."

"Once we're docked, they'll try to slave my propulsion systems, keep us from taking off without their say so."

"Then don't *let* them; we've got programs for that."

"They might notice."

"We're a courier craft; not letting anybody tell us where to go is part of the job." I turned to the Preacher. "Give me a list of the drugs we need for Marus."

She nodded, and her eyes stuttered with a wireless signal; the list appeared in my HUD. "Thank you," I said, heading for the hold. "You two stay on board, and don't . . . just . . . don't *anything*."

"We'll try to control ourselves," Esa drawled. I ignored her; I had other things on my mind.

It had been nearly three years since I'd seen Javi. Had I thought about what a reunion might be like? Sure, during boring moments on stakeouts, or on long interstellar cruises. In certain . . . lonelier moments in my bunk, maybe those daydreams had taken on a certain erotic sheen—I'd admit to that. But at no point had I pictured *me* needing *his* help—the stories I invented for myself usually went the other way around. Which at the time had definitely seemed more likely.

Anyway, none of that mattered. I was here for Marus. Javier would understand that; Marus had been his friend too.

Of course, neither of us had lifted a finger when he'd been exiled.

Not that he would know that—he'd been long gone by then. Still, it made me uncomfortable; always had, really. I knew *why* he'd done what he did. That didn't mean I agreed with him, or thought it was the right choice. But we had been close, and when I'd had the chance to fight for him, I'd stayed silent. It wouldn't have mattered—his "trial" in absentia had been an afterthought, his exile a foregone conclusion; all I could have done by speaking up in his defense was damage my own standing with the council.

That didn't mean I felt good about it.

I stepped through the airlock just as Scheherazade gave a slight thump; we were docked on board Beyond Ending. As the ramp started to lower, I banished all the other thoughts from my mind—put myself in the headspace of the courier captain instead. Being surrounded by my armory helped.

I was here to make a delivery, and then to escort Ortega to wherever he had a return package for me; it was just a job, that's all. We'd be watched the whole time I was on board, pirates not in general being a particularly trustworthy lot. Honestly, that made me feel better—it meant certain uncomfortable conversations were much less likely, neither one of us capable of speaking freely.

Javier was waiting for me as the ramp lowered. He still looked good; I'd give him that. Same strong jaw, same hawkish nose, same slightly-too-wide eyes. I'd thought maybe, cut off from the medical expertise of the Justified, he'd have aged poorly, but if anything, he looked healthier—had put on some muscle where he'd been a little thin before. Then again, he'd always been younger than me, by a solid three decades, born after the pulse.

He was still tall, taller than me, which was fairly rare. Not that I'd expected that to change, but sometimes you wondered if your memories were exaggerating certain characteristics of people you hadn't seen in a while. Nope: still tall. He'd grown his hair out, too: had it tied low in a ponytail that vanished down his back. It looked amazingly stupid.

I held on to that thought as I walked down the ramp, slipping a slightly bored expression onto my face. Not that he still looked good, even better than I remembered; not how much I suddenly realized I missed him. That his hair was stupid.

"You Javier Ortega?" I drawled, scanning the rest of the docking bay. I'd expected at least a few other pirates, keeping tabs on the outsider who'd landed on their ship, but there was nothing—just Javi, and a few empty scout craft. Not even our escorts had docked.

I was expecting him to answer in kind, to probe at my cover story so that he could match it if it came up—we maybe hadn't parted on the best of terms, but I doubted he was pissed enough to sell me out to pirates, even if I had been ignoring his letters—but instead he moved quickly up the ramp and took me by the elbow, pulling me back inside Scheherazade's airlock.

"As always, your timing is amazingly terrible." He shook his head, keeping his voice pitched low. "We need to get the fuck *off* of Beyond Ending, and we need to do it *right goddamned now.*"

CHAPTER 14

It took me half a second to work through what he was saying. "Can't *do* that," I hissed back. "I'm here for your *help*, you moron; we can't leave without—"

"If we don't leave"—he glared at me, leaning close so that just in case anyone else *was* listening they wouldn't be able to make his words out—"we're going to be turned into just another bit of organic debris, along with everyone else on board. These pirates are about to start a fight they can't *win*. Get Schaz up and running—whatever you need help with, you'll have to get it elsewhere."

I stared up at him for just a moment—maybe a beat too long, but even for me, this was all happening *very* fast, and for once I was the one struggling to keep up. Javier was a lot of things, but making up a lie like that, just to get on board my ship—that wasn't something he was capable of.

Unless his years of exile had changed him.

Still, I wouldn't have come here if a part of me hadn't still trusted him. I nodded, then slapped open the airlock and we slipped inside, Javier already making his way toward the cockpit—he knew Scheherazade's layout almost as well as I did.

Better days.

"Javi!" Schaz squealed—or at least, as close to a squeal as the approximation of a Tyll aristocrat that was her voice could reach. "How have you—"

"Can it," I growled at her, pushing past Javier as I did. "We've apparently landed in even deeper shit than the deep *well* of shit we just left behind. Get us *out* of here, Schaz. How long 'til the hyperdrive is—"

"Eight minutes," she said, suddenly all professionalism again now that she realized we were about to be shot at. Javi followed me into the cockpit; I ducked into the pilot's seat, and he stopped, looking down at Esa, who was in her usual chair at the gunnery console.

"Hi, nice to meet you," he said. "Move."

"Do as he says, Esa," I told her, already prepping our systems for takeoff.

"What's happening?" she asked, moving over to the navigation seat instead. Javier slipped behind the gunnery console, already prepping Schaz's weapons.

"I don't know—ask Javi," I replied.

"I was halfway through the concourse—coming to meet you—when everybody started losing their goddamned minds," he said. "*Apparently* an entire Pax fleet just appeared on the far side of the system, headed this way and *not* in a chatty mood. Dozens of frigates, *hundreds* of fighters and scout craft. And five dreadnaughts."

I swallowed. Whatever this was, I *doubted* it was related to us—that was a far larger force than what we'd seen over Esa's homeworld. But it was also a far larger force than what the Pax would have needed to wipe Beyond Ending out of the stars; slaving the two supercraft together had extremely limited their mobility, and no matter how many guns the pirates had stacked onto them since then, she still couldn't adjust her firing angles enough to be a match for even *one* dreadnaught, let alone five of them.

"That sounds like overkill," I said, lifting us off from the dock. The pirates didn't try to stop us; they had other things on their minds at the moment.

"Yeah, it does." I could hear the glare in Javier's voice. "So why do I *not* think it's coincidence they dropped out of hyperspace *just* after your arrival?"

"They don't need five dreadnaughts to wipe out Beyond Ending; they *definitely* don't need five dreadnaughts to take down Scheherazade," I snapped back.

"Ordinarily I'd take offense at that, but—yeah, you're definitely right," Schaz agreed. "I'd be fucked."

"Can you scan anything out there?" I asked Schaz.

"Not until we're outside of their envelope," she replied.

"I take it you want me back in the tailgun?" the Preacher asked, still standing in the doorway, taking all of this in as it happened.

"Please," I nodded. "This . . . may get rough."

"That's an understatement," Schaz muttered.

"Maybe not—the pirates were scattering to their own ships," Javier pointed out, "and while they can't match the Pax fleet dreadnaught for dreadnaught, they've got them significantly outnumbered when it comes to smaller craft. Damned near every pirate on board Beyond Ending either has a ship in their own right, or is at least part of a ship's crew. That's several *hundred* pirate craft, all trying to get out of system at once. If the Pax are trying to find a single needle—say, *us*—"

"There is no 'us,'" I reminded him.

"Fine, Schaz, then—does that really matter right now?"

"We still don't know they're after us at all," Esa reminded him, her tone nervous. She turned to me. "Are they after us?" she asked.

"Better to assume they are and get the fuck *out* of here than stick around to be proven wrong," I told her. "Even if they don't want us *specifically,* they're Pax—they'll still make us dead just for not flying Pax colors. We're not Pax, therefore we're a challenge."

We broke out of the scan-deadening envelope surrounding Beyond Ending; my screens flooded with life and color. Javier wasn't wrong—it was a goddamned *shitstorm* out there, a carnival of death and chaos as the pirates and the fascists vied for control of the local escape vectors.

Beyond Ending was already trading fire with the Pax dreadnaughts. At the extreme ranges they were at, neither of the massive, city-sized supercraft was doing much damage—the question wasn't the stopping power of their weapons, but more the accuracy with which they could fire over such long distances, not to mention that this early in the conflict both ships had their shields fully charged—but as they closed, the attrition would start to tell. More and more shots would break through the shielding, and more and more systems on board would start to crash.

Meanwhile, smaller Pax craft were fanning out, trying to cut down as many of the pirate vessels as possible. Beyond Ending's orbit had brought it close enough to the gravity well of the supergiant planet in the system that the craft trying to flee had to *first* get clear of that before they had a shot at the vectors out, which meant the Pax had a few minutes to take potshots at them before they could activate their hyperdrives. In return, some of the pirates were spending those few minutes engaging the Pax head on—the dreadnaughts were mostly ignoring the smaller craft, which meant that the pirates had the Pax outnumbered by a clear margin. Ships were already going down in flames, and there were just as many Pax dropping off of my radar as there were pirates, maybe more.

Unfortunately, we were in the same boat. We had to get out of the gravity well too, and worse than that, *our* hyperdrive hadn't been sitting in a dock on Beyond Ending for days, being kept artificially cool. It would only take us a couple of minutes to get clear of the gravity, but after that, we'd still have to stay alive for another smallish forever before we could make the jump to hyperspace.

So I did the only thing I could, the last thing anyone would expect: I dove right into the bedlam before me, heading right for the heart of the fighting. If the Pax really were looking for us, they'd have to cut through a whole hell of a lot of chaos to do so.

CHAPTER 15

My world was nothing but fire and motion. I'd *done* this for over a century, and I was fucking *good* at it; it was all reflex now, all reaction and momentum, acting before I even knew I was acting, finding the pinpoint course that would get us clear of whatever chaos was closest, and opening up targets for the ship's guns. It was like a dance, reading your partner's steps and intentions and momentums, except in this case, I had a thousand partners, and they all wanted to kill me.

Thankfully, they *also* wanted to kill each other. "Who should I prioritize targeting?" the Preacher asked me. "Pirates or Pax?"

"Shoot whoever's shooting at us; that's your priority target," I replied, never taking my eyes off the twisting shocks of light and flame and metal filling the cockpit in front of us.

"They're *all* shooting at us!"

"Then shoot back," Javier said calmly, following words with action. He'd taken control of the omnidirectional laser batteries, slicing blue fire through the chaos of the void. That still left me with the forward guns, and I fired whenever someone drifted into my targeting solution, but I wasn't *seeking* targets—I was keeping us clear of the targeting solutions of all the other ships, letting Javi and the Preacher worry about cutting down anyone who got too close.

"Javi?" Scheherazade asked, even as she worked through a thousand different processes, making minute adjustments to power flow and engine settings and energy output. "Where's Bolivar?"

"He's around. I told him to launch as soon as I knew I'd be getting out with—"

"Here I am!" The incongruously cheery voice belonged to Javier's ship; unlike Scheherazade's fairly mellow character, Bolivar had always been a tremendously upbeat, high-energy personality. Maybe it said something about Javi and me, the way our ships had both settled into personalities over the years that complemented—or antagonized—their owners; I wasn't sure. Now was not the time to worry about it.

"Stick high to our six, Var, but stay out of the targeting solution for the rear turret," I told him. Bolivar was a smaller ship than Scheherazade, a dagger to her sword, not really built for combat, though he could certainly hold his own—but without a pilot on board, his effectiveness was cut in half, at least.

"I got it," he replied. "So good to see you again, by the way. Or hear from you, I guess, since—"

"Var? Not now."

"Got it. Also, you've got a drone swarm heading in your direction."

I swore and swerved, ducking and weaving a little too close to one of the larger pirate ships—maybe the drones would target *it* before they came after us. Drones were little more than a nuisance on their own in combat—really just overgrown void-capable versions of the stun variants that had attacked Esa's home settlement. They were more dangerous than lone missiles, but no match for a ship with a pilot.

Even as a nuisance, though, they were dangerous enough: they'd be rigged to maximize their effectiveness; with lasers modulated to swat at shields rather than penetrate hulls. The idea was that they would wear down any ships they came in contact with so that by the time the vessel they'd been biting at engaged an *actual* enemy, they'd be at significantly less than full strength.

The pirate craft—almost a frigate, but not quite large enough—ignored us in order to focus its fire on the drone swarm, trying to cut them down before the wave of Pax ships that would inevitably follow. We returned the favor, blowing right past it and into the heart of *another* scrum, this time at least a dozen different vessels all in close combat, dodging and weaving.

Javi took slices at *all* of them as we passed, not doing enough damage to bring any one ship down, but making sure they were all pushed back into defensive maneuvers, too busy worrying about their own survival to take after us. "How long 'til the hyperdrive's up and running, Schaz?" I asked.

"Another three minutes," she replied. "Also, the port shield is taking a battering—one of the Pax dreadnaughts is taking an interest in us."

I swore again, read my screens, and dove, then pulled up in a tight spin. The dreadnaught wasn't doing much more than occasionally sniping at us with a spare turret or two—most of its firepower was concentrated on Beyond Ending, and anyway, the guns on a dreadnaught were designed to take on *other* dreadnaughts or for sustained planetary bombardment, not to pick little nuisance craft out of the sky—but the *weakest* gun on a ship that size was still bigger than anything we had on board.

I pulled us out of the upward spin, curving back around toward Beyond Ending. Sheets of metal were flaking off of the twinned ships as the combined might of the Pax dreadnaughts pounded against its hull; the last gasp of its shielding was a broken shimmering crackle of electricity dissipating into the void. It wouldn't last much longer.

Still, the pirates were giving back as well as they could, filling the cosmos with laser fire, the lances of light tinged crimson so that the gunners could actually *see* what they were shooting. At least one of the Pax dreadnaughts was listing badly, out of the fight, explosions pockmarking its hull.

The outcome was only a matter of time—the pirate base simply couldn't hold up to the pounding it was taking long enough to remove all four of the remaining Pax supercraft from the fight—but I'd give them that; there were at least a few pirates on board willing to go down fighting rather than roll over for the Pax. I guess those were the ones that knew what Pax *did* to their captives.

I dove closer to the buckling curves of Beyond Ending, sending Schaz through flames erupting from its punctured hull, trying to lose the attention we'd picked up among the debris left behind in the wake of the slow-motion collapse of the twinned dreadnaughts. That also gave the Preacher a clearer shot at the smaller ships that had been pursuing us, and they either broke off or she *picked* them off as we came nearer and nearer to Beyond Ending's disintegrating hull.

"Bolivar, stick with us on the other side of the structure," I said over the comms, cutting my thrust to minimum, just above drifting, matching the pull of orbital gravity with the dreadnaughts and using their twinned bulk as a shield. The radar screens in front of me were slowly depopulating—the pirates were either being picked off by the Pax, or making it out of the gravity well and jumping to hyperspace. Which meant, shortly, we'd be alone with the Pax and the dying dreadnaughts. Not good.

"How long 'til the hyperdrive's ready?" I asked Schaz again.

"You want me to just send the countdown to your screens?" she replied, somewhat waspishly.

"No, I want you to just *tell* me," I replied.

"Two minutes." It had only been a minute since I asked. It felt like forever.

"Var—stay in this orbital path, and put full thrust in. We'll slingshot around the goddamned planet. That ought to buy us enough time for Schaz's hyperdrive to cool down."

"Sounds like a plan!" Bolivar agreed, still incongruously cheery.

"Schaz, send Var the coordinates for a nearby system—"

"Where—"

"I don't *care* where, just so long as it's not *here!*"

Something erupted from the surface of the dreadnaught below; we broke away and I kicked the throttle to full, roaring clear from the rest of the fighting, at least temporarily. Pax craft were immediately in pursuit—no question, they'd been *looking* for us—but we had the advantage; they first had to find us among all of the debris flaking off of Beyond Ending, then adjust course, *then* try and match speed, and we were accelerating all the while.

That didn't mean we were out of *firing* range, though, and I kept ducking and twisting, still trying to keep us in the grip of the orbital gravity. "I've got a *lot* of targets back here!" the Preacher warned, and over the comms I could hear the deafening loud thump of the rear turret as she fired again and again.

"Then you shouldn't have any problems picking some off," I replied, still focusing on the stick.

"That would be *easier* if you would *hold fucking still!*"

"I do that and we're all going to be a lot warmer for a little bit, and then real fucking cold, Preacher. Less than a minute; just—"

"*Now*, ready *now*," Schaz interjected. I pulled us out of the orbital path, still picking up speed as I clawed our way out of the gravity well; Bolivar was right behind. The void in my cockpit screens—and I'm sure all behind us as well—was a mass of flak and explosions, the Pax throwing everything they had at us. They knew we were on an exit trajectory.

"Missiles closing," Javi warned. "I'm cutting them down as fast as I can, but I'm not going to be able to get all of them; they're primed to explode as soon as—"

"Faster, faster, faster, *faster*," Bolivar was chanting; if he was a person, I'd say he was doing it under his breath, his voice rising with every iteration.

"Beyond Ending is splitting apart," Scheherazade reported. "That's it, this is done, we need to—"

We hit the edge of the gravity well and I punched us into hyperdrive just as everything around us became nothing but fire.

CHAPTER 16

There was a moment of quiet inside the cockpit, everyone trying to catch their breath. The stars streamed by outside, the very speed at which we were moving imparting an odd antipodean sense of stillness, especially after the combat.

The fight had lasted less than ten minutes, but it *felt* like it had gone on forever; from a purely subjective viewpoint, I would say we'd been in that combat longer than we held the observation tower back on Esa's homeworld. I would have been *wrong*, but that's what it felt like. Space combat always did, for whatever reason. That was one of the reasons I'd always been so drawn to it, ever since I'd first gripped a flight stick and guided a ship through enemy fire: the *intensity* of the thing, the sheer awesome *scope* of it.

Finally, Esa broke the stillness. "Can we . . . *please* . . . stop getting shot at?" she begged.

Without looking, Javier pointed at the girl. "I'm with her," he announced. "Why do you always get shot at?" he asked me. "Always. Like—always."

"You do get shot at a great deal," Scheherazade affirmed.

"None of this is my fault." I tried to glare them all into submission, but it didn't seem to be gaining me much ground.

"Fault? No." Javier shook his head. "Destiny? Maybe." And then he grinned at me, and suddenly the last three years just fell away. There was nothing standing between us; he hadn't deserted the Justified, I hadn't deserted him. It was the exact same grin he'd always given me after I pulled him out of some trouble he'd stirred up, the exact same grin he'd given me when we managed to meet up on some isolated world somewhere, light years from Sanctum or responsibility or any other living being. I grinned back before I could help myself.

Then it all came crashing back in. He had run; I had refused to follow, or even defend him. *And* we'd just crashed into whatever new life he'd managed to set up for himself, bringing *that* down around his ears as well. I didn't know for a fact that the Pax had come there looking for us, but I didn't *not* know it, either.

His smile slowly faded at the sight of whatever it was he saw on my face. "So," he said, leaning back against his chair, "how have *you* been?"

I laughed; I couldn't help it. "This is awkward," I admitted.

"It's not awkward," Scheherazade protested. "It doesn't *have* to be awkward, at least."

"Do you guys need the room, or something?" Esa asked, looking between the two of us.

I sighed, and shook my head. "No. Stay," I said. "If we're going to fight, it's not like there's anywhere on this ship you could *not* hear it, anyway. Schaz just isn't that big."

"I have a ladylike figure," Schaz said primly.

Javi laughed, out of nowhere. "What the *hell* is wrong with your voice?" he asked her.

"JackDoes," she replied, her tone full of murder.

"Ah. How'd you piss him off?"

"He's been trying to develop a sense of humor—I *think* he may be modeling it after someone currently on board, in fact. Someone who was never all that good at humor to begin with, despite their own certainty that they *were*."

"You mean me?" Javier tried to sound innocent. He was bad at it.

"I mean you, yes."

"Sorry we got your pirate base blown up," I said to Javi, standing from my chair and straightening. It wasn't exactly a rousing apology, but it was at least a start.

He shrugged. "It's not like it was my favorite place in the galaxy, anyway. But pirates are surprisingly willing to trade with you when no one else is."

"So that's what you've been doing? Making your living as a trader, a smuggler?"

"It's kept me flying," he admitted, scratching his chin. "After all, I spent years mapping systems that the Justified either didn't think were worth further investigation, or never got around to, but what's not worth it to a sect like ours—yours—can still be plenty profitable for one man."

I smiled, looking down. "So you're still an explorer at heart," I said.

"I am what I am," he sighed, staring at his hands. "I think we both know at this point that's not going to change. Anyway." He looked up at me, then past me, at the Preacher. "Javier Ortega," he said, extending a hand. "Nice shooting back there."

"And yourself," she answered, carefully returning his handshake. "I hear you're—"

"Can we do this later?" I interrupted. I was tired, and it came out crankier than I meant it to, but I couldn't help it—it had been a long day. "Javi, this is the Preacher—Preacher, this is Javi, like he already said. She's here looking after the girl. The girl's my charge."

"Your cargo, you mean." His tone was dry, just a hint of humor running underneath it.

"That's pretty much what she means, yeah," Esa agreed.

"On your way to Sanctum, huh, kid? Good luck—it's nice there. I kind of miss it. Anyway." Javier spread his hands before turning back to me; always the peacemaker. "You said back on Beyond Ending you were here for my help. What can I do for you?"

"Marus, he's—"

"Holy shit, Marus is on board?" he broke out into a broad grin as he turned, scanning the cockpit, like he was expecting his old Tyll friend to have been hiding in an air duct or something. "What's he—"

"He's hurt, Javi. Bad. He's slipped into *cort*."

The smile was erased from Javier's face in an instant. "How long?" he asked.

"A couple of days."

"So he's got a while yet. I have a supply stash not far from here." He shifted over to the navigation console, leaning across Esa to work in commands. "I set it up in case of . . . well, in case of exactly the sort of thing that just happened. Odds and ends, but I've got a good deal of medical gear—"

"Hypochondriac," I muttered, coming up behind him to peer over his shoulder. It was something I just *did*, old habits.

"Pragmatist," he replied, his tone fake-hurt. "Anyway, I'm fairly sure I've got some Tyll stuff that Schaz can break down and recompound into something that'll . . . well, wake him up, at least."

I nodded. "Good. Schaz, when we drop out of hyperspace, can you send these new coordinates over to Bolivar?" I asked.

"Will do, boss," she replied.

"You still calling her that?" Javier laughed at her.

"What does Bolivar call you these days?" she asked in return.

"'Dummy', usually," he said.

"He's always lacked a certain respect for his captain," Scheherazade replied primly. "The agents of the Justified are to be respected—"

"Thank you, Schaz—" I was almost touched.

"Even when they're stupid and wrong and making bad decisions."

I sighed. "Thank you, Schaz."

"Schaz—never change," Javier said, stepping away from the console.

"I know. I'm pretty much perfect."

Javier looked up at me. "So," he said. "*Are* we going to talk about it?"

I arched an eyebrow at him. "You have anything you've been waiting three years to say?" I asked.

"A few things, yeah."

"You planning on saying them?"

"Looking for the right moment."

"Then skip it for now. Let's get Marus taken care of."

CHAPTER 17

We jumped back into hyperspace, though not for long; Javier hadn't been exaggerating—a rarity—and his stash really was close. In the meantime, I did my best to steer clear of him, given that however this ended, I knew it wouldn't likely be with the two of us resuming our former relationship.

That task was made easier by Esa sticking to him like glue, staying right on his heels as he moved into the living quarters. The Preacher didn't know anything about me to tell her, and Schaz *wouldn't*—Javier, of course, would, mostly because he knew it would piss me off. "No, kid." He laughed at whatever she'd just asked him. "I'm not *quite* as old as she is." He rotated the kitchen module out of its housing with practiced ease, then started digging around in my cold box for something to drink. Make yourself right at home, Javier. "Didn't see much of the sect wars, myself."

"So she *was* a soldier," Esa said. "I knew it."

"I've *told* you that much," I said from the cockpit; they both ignored me.

"Yep." He nodded. "Soldier, gunner, tactician, one of the best pilots I've ever seen; if you name it and it involves some kind of fighting, she's done her share."

"And you?" she asked.

"I'm no slouch—especially not on the piloting front—and I know how to keep myself alive, but I'm not her." He looked sideways, caught me glaring at him, and raised his hands, one still grasping his glass. "And she's sending me some not-so-subtle signals that I ought to shut up now, anyway."

"Why won't you let anyone tell me *anything*?" Esa complained at me.

"You'll learn what you need to know at Sanctum. Javier's take on the galaxy is . . . a bit skewed."

"By what?"

"By Javier."

"By survival," he said as way of correction, adding in a grin to lessen the bite. "Galaxy looks a lot different from the sorts of places I *wind* up than when you're looking out from the shimmering towers of Sanctum."

"Oh, yeah, Javi. Because my life's been nothing but crystal palaces and silken sheets." I was officially failing in my "do not engage Javier" policy. I couldn't help it. He was just goddamned *frustrating*—what was I supposed to do, let it lie?

"There are *palaces*?" Esa asked.

"There are towers," I answered with a sigh. "The rest is Javier being Javier."

"How about the Pax?" she asked. "Can I ask him about them?"

The smile fell off of Javi's face in a hurry. "You can ask, kid," he said. "I don't think I can tell you anything you don't already know. What they can take, they take. What they can't take, they kill. What they can't kill, they do their damnedest to cripple, so it can't rise against them."

"But they're not *everywhere*, right? She"—and here, she pointed at me, the action almost accusatory—"she told me they didn't rule the galaxy or anything, but I still don't—it seems like there are a *lot* of them."

He had to laugh at that; she looked kind of pissed off, so he stifled it in a hurry. "Look, Esa; I get that you grew up on a kind of . . . backwater, yeah? No offense," he added.

"None taken. It was kind of a shithole."

"It wasn't that bad." The Preacher sounded vaguely affronted on behalf of her adopted home.

"As shitholes go, no." Esa shrugged.

"Point is, to someone who's spent most of their life on one world—which is most people, honestly—it can be tough to grasp just how *big* the galaxy is," Javier said. "There are tens of millions of Pax, yeah. Or at least, people living under Pax rule. Maybe even more than that—billions, possibly."

"That's . . . a lot," she said with a swallow.

"It is, and it isn't," he said. "Compared to your homeworld, it probably is. Those billions of people, though, they only represent a tiny *fraction* of the total galactic population. Not even a full percent of the whole—not even a percent of a percent. A handful of worlds that the Pax claim; that's it. Not even the biggest of the corporations—not those that are still running *or* those that didn't survive the pulse—could claim to have influence over even *half* the worlds out there, let alone *all* of them. The galaxy's just so damned big, *nobody* can control all of it. Even during the golden age there was never a central government—"

"That we know of," the Preacher added. "Most of the stories from that era of history are more legend than fact, anyway. It's entirely possible there *was* a galactic government, or even that some of the civilizations that came before—like the forerunners, those who built my kind—might have managed it. Just because we've never *seen* it done, doesn't mean it can't be."

"No, but people being people does," Javier disagreed. "You get enough individuals in a room and ask for a show of hands on *any* single issue, there will always be at least *some* full pockets. I don't care if the issue is something almost universal, like 'are babies cute'; there's always going to be at least *one* contrarian."

"I *hate* babies," Schaz put in, feeling her opinion was necessary at this point. "They smell and they're loud and they can't hold interesting conversations at *all*."

"Who hates *babies*?" the Preacher asked her, aghast.

"Me. Like I just said."

"Case in point," Javier tipped his drink in the direction of Schaz's core. "And that's just us, just a couple people in a room. A central government over something as big as a galaxy: it's just untenable."

"The Pax don't think so," Esa put in.

"The Pax are stupid," Javier reminded her. "Fascists usually are. It takes a combination of a pretty scary failure of empathy and a *total* lack of imagination to think that you can run the whole galaxy, when nobody else has ever been able to. Especially after the pulse."

Scheherazade's proximity alert started chiming; I ducked back into the cockpit, leaving them to their political discussion. Personally, I agreed with Javier, but that didn't mean a single institution couldn't *affect* the whole of the galaxy: just that they couldn't possibly *control* it. That was the difference between the Justified and a more formal government. We were closer to an intergalactic aid agency than anything else.

"Coming up on the system Javi marked, boss," Schaz told me as I slipped behind the stick. I pulled us out of hyperspace, studying the scans on the viewscreen as I did.

Not much to see—either in the mapping data or on the system coming into view as we dropped out of hyperspace. There was a lone populated world, one that hadn't been taken so far back by the pulse as to be robbed of electricity, but still well short of spaceflight. Javier always had been clever: that one planet would draw the attention of anyone who arrived in the system, and they wouldn't bother with any of the *other* celestial bodies, of which there were thousands, thanks to an asteroid belt ringing the inner worlds like an ocean of floating stone.

He'd hidden his stash on one of the larger asteroids in the belt; not even Schaz's scans could pick up anything interesting about it, just dense, common rock. We followed Bolivar in, both because of his more finely tuned instruments—this was what he had been built for, after all—and because he knew where the hell he was going.

The asteroid was the size of a small moon, and Javi being Javi, he hadn't just left his stash on the surface. No, he'd built it deep in a strange rift that ran halfway down to the core of the asteroid, because a constant low level of paranoia also helped in Javier's former profession. In his current profession, too, come to think of it.

Bolivar guided us deep into the crevice, until we were well below the point where scans would penetrate through the asteroid's metallic surface—you'd have to be right above this particular location, *and* have some pretty fancy scanners, *and* know what you were looking for, to find Javier's little emergency depot. Like I said: paranoia.

It was just a cave, of course, a natural formation in whatever process had left the massive rift we had descended into. Javi was a great many things, but he wasn't an engineer; he'd rigged up a simple shield generator to contain the atmosphere that he'd pumped in, and that was that. Too bad; I wouldn't have minded taking another pass at Schaz's damaged thrusters if he'd had a workshop. As it was, though, there was just the bare stone cavern, small enough that both ships could barely squeeze inside.

Javi and I exited Scheherazade's ramp, leaving the other two behind. The only light came from the floods on the ships; the only thing they illuminated was the stack of crates strewn haphazardly against the far wall. "Oh, very well organized," I told him, not bothering to try and hide the sarcasm.

He arched an eyebrow at me. "I'm sorry, were you expecting things to be alphabetized by scientific name?" he asked. "Or maybe in descending order of likelihood and severity of possible emergency. I've got better shit to do than spend a few days puttering around in all of my various stash houses, hauling crates around to suit the obsessive nature that I entirely lack."

"Do you?" I asked.

"Ever since I got kicked out of the Justified, yeah, I do," he replied, keeping his tone as bland as possible.

Still, I winced. "Fair point," I said.

"Thank you." He walked to a crate—seemingly at random, it's not like it was marked "Tyll medical supplies," or even anywhere near any *other* crate that might have had some sort of indicator as to why in the hell he went to this one in particular—and popped the mechanical lock. After a moment of rummaging, he emerged with a steel cylinder in his grasp. "This should do," he said, extending it toward me.

I took the medicine from him. "Thank you," I told him.

"My pleasure," he grinned. "You got me off of Beyond Ending intact, I should think that—"

I sighed. "No, dammit, Javi, I mean . . . I mean thank you. You didn't have to do this."

He nodded. "You're welcome. Marus is my friend too. Speaking of . . ." He gestured to the cylinder, locking his crate behind him again. "Let's go dose the old man. I'm sure he has some interesting stories to tell."

We ascended back inside Scheherazade; the Preacher had lain Marus out on the medical table again. I plugged the cylinder into one of Schaz's ports, and then ran an IV from there to Marus, finding a vein just above the second joint in his elbow. It was currently just a slow-drip saline solution, but now, once Schaz was ready, she could feed the drugs to Marus without any other aid from us.

"It will take me some time to synthesize the compound," Schaz said, "and then it will take a little bit for Marus to come out of *cort*, too. He may also still need medical attention when he does."

"How long until the hyperdrive's ready to jump again?" I asked.

"Factoring in exit time from this . . . really deep hole we're in, about fifteen minutes," she said. "It will be a few hours before Marus can wake up."

"All right. Bring up your maps; find me a broadcast tower on a nearby world, preferably somewhere friendly. We need to let Sanctum know what's been going on in here. I'm already overdue to be back with Esa."

"You don't want to head directly back there?" she asked. "If we plot a direct course, we can be home in just over a day."

I shook my head, and looked up at Javi. He smiled, and raised his hands. "I get it," he said. "You appreciate the help and all, but *me* helping *you* out of a jam won't be enough to clear my name with the council. In fact, you're going to leave me out of your report entirely, because not shooting me in the head would reflect badly on your ability to follow orders."

"Oh," Schaz said, sounding small. "Right."

"Javi, that's not—"

"It is; it's fine. And I, you know, I appreciate it. The whole 'not shooting me' thing."

Esa was watching the two of us. "This . . . doesn't seem right," she said slowly. "It doesn't seem fair. I mean, he's not a bad guy, right? He doesn't seem like a bad guy. He *helped* us. Can't we help him?"

He smiled at her. The look didn't quite reach his eyes, but maybe it was enough to fool a teenager. "Don't worry about it, kid," he told her. "I knew when I got on board this wasn't a grand reunion, just a brief hello. Like running into an old friend on the street, when you've both got places to be."

"You've got places to be?" I asked softly, before I could think better of it.

He shrugged. "I've got people that want to kill me," he said. "Probably more, now that at least a *few* of the pirates that got off of Beyond Ending may have put together my getting a surprise visitor, and then everything going straight to hell."

I sighed. "I didn't mean to make life more difficult for you."

"I know. Funny how it always seems to happen that way anyway, right?" He turned, and looked at the Preacher. "What about you?" he asked.

"What about me, what?" she said in return.

"You know she's never going to let you see Sanctum, yeah? She's witnessed her fair share of how the council reacts when you show up at their doorstep alongside somebody they don't think is supposed to be there."

"I can be . . . very persuasive."

"I'm sure you can, but persuasion has its limits," he replied. "Even if you persuaded *her*, it won't stop the council from doing something drastic when she gets back, and that's not saying anything about what they would do to *you*. The Justified are a great many things, and a great many of them are good, but make no mistake: they're zealots, just like all the other zealots who spent hundreds of years waging war on each other for no good goddamned reason before the pulse. After, too, for some of them."

I saw where this was going, and tried to stop it. "That's not—"

Javier ignored me, still talking directly to the Preacher. "They *will* think you're a danger to their grand cause, and they *will* deactivate you to keep you from telling anyone you know. Trust me: the only way you get to see a month from now is if you board Bolivar with me when I go." He turned to me. "Assuming she'll let you."

The Preacher looked at me. "Is that the way things are?" she asked, her tone blunt.

I didn't have a good answer, not off the top of my head.

"Come *on*," Esa said, her tone disbelieving, looking among all three of us. "We've been through some real *shit* to get here—is this really . . . just because of some stupid *rule*, we have to leave you guys behind?" She shook her head. "No."

"Esa, it's not—"

"No!" she insisted. "Seriously, what are you gonna say—that it's not that simple? It really is. *I'm* what you're here for, remember? I'm your stupid . . . package, your job, your cargo. You said I'd have a choice; well, I'm making one now. The Pax are still hunting us, which means they'll be hunting *them*, too, to *get* to us. How long will they last, huh? How long?" She shook her head yet again. "I'm saying no. I'm saying you either take them with us, or you leave me with them."

"Kid, she will knock you the fuck out and drag you unconscious to Sanctum," Javi said, his kind tone not matching the finality of his words.

I glared at him. "Why the hell would you say that?" I asked him. "Is that—do you really think that's who I am?"

"You planning to prove me wrong?" he asked.

I threw up my hands. "Schaz, get us out of here; get us to a broadcast tower," I said. "We can argue over this nonsense later. We'll contact Sanctum—I'll let them know what's been going on, and I'll make *every possible* argument that you two should be able to come with us. Then it will be in their hands."

"Yeah," Javier said softly. "Because god knows it wouldn't be fair for *you* to actually have to make a choice."

I won't lie: that hurt. "You have your own ship," I told him. "You might want to get back on board; I'm sure Bolivar is getting lonely."

He sighed. "That's not what I—"

"I'll go with him," the Preacher interrupted, standing. "If I'm going to be exiled with the man, I might as well see how well he treats his shackled slave."

"*Don't* call him that, please," Scheherazade said.

The two of them moved to the airlock and could barely wait for the ramp to lower before they got off of Scheherazade. The doors sealed behind them, and then Esa and I were alone inside our ship—the way it should have been, from the beginning.

"It wasn't true, right?" Esa asked into the silence. I couldn't tell if she was asking me, or Schaz. "The Justified wouldn't just kill them both."

"It's a complicated galaxy, Esa," I told her honestly. "Sometimes we have to do things that we don't like. Schaz, get us out of here. Suddenly I can feel the goddamned walls pressing in on me."

"Will do, boss," she murmured. Even she managed to sound slightly disappointed in me.

CHAPTER 18

I kept Esa occupied during the trip by having Schaz run training simulations for her at the gunnery station. If she was going to be on board, at least she could do something useful if we ran into trouble again. Plus, it kept her from asking more questions—Javier had come dangerously close to exposing information she shouldn't have yet, and I honestly don't know what I would have done if he had tipped my hand. At one point, I'd loved the man; I could be honest enough to admit that. Time and regret had a tendency to make you forget how infuriating people could be sometimes.

Scheherazade kept working on the compounds we'd need to wake Marus up, but we'd get to the broadcast tower before they were quite ready. That was fine with me—don't get me wrong, I was ready for my friend to be healed up, and to have someone else on board who would be more likely to defend the Justified from Javier's not-quite-baseless attacks, but now that I knew that was *going* to happen, it removed the pressure to make sure that it did. I wanted Marus *healed* more than I wanted him awake.

We emerged into the system where the tower was located; a busy little trade hub before the pulse, now home to two populated worlds—both thrown to well-short-of-spaceflight technological levels—that spun in their orbits around the twinned binary stars, locked into their own stories.

They were almost a microcosm of the galaxy as a whole; one had laid down their arms shortly after the pulse, the three separate sects that had been waging war on the surface coming together to form a new society, seeking answers for what had happened to them. They wouldn't get any; the pulse had guaranteed that. But it was a better world than it had been before—everything from average lifespan to infant-mortality rates to general quality of life had risen significantly, until it was no longer recognizable as the war-torn hellhole it had been. That was how the pulse had been *supposed* to work.

The other world had kept moving in the same direction it had been headed before the pulse hit: the same three sides as the other world, the same three former sects, but instead of laying down their arms, they'd remained locked in brutal combat, each sure it was the actions of one of the other sides that had caused the pulse. With most of their extreme weapons knocked out by the radiation, they'd settled into a long war of attrition, mining out the few pockets of fissile material the planet contained to launch nuclear strikes, the most advanced option to kill each other left to them. Now the world was locked in a nuclear winter, and the war still raged on.

What had been the difference between the two worlds? Why had one managed to achieve peace in the face of the chaos and strangeness of the pulse, and the other had only dug deeper into its war? The same three sects, the same basic species makeup, even roughly the same climates and landscape on the two planets, having both been terraformed to similar specifications. Different leaders, perhaps? Different reactions? It was like a coin toss that one side had won, the other had lost, and neither knew had ever happened.

Regardless, what we were looking for was on *neither* world. Instead, it was on one of the moons above, circling the war-ravaged planet. Once upon a time, one of the sects below had built a powerful broadcast antenna on the moon's surface, likely for contacting the stronghold of their sect, wherever that had been. In the century since the pulse, the sect below had lost their ability to reach out through the radiation, and the antenna had gone unused.

Well, *mostly* unused. The two planets hadn't been able to activate the tower, but that hadn't stopped enterprising travelers from making use of the facilities. The pulse had left both *worlds* with pre-spaceflight tech, but the moon itself, due to the random nature of the pulse, had been almost untouched. Passing travelers had used it to broadcast signals for decades now; currently, there were two ships set down just outside of the facility, easily visible to scans from orbit.

The lack of markings on their hulls and the laser-scoring visible to Scheherazade's cameras told the story of who they were quite clearly—more pirates, probably using the antenna to scan nearby systems for unwary travelers. Great.

The comms crackled to life. "What do you think?" Javier asked me, his tone all business—not trying to remind me of the fight we'd started, but also keeping his usual sly good nature out of his voice. "Two ships, anywhere from four or five hostiles inside, up to two dozen, depending on how much they don't like personal space. We don't *have* to use this tower—we can just move on, wake Marus up, send your broadcast from somewhere else."

I sighed, running a hand through my hair. "Odds are another tower will just have a similar reception waiting for us," I said. "Better the devil you know, and all that. It doesn't look like they know we're here—we've got the drop on them."

"Plus, making the galaxy safer from pirate scum; I never feel too bad about that, despite my recent furlough at Beyond Ending. If anything, it's reinforced the notion. I kind of *hated* it there."

Once upon a time, both of us had believed that sort of thing was our calling—clearing away threats to the innocent of the galaxy. Those days were long past us now. "Let's just get this done," I told him. "You ready for a fight?" Javier had never been the fighter I was—his former position with the Justified hadn't led him into combat nearly as much as mine did—but he wasn't exactly a babe in the woods, either.

"Always," he replied. "An unfortunate side effect of my recent circumstances. How do you want to handle it?"

"Simple," I replied. "We'll knock on the door."

CHAPTER 19

We had Bolivar and Scheherazade set us down a ways from the broadcast tower, on the dusty surface of the moon—"us" here being Javier, the Preacher, and myself, leaving Esa behind on Schaz despite her strenuous objections. The ships retreated to orbit with all their stealth systems activated, and the three of us began the hike to the antenna.

This particular moon had only ever had basic terraforming—atmosphere and normalized gravity, enough for a few facilities like the broadcast antenna, but not for any real manufacturing or agricultural work. Either it had been deemed unsuited for such during the golden age, with the planets nearby better candidates, or the wars had broken out before anyone could get that far. Either way, the surface was nothing but purplish dust and indigo rock; pretty in an abstract kind of way, but it got real monotonous, real quick, when you actually had to hike across it.

The tower rose up like a gleaming spike from the moon's surface, an antenna to the heavens meant to keep the world below in contact with the rest of the galaxy, now simply a net the pirates could spread to locate their next prey. I won't lie—yes, this was what we needed to do, it was part of my mission, it was a viable strategy to continue moving forward, but it also felt *good*, to be taking on those who were making life harder for the few space-faring peoples that remained in the galaxy. Violence was a tool in my toolkit: not the only one I used, but one of the more common ones. It felt good to use it for the same reasons I'd initially picked it up.

Our plan was simple enough; when we got close, Javier left the Preacher and me on a high ridge—both of us armed with gauss rifles, since, for a change, the lack of radiation in the atmosphere wouldn't eat through them and force us to rush our shots—and he snuck down to the low plain below, where the pirates had left their ships. The Preacher and I watched his progress through our scopes as he crept to the belly of each craft and affixed charges to their engines.

If there had been a point where my plan would have failed, it would have been there—just an unlucky break: if one of the pirates strolled out of the facility to retrieve something from their holds, or if there was one already on board and she decided now was a good time to head back into the low handful of buildings clustered beneath the rise of the tower, we would have been in for a protracted fight. Luckily, Javi set the charges and returned to our position above with the pirates none the wiser; however they were killing time inside, it apparently didn't require frequent trips out to their vessels.

He grinned at me when he got back—regardless of our fight earlier, he did still love this kind of thing, same as I did—and then he triggered the detonator.

The explosives he'd planted weren't enough to completely destroy the pirates' ships, but they did ruin them beyond repair, and more importantly to the plan, they made one *hell* of a racket. I'm sure it came as quite a shock to the outbuildings' current inhabitants when twin fireballs suddenly erupted from their only way *off* of the desolate surface of the moon—they'd had the antenna trained so hard on nearby systems that they hadn't picked up the danger much closer to them, having long since written off the two planets as no threat. Of course, both Scheherazade and Bolivar had advanced stealth systems; those had also helped.

The pirates came boiling out of the facility like we'd kicked over a nest of ants. Some tried desperately to put out the fires consuming their ships—regardless of the viability of the craft, they still didn't want the flames to spread to the tower compound itself—while others cast desperately around, trying to figure out if they were under attack or if it was just some sort of terrible engineering malfunction. Still others simply cursed and swore and shook their fists, blind rage overcoming any other instincts they had. It was funny, the way different people will react to bad situations.

Of course, regardless of their reactions, they all met the same end. The Preacher and I didn't have to fire a shot—the rifles had been more to cover Javier. We had more powerful tools than that at our disposal.

It was over almost as soon as it began; once Schaz and Bolivar dropped out of the sky and started scything lasers through their ranks, there was nowhere for their targets to run. At least a dozen of the pirates had emerged from the facility; none of that number made it back inside.

We entered the facility, leaving our rifles at the door. Gauss rifles were great for long-range engagement, but less useful in close quarters, just too unwieldy. There were a few bandits left inside—mostly those too drunk to react to the explosions—and they were still scrambling to get outfitted, which meant that most of them lacked kinetic shielding units.

In a tight-exchange gunfight like that, if one side has shielding and the other doesn't, the fight has already been decided; it just has to play out, and in close quarters, it'll play out quickly. It did; we were left standing, and they were not.

Was it a fair fight? No. Was it an ambush? Yes. Exactly the *same* type of ambush I was sure they'd laid for dozens of ships trying to make their way through the galaxy, the same ambush they would have laid for us if we'd been unlucky enough for them to see us coming. I didn't feel bad about it in the least. There had been close to two dozen of them; that was two dozen pirates that wouldn't be preying on the few travelers left still trying to knit the galaxy back together. It was a small victory, but I'd take it.

They'd clearly been living here for a while; they'd converted the interior of the facility into a kind of pirate playground, with a great deal of stolen weaponry, intoxicants, and other loot. I left Javi pawing through all of that, looking for anything useful, and went to send my message back to Sanctum. The Preacher returned outside to fetch our rifles, then went to meet Scheherazade and Bolivar, who had descended from orbit to land slightly away from the still-burning pirate craft.

I'd already figured out roughly the message I wanted to send, had agonized over it, in fact, through much of the trip here. I didn't know that it would do any real good, but it was the best I could manage. In clear, calm terms, I laid out everything that had happened since my last communication, which was when I had been about to descend to Esa's homeworld in search of her; I made sure to commend both the Preacher and Javier for their help. Sanctum couldn't get too pissed at me for bringing them this far, not with as sideways as everything *else* had gone on this particular run.

Then I shut down the antenna—for good measure running an electrical charge through its systems and frying them straight through; if another group of pirates wanted to use the tower to search for prey, they'd be facing weeks of repairs at minimum before that was a viable plan—and headed back through the pirate den. We were done here.

That was when Schaz contacted me to tell me Marus was awake.

CHAPTER 20

I took the ramp at not quite a run, waiting impatiently for the airlock. When it finally cycled, I made my way to the living quarters, and there was Marus, right as rain—or, at least, not unconscious.

He still looked inordinately tired, but his color was back to a healthy neon green; by Tyll standards, Marus was dashingly handsome, which meant wide, nearly black eyes and a thick, muscular jaw. He ran his hand over the stony plates that covered the top of his head—darkened to a stormy blue-gray, a sign of his advancing age—and smiled at me as I entered.

"Good to see you," he offered. "Thanks for the lift."

"Yeah, well, if I'd known I was going to be picking you up, I would have stopped by an intergalactic deli, gotten some sandwiches or something," I told him. It was a little lame, I know; I was still grinning like an idiot. It was good to see my friend up and around.

He winced as he stretched his muscles, finding new aches where the *cort* had kept him in one position for too long. "Khonnerhonn?" he asked, though I could tell by his tone he already knew the answer.

I shook my head. "I'm sorry, Marus," I told him. "He . . . by the time we got there, he was already going."

He looked down for a moment, composing himself. Tyll shied away from big displays of emotion; just part of their cultural makeup. "Last thing I remember was the Pax getting a missile through," he said. "Khonn was doing his best, but there were . . . just too many of them."

"You sent a message," I offered. "Set it to repeat, on a Justified frequency. That's how we found you."

He nodded slowly. "I . . . I *think* I remember that," he said. "But there were Pax, all around, they . . . came out of nowhere. Hit us a couple times before we could even get out-system; we kept running, and they kept chasing, getting in a few licks between each jump."

"Khonn kept running, after," I told him. "Finally gave them the slip, even though . . . he knew he didn't have long. He knew we'd come for you, though, at the end. He knew we were there, knew that you'd survive."

"Good." He took a drink of water, and said no more. It wasn't his way.

"Holy hell, Marus; you've seen better days." Javier had joined us.

Marus broke into a broad grin when he saw him standing at the airlock. "Javier Ortega, may my pate rust over. Things must have gotten real bad for her to have dug *you* up. Are we about to die, or what?" He held out a hand; despite Javier's choices, Marus had never held those against him.

Javier wouldn't have known that, but he shook Marus's outstretched hand firmly anyway. "Probably," he admitted. "So you're not going to demand that she shoot me in the head here and now?"

Marus shook his head. "I was one of the ones who spoke *up* for you, brother," he replied.

"Good to know *someone* did," Javi replied, firmly not looking at me. I ignored him.

Marus looked between the two of us. "Don't give her a hard time, man," he said. "We all knew *why* you did what you did; it was the sort of thing the Justified were *supposed* to do, were built to do, before we became . . . sidetracked."

"'An answer to the pulse is the greatest good, our ultimate responsibility to the galaxy,' and all that," Javi nodded. "Don't worry about it, Marus. I knew what I was doing when I did it."

"Yeah, well, she won't say it, but it hit her hard. She doesn't need you twisting the knife."

"Marus." I shook my head softly.

He sighed. "Fine. You two can have your spat; I'll stay out of it. Where the hell *are* we, anyway?"

"A few jumps out of Sanctum," I told him. "Do you know *why* the Pax hit you? They're behaving strangely, all over; I've run into them twice on this trip, both in places you wouldn't expect them to be. And that's not counting them hitting you."

"No idea, but they're up to *something*—you're right about that. There were . . . let me start at the beginning."

"Do that. Last time I saw *you*, you were on your way to a well-deserved furlough. Something about going mountain climbing somewhere, because *that's* a good idea for a guy your age."

He laughed. "Never even got to start that trip," he replied. "Got a message from one of my contacts, an urgent request for help. Khonn and I headed out there at full speed—she'd asked us to meet her at Marlotelle."

I nodded; I'd been there before as well. Marlotelle was a trading station, a little off the galactic beaten path, but still at the intersection of several well-used vectors connecting only lightly pulsed sectors of the galaxy. It should have been well outside of Pax influence, though so should Beyond Ending, for that matter.

Marus took another drink of water, then continued. "When I arrived, there was no sign of her, but we'd met there before, and I checked one of the dead drops we'd used: found a message, a data stick. Khonn and I had just started to decrypt it when the Pax hit us. I suppose whatever it was"—he shook his head—"it's gone now."

"Maybe not," Scheherazade said. "The boss told me to pull everything from Khonnerhonn's drives that I could, to prioritize anything with strange encryption. It's . . . I didn't like doing that, rooting through his files, but . . ."

"He'd understand, Schaz," Marus told her. "Did you find anything?"

"I *think* so. An encrypted file that had recently been downloaded. I've been running background processes, trying to crack it, but . . ."

"No luck? Bring it up; let me take a look." Marus hopped gingerly off the table, made his way to the vid screen on the central table. The keyboard rotated out of its housing; coding and lines of text started flashing across the screen, far faster than I could follow. There are things I am good at, but this sort of work was not among them.

Marus pulled up a chair and started typing away. Javier and I looked at each other, then back to Marus, letting the sound of the clacking keyboard fill the silence. Whatever we had to say to each other, it could wait. Khonnerhonn had died to get us the information behind this wall of encryption; I hoped to hell it was worth it.

A flash of something new on the screen, then a sharp intake of breath from

Marus. I might have attributed it to lingering soreness from the *cort*, but there was something other than pain in the noise. "Oh," he said quietly. "Oh, *no*."

"What?" I asked. "What is it?"

"It's the Pax," he replied, still staring at the monitor, and I suddenly knew what I was hearing in his voice. Fear. A great deal of fear. "That's what my contact was trying to tell me; that's why they hit us so hard. They couldn't risk this getting back to us."

"Enough with the suspense, Marus," Javier told him. "What *is* it?"

"I don't know how, and I don't know . . . but this is what they've been preparing for. I don't . . . we may not have enough time." He looked up at us both. "They're putting together a massive fleet, every ship they've got, plus more. They're going to hit us. They know where Sanctum *is*."

ACT
THREE

CHAPTER 1

I licked my lips, my heart suddenly pounding out of my chest. I tried to convince myself that I'd *heard* him wrong, because it wasn't possible; we were all so goddamned *careful*. We'd given up and sacrificed and *worked* to make sure that nobody could find Sanctum, *nobody*, and now Marus was telling me that had all been for nothing.

"How?" I asked him. "How has—"

He shook his head, still staring at the monitor. "I don't know. They found—*something*, my contact didn't know what, and he didn't know *where* they found it, but she said they came into a massive armory somewhere. Maybe an old corporate world that was overlooked after—I don't *know*. She says here"—he traced a line on the screen with his finger—"dozens of dreadnaughts, *hundreds* of ships, none of them craft she'd seen in Pax shipyards before. When she was preparing this message to me they were busy launching exploratory raids with their older craft, finishing up operations *everywhere* so that they could be ready when the time came to . . . to . . ." He shook his head, his six-fingered hands gripping the side of the monitor hard enough that his knuckles were a paler shade of green than the rest of his skin. "After that, they were to withdraw *all* their forces to the core Pax territories, preparing everything they had—all their old ships *and* all the new ones—for a single strike, overwhelming force."

"But that doesn't mean—"

He spun the monitor so that I could see it: a single vector, a hyperspace route, stretching across the galaxy. Ending at Sanctum's home system. Like an arrow, aimed at the heart of a target. Our heart. "They *know*," Marus said again. "I don't know how they know, but they know. That's their approach route: the route they were planning to take once they were all together at the Pax core system. They may well have already left."

It couldn't be. We weren't—it didn't make any *sense*.

Except it did. Of course it did. That was why they'd been so willing to sacrifice the old dreadnaught over Esa's homeworld, to risk those that had taken on the pirates at Beyond Ending. They didn't have the *crew*, not to man all of their old vessels and their newer acquisitions both, so they were shedding the weaker craft in a series of bold attacks meant to pave the way for their offensive. No more worrying about the pirates from Beyond Ending harrying their territories while they were off making their assault—they had more firepower than they knew what to do with, so they wiped the pirate refuge off the map.

They hadn't hit Esa's homeworld just because they were looking to add her strength to their ranks. They'd hit Esa's homeworld because they'd wanted to add her strength to their ranks *in preparation* for their upcoming offensive. They'd wanted a gifted child to lead the charge on Sanctum's own.

Marus was right—the map was right. If they knew where Sanctum was, and clearly they *did*, then attacking was a foregone conclusion. It was the Pax way.

That meant there was a Pax armada—more than just that, multiple armadas, a force so big I didn't even know the term for it, a force the size of which the universe hadn't seen since before the pulse—preparing to hit Sanctum, preparing to hit the world where all my friends lived, where I'd taken all the children I'd rescued over the years and told them they would be *safe*. I couldn't be made a liar like this. Not like this.

"Schaz," I said, my voice little more than a croak. "Set course for Sanctum. Now. *Now*."

"Yes, boss." All the usual joking, the good-natured humor and the dry wit—it was all gone from Scheherazade's voice. She was scared too.

"Remember . . ." I tried to think about whatever I was forgetting, but there was too much. The enormity of this wouldn't go away, just kept filling my mind, blocking everything else out. "Remember to send Bolivar our vector," I reminded Schaz dully. "We'll need to link up with him, *before* we start our approach." Otherwise Sanctum control might just blast him out of the sky.

"Got it."

"We could . . . the broadcast tower," Javier suggested, flailing for ideas, doing what he always did, trying to solve things, trying to solve everything. "We could send a message, we could . . ."

I shook my head. "We'd arrive at Sanctum well before a broadcast, anyway," I reminded him. "Besides, I fried the tower after I sent my own message out." That felt like it had been so long ago—half an hour, if that—that I could barely remember why I'd done it: to keep pirates from using it to locate new prey, that's right. It seemed so unimportant now.

"What . . . what does that *mean*?" Esa asked, looking among the faces of the adults in the room, all of whom probably looked as shell-shocked as I felt. I wasn't up to looking at any of them; I was still trying to process the enormity of this.

Marus sighed heavily, still staring at the code racing past on the screen. "Sanctum relies on deception and discretion and disinformation to stay safe," he told her, watching the monitor as if he could *will* what it said to change. "That decision was made . . . many years before you were born. If no one can *find* the Justified, no one can attack the Justified. The location of our base was chosen very *specifically* because it would be hard to find, hard to get to. It's why . . ." He made a futile, almost helpless gesture in Javier's direction as he finally turned in his chair.

"It's why they drummed me out," Javi said simply, reaching behind his head to untie his hair. He ran his hands through it, like he was trying to scratch an itch inside his skull. "It's also why I knew they'd take in the refugees I brought with me. The more people who know the location of Sanctum, the less safe it is. If they didn't want to kill them *all*, they didn't have any choice but to absorb them. They couldn't just let them go."

"Most people who live there don't *leave*," Marus said. "They help the Justified in their own way, but agents, operatives, are the only ones who go out-system; agents like us, like . . ." He looked at Javi, then looked away. "Sorry," he said.

Javier shrugged. "I was an agent, once. It's a fair thing to forget. Sometimes I do too."

"Will they remember, when we get back there?" the Preacher asked him. "Are you walking into an execution, Ortega?"

He shook his head. "I hope not," he said.

"He won't be," I said firmly. This was just too big to worry about one rogue operative returning to the fold. "Not after what we're bringing with us. They might want to kill him later, but with this news, it's going to be all hands on deck."

"You think you can *fight* this?" the Preacher asked me.

I nodded. "We have to," I replied. "We don't have any other choice."

"You can *run*. Pack up everyone living there, burn everything else down behind you; don't leave anything for the Pax to find." She said it like she'd done it before—not from the Pax, maybe, but the running part. The leaving it all behind part. "There are millions of uninhabited worlds out there, terraformed—or nearly—and just ready for a population. Just *run*."

"Can't." I'd been a soldier, once—a lifetime ago. I knew how this would work.

"Why the *hell not*?"

"Don't have enough ships, for one," Marus said, running a hand down his pate. "Even if we got the old frigates out of mothballs—and they've been that way for a century, it would take some serious work to get them running again—I doubt we could fit the whole population of Sanctum on board. There are *millions* of people living there . . . whoever the hell you are. Millions." He looked up at the Preacher, then at me. "Who *is* this, by the way?" he asked.

I waved him off. "Ships aren't the only problem," I told the Barious. "Sanctum's a dead-end street, very specifically. You'll understand when we get there. There's only one way in and one way out; we picked it for that very reason."

"You hid your bolt-hole someplace with no escape route?" The Preacher couldn't help the note of disdain that crept into her voice; it was almost closer to shock. She truly couldn't imagine such a thing.

"I told you"—I shook my head—"when the decision was made, we set up somewhere that we *wouldn't have* to fight over. Someplace no one could find us, someplace no one would even think to *look*."

"Will someone . . . will someone tell me what the hell is going on?" Esa burst out, finally unable to contain herself. "A few days ago I was just an orphan, living on a planet I *knew* I was never going to get off of. Now all of a sudden there are pirates and assholes called the Pax and fights among the stars and now everybody's *real* goddamned scared and I . . . don't . . . know . . . *why*. *Why* are the Pax coming after you so hard? You keep telling me that the galaxy's huge, and they're just a little part of it—so why are they so hell-bent on tearing you apart? Are you even anywhere *near* their goddamned empire? What have you done to piss them off this bad?"

I looked at Marus, who nodded, ever so slightly. "They know," he said to me. "They *have* to. That's why . . . it's the only thing that explains it," he said.

"They know *what*?" Esa asked.

"They know that we're the reason the universe is the way it is," I told her. "They know that we caused the pulse."

CHAPTER 2

You what?" the Preacher asked. A simple question, one she'd been trying to answer for a century. There was a lurch as Schaz jumped into hyperspace; no one was paying attention. "You *what?*" The first time she asked, the question had been shocked, almost quiet: the second time it was full of rage.

I don't think she even knew she'd taken a few steps toward me, that her hands were balled into metal fists. "Easy, Preacher," Javi said. His hand was on his gun. "Now's not the time for—"

"You're telling me that you . . . you *people* have known what caused the pulse, that . . . that you were the *ones* that caused it, and you're telling me *easy?*" She whipped around to glare at him, noticed that she was closer to violence than she'd thought. It was understandable. With an actual effort, she forced herself to lower her fists, but the anger in her voice hadn't faded a jot. "Fuck you. Fuck both of you; fuck all of you. Start talking. Start talking *now.*"

"Why?" Esa asked me. "Why would you . . ." She was staring right at me, searching my face, trying to find answers. "All the stories I grew up with, all the stories about . . . life was supposed to be so much better, before the pulse. Easier. Why would you take that *away?*"

"Because your stories were lies," I told her, my voice as even as I could manage. With a sigh, I took a seat in one of the unclaimed chairs. If the Preacher wanted to beat me to death, she was welcome to try. Maybe I even had it coming.

I looked the Barious square in the eye. "Now you see why I didn't want to take you to Sanctum? Now you understand why we have to hide?"

"I understand fuck-all," she snapped. "I want answers, Justified. *Now.*"

I looked at Esa "This was supposed to happen in a classroom," I told her. "I wasn't supposed to—you were supposed to learn about this with . . . charts, and videos, and stories to make you understand what happened. I wasn't . . . . I shouldn't be the one to tell you this."

"But now you have," she answered stonily. "I think the Preacher's right. I think you had better tell us everything."

"Tell us why we shouldn't just let the Pax roll right over you," the Preacher spat. "Because right now, that would seem like justice; it would seem *justified*." She snarled the last word.

"Your stories." It wasn't me who started talking; it was Marus, speaking to Esa. "The ones about how much easier life was, before the pulse. In some ways, they were right. Medicine was better; it was easier to grow crops, to feed people. In a perfect galaxy. But the galaxy wasn't perfect. More people starved to death, died from disease, every *year* in the old universe than do in a decade now."

"Because there were more *people*," the Preacher dismissed him. "What you did was tantamount to genocide."

"We didn't mean to," he replied to her, keeping his voice even. "But it's a false equivalency, to say that life was so much better before the pulse than after. Yes, the technologies we wiped out had the potential to improve quality of life on a great many worlds. But that wasn't what they were actually *used* for, and you know it. You were alive before, just like I was."

"Of course." She managed something that was almost a laugh. "Of course. The Justified and the Repentant. You always thought you were better than everyone else, smarter, more *moral*, trying to be a police force for the entire galaxy, ready to tell everyone else how they should think, how they should be. Of *course* you think you'd have the right to unleash something like that on the entire—"

"That *isn't what happened*," I said again. "It was an accident."

"Bullshit."

"You want answers, fine. And you don't have to believe us. But you said to start talking, and we're talking. You want to listen, or you want to keep trying to make everything fit how you *think* the galaxy works?"

"I want answers," Esa said, her voice surprisingly firm. "Tell me why. You said it was an accident. Accidents don't just happen at random. What were you *trying* to do?"

"The galaxy . . ." Marus ran a hand across the stony plates on his skull. "The sects that controlled the galaxy, before. There were thousands of them, tens of thousands, each representing different ideas, different ideals, different people. They . . . disagreed."

The Preacher snorted. "They killed each other."

"Yes." He looked up at her. "They did. Over and over and over again, all the time. Every single populated world in the galaxy, every *single one*, was involved in one war or another. Everything, everyone in the galaxy was defined by those conflicts."

"So you did it . . . the pulse, it was to stop these wars? Is that . . ." Esa shook her head. "That's not enough."

"It wasn't supposed to do . . . it wasn't supposed to *stop* the wars," I told her. "But as the conflicts escalated, so did the weaponry the sects used. You think what the Pax did to your home was bad? That was *nothing* back then, a minor skirmish. As would have been the fighting at Beyond Ending. Back then, whole *worlds* died in instants, thanks to the bigger, better, badder tools of mass destruction that the forward march of technology gave us access to."

"Toxic dispersal generators that could poison an entire atmosphere in hours," Marus listed an example in a wooden, emotionless voice. "Singularity missiles that could *create* black holes. Solar-fusion destabilizers that could cause entire *stars* to go supernova. Those examples aren't theoretical. They were *used*. We—the sentient, supposedly deserving races—had conquered the galaxy, and bit by bit, we were destroying it. Billions were dying every day, every single *day*. Billions."

"And how many *hundreds* of billions did the pulse kill?" the Preacher responded bitterly.

"None." He stared at her, almost daring her to contradict him. "Not a single death came from the pulse itself. It was built that way on purpose. Ships weren't knocked out of the sky; they were left with enough power to coast to a landing. Fusion reactors didn't go critical; they just slowly drained their energy, became inert. The very first day after the pulse, billions *didn't* die that otherwise would have, if things had just gone on as normal. Because the weapons that would have killed them were useless."

"And the billions after that?" she asked. "The billions that suddenly didn't have access to medicines, to surgical AIs? Those on planets that didn't have arable land, that depended on interplanetary or interstellar trade to feed themselves? How many of *those* deaths are on your hands, do you think?"

"All of them," he replied simply. "Like she said"—he nodded in my direction—"what happened wasn't *supposed* to happen. Not like that."

"Then what was?" the Preacher asked.

CHAPTER 3

The pulse—what became the pulse—it was meant to take out weapons," I told her. "It was meant to be localized, to be aimed. To destabilize and disrupt the production facilities where the various sects were building their planet-killers. That's all it was supposed to do."

"So you fucked up," the Preacher choked back something that was almost a laugh. "Of course. Of *course* that's all it was. The biggest catastrophe—the biggest *change* in thousands of years to how life in the galaxy was lived, and it's because you noble-intentions-having *motherfuckers* just couldn't stop yourselves from trying to make things better."

"Not better," Marus shook his head. "Just not *worse*. You were alive back then. How often did you get news of a new planet being destroyed, being completely wiped out, or rendered completely uninhabitable? How often? Before I was born, it happened every decade. A desperate sect would do something unforgivable, and all the other sects would turn on them, repudiate them, scatter them to the interstellar winds. By the time I joined the Justified, it was once a year, and the condemnation was minor, at best. By the time I voted to use the pulse—and *yes*, we held a vote, and *yes*, I voted for it—it was every other *day*. We didn't think we could stop the wars, that wasn't ever our intent, but we thought we could at least slow the bleeding."

"You realize your noble intentions mean nothing to me, right?" she told him. "Your self-justifications, your desperate need to defend what you did, all the flagellation you've engaged in over the last century; it means nothing."

He nodded, looking away. "I do."

"So it was . . . a weapon." Esa was still struggling to understand. "A weapon that only destroyed other weapons. That's what it was *supposed* to be."

"It was," I nodded. "But we used it before we were ready. When we were still designing it, still getting it prepared for its test deployment, one of our intelligence operatives brought us word that another sect —one that had long objected to our policies, our way of life—"

"Your way of inserting yourself into conflicts that you hadn't been involved in, of telling everyone else how to live," the Preacher interjected.

"Fine, *yes*, if that makes you feel better," I snapped at her. "The bastards were aiming a fusion laser straight at our home, a laser that would have cut through the crust and destabilized the core of our world, but pretend like we would have *deserved that*, Preacher, if it's what you need to think. Millions of people lived on that planet—our friends, our families. They all would have been killed, and not even all at once, not in a fierce flash of fire, but over *days* of chaos and collapse as that world shook itself to pieces. Is that how you think the Justified deserved to die, Preacher? Did *anyone* deserve that kind of death, any of the billions that died that way, or worse?"

"So you used it," Esa said; how the child was the calmest voice in the room, I'm sure I didn't know. "The pulse, I mean, the . . . whatever it was, before. You . . . fired it, or whatever, at this other sect, this sect planning to kill you."

"It wasn't fired," I told her, calming myself with real effort. "It had to be put in place by an infiltration team, on the ground in the target area; it was far too delicate to launch in a missile. But yes, we did."

"He . . . Marus said that he voted for it." She waved at him vaguely, as though she didn't have the energy to even turn and look at him. "Did you?"

"I did more than that," I sighed, running a hand through my hair. "I was part of the platoon that set the damn thing."

"So what went wrong?" the Preacher asked.

"I'm not a physicist, I'm not a . . . I don't know. We've been studying it for the past hundred years, trying to answer that question, and all I can tell you is that we don't *know*. It was supposed to be localized, it was supposed to irradiate the tech in a specific facility—not even the whole world, just a thousand square miles, rendered technologically inert. Instead . . ."

"You're right," Marus told her. "We didn't know what we were doing; it was our mistake. We own that."

"You made my species unable to reproduce." There, the Preacher finally said it. The reason she was so angry, the reason she had been searching, trying to hold someone, anyone accountable for the pulse. "You doomed us to a slow-motion extinction. Every Barious that dies is one fewer Barious the galaxy will ever see. I don't think there are more than a few million of us left now. In a hundred years, that number will be down to the thousands. A hundred years past that, it may be dozens. And after that . . ." She looked down, at her hands, as though she couldn't trust herself to look at us. "You wiped us *out*," she whispered. "You *killed my people*, and that's all you can say? That it was a mistake? That you *own* it?"

"The pulse was designed, very specifically, to leave Barious immune," Marus said. "But we never . . . it was never meant to be used near Barious production facilities. There wasn't one within a dozen light-years of where we set it off. I'm . . . I'm sorry."

"Fuck you," she murmured, the words gentle, almost astonished. "Fuck your sorry." She looked up at both of us, her face contorted into a mask of pain. "All these years, we thought it was the forerunners, our creators, those that *built* us. We thought they were the only ones who could have . . . we thought we'd done something *wrong*, something to deserve this, tarnished their legacy somehow, even though we didn't even remember what that legacy *was*. But it was never our forerunners at all—it was just you, screwing around with tech you didn't understand, trying to make the galaxy *better*."

"We did use ancient tech in the design," Marus admitted. "Probably tech from the lost race that built the Barious. We found it, dug it up, out of a ruined . . ." He shook his head. That part didn't matter. "If that . . . if that helps. I don't know that it does."

"It doesn't. Not at all."

"But what *happened*?" Esa asked again. "You set off this . . . this weapon, this weapon-killing weapon, and then what?"

I spread my hands. "We don't know. It worked—it knocked out the facility—and then it just . . . spread. In minutes, it had taken over the entire planet. In hours, the whole of that solar system. And it only got faster as it went further, which . . . that's not how things work. The whole concept was a 'fuck off' to the very idea of physics."

"The first use was only supposed to knock the facility back to where they couldn't build weapons of mass destruction any longer," Marus added. "It wasn't even supposed to send them to pre-spaceflight. We didn't even know it could *do* that."

"So it really was random," Esa said. "That some worlds only lost top-of-the-line tech, and others—mine—were pushed all the way back to where internal combustion engines weren't possible."

I half-smiled. "How do you even know what the hell an internal combustion engine *is*?" I asked her.

"There was a man in town, he kept claiming he'd . . ." She waved me away. "It's not important," she replied. "What's important is what happened after that."

She was still looking at me when she asked the implied question, but I pointed her at Marus. "Best ask him," I said. "I wasn't around for the aftermath; I was stuck on the same world where we'd set off the bomb. For years, actually. The Justified were in disarray, just like everyone else—they didn't have the resources to spare, trying to pick up a platoon that was likely dead anyway."

"We tried to figure it out, of course," Marus shrugged. "Tried to discover what went wrong, looked for a way to reverse it. But instead of *that*, we found the other thing. Discovered them almost on accident."

"Me," Esa said softly.

"You," he nodded. "The first of the gifted children—as far as we know—was born on our former homeworld, to a Justified mother. In studying *that* child, we learned that there must be others, then found them: the next generation. You."

"And once you learned about *us*—"

"We learned about the other thing, the impossibly scarier thing. That the pulse wasn't done, that it was still having effects, still intensifying, that it was on its way back around. Like ripples in a teacup that hit the porcelain edge and return to the center.

"The first pulse had spread outward from its origin point, all the way to the edges of the galaxy. Instead of moving on, though, into whatever . . . nothing . . . lies out there, it just . . . stopped, instead. Stopped moving, and started churning. *Building* on itself. Preparing to double *back* on its prior course. There's a theory—hotly debated, even amongst our own—that it's *waiting* for something, to hit critical mass somehow. Maybe even for a certain number of gifted children to be born; we know they're linked somehow, not just the children and the radiation, but the children and the pulse itself. But waiting or not, *purposeful* or not, it's still *out* there, out in the black beyond the ends of the galaxy, building strength. We unleashed it. *We* have to be responsible for when it returns. And to do that, the only way we figured out how to stop it—"

"Me." Esa's jaw worked for a moment, like she had something to say, then clamped shut. She breathed in, once, then out. "You need me, and kids like me. Our gifts were created by the pulse. You think *our* gifts can stop it, when it returns. By . . . *how?* What does that even *mean?* You think we—your fucking 'next generation,' you think we can just join hands and sing songs and it'll just *turn around?*"

"Your gifts are a product of the pulse, a sort of . . . accelerated mutagenic evolution," Marus told her, keeping his voice even. "Brought on by exposure to intense plumes of pulse radiation. They allow you to interact with matter, with energy, in ways no other beings can. Yes. We think you can stop it. If you work *together.* If there are enough of you. You can stop it—or you can at least hold it off."

"So you need us . . ." She was almost whispering. "You need us to clean up *your* mistake."

I laughed; I couldn't help it. "Not even to clean it up, really," I said. "Just to stop it from happening again. We don't think the next generation can *fix* the pulse, Esa. What's done is done; the old galaxy is gone, and it's not coming back, not any more than the Preacher's long-lost creators are. We don't need to clean *up* our mistake—we just want to avoid something worse."

CHAPTER 4

Esa sighed, looked away from all of us, like she could stare through Scheherazade's hull, like she could see right to the hole we'd unintentionally ripped in the universe. She'd thought I'd come for her because she was special. In a way, that was still true. But it was just another case of one generation passing its sins on to another.

"What about you?" she asked Javier finally. "You've been awfully quiet."

He spread his hands. "I was born after all of this happened, like you. This is all just . . . history to me."

"That's it? You signed on with the Justified, even after you learned what they'd done?"

"It was a little more complicated than that," he shrugged. "I owed them."

"And that's all that matters to you," the Preacher asked him, almost aghast. "Your own personal debt, your own . . . what they *did*, it doesn't matter, because it didn't happen to you?"

He fixed her with a look that would have pinned a lesser person to the spot. "I fought my wars, Preacher. I paid my dues." His voice was low, barely a whisper.

She just glared back. "And that's all that matters." Her mechanical voice didn't quite sneer, but it came close. "Your own story, your own suffering."

"That's all that matters to anyone. Even you. You want to know *my* story? Fine. *I* grew up on an absolute hellhole. Mountains and glaciers, for the most part, very little arable land. Didn't matter before the pulse. Food got shipped in. You know what happened after?"

"I can—"

He shook his head. "Don't try. You don't. You might think you do. You'd be wrong. See, I was *born* after, like I said. As far as I knew, all the old stories about the galaxy above, star freighters dropping down out of the atmosphere with thousands of tons of food? Fairy tales. Might as well have called it manna from heaven. The world *I* was born on was a feudal nightmare, ruled by petty tyrants who seized whatever power they could, who used the chaos to make themselves *kings*. Keeping people in line with the threat of those who had gone completely mad in the aftermath, become savages and cannibals." I hadn't known that. Javier wasn't one to talk about his past much. "So, yeah: I wasn't *alive* when the pulse went off, but don't you dare say it didn't *happen* to me. Every life in this galaxy was touched by the Justified's mistake. Even mine."

"But you still joined them."

"I did. Like I said: I owed them."

"The wrongs they did, the—"

"Doesn't matter. They did wrong, yes. And they're trying to fix that wrong, or at least keep it from getting worse. But maybe that doesn't mean much to you; good intentions. Fine." He shook his head. "You know where I'd be, if they hadn't showed up on that dying world when they did? I do. Dead. Dead, or a monster myself. And neither one would have been pretty. I'm not *responsible* for what the Justified did before I was born, not any more than I'm responsible for what any other Justified does, any Justified that's not me. I owed them, and they turned that debt around and gave me the opportunity to do *good* with it, and they got me off of that shithole world I'd grown up on in the bargain. You're damned right I took them up on it."

"Until we kicked you out," Marus reminded him. "For doing good, I mean."

Javier gave him something that was almost a grin, though there was still something mean behind his eyes, the remnants of his anger. "Whose side are you on, old man?" he asked.

"I'm on the side of what's right," Marus replied. "What we did, causing the pulse; I'm still not convinced it wasn't the right thing to *try*, but knowing now what we didn't know then, of course it wasn't the right thing to *do*. What we've done since—trying to stop the damage from compounding, gathering together the next generation, preparing them so that they can stop the pulse from returning—*that's* right. Kicking you out because you tried to save more people; that wasn't." He turned to the Preacher. "Do you want to ask me?" he said, his voice even.

"Ask you what? I already know that you *voted* for it. As if an act of tyranny by a democracy of few could—"

"Do you want to ask me if I still owe something. For my part in it. For my piece. Do you want to ask what I still owe."

The Preacher swallowed, nodded once, the motion hard, a single sharp jerk.

"Everything," Marus said simply, spreading his hands, the webbing between his fingers almost glowing in the light.

She looked away from him, but I could still see her face, all that rage and the pain and the fear, her steel mask probably less impassive than she would have liked it to be. She was working through all the new information, changing truths that had been at the fundamental core of her being for over a hundred years, and she didn't like *any* of it.

Better blind and unafraid than to *know* you can see and only find darkness anyway.

"And how do you plan on *paying* that debt?" she asked Marus finally. "All the lives, all the pain—how could you possibly pay that off?"

"A little bit every day," he replied, matching her anger with his own calm. "I may never touch all of it—I may never come close. But a little's better than nothing. And nothing's how much I'll be able to repay—how much *any* of us will be able to pay—if the Pax reach Sanctum."

And there it was. Regardless of what we'd done, Marus and I—regardless of what we'd continued to do. Right or wrong, what was in the past was in the *past*. We had to deal with what was ahead of us.

"So now you know," I told the Preacher, my arms folded across my chest.

"And if I say I'm going to expose the whole thing: tell the whole universe what you did, who they should blame?" The way she was looking at me, it was clear she didn't actually have to ask.

"You know I won't let you do that," I said evenly.

"Maybe the Pax *should* wipe you out, then." Her voice was bitter as she said it. "Maybe it's what you deserve."

"Maybe. Maybe not. If you can stand back and let millions die—plenty of whom weren't even born back then—for a mistake we made a hundred years ago, maybe that's who you are. But maybe you haven't considered what it would mean for the Pax to take Sanctum."

"The loss of a dead-end bolt-hole in a nothing system? Would it really mean all that much at all? Despite the bill for your actions finally coming due."

I nodded. "Ignore the fact that we've been studying the pulse for a hundred years—that, with what we know, we could re-create it, if we wanted to. Ignore the fact that, even if we tried to wipe all that data *out*, the Pax would get at least some of it, that they'd then likely be able to use the pulse against their enemies, otherwise known as *everyone*. Ignore the fact that, no matter how much you may want to blame us for what happened, the Justified are still a force of good in this galaxy. There's also the fact that we've built a school, a place for gifted children, changed children. Like Esa."

I looked at the girl when I said it; she closed her eyes. She'd been quiet for a while now—too long. "They came for me on my homeworld," she said. "Were willing to sacrifice one of their big ships, just to get me. You said it was for my . . . my gifts, before. That they wanted to make a soldier out of me."

"Well, they don't care about stopping the pulse from returning," Marus told her. "I can promise you that."

"And the other children?" she asked. "The other ones at Sanctum, the other—all the other kids," she glared at me, "the others that you've taken from their homes. If the Pax get to them . . ."

"They want you for your abilities," Javier nodded. "As far as the Justified are concerned, the gifts you—and those like you—are born with, those are just . . . secondary, useful only in the sense that they let us *identify* you as those changed by the pulse, and thus those who can guard against its return, eventually. Those who can stop it. To the Pax, though . . ."

"The Pax are a great many things," Marus continued, picking up the thread. "But you have to give it to them—they are *completely* blind to species prejudice. They think they're the answer to everything that ails the galaxy, that if everyone came together under their rule, under their *rules*, there would be no more war, no more conflict. The strong would rule the weak, and the weak would submit. Because they would have no other choice."

"Even if they have to kill two-thirds of the galaxy to get there," I murmured.

"And how is that any different from what the Justified did?" Esa asked me. From the Preacher, I could have shrugged it off. From the girl, it hurt.

I didn't let that show as I shook my head. "Not important. What is important is—they will *make* those they capture into Pax. They're very good at it; they've had enough practice. Whatever you want to call what the Pax do to their 'recruits'—brainwashing, lobotomization, pick your poison, it's a little of both: there's an element of both surgery and powerful chemical rebalancing involved—they've honed it to a science.

"Point is, they wouldn't just do that to the *slaves* they took from Sanctum. They'd do it to all the other children, the others like you. The gifted. We took you from your homeworlds because we needed you to stop the pulse from coming back, and because we wanted to give you lives where you could . . . *know* your place in this galaxy. Serve a purpose. The Pax want to make you soldiers, and the only purpose you will serve then will be death. The gifts you were born with, the gifts the pulse radiation left you with—they vary, but almost *all* of them would be devastating in combat, if properly trained."

"So those are my options," she said. "Join the Justified's cult, and train my gifts to try and stop the pulse when it returns—*if* it returns. Or be taken by the Pax, and be brainwashed into using . . . what I can do . . . to unite the galaxy under their rule."

"Oh, they still wouldn't be able to unite the galaxy, not even with an army of kids like you," Javier told her. "They'd still fail, eventually."

"And leave a trail of dead behind them that would stretch between the stars," Marus added. "The legacy of the Justified may be a heavy weight to bear, Esa—it is for me. But it's a feather compared to what the Pax will make you do. If they catch you."

She looked at me, tears drying on her cheeks, utterly betrayed. This was why my superiors told us not to form bonds with the children we rescued; this was why I didn't tell them my name. It was always the person who'd pulled them out of their old life that they blamed, when the new life they were presented with turned out to involve just as much compromise and difficulty as their old one. "I don't see that's much of a choice at all," she said.

I could see it, behind her eyes—she'd made her decision. Maybe the first true adult choice she'd ever make. I just hoped it wouldn't be the last.

Ultimately, though, it was beside the point. Esa's broken heart would heal, eventually; being among kids like her, at Sanctum—that would help. Didn't matter if she hated me; if that part never healed. That was my own price to pay. For now, we still had the Pax invasion force to deal with. "And you?" I asked, turning to the Preacher.

"You'll throw me out the airlock if I disagree; what do you expect me to say?" she asked.

"I'll throw you out the airlock if you threaten us, yes," I nodded. "That doesn't mean I'm going to ask you to fight. Not if you don't want to. You can sit this out. Granted, that sitting'll be done in a jail cell in Sanctum, and if the Pax break through, they'll either kill you or fry out your programming trying to turn you into one of them, but still. If you can't bring yourself to fight on the side of the Justified, I won't ask you to."

She almost smiled at that. "You're not one to soften a blow, are you?"

"You soften a blow, it just means you have to throw more of them," I replied. "You still haven't answered my question."

She nodded, just a tiny fraction. "I'll help you fight," she said. "But when this is done, I want access to your research, access to your records. I want to know *everything*."

I shook my head. "I can't promise you that; it's not in my authority to grant."

"But you'll try."

"I'll try." I would, too. She'd earned that.

She nodded, once, and then was silent. I turned to Javi.

"You don't have to ask," he told me, raising a hand. "I'll help. You know I will. Unless the council decides to shoot me on sight, of course. I won't be very good to you then."

"You can still take Bolivar and run," I reminded him gently. "As soon as we get in-system, we could link up, get you on board; you could be out of here, well clear by the time the Pax show up." It would tear me up to watch him go—I could admit that to myself, if not to him—but I'd done it before, and I'd survived. I'd survive it again. Though maybe not for long, not with what we were facing.

He shook his head, something sad in his face as he did it. "If you're asking me to do that, you never knew me at all," he said.

"I'm not asking. I'm giving you the option."

"Well, I'm not taking it."

"Good." I tried not to put too much meaning into that single word, but at least some of what I felt made its way in there. Javier looked up at me and smiled when he heard it. It was a sad smile, and more than a little bitter—as much hurt there as anything else—but at least he was still capable of hearing the things I didn't say. At least we still had that.

I looked around the room. Marus, Javier, the Preacher, Esa. Myself. A spy, a smuggler, a cleric, a child, a soldier. Not a single one of us was capable of changing the course of a war. We wouldn't do much in a fight against the Pax—this was going to be so much bigger than us, so much bigger than Schaz or Bolivar—but if we could get there, if we could warn them, at least we could give Sanctum a fighting chance.

"Get some sleep," I told the others, uncrossing my arms and leaning off the wall. "When we get to Sanctum, there likely won't be time to rest. There will be a great deal of work to do before we're prepared to take on the Pax fleet."

"You think you can?" the Preacher asked me. "Everything else aside, I'm asking . . . logistically, I suppose. Even with advanced warning, *can* the Justified hold off a Pax invasion armada?"

I gave her a tired grin. "I guess we'll find out," I replied.

CHAPTER 5

We didn't talk to each other much on the last leg of the journey to Sanctum. That wasn't an easy thing to do on a ship Scheherazade's size, but we managed it; we were all wrestling with different demons, and none of us particularly wanted company.

Marus spent most of the trip hooked up to Scheherazade's medical suite, getting his biochemicals back into balance. We'd healed up the burns he'd taken when Khonnerhonn's systems had overloaded, but he was still drained from his overlong stay in *cort*, malnourished and dehydrated.

Javier sat in the cockpit for the most part. He might have slept, but mostly he just talked quietly to Schaz. They'd always liked each other, and Schaz didn't even have Bolivar for company at the moment; ships couldn't communicate in hyperspace. I didn't begrudge her the conversation, though I had an idea that this would only encourage her entreaties for me to somehow heal the rift between Javi and myself. Like all it would take was a kind word or two.

The Preacher meditated in the turret. I don't know what she thought about. I mean, I could guess, but I would probably be wrong. Barious can be hard to figure out sometimes. They're almost like other sentient species, until they're entirely not.

Esa stayed in the living quarters. Her mind I could read a lot better than the Preacher's, just by the expression on her face: she was wondering what she'd gotten herself into, if maybe she wouldn't have been better off staying on her homeworld. Sure, it had bandits and food shortages and all sorts of dangers; sure, it lacked fancy tech and resources and answers to questions she never knew she'd had; and sure, it was currently under Pax occupation, but at the moment, it still had to seem maybe the better alternative than what she was flying into.

As for myself, I took my own advice, and slept. Pretty much everyone on board was angry with me, for one reason or another, and there wasn't a great deal I could do about it. That was fine—to be expected, really. So I just sacked out, rotated one of the bunks built into the walls into position and told Schaz to wake me when we neared Justified space.

She did that.

She did it quietly; she always did, when we had company. I stretched, and yawned. Did that quietly too. Old habits, from back home when I spent most of my time bunked down with a whole platoon and privacy was a kind of myth, something the officers got maybe once a month or so.

Marus was out of the medbay, talking to Esa, quietly, but he actually had her smiling, which must have taken some work. "Eels," he was saying. I listened, without letting them know I was awake. "Mutated eels, some of them six, maybe seven feet. Teeth as long as your hand."

"What are 'eels'?" she asked.

"Big fish. Big, long, mean fish. From human worlds, I think, originally, though you find them in a great many oceans. They eat almost everything."

"And she was—"

"Had no idea, no." He chuckled; I glared, though neither of them was paying attention to me. Why did he *always* have to tell this story? "Remember, she didn't grow up anywhere near an ocean. Learned to swim in reservoirs, quarries—wasn't used to the idea that there might be things *living* under the water. I was just about to call out to her when the first of them—"

I made my presence known, primarily by kicking the back of Esa's chair. "What?" she asked, more than a bit sullenly. Well, she was due that much. "We were about to get to the good part."

"You mean where I almost got *eaten*?"

"Yeah." The "obviously" was implied.

"I'll spoil it for you: I didn't. Now, you can stay mad at me all you like," I told her, "but you're still going to want to see this." Then I turned and headed for the cockpit without waiting to see if she was going to follow.

Javi was still in the gunnery chair; I slid past him. He reached out—not by much, just a slight motion of his hand—and brushed my arm as I did. A tiny moment of human contact, of support. He was still on my side, or, at least, was doing his best not to hate me at the moment. It meant a great deal, not that I'd tell him that.

I sat in the cockpit and took the stick. "You want control for the approach?" Scheherazade asked me.

"Better give it to me, yeah," I replied. "I know you can do it, but I can do it faster, and every second counts."

"Plus you want to think about piloting, rather than—"

"Just give me the damn stick, Scheherazade."

Javier chuckled softly. I turned in my chair and gave him a dirty look. "Don't glare at me," he said. "I wasn't the one telling the eels story."

"I hate that story. I don't know why everyone thinks it's so funny."

"Mostly because of how Marus tells it. I mean . . . it is pretty great. When he makes the faces and all." I ignored him, started checking my instruments instead. As I did, I turned slightly, on the pretext of setting some of the toggles above me—saw that Esa had slipped in, to sit quietly in the navigator's chair. She was still sulking, but she was here. That was good. Regardless of how this turned out, she deserved to see this.

I shifted us out of hyperspace, and the Justified's home system filled the viewscreens, both the cockpit window itself and the various monitors taking their feeds from the forward cameras.

"Oh, god," Esa breathed, forgetting, for a moment, how angry she was at all of us.

"Yeah," Javier agreed. "'Behold, the glory of destruction, and the beauty that it has wrought in its wake.'" His voice was caught somewhere between sarcasm and reverence; I don't know what he was quoting from, but it was apt.

Once upon a time, this solar system had been home to four separate stars—a binary pair at the center, orbited in turn by two smaller suns, themselves orbited by small clusters of planets, nearly a dozen, filling out the spaces between the stars. There were half a hundred moons as well, most surrounding the outer gas giants, though each world had at least a pair. It had been a ridiculous wealth of terraformable worlds, by any galactic standard. That was before the sect wars.

The two outer stars had both been collapsed into black holes, not by natural cosmic forces, but by the exact sort of weapons the pulse had been designed to render inert. The sucking voids spun and whirled at the edges of the system, their presence a constant reminder of the wars that had swept through here long before the Justified arrived.

Like dancers in counterpoint, the black holes bracketed the system on either side, bending and twisting the light of the cosmic firmament as they drew it toward them like ribbons in a gale. Most of the planets had been destroyed as well, in one manner or another, each terrifying in its own way, each leaving behind a painfully gorgeous vista that you could never forget had been created by the havoc that had also caused the deaths of untold civilians.

Some of the rocky planets had been shattered from within, broken into a billion pieces, filling the inner system with metallic shards that reflected the two surviving stars' light toward us, and toward the two black holes, creating a constant stream of light as the voids *ate* the illumination. A few of the worlds had been split in half or broken up into their component plates by coring, their orbits still strong enough to hold them *mostly* together, haunting facades of the complete spheres they had once been. Still others—mostly moons—had been completely pulverized, forming a faint ring that wove throughout the system, as well as smaller halos around the three planets that remained.

In all the systems I've traveled to—and I've seen hundreds, maybe thousands—I'd never seen anything of its like. When I'd first reached this system, after I'd finally managed to evacuate the world where we'd set off the pulse bomb—this hadn't been where the Justified's original home base had been; it had been soaked with pulse rads and unusable, so we'd retreated to this bolt-hole instead, realizing that we'd have to stay hidden if anyone in the greater galaxy ever learned the extent of the great sin we'd committed— I'd been both awed by the terrifying grandeur of the sight, and reminded that *this* was why we'd done what we'd done, regardless of how the consequences had played out.

Javi's quote was right—it was easily one of the most beautiful sights I had ever seen or ever would see, and it had come at the cost of billions of lives.

"What . . . what *is* it all?" Esa whispered.

"The remnants of a sect lost to history." It wasn't any of us that spoke; instead, it was a deep, resonant bass voice, modeled after a human male, broadcast from Schaz's comm systems. Esa jumped when she heard it; the voice laughed. "Forgive me, young one. Scheherazade patched me in to you, and I always like to greet new arrivals to Sanctum."

". . . Thanks?" she said, her voice unsure.

"We've got news, John," I told him. "Bad news." John—John Henry, in full—was Sanctum's resident AI. He acted as a kind of mentor and father figure to everyone on Sanctum, especially to the smaller, younger ship intelligences, but he had a soft spot for the kids I brought in, as well.

"I know; Scheherazade has already sent me the data you recovered," he replied. For whatever reason, John Henry hated using nicknames. Scheherazade was always "Scheherazade," never "Schaz." He barely tolerated us calling him just "John." "I'm convening the council as we speak; they'll want to debrief you in person when you arrive. They're . . . not likely to be happy with the friends you've brought along, you know."

"The council's never happy with me; I'll survive."

"We can hope," he replied. That wasn't ominous at all. "I'll talk to you again once you've addressed them."

"I'm not sure we'll be able to handle the anticipation," I told him dryly.

"In that case," he said, "have Marus tell the story about the time you were almost eaten by eels. That should help pass the time."

Goddammit. Never try to match wits against a supercomputer with a brain the size of a city block.

CHAPTER 6

So this is the Justified's great hiding place." The Preacher had joined us in the cockpit, was staring out at the broken system we called home. "Where you retreated to lick your wounds after your great crime. No wonder no one can find you."

"It's kept us safe for a century," I agreed, not rising to her bait.

"I can see why." As horrible as the acts that had ripped these worlds apart were, the Preacher was right—they had left the system an eminently defensible location. Interstellar scans wouldn't even *read* any habitable worlds—there was too much interference from the chaos the various attacks had left behind.

Once someone arrived from hyperspace, the twin black holes and the debris from the shattered planets left only one route toward Sanctum itself. There was no other approach toward the habitable zone; if incoming ships tried a different route, regardless of how fast or agile they were, they'd either be sucked into the black holes or ripped to shreds by the rain of razor-sharp detritus spinning through most of the system. Even a dreadnaught couldn't stand up to that level of bombardment.

Anyone coming to attack us—like, say, a Pax flotilla currently outfitting for that very same push—would be forced through that single avenue between the black holes, limited in the amount of ships they could move into the system at any one time.

"It won't be enough," the Preacher said.

"I know." She wasn't wrong there, either. Most of Sanctum's defenses were built around hiding its location from the larger galaxy; the Pax already knew where we were. They'd force through as quickly as possible, even with the bottleneck of the approach, and once they cleared the black holes and the debris field, we'd be at their mercy. Their dreadnaughts would slip into orbit above Sanctum, and pound us to dust. The city was shielded, of course, and had an anti-orbital gun of its own, but no shield could stand up to that level of sustained attack, and the single major gun in Sanctum—despite being one of the most powerful in existence—still wouldn't be able to drop *all* the dreadnaughts the Pax were bringing, if Marus's intelligence was right.

I took us through the dangerous approach, weaving an old path through the interplanetary wreckage. "Take a good look," I reminded Esa. "This is what the sect wars left behind."

"Why would someone *do* all of this?" she asked.

"Because there were worlds they wanted, and couldn't have, so they decided no one would have them. Because their enemies lived here, and they couldn't root them out with conventional warfare, so they got desperate, and used more terrible tools instead."

"Who *were* they, though? The people that did this, the people that lived here? Before the Justified, I mean?"

"Doesn't really matter. Not anymore. Both were sects that have been long lost to history, that were fading in their power since well before the pulse. Those who lived here, of course, thanks to all that." I nodded out the cockpit window. "And the winners, as well. This likely wasn't a victory for them— it was their last, desperate attempt to . . ." I didn't know the words, how to put it. To leave their mark. To prove that they mattered. Instead, among all the spread of the massive void that was the galaxy, *this* was the only way they would be remembered. For the destruction they'd left in their wake.

We hadn't meant for the pulse to do what it did. But it *had* prevented something like this from happening ever again. No matter what Esa or the Preacher thought, the act of setting off the pulse—the question of whether it had been wrong or right—wasn't so cut-and-dried.

"It was mostly Reint in-system," I told Esa, trying to answer her question, not just pass on my own sudden melancholy. "There are still pockets of them, here and there, on the few habitable slivers of land left. Devolved into primal chaos."

"And you've just . . . *left* them, like that?"

"We didn't have much of a choice." I didn't get into why; if I was right about some of the decisions the council would make, I'd be delving into that soon enough.

"That's *awful.*"

"They had their reasons." The support came from a surprising quarter: the Preacher. "Which world has your bolt-hole?" She used the question to smoothly deflect Esa's attention from the other remaining planets below.

I pointed through the cockpit. "There. The tidally locked moon over the second planet."

It wasn't easy to pick out through the chaos; our approach had angled us toward that second planet, a large frozen world that still orbited the binary stars at the center of the system. It hadn't always been an icy hell—while it had escaped direct attack, the various other changes to the system's geography had pulled it out of its normal orbit, ceasing its rotation almost completely and locking it in an elliptical path around the stars. The side we *couldn't* see was constantly scorched by the heat of the binaries, and the other half was a frozen waste, leaving only a sliver at anything even close to survivable temperatures.

The same thing had happened to the rotation of the moon above, where Sanctum was hidden. A single crescent no more than a hundred miles wide was the only habitable area on the whole planetary body, where the planet below blocked the boiling heat from the twin stars, yet reflected enough heat for organic beings to survive. The rest of the moon was either boiling oceans of liquid crystal, or frozen, jagged wastes—beautiful, and deadly.

That was another reason we'd chosen to locate Sanctum on that particular moon—the locked rotation. Dreadnaughts couldn't bombard the city until they'd put themselves in orbit around the planet below, meaning that they needed to position themselves between the icy wasteland and the crystal fields of the moon before they had an angle of attack. They couldn't fire during their approach—they'd have to circle the moon before Sanctum came into their firing solutions.

"All right, we're through the difficult stuff," I told Schaz, releasing the stick. "You can take control again."

"Thank you ever so much," she said dryly. Schaz didn't *think* I was actually a better pilot than she was, at least when we weren't in combat, which was one of the reasons I *was.* AI are programmed to react in a certain manner in a certain way under the assumption that everything around them is going to follow the same rules, which meant that yes, Schaz was better at minute shifts in our heading and meticulously fine-tuned course corrections than I was, but once things started getting complicated, she wouldn't be able to keep up. I'd met very few AIs I'd want on the stick over any given human pilot in chaotic conditions—in combat, or just when threading a needle through spinning fields of death, like we'd just done.

"So what happens now?" Esa asked.

I took a deep breath. "When we land, you'll be taken to orientation," I told her. "You'll be put in a group of other kids who have relatively recently arrived, in the last few months or so. Try to be nice—some of the things I've told you they won't know yet. After that—"

She waved me away. "I don't—I'm not asking what superpower school is like," she said witheringly. "I'm not worried about the first day of *class*. From everything I've heard, we're not likely to survive to graduation anyway. I mean what happens with the attack?"

"That," I told her, "depends on the council."

"Which is why you're going to go shout at them as soon as we land."

"You heard John Henry. I've already been summoned."

"Yeah. Which means you're going to go shout at them."

"I'm not going to shout."

"You're probably going to shout," Schaz weighed in.

"Not if they're not idiots," I told her.

". . . You're probably going to shout."

CHAPTER 7

The moon passing beneath Schaz's body was a barren landscape of strange, twisting crystalline formations, all violet reflection and turquoise shards of climbing minerals. Sanctum's homeworld was a great deal of things, but it was also very pretty. Even the boiling seas, where the light from the suns raised the temperatures to past the crystals' melting point—leading to constant storms of razor-like shards on the edge of the temperature differential—had a certain glorious awe to them.

The city itself—and that's what it was, not just a colony, or a military base, but a *city*, populated by people from all over the galaxy, people trying to make that galaxy better, even if they could only do so from hiding—was built across a mountainside, overlooking a crater filled with a pellucid sea of indigo-to-red crystal, the formations frozen in sweeping waves when the destruction that had swept through the system had locked the moon's orbit in place. The mountain itself rose up from out of that sweep of crystal, its rocky outcroppings at first studded with the growths as well, then less and less as it climbed higher. The lights of Sanctum shone from the peak, a beacon even in the constant daylight—a beacon the Pax were coming to snuff out.

Scheherazade set down on one of the landing platforms jutting out from the mountainside. Sanctum clung to the side of the rock in platforms and bridges, the peak drilled almost hollow so that the city was held just as much within the stone as it was anchored to the outside. The landing platform was already buzzing with activity, people running around, trying to prepare for what was coming. I doubted they *could*, but it was good to know the council weren't completely sticking their heads in the sand.

When we disembarked, I grabbed the nearest technician I could find, a Reint called SamMay. She was taller than most of her species, which meant she came almost all the way up to my chin; she grinned as she saw me. The technicians always liked me, for some reason—despite the fact that Schaz could be . . . *particular* about how, exactly, they worked on her, though she was usually effusive with her praise when they finally got something the way she liked it.

The Reint as a species had evolved down a tributary of the evolutionary river closer to reptilian than mammalian; SamMay's scales were a latticed pattern of neon orange and pink, and her fingers still ended in the retractable talons that meant Reint were handy mechanics, given that those talons were hard enough—and sharp enough—to double for most of the tools in a toolkit.

"Get a crew together, whoever you can find," I told her. I wasn't trying to be rude; you just sometimes have to be . . . abrupt with Reint, or else they'll simply wander off and do something else entirely. "I need Schaz patched, rearmed, and in prime condition as soon as possible. Take a look at her maneuvering thrusters in particular—at least three took some bad hits."

"Can do." SamMay shrugged, blinking her nictitating membrane at me.

"Also don't let JackDoes anywhere near her."

She laughed, or the Reint equivalent, which was a kind of hissing through her front row of sharp teeth. "As soon as he heard you were back, he ran away to hide," she told me, her long, fanged jaws giving her speech a sibilance lacking from most other species.

"Well, it's his lucky day; I've got other shit to deal with. When I *do* find time, though, he's going to regret messing with my AI. I did *not* appreciate the joke."

"He said you were going to try and throw him off the mountain."

"You ever known me to try something and fail?"

"I have not, no," she admitted.

"Then tell JackDoes that after all this shit is over, he'd better present himself to Schaz and apologize, profusely. If he doesn't, it'll be a long drop and a sudden stop for him. Meanwhile—get Schaz looked over."

"I got it, I got it."

"Thanks, SamMay."

"No problem. Council's probably waiting on you."

I sighed. "I know."

SamMay darted off, already hollering to get the attention of some of the other technicians; I turned back to the ramp, where the others were waiting. "Marus, can you take Esa to orientation?" I asked him.

He nodded. "I'll join you after," he said.

"You really ought to get to the infirmary."

He grinned. Amazing he could still manage it. "I'll join you after," he repeated. "Come along, Esa."

The girl stared at me for a moment, like she was trying to think of something to say. I just nodded at her, and she nodded back—that was enough, it covered what neither of us wanted to try and find a way to speak out loud. She whispered something to the Preacher, then followed Marus into the bustle of the hangar.

She was almost at the door when she turned around; apparently she'd thought better about the "not saying anything" bit. "Good luck!" she shouted across the space at me, waving.

"Thanks, kid," I said back. I'm not sure if she heard.

"And me?" Javier asked, coming to stand at my shoulder and watch Esa walk away.

"Up to you," I shrugged. "You can do whatever you like—just remember that most of the people here still think of you as a traitor and a deserter. I'll do my best to convince the council not to shoot you in the head right away, but until then . . ."

"Yeah, maybe I'll just stay on board Bolivar. He's probably getting lonely anyway."

"Seems like a good plan."

"I'll come with you," the Preacher told me.

I looked over at her. That hadn't been what I was expecting. "They may not even let you into the council chambers," I reminded her. "I wasn't exactly supposed to bring home strays with me."

"I know. But I want to see the people who rule this place myself. Look them in the eye and make sure they truly understand what they've done, and what they're facing."

I sighed. "'Rule' might be too strong a term," I told her. "Most of the time they can't even agree what to have for lunch."

"That's democracy for you. I suppose if you were in charge, you'd just *decide* what was for lunch, and that's what everyone would have."

"If I was in charge, we'd just eat whatever we had the most of, until that wasn't the thing we had the most of anymore. It's the same thing I do on board Scheherazade. Much simpler."

"You're a tyrant at heart, you know that?"

"I've spent most of the last century escorting teenagers, usually through pretty hairy situations. Of *course* I've developed a dictatorial streak; there's no other way to get them to listen." We started making our way into the hangar, heading toward the council chambers. I didn't know if it was actually wise, taking the Preacher with me, flaunting the rules I was breaking just when I needed the council to hear what I had to say, but it made me feel surprisingly good that the Preacher had chosen to come with me.

I knew she was still angry, both with the Justified as a whole and with me personally, so it was a nice gesture on her part to offer me some solidarity, from an outside perspective, at least. I appreciated it.

We stepped into the stone-and-rose corridors of the military base that occupied this side of the mountain—the interior crystals spreading through the rock like veins of ore—and made our way toward the city itself.

Time to see what the council had to say.

CHAPTER 8

That vein of rose-colored crystal that grew out of the interior of the mountain—a glittering sweep of shards reflecting the light—slowly gave way to amber veins, instead, and then pink, the colors refracting in dazzling patterns on the floors. The people who had built this place—people here long before the Justified—had placed careful spotlights in cunningly concealed positions all throughout the caverns, letting the illumination bounce and spread and sweep, bathing the whole place in kaleidoscopic colors that sometimes made it look less like a city and more like an art installation. They'd built something as beautiful as this, and someone had still come to murder them all. That was the way the galaxy had worked, before the pulse.

The council chambers were located down a stretch of open corridors bathed in an azure swath of crystal-reflected light, the cool, calming blues making the whole section feel like it was underwater. I think when the Justified who found this place were laying out their new headquarters, maybe they thought reserving that sector of the city for their major forum might help cooler voices prevail. It never seemed to work that way.

"You've been advocating for us to retake those guns for decades now." The council was busy sniping at each other as I stepped into the chamber, the various council members seated on a semicircular raised platform above the doors; the speaker was named Helliot, a bad-tempered Vyriat who was probably leading the vote to take me into custody as soon as I arrived.

If Reint and Tyll were vaguely reptilian, and Wulf were vaguely lupine, the Vyriat were closer to cephalopods than any other creature from the human sphere: amphibious, like the Reint, they were covered in waving tendrils and fine cilia that tended to stand on end when they were upset, meaning Helliot currently looked like a pincushion.

"It's a waste of resources, a pipe dream!" Oblivious to our entrance, she continued her tirade, her iridescent skin shimmering with barely contained fury as she shouted across the table. The target of her ire was Criat Long-run, the Wulf council member who headed up my division; he glared back, but was holding his tongue, for now. *That* likely wouldn't last long. "Even if we *took* the planetside guns," Helliot spat at him, "which is still a big 'if,' the radiation would cook them as fast as we could repair them. We have no idea—"

"If we don't retake the anti-orbital cannons, we'll all die here." I cut Helliot off before Criat could form his own response, which likely would have involved a great deal of swearing. If the council was going to throw me in jail anyway, might as well do it for as many reasons as possible, and keep some of the heat off of my boss. "It's really that simple. We don't have the defenses otherwise."

The Vyriat glared at me, the swirling colors under her skin amplifying the narrowing shift of her three eyes. "Do you really think your voice carries *any* weight here?" she asked, her tentacles waving disdainfully in my direction. "You brought this down upon us, and you've broken I don't even know how many regulations just by doing so. Your fate—"

"She brought us warning, Helliot," Criat rumbled at her, speaking slowly to control his own temper. "Don't shoot the messenger." Old legends said that when humans had first encountered the Wulf—the first sentient species we'd met outside of our own world—we first took them for "werewolves," old fairy tales about men who became more canid than man. That was about as apt a description of the Wulf as any. Even their name was a corruption of the lupine species from our homeworld; what the Wulf called themselves was unpronounceable to most other species, and so the name humans had given them had spread through the universal lexicon instead.

With the level of fury contained in Criat's glare, I wasn't surprised those early humans had looked at Wulf and seen beasts: I sure as hell wouldn't want that much Wulf *that* angry in my direction. Of course, his antagonism of Helliot was as much in general principle as in defense of *me*; they'd never gotten along real well.

"Oh, I can think of plenty of other reasons to shoot her," Helliot replied, her tone like acid.

"Shoot me or not, that's up to you," I replied. "But why are the cannons even under discussion? You've read the report I sent in, the report Marus's sources—"

"A *single* source, from a single agent." The objection came from one of Helliot's cronies on the council—Bathus, a Tyll who headed up the research division, old enough that his rocky pate was nearly black and his skin was faded from bright neon hues to an almost pastel shade of green typical of older Tyll. Still, I shouldn't sell him short—he always backed Helliot's plays because she made sure his scientists always had what they needed, not out of any personal stake.

Of course, whether I respected him or not didn't matter; he was still cutting our argument out from under us. "You expect us to scramble and waste precious time," he drawled, tapping his six fingers against the railing before him, "without even confirmation that this is a true threat?"

"The Pax *are* mobilizing," I said evenly. "I've seen that with my own eyes."

"And we're just supposed to—"

"Whether she's broken regulations or not, she is still an operative of the Justified, and can be trusted as such," Criat reminded Bathus, the bass register of his voice heavy with a reminder of the weight we all carried. "As is Marus. If we start doubting each other, we are truly doomed."

"A fair point." MelWill, small even for Reint standards, had to use a microphone to be heard, and was seated on a raised chair to even *reach* that microphone. She was the head of the engineering division, mostly comprised of Reint and Tyll, and a bona fide hero to everyone within Sanctum. Our tech, our defenses, and the theory that the next generation could be used to turn back the next tide of the pulse: all of it, all MelWill's work. Without her, the Justified would have fallen apart long ago: she'd given us new purpose in the dark years after we'd begun to understand what we'd unleashed. That discovery alone went a long way to explain the near-veneration she received—and deserved—from the rank and file Justified.

"It's not their word I don't trust, it's their source." Bathus switched tactics smoothly, not willing to take on MelWill—and her legend—directly. As Bathus headed up the science division, the two of them worked closely together: he couldn't afford to alienate either MelWill herself, or the engineering corps his scientists depended on. "One strung-out junkie on *one* trade station is simply not enough intelligence for us to uproot—"

Criat's fur was fairly standing on end. "If Sanctum is pounded into dust by a sustained barrage from multiple dreadnaughts, I imagine your precious projects will be set back *significantly* farther."

"We always knew this day might come." Acheron427 was the new speaker, the Barious who headed up the next-generation research initiative, otherwise known as the school that Esa would be attending. Tall for a Barious, and missing an arm—without the Barious factories online, she couldn't replace it, and she refused to wear a normal prosthetic instead, though whether she was making some kind of statement with that refusal I'd never been quite sure.

I didn't look away from the council, but I could feel the Preacher stiffen beside me as she realized there were Barious not just in the Justified ranks, but this high up in our command structure. "We've hidden Sanctum well, but nothing stays hidden forever," Acheron continued, her gaze flicking over the Preacher, then back to the other counselors. "Criat is right—regardless of whether the cannons *should* have been retaken years ago, they *must* be retaken now."

"My agent's information, sadly, did not include a timetable." Aoka was the head of the intelligence division, Marus's boss. Despite the fact that he was a Vyriat, like Helliot—all tentacles and slick, bulbous skin in hues that shifted depending on their moods—the two of them despised each other, always had. By nature Aoka was secretive, distrustful, and cryptic for the sake of being cryptic: all to be expected from a spymaster. "We don't know if we even have *time* to reactivate the cannons. We have to consider evacuation."

Criat shook his head, sending fur flying. "Not possible. We simply do not have enough ships. Less than a quarter of Sanctum could be—"

"I was not considering evacuating everyone, my friend." Aoka smiled. The two were usually allies on the council—much like Bathus and MelWill, Aoka and Criat often worked closely together, Criat's operatives carrying out retrievals or raids based on intelligence from Aoka's spies—but this particular issue seemed to be drawing all new battle lines. "Merely Acheron's students, their instructors, other key personnel. The next generation *must* survive. Everything else is secondary."

"And I suppose that 'key personnel' would include ourselves." The last member of the council, Seamus, was human: in charge of the day-to-day operations of Sanctum, including security, he had a surprising amount of pull for someone who managed duties the rest tended to think of as "menial." Still, when they wanted something done, it was Seamus and his workers who *got* it done, and they all owed him for one rush job or another.

Unremarkable in every single way, from his shoes to his haircut, I had a feeling Seamus cultivated that appearance very much on purpose: he didn't *want* you to think about him until you needed something. He shook his head now, looking carefully at each council member in turn. "We are the Justified. We stand together, or not at all." His gaze shifted to my boss. "I'm with Criat. We need to get working on the anti-orbital guns, and we need to start yesterday."

Their argument was an old one, a discussion that had been going on for as long as Sanctum had been settled by the Justified. When they'd first arrived here—I hadn't been present for the initial argument, still being stuck on the world where we'd set off the pulse bomb—Sanctum itself had been the obvious choice for a safe haven. The few remaining pockets of Reint on the other worlds had already collapsed into chaos, their very presence forming a kind of natural camouflage—anyone who somehow made it past the black holes and debris fields to scan the system would just find the few habitable spots overrun with devolved Reint, and devolved Reint were not something to fuck with.

That, however, meant that the defenses the Reint sect had built to deal with an enemy incursion—before their worlds had been attacked, before they themselves had descended into base savagery—had also been left unmaintained, and the Justified had chosen to leave them that way. A system emptied of all but devolved Reint would be overlooked; a system emptied of all but devolved Reint and curiously well-maintained defenses was worth a second glance.

The former occupants had originally built hundreds of anti-orbital cannons, seeded throughout the system—weapons powerful enough to trade fire with a dreadnaught—but whatever mystery devastation had torn their worlds apart, less than a dozen had survived. Three of the big guns were based on the same moon as Sanctum; the rest were scattered throughout the three remaining worlds, all of which had been affected by the pulse to greater or lesser degrees.

The council had been bickering over the issue for decades, some arguing that we should retake the cannons just in case we needed to mount a more muscular defense of Sanctum than "run and hide," the others arguing that an operational cannon facility would make a lie of our carefully constructed smokescreen. Devolved Reint, after all—the only local population other than us, creatures long since fallen back to their basest predatory urges—couldn't *hold* a wrench, much less maintain an anti-orbital gun.

"A compromise." Aoka held up a tendril. Of course the spymaster was the one to offer a neutral path. "Of the eight cannons that still *might* be operational—regardless of the pulse, we do not know if lack of maintenance and the basic laws of entropy have rendered them useless—three are located on this very moon. Let's send engineers to those three, to try and reclaim those facilities, at least until this threat has been dealt with. Then we can argue about whether or not they should continue to be maintained."

An optimistic outlook. Not a bad idea; the only problem was that the cannons he was talking about were on the opposite side of the moon, facing the entrance to the system and the pathway between the black holes. They could bombard the Pax fleet while it approached, yes, but the enemy would have defilade from the guns as soon as they circled the moon and arrived above Sanctum itself.

"A half-measure." Criat shook his head. "We need *at least* six cannons—the three on the far side of this moon, yes, but also at least three more. We *will* need additional firepower to stop the Pax than what we already have. This is a fact. I do not say that bringing the weapons back online will ensure our survival, merely that we are doomed if we do not."

"Of the five remaining cannon scattered about the system, three are locked into firing positions that would render them useless in any fight," MelWill pointed out. "Left that way in the wake of the chaos that broke these worlds apart. So your 'six' is unobtainable, regardless of desire. The three on the moon, yes, we can reach those with minimal difficulty: there seems to be no disagreement on this point, correct?" She looked around at the other council members, nodded when she heard no objections, and continued, raising up two talons. "That leaves two cannon remaining, those on the planet directly below: in an ideal position to fire up at anyone attempting to bombard Sanctum itself."

"The cold will have destroyed them years ago." Helliot dismissed her with a wave of her tentacle. "Even if it did not, that world is choked with radiation, pushed back by the pulse to a pre-spaceflight era. Keeping them running during a fight would require a massive effort, one we simply cannot spare the engineers for."

"Oh, I'm sorry," MelWill told her, her voice cool. MelWill did *not* like being told what her own people were capable of. "I didn't realize *you* were the head of the engineering department."

That shut Helliot up, at least for a bit; MelWill continued as if she'd never been interrupted in the first place. "First we must ascertain whether the *lunar* guns can be repaired, the three on the surface of this moon," she said. "If there's no hope of fixing them, there's *absolutely* no hope of fixing the guns below. So. I'll send exploratory teams to each of the three guns on the outward face of this moon. If my teams tell us that there's at least a *chance* the lunar guns can be made operational, we can consider expeditions to the two on the surface below."

"And the risks involved?" Seamus asked her. "You'd send your engineers onto a pulsed world?"

She shook her head. "The pulse is not the danger; we all know what prowls the world below. It would take a sizeable military force to reclaim facilities overrun by those . . . things."

"You mock your own kind?" Aoka raised a tentacled eyebrow.

"I pity them," MelWill replied calmly. "And I know how dangerous they are. You here on the council have always spoken of the devolved Reint we share this system with as if you truly understood the threat they represent; you do not. I do. Without soldiers to protect them, it would be certain death for my engineers."

She wasn't wrong. Most species on the pathway to the interstellar technologies that had allowed the golden age—fusion reactors, hyperdrives, AI—to exist at all had evolved from stone tools to spaceflight in a certain window of time, all driven to conquer the world around them mainly in order not to be killed off by the ecological dangers of their specific planets. The

Reint had taken nearly six times as long, simply because, on their homeworld, they already *were* the apex predator, and not because of their mental capacity.

Quick, silent, and possessed of singular hunting instincts, the key Reint steps on the technological ladder hadn't been fire or sailing or the wheel. Instead they had been basic social structures, things the other species took for granted. The Reint *forced* themselves to be massively social creatures, a cultural habit deeply ingrained by hundreds of thousands of years of rigid adherence, because if they didn't, they quickly returned to the alpha predator state of "eat everything you can find, unless it can be fucked" that had nearly wiped out every *other* species of fauna on their homeworld.

After the pulse, when much of the social order had collapsed, not *all* Reint colonies had devolved back to their pre-sapient state, but those few that had were nightmare factories. I'd tangled with them before, and still had the scars; I wasn't in any hurry to do so again.

Even still, I raised my voice, because I didn't see that there was another option. "I'll go," I said. "I'll check out the other two cannons. If I can clear them of Reint, we can send in engineers. If I can't, I'll get eaten, and the council won't have to worry about what to do with me after."

CHAPTER 9

For a moment, the council just stared at me, as if unsure that those words had just come out of my mouth. I couldn't blame them; I wasn't entirely sure they had either, and I had said them.

Marus joined me, coming to stand at my elbow. He took in the silence in a single look, then asked under his breath, "What exactly have you done?"

I gave him a mild shrug. It was hard to explain.

Finally, Helliot laughed, a disbelieving bubbling sound that filled the azure chamber. "I'd been planning on calling for your execution when this was all done, anyway," she told me. "If you want to walk into it instead, be my guest."

I don't know what I'd done to piss the Vyriat leader off, or when, but whatever it was, she'd been holding a grudge against me for quite some time. "Happy to oblige," I grated at her.

"Great—let your anger make the decision for you. Smart." Funny, Marus didn't *sound* complimentary. "Well, you're not going alone," he sighed. "I'll go with you."

"That's not for you to decide, Marus," Aoka told him pointedly, his boss trying to keep his operative alive.

"Actually, it is," Marus responded. "Khonnerhonn is gone, killed by the Pax. I don't have a ship—I won't be any good in the upcoming fight. I can at least help clear the guns."

"You'll need more help than that," Seamus said, ever the pragmatist. "The both of you. I'll ask for volunteers—"

"No. Absolutely not." Helliot again. Of course. "If she wants to throw her life away on a fool's errand, all the better, but we will *not* waste personnel on her execution. Neither Marus nor any of the security forces can be allowed to accompany her."

"The coming battle will take place in the void, Helliot," Criat sighed, looking at me with something like disappointment in his brown eyes. I couldn't blame him; if I'd been in charge of me, I'd want to slap me silly too. His agents were taught to keep themselves alive at all costs, and I'd just thrown that out the window. "The Pax aren't coming to assault Sanctum from the ground; they'll hang in orbit between the planet and the moon and pound us to dust with their long guns. A few platoons of tactical soldiers won't make a difference, even if we do get enough frigates running before they arrive to load up boarding parties."

"It's not worth a single soldier's life to—"

"I would spend the lives of every soldier under my command to ensure we get those guns back," Seamus undercut her. His tone was mild, but all the same, he was pissed. "And don't discount the abilities of the men and women under my command so easily. If I tell them to clear those guns, they'll clear those guns. Whether or not the guns'll be in any shape to use, after, well . . ." He threw MelWill a crooked grin. "That's engineering's problem."

"Great," MelWill sighed. "As if we didn't have enough to worry about."

"I would like to point something out at this juncture." John Henry's voice filled the auditorium; we all paused expectantly. He wasn't a member of the council per se, but as the AI responsible for most of Sanctum's functions, his voice carried a great deal of weight in the room. "Based on my analysis of the intelligence Marus has brought us, we have somewhere between a week and three before the Pax arrive, depending on whether or not they know *we* know they are on their way.

"A week may or may not be enough time to get the frigates up and running, and it may or may not be enough time to plan a worst-case-scenario evacuation, but it *is* enough time to try and reclaim the guns. Whether those attempts will succeed or fail, I have no way of telling; I have no sensors on the world below, or even on the emplacements on this very moon. But we *do* have plenty of time to at least try.

"This isn't an 'if/or' scenario; they can reconnoiter the emplacements, and decide then exactly what sort of force will be required to retake them from the Reint, if indeed it will be possible at all. In the meantime, there is plenty of other work to be done. Repairing the frigates, calling back the operatives we have scattered about the cosmos, seeding the bottleneck with mines and other traps to slow the inevitable Pax advance.

"If we are going to win this fight—and I won't bore you with calculations on what our odds are; suffice it to say they are *not* in our favor—we need to be working, not bickering. To succeed, every department of Sanctum will have to operate at their peak abilities, not spend time trying to undercut the others. You've achieved what you set out to achieve today—you're all aware of the threat, and the various steps that will need to be taken to counter it.

"I suggest adjourning at this point and letting each department start their own work. Further discussion will only belabor our differences, not remind us of our common cause: not just our own survival, but the survival of the work we do. It is not a hyperbolic statement to make to say that the fate of the entire galaxy is at stake here: not just from what the Pax may become if they abduct the children under our protection, but from what will occur if Sanctum— and the Justified—fall.

"The Pax intend to destroy us, in order to make themselves stronger. They do not care that in doing so, they may well doom the entire galaxy to another pulsed age, one that might make the current era seem a halcyon epoch in comparison. No one else in the galaxy is working to prevent the pulse from returning; no one else is aware of that inevitable threat, and it is not information we can share without endangering ourselves further. We are the line. Therefore, it falls to us to defend ourselves. There will be no help coming.

"Is there any disagreement on any of the points I have made?" You could almost feel the AI watching us all in turn, to see if anyone would object. They did not; John Henry was many things, but unreasonable had never been one of them. "Good. Then let us get to work."

"One more issue before we begin," Acheron said, pointing at me. "The stranger she has brought into our midst, and the traitor Javier Ortega. What will we do with them?"

"You could ask me directly, you know," the Preacher told her, her tone acidic at being so slighted by a member of her own race.

"I could, but the question wasn't for you," Acheron replied indifferently.

"Let them join her assault on the Reint," Helliot said with a shivering motion in her tentacles, the Vyriat equivalent of a shrug. "If they die with her, the problem is taken off our hands. If they do not, we can consider their success a mark in their favor."

"You're kind of a bitch, huh?" the Preacher asked mildly. I choked back a snort of laughter; it hadn't been what I was expecting.

"It's why she's so good at her job," Seamus said, a hint of a smile on his own face. "Do you object to joining the assault?"

"Do I have any choice?"

"Not really, no."

"So I guess I have no objections—no useful ones, at least." She sounded more like she was being dragged to some less-than-ideal social outing than being forced to face down prehistoric killing machines.

"Then there we go." Seamus turned back to me, and nodded. "I'll send word to my men to meet you at the armory. We won't be able to spare a craft, not with all the other work that'll need doing, so you'll have to give them a lift. You can resupply there if you need to."

"Will do," I nodded.

"Also, try not to get yourself killed," Seamus added, a full-on smile on his face this time. "We *really* need those guns."

"Will *also* do."

"One more thing," Criat rumbled. I winced; I'd worked for him long enough to know when he was pissed. "Before you take off on this daring adventure to commit suicide, kindly send Javier to me. I'd like a word with my wayward friend." Exploration and cartography had also fallen within my boss's purview; Javi had answered to Criat before he'd gone off the reservation. Several members of the council had blamed Criat's loose hand for Javier's actions. I doubted Javi was in for a fun conversation.

I grinned at my boss. "If I tell him that, he might take off running instead."

"Then knock his ass out and *drag* him to me. I have some words to exchange with him. Words about his parentage, and the sexual proclivities of his mother. What's the human expression I'm looking for?"

"Probably 'motherfucker,' my friend," Seamus answered him.

"Right. Motherfucker. I'll have to remember to call him that, specifically. It's always nice when you can insult someone in their own species's argot."

CHAPTER 10

On my way to the armory, I had Schaz tell Bolivar to tell Javier to meet Criat; at least I didn't have to do that in person. "What the hell have you gotten us into?" Marus asked me from my elbow as we walked.

"It seemed like a good idea at the time," I shrugged. All around us, Sanctum bustled with activity; the directors were already busy giving orders to their various units. We had a week, maybe more, but every single second would count. Sanctum had hidden us for a century—we'd never had an attack like this in our history in this place.

"Did it? Did it really?"

"You don't have to go along, you know," the Preacher told him.

"I know," he agreed with her. "I'm kind of regretting it."

"So why did you volunteer?"

He grinned at me. "It seemed like a good idea at the time."

I smiled back. Always nice to have friends.

We made our way through the city, back toward the hangars built into the mountainside, where the military installations were located—specifically, the armory. I'd visited often, since it also doubled as Seamus's quartermaster facility, where any outgoing agents picked up whatever gear they'd need. Ordinarily, I'd be getting chewed out for leaving behind so many working tools on Esa's homeworld, but we had bigger problems to worry about now.

Seamus's troops were already assembled, strapping on heavy ordnance. Their lieutenant was a Mahren named Sahluk, small for his species, which meant he only towered over me by a foot or so, his shoulders wider than Marus and me standing side by side. His rocky slate-like skin was shot through with veins of copper, making a strange contrast to the metal exosuit he was attaching around himself.

"You got us into some trouble, huh?" he said to me as I entered. Mahren can be kind of hard to read—their facial expressions tend to be incredibly subtle, meaning it was slightly hard to tell if he was being sarcastic or serious. I'd worked with Sahluk a few times before, though, and I was banking on the former.

"You know, just had a few strays follow me home," I returned his mild tone. "Nothing serious."

He chuckled. It sounded like a minor earthquake. "Well, good to have you back in the field," he said.

"I *knew* you weren't just a glorified babysitter," the Preacher told me.

"Yes, you're very smart," I sighed. "It helps that I *told* you I wasn't, multiple times."

"What, you didn't think she was a soldier?" Seamus asked the Preacher.

"I *knew* she *was*—she just wouldn't admit it, not outright."

Seamus laughed. "You've been spending too much time with Marus," he told me. "Some of that spycraft, keep-your-secrets-close nonsense is rubbing off on you."

"I am standing right here, Sahluk," Marus pointed out mildly.

"I didn't say you weren't *good* at it," Sahluk replied, feigning a slightly injured tone. "Just that it's not, you know, for everybody." He rapped his rocky knuckles against his exosuit, indicating the massive frame inside. "I'm not really built for covert infiltration."

"We all have our gifts," Marus shrugged.

Sahluk just laughed, turning back to me. "You want one of these?" he asked, tapping his exosuit again.

I considered it, but shook my head. The suits were great for heavy combat—if nothing else, they let you use far larger guns than any sentient species was strong enough to carry on its own. An exo-wearing trooper was a force to be reckoned with on a battlefield, simultaneously their own base of fire *and* forward cover for other troopers, given the heavy armor they wore. We weren't headed toward a conventional battlefield, though, and I had always valued speed and agility over sheer firepower.

"I'll let your guys handle the big guns," I told him. "I'll try to pick the Reint off before they can peel you out of those things like rations out of a tin can."

He nodded. "Suit yourself." With negligible effort—his own massive strength helped, but it was mainly the exosuit—he lifted a spare battery pack from the floor, and attached it to one of his crew, a big Wulf. She grunted with satisfaction as her suit powered up and she was able to actually move again, the fusion battery charging the servos and pistons that made up the suit. Sahluk checked the rest of his platoon; they were all suited up and powered on as well.

"You guys volunteered for this detail, right?" Marus asked him. We were headed into a bad situation; he wanted to make sure they all understood that.

"We did indeed," Sahluk replied. "You know how boring it gets around here with nothing to do but everyday policing? It's enough to make a fella wish for a minor riot."

"You should have been in there with the council before," the Preacher told him, her tone dry. "You almost got one."

He arched a coppery eyebrow at her. "Not impressed with Sanctum so far, outsider?"

"I'd hoped the forces that damned the galaxy would be slightly more impressive, yes. Instead you squabble like children, no different from the sects that you shut down."

"We're people, Barious. Just like other people."

"You didn't—"

"Stow it." This from one of Sahluk's platoon, a Barious herself. She pointed a metallic finger at the Preacher. "Everything you think you know, right now, everything you're feeling—it's been felt. You've got nothing new to add. You got dragged into this, fine, but now you've got an opportunity to *do* something. If you're going to take it, quit whining. If not, go back to pining for our creators to return and save you from having to make any decisions on your own. It won't *help*, but I'm sure it'll make you feel better."

A strange moment passed between the two of them as they stared each other down; I could tell by the slightly flickering light in their eyes that they were continuing their little exchange, information flowing between them at a far faster rate than auditory communication would allow. Whether their little consultation was a philosophical debate of ideas, or simply an exchange of Barious-specific anatomical and scatological insults, I had no idea.

Sahluk looked between the two of them. His big, exosuited hand curled into a fist. If it came to a fight, he could put either one of them through a goddamned wall, and that was without the suit's help. Barious were strong—built internally not far from the exosuits the soldiers wore, all servos and pistons and tensile strength—but Mahren were absolute forces of nature. "All good?" Sahluk asked his soldier quietly.

She tilted her head quizzically, still looking at the Preacher. "Depends," she said.

The Preacher gave a single sharp jerk of her head. Whatever they'd discussed in their little exchange of ideas, she hadn't liked it, but she wasn't bitching, either.

The other Barious nodded as well. "All good," she told Sahluk.

He reached down and hefted his primary weapon, already cabled to his exosuit: a semiautomatic grenade launcher that I wouldn't have been able to lift even if I *had* been suited up. "Then let's go kick some ass," he said.

I pointed at his weapon; it was the kind of gun you strapped on when you didn't just want to *storm* an enemy compound, you wanted to level it, and for whatever reason you couldn't do so from the air. "You know we want to leave the facility intact, right?" I asked.

He just grinned at me. It probably wasn't as comforting as he imagined.

CHAPTER 11

Making my way back to Scheherazade with a heavily armored platoon of exosuited shock troopers at my back made me feel like I was leading a terrible parade. The various streams of people headed here and there on their errands to harden Sanctum parted like a river as we passed. I didn't know if we could clear the two guns with just under twenty soldiers, but I felt a great deal better about our odds than when it had just been Javier, Marus, the Preacher, and myself.

Schaz, however, felt differently. "No," she said, broadcasting her dissent through the speakers near her ramp, so that all of Sahluk's troops could hear her. "No, no, no. They won't all fit. I'm not rated to carry—"

"You'll be fine, dear," I said soothingly, managing not to roll my eyes.

"We work hard to keep my interior clean—look at them! They're going to leak oil and lubricant all over my nice, shiny floors! I've had JackDoes working hard to clean out the mess Marus made by nearly dying in my medbay—JackDoes has apologized, by the way—"

"Am *I* supposed to?" Marus asked wryly; I shook my head.

Schaz was still in full voice. "—and there's no way twenty heavily armed soldiers aren't going to make *another mess*, right after I've gotten the first one all cleaned up."

"If JackDoes has apologized, why isn't your voice fixed?" I asked, trying to distract her.

It didn't work. "He says it will take a few cycles to boot back up—a week or so. Meanwhile—"

"Come on, Schaz. It's for the good of Sanctum."

"But my *floors!*"

Sahluk was laughing; I suppose he couldn't help it. Over the years, spending so much time with only Schaz for company, I'd given her significantly more . . . leeway, I suppose, to develop her own personality. Most agents had their ships reset after a while, to clear them of exactly this sort of hiccup, but I was resistant to that sort of thing. I hadn't really expected Schaz to develop a borderline obsessive-compulsive need for cleanliness—due, I'm sure, to my own spartan tendencies—but she had, anyway. It had become more and more pronounced over the last few years, and I would have felt boorish to ask one of the AI techs to purge her of a part of her personality just because it was occasionally an inconvenience.

"We promise, sir." Sahluk managed to stop chuckling long enough to get the words out.

"Ma'am," I corrected him, under my breath.

"Ma'am," he adjusted. "We'll take the utmost care with your floors. We may be big, but we're surprisingly graceful."

"You'd better," she grumbled.

"Oh, please tell me you fellas are here to arrest me." Javier was approaching, taking in the platoon of heavily armed soldiers standing around Schaz's ramp. The expression on his face told me that his conversation with Criat had been exactly as fun as I would have expected it to be. "Throw me in a cell; just don't let Criat shout at me again. He called me . . . *things*."

"No such luck, Ortega." Sahluk had shut down his friendly demeanor; apparently, he wasn't exactly pleased to be partnered up with a theoretical traitor on this mission.

Javi looked Sahluk up and down. "We going to have a problem?" he asked.

"You planning to betray Sanctum again?"

"No," Javier shrugged. "But I didn't think I was doing that the first time, either."

"Let it lie, boss." This from one of Sahluk's people, his sergeant, by the rank bars on his suit. A Tyll—not what you would expect from security, but people are allowed to stray from their species's typical cultural roles, after all.

Sahluk looked Javier up and down once more. "Yeah," he said finally. He turned, and marched up Scheherazade's lowered ramp without another word.

"Appreciate it," Javi told the Tyll sergeant.

The sergeant gave him a wry grin. "Not as much as I do," he said. "My family and I were on board the refugee fleet you saved from the Filt. Sanctum may have a long memory as far as what happened that day, but we're part of Sanctum now, and we don't forget either." With a whine of servos in his exosuit, he held out an armored hand to Javi. Javier shook it, and grinned.

"My genuine pleasure, sir," he said.

"Right." I sighed. "Can we get on board and start this suicide mission already? I can practically feel Schaz having a nervous breakdown about her floors."

CHAPTER 12

We packed inside Scheherazade. It felt uncomfortably like being sealed inside a ration pack. Thankfully, my seat in the cockpit was relatively free of hulking security officers in heavy exosuits, so once I squeezed past I still had some elbow room. Javier and the Preacher took the main consoles while Marus folded down one of the jump seats, with Sahluk sliding in and standing next to him; the rest got as comfortable as they could in the living quarters. I think one of them wound up standing in the shower.

"With this much weight on board, I don't know that I'm even going to be able to break atmosphere," Schaz grumbled, but she proceeded to do just that, taking us out of the hangar and into orbit around the world Sanctum hung above, all icy winds and frozen mountain ranges.

"All right," I said to Sahluk, turning in my chair. "We've got two guns to check and clear, both on the planet below us." I tapped a few buttons on Schaz's control panel, and turned the cockpit window into a viewscreen. A tactical view of the freezing planet lit up the glass, showing topography and rough estimates of the Reint populations.

Unlike the moon housing Sanctum, the world below us hadn't quite been locked on its axis, its rotation instead had just slowed to a crawl. Viewed as a gunnery position, that was ideal—it meant that the cannons wouldn't rotate out of their firing solution for quite some time. From the perspective of clearing the emplacements, though, it made things more difficult.

The various chaos that had been done to the system had led to extreme global warming on this particular world, but the longer any given side of the planet faced away from the binary stars the colder it grew, the bleak constant night broken only by a sliver of sunlight from the other binary star every few chronological days. The deep cold would hamper our efforts, but hopefully it would also make the Reint slightly sluggish, due to their cold-blooded physiology.

"The first gun—Alpha—is up in the mountains, here." I indicated a position on a raised piece of topography. In the living quarters behind me, the holoprojector was displaying the same map and marking where I was touching, and Schaz was transmitting my voice to the soldiers back there as well. "That's the safest bet; it's colder, which means it's less likely the devolved Reint will have turned it into a hunting ground. For the upcoming fight, though, it's not as useful to us—it doesn't have an angle on Sanctum, which means it won't have an angle on any dreadnaughts that get into orbit *over* Sanctum, just on their approach."

I shifted the map south, the topographical ridges fading away as I moved the view to an area lower on the planet's surface. "The second gun—Bravo—is about a thousand kilometers away from the first, closer to the equator. It *does* have an angle on Sanctum, and it will also be the easier gun for the engineers to bring back online, because its fusion reactor is still running. Just a trickle, but still running."

"The pulse didn't take that out?" the Preacher asked.

I shook my head. "This world got knocked back pre-spaceflight, not prefusion. Most of our higher-tier weapons will get chewed through by the rads eventually, and the exosuits too, but fusion energy in general remains unaffected."

"And the reason we're not heading to Bravo automatically?" Sahluk asked. "If it's both the more useful gun, and the easiest to bring back online?"

"Because it's warmer, both by its equatorial placement and *because* the fusion reactor's still running. It's also smack in the middle of a prior population center. Heat mapping shows high concentrations of Reint still living there over the years, which means it may be crawling with hostiles, especially given the warmth of the reactor."

"So it's the harder target."

"Significantly, yes."

"How do you know all this?" the Preacher asked me. "I've been with you since we arrived; you didn't have time to do this much research."

Marus grinned at her. "Criat has been trying to convince the council to retake the guns for decades," he said. "He's spent that whole time forcing his agents to study the various emplacements, just on the off chance he ever actually won his argument with Helliot; she's had this assault in the back of her mind since we first settled on Sanctum."

"When *you* settled on Sanctum, *I* was still getting shot at in the chaos left in the wake of the pulse bomb," I reminded him dryly. "But, yes; I've known for a long time I'd be involved, one way or another, in a campaign to reclaim the cannons. Eventually."

"We take the hard target first," Sahluk said decisively, reaching up to tap the hologram. "Bravo emplacement. If we succeed, it'll take the engineers less time to get it back online, because its reactor is still active, and they can be ready to move on the other facility in short order. If we get repulsed, we can always pull back, try for Alpha instead. Once we're successful there we can retreat back to Sanctum and beg for enough reinforcements to try *again* at Bravo gun, while the engineers get to work on Alpha."

"Got it. Scheherazade?"

"Laying in a course," she confirmed. "Bravo target selected."

"Do you have a closer view of the facility?" Sahluk asked.

I zeroed in on the map, bringing up a composite of satellite imagery. Sahluk frowned; I couldn't blame him. There was nothing good about the position.

The anti-orbital cannon had been the centerpiece of a military installation built directly into the middle of a major metropolitan area—a common tactic during the sect wars. By building the facilities that would be targets for enemy raids in the midst of civilian populations, any enemy that wanted to attack was in for street-by-street fighting if they went in on foot, or would be forced to inflict massive civilian casualties if they tried bombarding the site from orbit.

Some sects wouldn't have cared, but others with more open-minded philosophies wouldn't have wanted to risk the backlash that would have arisen from their own citizens in the light of indiscriminate civilian murder, not to mention hardening the will of whatever insurgency was left on the bombarded world.

What *that* meant was that the gun had become one of the few sources of warmth for the Reint who had survived the devastation of their world—the only place for miles where they could rouse from the cold-blooded torpor enough to start a hunt. The rest was just crumbling city, warrens of concrete. The Reint were crammed nearly on top of each other inside the complex, or as close as their predatory instincts could stand.

"I had my platoon load fence-linked turrets into your hold," Sahluk said, turning away from the map. "We'll have to set those up in a perimeter around the facility, facing outward—that will hold off the Reint attacking from outside the position. Hopefully most of those in the interior will be off hunting, and we'll be able to construct the perimeter before they can get back."

"Don't lose your tags," his sergeant—the Tyll from the refugee fleet—added. "Those are what'll keep the turrets from targeting you if you wind up in front of the guns. They'll shoot at anything that moves, otherwise." The Preacher and Javier had been given provisional tags earlier—Marus and I wore them constantly anyway, so we were good there.

I nodded to Sahluk; it was a good plan. "You've fought devolved Reint before," I said.

"I have," he agreed. "Have you?"

I pulled down the collar of my jacket, showing off an ugly scar running up the side of my neck. "Yeah, you have," he agreed. "So you understand. Reint don't hunt in packs, but they will *watch* each other. If they see a few getting blasted to pieces by turrets or electrified by a shield fence, they'll learn where *not* to attack."

"But while we're setting up the fences, we'll still have to deal with both the Reint coming at us from the city, and those from inside the installation itself," I pointed out. "We'll be hit from both sides."

"Two options, then," he said. "We can stick together in one group, setting up the turrets one by one. Safer, but also slower, which means more time for the Reint to attack. Second option would be to split into two teams, each take a direction on the perimeter, meet back up on the far side. Faster, but each group would have half as many guns."

"There will be more Reint out in the city than inside the facility itself, even with the reactor warming the place," the Preacher pointed out. "As you said: they'll be hunting. My vote—if I get one—would be for the two teams, to shut that angle of approach off as soon as possible."

"Easy for you to say," Javier pointed out, his voice a touch sour. "You're made of metal; they're not going to try and *eat* you."

"They *will* try and eat me," I put in, "and I still vote for the second option. We're on a timetable here. A week or so may seem like a long time now, but every extra hour we can buy means more time for the engineers to work on the gun, more time for them to tweak it, to increase range, power flow, accuracy, all those sorts of things. Faster outweighs safer here."

"Unless we lose people doing things the faster way," Marus pointed out. "That just means clearing the facility itself will go slower, in the long run. And we'll be down another gun in the fight to come."

"It's your platoon," I told Sahluk. "It's your choice."

He stared at the screen a moment longer. "Faster," he agreed. "Two teams. Not *just* because we want the gun up and running as soon as possible, but because the longer we're making a commotion without the fences up, the more Reint are going to be drawn toward us from the outlying districts of the city."

"Also, I'll have to bug out after I drop the turrets," Schaz pointed out. "Too many rads. I can feed you scans from orbit, but those won't do you much good when you're inside the facility itself. It's hardened against that kind of observation, because of course it is, it was a military installation. Still, once I've cooled off in orbit for a while, I can swing back down, try and create a firewall between you and the rest of the city. If nothing else, I'll bring some of the buildings down—give you a clear line of sight, and hopefully make so much noise doing it that I scare some of the Reint off."

"Shock and awe," Sahluk grinned. "It's been, what, ten generations since these Reint have even seen spacecraft? In their devolved state, they won't have any way to contextualize why a thing flying through the sky is burning them to a crisp. I like it."

"Speaking of rads, though, it is hot down there," I pointed out to Sahluk. I tapped at the pauldron of his exosuit with one knuckle. "These won't last forever; the tech will cook out."

"Maybe not, but they'll last long enough for us to set up a perimeter, especially since we're taking the faster path," he said, before grinning at me. "Criat's agents aren't the only ones who have been planning this op for a while, you know."

Marus smiled slightly. "I *thought* Seamus was more eager than I expected him to be to dive into this," he said.

"The boss has never had as much faith as . . . certain other council members that the difficult navigational aspects of this system would be enough to protect us forever," Sahluk replied. "He likes his contingencies."

I grinned at that. Seamus had been born Justified—unlike myself or Javier, who'd been inducted later in life. He knew departmental politics backward and forward, and unlike Criat, who had a typically Wulf-like lack of restraint when it came to holding his temper, Seamus was perfectly capable of playing three council sides against each other for whatever he considered the greater good. Justified were a lot of things, but we tended toward ruthless pragmatism, as a rule.

"And after your tech *does* go?" Javier asked Sahluk. "Once your fancy suits are no good, we'll still have to clear the gun installation itself, you know."

Sahluk raised a stony eyebrow at him. "We may spend most of our time on Sanctum, but that doesn't mean we're not trained for rad-soaked combat," he replied, his tone cold. "We can strip out of the suits in less than three seconds, and we all carry ballistic backups. Don't worry your pretty little head, Ortega—we may not have as much firepower going into the facility as we do on landing, but we'll still keep you safe from the scary Reint. Unless, you know, we decide not to."

Marus sighed. "Can you two be dicks to each other later?" he asked.

"If there is a later, sure," Javier shrugged. "I can even be a dick in the middle of a firefight, if I have to."

"That much I remember," Marus told him dryly.

"So." I stared at the satellite feed for a moment longer, almost willing myself to see the Reint holed up in the crumbling buildings. I couldn't, of course—for one, some of these images were years old, if not decades, and for another, devolved Reint were very, very good at hiding. "That's the plan."

"That's the plan," Sahluk nodded.

"Schaz, give me a weather report on the city."

"There's a storm front moving in, and it looks like once it gets there, it'll stay awhile," she replied promptly. "Not just rain, either—freezing sleet and hail mixed in, just short of snow."

"Wonderful."

CHAPTER 13

Schaz threaded her way through the field of debris that encircled the nearly frozen world, found a path through, and plunged into the atmosphere below. The radiation alarms started squawking immediately; I shut them off with an irritated slap. Schaz knew what she was doing.

We hit the storm front before we were above Bravo itself, our view of the approach limited to boiling clouds and sheets of icy rainfall. Scheherazade spent the flight muttering about her paint job.

She took us lower, down through the clouds, and suddenly the city—the former city—loomed below us. Even after decades of landing on worlds shut down by the pulse, it was hard to ignore the strange twitch at the base of my spine that came from seeing buildings unlit, streets abandoned, structures half-collapsed under the weight of time and lack of maintenance. I knew *why* it was that way, but that didn't stop it from reading as wrong, off, strange.

The cannon was the biggest thing in the former metropolis, of course, towering over the other buildings by several magnitudes. Its scale didn't fit with everything around it—it seemed less a part of the silent city than something out of place, a tool dropped by some world—striding colossus rather than the installation the rest of the settlement had grown up around. Still, there were lights, here and there, in the complex of buildings below, barely visible through the rain: the reactor was still active. Even after all these years. The Reint sect that had occupied this city had built their fusion tech to *last*, I'd give them that.

Shame we were about to drop on top of a nest of their bloodthirsty descendants.

As the big gun loomed above us, Schaz did a slow circle of the complex, dropping the turrets as she went, the occasional flash of lightning illuminating the cracked concrete below, her target areas. We'd have to set up the weapons ourselves, and we couldn't bring them online until they were all connected: linked, they could resist pulse radiation for quite some time, reinforcing each other and drawing the radiation in a continuous loop around the facility. If we activated them before that connection was established, however, the rads would eat away at their guts, make them useless before we could get any work done on the gun.

"I won't be able to set down," Schaz told us. "You'll have to use the ropes."

"Yeah, I figured," I agreed. "Get us into position above the southernmost turret position. Do a sweep if you can, then get out of this atmosphere before the rads start to play merry hell with your internals."

"It always feels like I'm running a mild fever when I do this," she sighed, more to herself than anyone else.

Sahluk's troops had already pressed themselves close to the airlock; it whined open, and Scheherazade dropped descent ropes down to the ground. The storm roared past her ramp, sucking all the heat from the interior of the ship. The soldiers descended three at a time, one to each rope, leaping into the teeth of the lashing rain.

Marus, Javier, and I were the last out; I checked my rifle, then grabbed the swinging line. "Stay safe," Schaz told me.

"You too," I replied, then stepped out into the storm.

I slid downward through the freezing rain, touching down on the cracked pavement below. Sahluk's troops had already formed a loose circle around the first turret, and the Preacher was kneeling beside the hunk of inert metal, along with the other Barious, both of them with palms pressed against its side, communicating with the computer within in ways that only their kind understood.

"Any movement?" I asked Sahluk, having to shout to be heard over the storm.

He shook his stony head, surveying the buildings that rose up out of the rain around us, looming up like ghosts of the civilization that had once spanned this world. In this mess, the Reint might be right on top of us before we'd even notice.

"Maybe we're lucky, and the storm's keeping them inside," Javier suggested, standing close to me with his own rifle raised.

"In all your life, have you ever been lucky?" I asked him.

"Well, I met you," he shrugged, still not taking his eyes off the buildings beyond. It was an unexpectedly sweet thing to say.

"How long at each gun?" I asked the Preacher, mainly because I didn't know how to respond to Javi.

"Almost . . . there," she replied. "Almost . . . done. It's online." She and the other Barious stood; the gun gave a quiet whine, barely audible over the patter of the frozen rain, but otherwise was unchanged. It wouldn't try to go active until we'd networked it with the others.

"Move," Sahluk barked at his men, all business now that we were in enemy territory. "Squads one and two, circle the perimeter clockwise. You see something, don't shout, just fire. There's nothing but hostiles here. Squad three, you're with me and our guests, counterclockwise. The faster we get this done, the faster we can get inside the facility and out of this fucking rain." I don't know if the cold actually bothered the big Mahren that much, but he knew it would be uncomfortable for his troopers.

The two groups split apart; the second Barious went with the clockwise group, so that each of us would have a synthetic to "speak" with the turrets. Our merry little band moved on through the rain, making our way to the second gun, the empty city spreading out around us like a landscape from perdition.

The second turret gave us little trouble, and no sign of Reint yet.

The third was slightly harder to get to. Schaz had dropped it onto the roof of a building just outside the chain-link fence that ran around the installation. A good idea in theory, and useful placement once we got the guns online, but its elevation meant we had to climb up *to* the turret before we could even start to get it activated.

Sahluk and most of his squad stayed behind on the ground, covering the facility, leaving my team to climb up the structure to the turret, easier for us without the added bulk of the exosuits. Granted, Sahluk's team could have made their way up the structure by using the brute force of the suits to punch through the walls for handholds, but the state the building was in, that might have brought the whole thing crashing down.

Climbing slick concrete in freezing rain: not very fun.

Still, we made it up to the roof without incident, and the Preacher knelt by the turret while Javier, Marus, and I went splitting off to different corners to watch the silent city beyond the structure.

It was almost like the city was sleeping, like we were in the dead of night, and as soon as the sun arose and the blanket of rain swept away the nonexistent citizens would wake, would turn on their lights, and this place would go back to the way it should be. It never would, of course—even if our best future came to be and the return of the pulse was averted by the ultimate efforts of the gifted children I and the other operatives had gathered, pulsed worlds world still *be* pulsed; there was no changing that. Not to mention the fact that *this* world was still ruined, had been ruined long *before* the pulse— but that was what it looked like, anyway.

The sharp crack of a rifle shot, and a brief flash of muzzle flare in the darkness: Javier's corner. I ignored the impulse to run over to him and provide more fire, kept my eyes peeled on my own section of the city, my HUD dancing with overlays, trying to scan for any kind of movement out in the rain. "What have you got?" I shouted into my comms.

"Movement," he replied. "A half-dozen of them, at least. They scattered when I winged one of them, but they'll be back."

That was when Sahluk's squad below opened fire, the sound coming from the opposite end of the roof, back in the direction of the facility. The Reint had figured out we were here.

CHAPTER 14

This time I *did* run to the far side of the roof, back toward the Preacher and the turret. That was far too much gunfire coming from Sahluk's squad. A shot here and there, to pick off individual Reint creeping toward us, sure—much like what I'd heard from Javier—but this was sustained, and it was frantic, and it was only getting worse.

As I approached the edge of the roof I slid through the wash of water, coming up in a firing position on one knee, my rifle already raised, seeking targets. There were plenty to choose from.

The Reint were absolutely *boiling* out of the facility, their mottled scales twisting together, giving them the appearance of halos from where the rain was bouncing off their ever-so-slightly iridescent skin. They were charging Sahluk's position; he and his men were letting loose, their big guns roaring, tearing through the darkness and the rain to chase the Reint across the open ground, but there were a great many targets to choose from, and they were *fast*, so much faster than their civilized counterparts. You forget the advantages we lost by hundreds of thousands of years of purposefully suppressing the predator side of our nature.

This was wrong. This was all, all wrong. Devolved Reint didn't act like this. They didn't attack en masse, they didn't move in groups, they didn't work together at *all*. I thought I could even hear them *communicating*, a strange tonal collection of whistles and cries, just below the chaos of the gunfire. That was wrong too—that wasn't what Reint *did*, not how they spoke, devolved or otherwise. This was very, very wrong.

Time to worry about that later. For now, there were targets, and they were attacking, and while they weren't anywhere close to overrunning Sahluk's position, the more he and his men used their big guns, the faster they'd invite the pulse radiation to render their weapons useless hunks of metal that they'd have to leave behind.

Every aggressor I put down with my rifle—still the same gunpowder-round weapon I always carried on rad-soaked worlds, nothing about it inviting degradation by the radiation in the atmosphere—was one fewer the soldiers below would have to fire on, one less shot to eat through the rad shielding on their guns.

I let my HUD mark targets until my vision was swarming with red dots like aggressive fireflies, and then I started chasing them, letting them lead my rifle barrel, then overtaking them as they slowed or changed position—which they did rapidly and without warning—and firing in the split-second pause before they started moving again. I'm not saying I hit every shot, but I landed my share. This wasn't the first time I'd fought devolved Reint, and no matter that their behavior was odd, they still *moved* the same. Fast.

"How we doing on that turret, Preacher?" I shouted over the rain and the gunfire.

"Almost there!" she shouted back.

"Javi? Marus?" They were still in their positions on the corners of the roof behind me; I couldn't hear them firing, but that might have simply been because of the cacophony below.

"Movement, but they're not coming forward!" Marus shouted back. "I don't—"

"Oh, fuck yes they are!" And now Javier was definitely firing, and I cursed, making a decision, right or wrong. I spun and stood and raced back to their side of the roof, reloading my rifle as I went.

The Reint in the city were pouring out of the buildings now, the same way they were coming out of the facility, and there were a *lot* of them. They were behaving just as oddly as the Reint attacking Sahluk below, moving almost like birds on the wing, as if ruled by a single collective mind. Regardless, they were coming teeth bared and claws out, trying to climb the building and have us for dinner.

We didn't have the firepower Sahluk's team did, and there were a great many *more* Reint on our side. "Preacher!" I shouted, firing down as fast as I could, trying to pick the reptilian forms off even as they climbed, their claws anchoring them as steadily as if they'd pounded in pitons.

"Done!" she shouted back, standing away from the turret.

Our comms buzzed to life: Sahluk. "Jump!" he shouted. "We'll spread a—"

We didn't wait; we knew what he was going to say. All three of us—Marus, Javier, and I—bolted to that side of the roof and simply leapt, not even looking. We fell with the freezing rain, then hit the antigrav field below before we could smash into the concrete and break half the bones in our bodies. The field collapsed, boiled away by the rads, but we were unharmed and we were down and the turret was up.

The Preacher, of course, hadn't trusted Sahluk's field; she'd just jumped, well clear of the building, trusting her metal construction to handle the landing instead. She wasn't wrong, though the long-abandoned vehicle she crushed where she hit didn't take it nearly as well.

"Move!" I shouted to Sahluk. "Move to the next turret! They are *still fucking coming!*"

And they were.

CHAPTER 15

We moved as a mobile base of fire, the heavy guns of Sahluk's squad cutting us a path to the next turret. The Reint had realized by now that a direct attack wasn't getting them anywhere—they may have been devolved, but not so far that they couldn't recognize the corpses of their own kind, burnt down and scattered across the rain-slick pavement. Now, they watched, and hid, scrambling through the downpour, trying to find somewhere to lay in ambush.

Or, most of them did: some of the others were busy claiming the corpses of the fallen. Enough fauna had survived on this world that life hadn't gone extinct, there *was* still a food chain—on which the Reint sat comfortably on top—but that didn't mean prey was *easy* to come by, and cannibalism had become a common trait in the pre-sapient Reint wasteland that had once been a thriving metropolis.

The Preacher got the next turret up and running before the massed Reint charged again. Four down, four to go. The devolved predators hissed and screamed in the distance, both inside the complex to our left and out in the city; it sounded like the storm had come alive, thick with fury and howls.

"We can't keep this up for much longer," Sahluk warned me. "We weren't expecting this kind of opposition; our suits won't hold up to the rads if we're burning energy this fast."

"Why are they doing this?" Javier asked. "Why are they behaving this way? It doesn't make any sense."

I shook my head. "Doesn't matter. It's been dozens of generations since the pulse; they've been changed by it, just like every other world was changed. We know our objectives: get the turrets up, clear the gun. We need to keep moving."

Sahluk launched a grenade into an outbuilding on our path to the next turret; the round smashed through a mostly broken window and exploded inside with a dull thump. The metal of the building split and caved, and Reint came boiling out into the rain, looking for new cover. If he'd left it alone, our path would have taken us right beside the structure, and they would have been close enough to use their talons and fangs before we knew they were there.

"This turret's up," the Preacher reported, standing from beside her target.

"Good. Move," Sahluk said, reloading his launcher.

That was when a lone Reint came out of nowhere and hit him from the side, its claws scrabbling at his suit. The big Mahren cried out in pain and fury, dropping to one knee to try and hold it off—it couldn't get through the metal, but he still had exposed skin where the suit gapped, and as hard as his flesh was compared to other species', it wasn't as hard as Reint talons.

I drew my pistol, put it to the side of the Reint's head, and fired, blowing its brains out into the rain. Sahluk pushed the corpse off of him and stood, bleeding. He had a nasty gash across his cheek, but at least it wasn't high enough that the blood would get into his eyes. "I hate this place," he growled.

"Whatever happened to being excited to see some action?" Javier asked him.

"There's action and then there's a clusterfuck," he replied, lifting his grenade launcher again. "We're firmly into the latter territory."

"They're massing for another charge," the Preacher warned, her ocular implants seeing farther in the frozen rain than any of us could. "Between us and the next turret."

"We go through them," Sahluk said. "We—"

"Oh, dear." Scheherazade, on my comms. "This seems worse than I'd expected. There really are a great *many* of them, aren't there?"

"Tell me you're on approach," I begged her.

"I am indeed. You might want to tell everyone else in your party to hold still."

I turned to the others. "Scheherazade's coming in hot!" I shouted. "Don't move!"

I hoped they heard me, because before I could say anything else, Schaz had appeared out of the stormy skies, her guns blazing.

She was using her forward cannon to blast apart the buildings closest to the fence line, scattering Reint in any given direction as they tried to escape the fire and the rubble. Those that moved further back into the city survived—those that moved closer to us found themselves in the firing solution of the lasers mounted on her wings. The blue lines of heat carved in arcane figures across the pavement, leaving a path of glowing orange behind them—and the corpses of our attackers, of course, most cut right the hell in two.

Even over the wash of the thunderstorm, the smell was horrific, burning flesh and seared metal. By the time Schaz moved on, there wasn't a Reint left standing anywhere out in the open. They were fast, but not faster than sustained laser fire.

"Go!" I shouted to the others almost as soon as she'd headed off to make her circle of the entire compound. "Get to the next turret before they can recover!"

CHAPTER 16

Schaz had bought us time—time we desperately needed. We moved along the path of the destruction she'd wreaked, a terrible study of contrasts—the heat coming off the fires left behind in her lasers' wake stark against the waves of freezing cold rain still lashing us from the skies above. The Preacher got the next turret up, and the next, without the Reint launching another sustained counterattack.

By the time we'd reached the second-to-last turret, though, they'd recovered, howling like mad out in the storms. I don't know how many Reint were out in the city, but it felt like we'd killed at least half a hundred of them, not even counting Scheherazade's bombardment, and they just kept coming. We'd had another handful of close calls as Reint who'd hidden themselves in our path leapt out in ambush, but we'd managed to get clear of them without any casualties so far.

We were close enough to the end of our circuit that, from our position at the second-to-last turret, we could actually see the other squads through the rain, those that had gone counterclockwise around the facility. At least one of them carried a flame unit, and the waves of fire made it easy to pick out their position. We'd both reach the last turret at roughly the same time.

"Sergeant," Sahluk told his second in command, the Tyll who had been one of the refugees Javier had rescued. "Take these two and make for that last turret." He gestured at Javi and me, not even taking his hand off his gun. "Set up a base of fire so you can support the other squads on their way to join you."

"You sure that's wise?" I asked him. "We're already split up as it is."

"The sooner you can clear the area around the turret, the sooner we can get it up and running," he replied. "The sooner you can do *that*, the sooner all we have to worry about is what's inside the facility. I'll breathe a lot easier with those big guns online, keeping the bastards in the city back."

I nodded, and dashed off into the rain: he was in command, it was his call. My rifle held close to my chest, I concentrated on *moving*, on clearing the open ground as fast as possible, trusting in the others to cover me as my footfalls slapped against the wet pavement.

The last turret was on another rooftop, a former carpark, I think. Even through the rain I could hear the hissing noises of the Reint holed up inside, the sound of clicking talons on the concrete giving away their position.

The sergeant—who was carrying a big laser repeater, an only slightly smaller version of the guns Schaz had used to cook her way through the waves of the Reint—hit the building first, just ahead of me; he busted in a window and opened fire, destroying the vehicles within that the predators had been using for cover. I stood right beside him and picked my shots, Reint backlit by the flames inside as they darted away from the chaos his big gun had unleashed. Javier covered the both of us, firing at the Reint coming from the facility itself, streaming across the open ground, drawn by the noise and fire of our attack.

"Go on up; clear the roof," the sergeant told us. "I'll hold here."

"No," I shook my head. "I'm not leaving you alone in this mess; no way."

He frowned at me. "I'm second in command to—"

"You're not in command of us, friend," Javier told him wryly. "And trust me: giving her orders has never achieved anything. For anyone. Ever."

The Tyll sergeant opened his mouth to respond; that was when the Reint dropped on him from the roof above.

Its weight carried him to the ground, his cannon caught between its body and his own. I couldn't shoot—the round would go right through the smaller creature and hit the sergeant—so I hit it with my rifle butt instead, trying to draw its attention, but it was intent on its victim, clawing and slashing as he screamed. It hissed, a different sound from the noise the others had made before—guttural, almost gurgling—and we all knew what was coming and there wasn't time to do a damned thing to stop it.

The Reint had evolved a great deal of predatory tools in the millions of years between crawling out of the rough seas and becoming the dominant predator on their homeworld. An innate knowledge of ambush tactics; talons, fangs, the spike on the tip of their tail; dense muscle tissue that made them far stronger than their smallish size would seem; a kind of minor echolocation, which was what most of their hisses and howls were likely about.

One of the other abilities they had, though, was one modern Reint almost never used—some had even evolved past it, the organs vestigial and useless—which was why we'd forgotten they *could*: the ability to spit out a cloud of caustic expectorant.

The Reint on top of the sergeant spat it directly in his face.

He screamed, horribly. I dropped my rifle and grabbed the Reint underneath the bunched muscles of its forearms, hauling backward and ducking at the same time as it twisted to try and bite at me. I couldn't make it let go of the exosuit, but I at least pulled its upper body back, and that gave Javier a clear shot at its head, which he blew clean off.

The sergeant was still screaming. I let both of them drop, then pushed my way past the dead Reint—even without a head, its muscle memory meant it still had a tight grip on his suit—and fumbled at the aid spray on my belt. Javi got there first, discharging an entire canister into the Tyll's face, then jamming his hand through the hardening foam, right into the sergeant's mouth. It couldn't have been comfortable for either of them, but at least when he pulled his hand back, the man could *breathe*, though those breaths were coming fast and shallow, broken only by moans of pain.

A clicking sound behind me was my only warning; still kneeling beside the downed Tyll, I drew my pistol and turned, firing even as the Reint leapt from the window we'd just been standing in. That was the thing about devolved Reint—give them even a fraction of an opportunity, and they'd take it.

I managed to get two shots off, both of which hit the creature center mass, but they weren't enough to stop the predator's momentum, and he hit me full-on, still snapping and slashing even as death took hold. *I* wasn't wearing a fancy exosuit, and I took a couple of nasty gashes before I could throw the dying Reint off me and put another round through its skull.

"*Fuck,*" I swore, just on general principle, kneeling in the rain and reloading my revolver, empty shell casings spilling from my fingers as I pulled them clear. Javier was firing in every direction, trying to cover both me and the sergeant; ignoring my wounds for now, I holstered the reloaded revolver then picked up my rifle again, doing the same. Both squads were closing on our position—we had been meant to lay down fire for their approach, but now it was the other way around as they fired into the Reint striking for us.

The Preacher reached us first, firing with the strange arm-cannon I'd last seen her use on the observation tower; she took in the scene at a glance, realized we were capable of covering ourselves, and leapt for a drainpipe on the side of the building, shimmying up the length of it in a manner not entirely unlike the Reint themselves.

"Go after her," I told Javi, taking up position beside the wounded sergeant and firing toward the Reint charging at us from the facility. "I got this here, and she'll need cover."

He nodded, and went, moving quickly up the same pipe, if not quite as quickly as the Preacher.

Sahluk reached me next, the rest of his men shortly behind. I made sure to pick out Marus; no, I didn't want any of Sahluk's people to have been hurt either, we were all Justified, but Marus was my friend.

Sahluk knelt beside his sergeant, checking for a pulse. "He's still alive," I told him, "and stable. But he's out of this fight." And probably scarred for life. Medical nanotech is good for a great many things, but there are some kinds of damage even the tiny machines couldn't undo. I didn't know it for a fact, but I'd imagine getting a faceful of highly caustic gas was one of them.

Sahluk's rocky eyelids fluttered for a moment, making his face look like a mountainside under the waterfall of the wash of rain. It was the only sign that he was regretting his call. That was part of being a leader—not just making the decisions, but bottling up your guilt when a decision you'd made went bad. We might have lost someone else if we'd stayed together, but then again, we might not, and he'd have to live with that.

A high-pitched hum cut through the chaos of the storm, and then there was a flash of light; the Preacher had the last turret up and running, and all of the units were online now. Beams of solid green arched out from the turret beside her to the next on either side, and from there to the next, and from there to the *next*, and then the automated guns were roaring, chewing through the city, picking out telltale signs of Reint movement and pouring lead into those positions. At least one made a dash for the grid of laser, diving for a gap in the bright green lines: it was promptly flash-fried as the lasers detected his approach and sliced downward, the corpse dropping to either side of the pavement, both halves still smoking even in the icy rain.

The perimeter was established; we were safe from attack from the city. Now we just had the facility to clear.

CHAPTER 17

In addition to the Tyll sergeant, two members of the other teams had been injured. None as badly as our man, but they were both out of the fight, on the casualty lists. Another had been killed outright, the Wulf Sahluk had been fitting with an exosuit when I'd first joined the platoon. I hadn't even learned her name. I could try and deny it, but the truth was, I'd avoided that on purpose—I'd known we weren't all going home.

Would we have avoided those losses if we'd stayed in one group? Maybe. Or maybe we would have taken more; maybe we wouldn't have been able to get the turret perimeter up at all, and would have been forced to retreat. A call had been made; now we had to live with it.

We winched the wounded, and the body of the fallen, back up to Schaz. Marus went with them, to keep them stable on the trip back to Sanctum. He'd return with the first batch of engineers, those who would be working on the anti-orbital cannon, and those who would be keeping the turret perimeter running. In the rad-soaked atmosphere of this world, it would take constant maintenance to keep the fence and the gun active.

The Reint had stopped charging the barrier. The guns had laid out enough corpses in the rain that the others, those who had been watching, had realized this was a target they couldn't penetrate. As we worked to load the wounded onto Scheherazade, we saw others, scavengers, slither through the mist and the downpour to steal away with the corpses of their own dead, making meals out of those who had tried and failed to breach the perimeter. The weak feeding on the strong until they became strong themselves. There was something uncomfortably similar to Pax philosophy in that.

Schaz headed back out, and we were alone again in the rain.

"What does a downpour like this make you think of?" Javier asked the question as we watched Schaz vanish into the rolling mass of clouds.

I thought about it for a moment, my rifle still cradled in my arms. "The front, on the world where I was raised," I said finally, still staring up into the storm. "When it rained like this, the enemy snipers couldn't get a clear shot. Ours, either. Meant you were more likely to turn a corner and find an enemy patrol, just as lost as you were."

He was staring at me; I could tell, even though I was still watching the skies, thinking back. Everything had always come back around to war. Seemed like it always did. Didn't know if that was about me, or if that was just the way the galaxy worked.

"That's not what I think of," he told me.

"Then what?" I asked.

I could hear the smile in his voice when he said, "I think of that cloud-burst we got caught in, our first mission together. We were trying to break through the Antioch perimeter, to get to the spaceport and get clear, and then all of a sudden it was just *pouring*, and we were freezing, hunted, and lost. You remember that?"

"I remember that," I replied, the words almost lost in the storm. He'd kissed me. No; I'd kissed him. It had been a harder fight than it should have, to get clear, after, because we—

No point in dwelling on that. No point in thinking about it. It was done; it was past; we couldn't get it back. I didn't know why he was even mentioning it now.

"All that we went through, after." He shook his head again. "All I'd gone through, before." He was still staring at me. "I'm still glad I kissed you."

"I kissed *you*," I told him with a frown, turning to face him.

"Yeah," he grinned back, shifting his rifle in his arms. "Maybe."

I shook my head, went back to watching the sky. Schaz was long gone. No point in dwelling on the past, what might have been, what *had* been. We'd made our choices, choices that cut deeper than a single moment that felt life-times gone. Now, we lived with them.

Not that we'd necessarily be doing so much longer. The Pax were still on their way.

"Ready to start?" Sahluk asked me.

I turned back to him. Most of his platoon had stripped out of their exo-suits, though a handful of them still had a little juice left. They were tired, and worn, but there was a look in their eyes—I'd seen it before, on other battlefields. We'd lost some already, and the mission wasn't done. If we couldn't see it through, it would all be for nothing. They weren't going to let that happen.

"Ready to start," I nodded.

We stared at the facility for a moment, trying to decide how to do this. Three floors, built around the gun itself, and an equal number of basements, all filled with nooks and crannies likely teeming with Reint, those who hadn't joined the attacks earlier. The reactor would be below, which meant we'd have to clear the floors above first. Time to get to work.

"Who are we?" Sahluk roared at his soldiers.

Spines stiffened; guns were raised. "We are the Justified and the Repentant!" came the response.

"Do any of you feel particularly repentant *today*?" Sahluk shouted into the freezing rain.

"No, *sir!*"

"Good to know," he growled, then turned and began stalking toward the facility. He didn't have to motion for them to follow. Tired, worn, bruised—their commander was moving, and they went after.

"Some things don't change," Javier said to me as we moved to follow. I couldn't help but answer with a grin. That particular call-and-response had been around since even before I joined the Justified.

We started at the entrance closest to us, put guns at the windows, then breached the door. The plan was to make our way up to the top of the facility, where it connected to the gun itself. Every member of the team, even Javier, had added an upgraded combat package to their HUD at some point in the past, and we all had our motion tracking dialed up, resulting in our vision being filled with soft waves. When the waves were even and unbroken, a steady line, the trackers weren't picking up anything—when they started to bounce and twitch, something was moving in the direction of the disturbance.

The interior of the facility felt like a ghost town. Nothing was moving beyond the drip of water here and there, a trickle compared to the roar outside. It might have just been days since the gun was abandoned, not decades. We could still hear the downpour on the other side of the exterior walls; at least we were out of the rain. It would have felt like *more* of an improvement if we hadn't been expecting Reint to leap out of every shadow or to drop down from the ceilings onto our heads.

We only found two Reint hiding on the ground floor. That wasn't surprising—those who had claimed the lower floors would have been the strongest, the fastest, and so had likely been the same who had charged us in the initial attack. One of the two tried to run; the other tried to attack. We executed them both.

Generations ago, their ancestors had been sapient species, thinking, sentient beings like the Reint we worked with every day back at Sanctum. Now, they were just animals—incredibly dangerous animals. Even if we tranquilized them and brought them back to Sanctum, they would never return to the state their forebears had been in.

Not that it would have mattered, even if they might have. We still would have killed them. The stakes were just too high for hand-wringing now.

No repentance. Not today.

The second floor was more populated, with more aggressive members of the devolved race, those smart enough to know that charging the fence was just going to get them killed. They tried to mount an ambush, hiding in the air ducts, waiting to drop down on us from above. Thankfully, Javier spotted one slipping through a grate, and one of Sahluk's troops still had a flame unit running off his exosuit. He filled the ductwork with fire.

The smell was atrocious. We picked lots on who got to stick their head inside to make sure they were all dead; the Preacher lost, and she did so with a sigh, shutting her olfactory receptors off.

Outside, we could still hear the turrets chatter every once in a while as the Reint out in the city tried to determine the limits of the autoguns' range. Between that and the howling storm, the powered-down facility was feeling more ominous by the moment. I was perfectly happy when the Preacher climbed back down from the vents and gave us the okay to move on.

Up to the top floor. Again, the Reint there had organized, something I thought devolved Reint would never do. They were clever. They attacked en masse from the front, forcing us to fall back into a kind of storeroom under a field of fire—only the storeroom wasn't safe either, because that was where the ambush was pushing us: they'd laid a trap.

More Reint were lying in wait on the highest shelves, near the ceiling; we didn't know they were there, because they weren't moving, weren't setting off the motion detectors. As soon as we shut the door to the main hallway, before we could turn our attention to clearing the room, they attacked.

The storeroom was too tight for me to get my rifle to bear, and they were on us too quick for me to pull my pistol. For the first time since landing on this planet I had to use my fists, activating my melee implants and wading into the fight.

The Reint were quick, and they were mean, and they had a dozen awful little tricks like the gas-spitting at their disposal, but they didn't have tech that turned a jab into a sledgehammer blow or a body hook into an electrical discharge. We fought them off.

The extent of the injuries was that one of Sahluk's soldiers, a human, lost an ear. He cursed a great deal as we sprayed him down with medical foam, but it wouldn't keep him out of combat. Once we got him back to a proper medical facility, the doctors on Sanctum might even be able to grow it back for him. Maybe. You could never quite tell, especially not when it had been gnawed off and ripped free rather than removed by a clean cut.

After that, we used the last of the flame units to burn out the Reint who had herded us into the storeroom. Top floor cleared. I was truly beginning to hate this place.

We swept again on our way back down—three more Reint, lying in wait, met bad ends—and then the aboveground levels of the facility were cleared.

That meant it was time to descend to the basement, where the fusion reactor was putting out the barest trickle of heat. Where most of the Reint inside would be concentrated.

We weren't done yet.

CHAPTER 18

The two stairwells we tried were blocked by rubble—possibly a purposeful act by the Reint who nested below, making it difficult for competitors to track them to their lair. That meant we had to pry open one of the elevator shafts, and what we found wasn't good.

"Oh, shit," Javier said, with typical understatement.

Oh, shit was right. The elevator went down all the way to the bottom, the third subbasement, but we couldn't see that far down. Not because of the lack of lighting—we all had low-light-level illumination on our HUDs—but because the bottom of the shaft was filled with brackish water, perhaps ten feet deep if I remembered the facility diagrams right. There was a leak somewhere in the facility, and over the years, the bottom floor had become completely flooded.

"How the hell is the reactor even running?" Sahluk wondered. He casually ripped a piece of rebar from the wall—that wasn't because of his exosuit, he'd abandoned that earlier; he was just that goddamned strong—and dropped it into the murk below. Two Reint boiled out, bursting from the black pool; we cut them down.

The Preacher lowered her rifle, answering his question as the echoes of the gunshots faded. "The bottom floor would just be piping and circulation," she told him. "It'll all be watertight, much more so than the building itself."

"We still have to clear that mess," Javier reminded her. "And I don't know about the rest of you, but I can't breathe under water, and I certainly have no desire to skindive into . . . that." He wasn't just worried about infection or jagged metal; Reint were amphibious, as the two we'd just killed had proven. There was a good chance the nesting grounds were hidden somewhere in the flooded basement, and Reint were twice as dangerous underwater as they were on dry land, simply by virtue of the fact that most of us were *not*.

"We won't have to." The Preacher had a smile on her metal mouth that could only be described as cruel. "All we'll have to do is get the fusion reactor back to full power. Without resetting the heat circulators."

Sahluk made a noise; it wasn't a happy one. Yes, we were here to kill the Reint, and we'd do it by any means necessary. From a coolly logical perspective, the Preacher's plan was infallible—it would mean clearing the flooded basement in one fell swoop, or at least driving the Reint in the water below up to the surface, real fast. That was because powering up the reactor without pushing the excess heat it created back into its core would bring the water below to a full boil in moments. Most of the Reint would be cooked alive.

"We still have to clear the other two floors first," Sahluk reminded everyone. He'd go along with the Preacher's plan—it meant fewer Reint for his soldiers to fight one on one—but he didn't like it, and neither did I. It was cruel. "If they're nesting below, this will get ugly." He turned to me. "You better send a message to your ship. It won't catch up to her until she's back at Sanctum, but the first team of engineers will need to know that they'll have to bring equipment to pump all this shit out before they can get started."

I nodded, and did so, sending Schaz a video feed of the whole clearing operation so far. That way the engineers could study the structure on their flight over, figuring out where to start first with the repairs. Some of them would be Reint—the reptilian people had an affinity for that sort of work— and I didn't envy them watching us kill dozens of their species on the feed, but we all did what we had to do.

"First level," Sahluk said when I was done. "I want the two Barious on point."

"That's because Reint don't like the taste of metal," Sahluk's Barious trooper told the Preacher.

"I'd gathered that," she replied flatly, apparently still a little annoyed with her fellow synthetic over their information exchange back on Sanctum.

They swung down on the elevator cables, prying open the doors to the first basement. We watched from above, covering them, waiting for something—anything—to hit. We didn't have to wait long.

No sooner had they forced the doors open than a Reint bolted through, colliding with the Preacher and carrying her down into the murk below with a splash.

I cursed and aimed, but there was nothing I could see; just the thrashing, sloshing water below as the Preacher fought the Reint hand to hand underneath the surface of the liquid. The other Barious dived in after her, and soon the water stilled, broken eventually by the corpse of the dead Reint, floating to the surface.

The Preacher and the other Barious climbed out, hand over hand up the cable. "Door's open," the Preacher said mildly, shaking her head like a dog, flinging water from her metal skin.

"Have a nice swim?" Javier asked her.

"I've noticed over the years that organic humor leaves a great deal to be desired," she replied dryly. "I think it has something to do with the fact that every single one of you thinks you're far funnier than you actually are." She leapt from the rope, through the now-opened door on the first basement. She'd lost her rifle in the scuffle—one she'd claimed from one of our injured, retreating to Sanctum—but there were two sharp blasts anyway: the energy weapon she had built into her wrist. The other Barious, still hanging from the cable, fired through as well, expertly controlling the recoil even with a one-handed grip on her gun.

"Clear," the Preacher called from inside.

"I hate this place," Javier muttered, slinging his rifle on his back and reaching for the cable. "I hate everything about it."

"Just keep reminding yourself that in a week or so, this gun might be the only thing standing between us and a Pax armada," I told him.

"Oh, I'm not saying I won't be grateful for it; just that I also hate it. I'm a man of contradictions."

"You're a man of lots of things. Now get to shimmying; the sooner we get down there, the sooner we can get this done."

CHAPTER 19

I reached out and grasped the cable. It was slick with moisture; I didn't know if that was leftover lubricant from back when it had still run, or built-up gunk from the soaked atmosphere inside the derelict facility. Either way, I had to trigger my implants just a bit to get a tight grasp on the thing, so I didn't immediately lose my grip and follow the Preacher's path down into the water below. I doubted *I* could win a one-on-one fight with a Reint underneath the surface, so I was careful with my hold on the cable.

I slid down, and vaulted into the hallway. The facility above had still been relatively clear of debris—junked and damaged, but clear. Not so down in the basements. The Reint who had been nesting here had piled up all sorts of crap, creating narrow alleys out of wide corridors. Everything seemed to have sharp edges. My HUD had switched over to full night vision, giving everything an eerie green glow that made the hallway seem like it was rotting, turning the detritus-scattered halls into a kind of gangrenous maze.

We started checking rooms.

The first few Reint we found were torpid, slow moving, the heat of the reactor slowing their reactions and dulling their senses. As much as we could, we finished them with knives and our hands, trying to keep the sound level to a minimum. It worked, but only for a while.

We could start to hear movement in the other rooms. Movement, then hissing, then the clicking sound of Reint talons on metal; the predators were shaking off their torpor as they realized the basement had been breached. Then the screaming started.

They knew we were here. They knew someone had invaded their nest. The fighting above hadn't concerned them—Reint were used to everything around them trying to kill each other, all the time; the Reint homeworld had been . . . kind of a terrible place—but now that we'd come below, they were *angry.* We'd breached the pheromone trails that marked their territory, warning off other Reint, and they were going to tear us apart for it.

None of Sahluk's troops had their exosuits anymore; we were down to ballistic weapons, and whatever close-quarters tools or implants we had. Every room we checked had at least a few Reint waiting for us, usually with an ambush prepared. The question was never *if* a room would be occupied—it was where the Reint would be hiding, where they would leap from. The staccato sound of gunfire—silence, then deafeningly loud, then silent again—became a kind of constant ringing, echoing down and back through the basements.

By the time we cleared the first level, leaving the wet concrete dripping with gore, two more of Sahluk's squad were injured. Neither was completely incapacitated, but their effectiveness was degraded significantly. I could tell Sahluk was struggling with the question of whether or not to send them back upstairs, but if a fleeing Reint made it through our sweep and past us to the elevators, they'd be easy targets. He kept them with us, in the center of our grouping.

We descended to the second basement level, our feet treading through a slight scum of water that rippled and washed in waves down the stairs. The murk was ankle deep on the landing, and well over knee deep in the hallway beyond. Deep enough that a Reint could hide itself under the water by lying prone, and wait until we were nearly on top of it to burst free.

Whether they'd somehow done this on purpose—ripped open the roof above to let the water in—or it was just a happy accident, the basements now resembled the Reint homeworld, which was all swamps and tropical forests and things with lots of *teeth.* Purposefully or not, it had become as close to their natural hunting ground as a concrete and metal structure could be, exactly the kind of morass they'd evolved to stalk prey in.

It was also getting warmer; I was sweating into my body armor. That should have been a good sign—it meant we were getting closer to the reactor— but we were all decked out in cold-weather gear, clothing designed to make subfreezing temperatures feel temperate. We took a moment to strip most of it off. The Reint chose that moment to attack, because of course they did. They were predators; they recognized hesitation, innately.

We cut them down, but two more of ours were wounded, and one more was killed, his throat slashed by a Reint who burst through a pile of debris.

I was glad the lime coloring of my night vision couldn't show me the eddies of blood that must have been creeping through the water between my knees.

Finally, we reached the fusion reactor itself, or at least the catwalks and maintenance shafts that surrounded it. We set up a breach profile at the door, with Sahluk doing the breaching. He ripped the damn thing clear out of its housing and threw it at the hissing pile of Reint on the other side, disrupting their ambush. We opened fire before they could recover, the bright flashes popping in our HUDs. Right up next to the reactor was where it was warmest, so that's where the alphas of the Reint had congregated—the biggest, the strongest, the fastest, the deadliest.

We lost another of our team before we could even get into the reactor room proper, Sahluk's man cut down as a Reint we'd missed somehow in the hallways behind took advantage of the chaos in front of us to grab him and tear half his face off. He didn't even manage to scream; we never would have known it had happened, except the Preacher saw the motion from the corner of her eye and blasted the Reint in two with her energy cannon.

Nothing we could have done; the Preacher salvaged the man's rifle, and we pressed forward, into the reactor room itself. The open space was ten times as big as Scheherazade's entire interior, full of pipes and chains and catwalks, the reactor machinery taking up all three floors of the basement, leaving it open to the standing brackish water that flooded up from below, creating a wide pool at the very center of the complex, surrounding the massive reactor itself.

That's where the Reint were emerging from. They just kept coming up out of the murk, their claws skittering on the metal gratings as they emerged dripping from the pool and lunged across the space at us. It was like the water below was boiling already, there was so much movement down there.

Javier and the Preacher moved to the reactor's controls as the rest of us covered them. Sahluk's Barious team member moved with them as well, her gun raised and firing: apparently whatever had been in that little exchange of ideas they'd had back in Sanctum, the Preacher had come out on top as far as who should be allowed to do the technical work. She knelt in front of the control panel, breaking open an access port and pulling some of the wiring free so that she could plug it into her arm like a junkie after a fix.

I'd fired my rifle dry, so I tossed it aside. Maybe I'd be able to find it later, maybe not. I drew my pistol instead, began picking my shots more carefully. We didn't speak, none of us. We all knew what would happen here—either the Reint would overwhelm us, and we'd fail, or the Preacher would succeed, and every single Reint who didn't boil to death in the basement below our feet would come up out of the water surrounding the reactor. They'd emerge maddened by pain and with only one thought: to get out. The only way out available to them would be through us.

"It's heating up!" the Preacher called out, unplugging from the console and stepping back, lifting her rifle as she did so, the weapon still bloodstained from the hands of the soldier she'd taken it from.

The Reint were calling out to each other under the water below, a kind of burbling howl distorted by the liquid. They were coming.

CHAPTER 20

It was ugly. It was endless. They just kept coming. We hadn't planned for this—devolved Reint were territorial by nature: there should have been a dozen at most down in the basements. There just wasn't enough *space* for more of them to share, given the room they needed before they would start killing each other off. Except these Reint were *different*, had been willing to cram nearly on top of each other, and there must have been half a hundred in the flooded basement below.

The water sloshing around our knees—now choked with Reint blood and viscera—was growing warm, and it was quite a ways away from the reactor's piping a floor beneath us, the heat source that was making the basement literally boil.

The clouds of steam rising from the brackish foulness didn't help our visibility, nor did the fluctuating light leaking from the reactor itself, bathing the mist and murk in shades of indigo and violet like a strobe. I'd dialed down my HUD's light levels as the illumination from the reactor had increased, and now I was firing at motion more than anything else, the spikes and ripples in the waves from my tracker seemingly everywhere, the clouds of steam eddying and shifting this way and that, broken every few seconds by another Reint charging our position.

Finally, it was over. There was no signal, no last defiant charge—just an end to the screaming, and no more forms exploding up from the superheated water to try and tear our faces off. Reint bodies floated past us in the wash, broken like dolls and riddled with bullet holes.

The light from the reactor steadied into a constant glow, and the Preacher activated the heat circulators, meaning the boiling died down almost immediately. The smell of death and cooked reptilian meat was thick in the air, enough that I tried not to breathe as much as possible.

Sahluk was panting, kneeling near the center of the room. He'd lost his rifle early on, had fallen back on hand-to-hand tactics, almost daring the Reint to come at him because he was stronger than the rest of us, with tougher skin. It had worked—he'd pulled the more aggressive away from those of us who still had their guns, let us fire more freely, but he hadn't gotten away clean. I moved to take at least some of his weight as he stumbled; Javier reached him just after me and applied a medical foam to his damaged face.

I'd known when he took the wound that he would lose the eye.

"Sound off!" he shouted to his men, nothing in his voice giving away how badly he was hurt. One by one, his troops responded. Two of the wounded had been dragged away in the chaos. Maybe we'd find them somewhere in the rest of the facility; maybe not. The overhead lights were beginning to come up, those that still worked, giving the basement a patchy glow.

It was an ugly place, full of death and carnage. Four more of ours had died in the fighting, among them the other Barious. The synthetic species was tough, but three Reint had pinned her down as a fourth ripped her head entirely free of her body. Even Barious couldn't survive that. Almost half of the soldiers who had entered the complex wouldn't be coming back out again.

A nothing price to pay, if it meant we got the cannon back in working order.

I hated to think like that; I did. But the Pax were still coming—having this gun online, if the engineers could get it back to full operation, meant that we'd be able to pound their dreadnaughts as they moved into a firing solution over Sanctum. If they wanted to be able to bombard our home with impunity, they'd likely have to take this gun first. That could save hundreds of lives, thousands, maybe even turn the tide of the coming fight. The cold, hard math was still very much on our side.

It didn't feel like that, watching the soldiers prepare their comrades' bodies for extraction, trying to keep them out of the water made pale pink with blood, both their own and that of the Reint we'd cut down.

"We're not done yet," Sahluk growled at his troops. "We've cleared most of them, but I want this facility checked again, and again, before the techs get here. Top to bottom, at least two more times. Plenty of Reint got past us, I'm sure—they could still be hiding elsewhere in the building." He turned to me, which was easy, given that I was the only thing keeping him standing.

"Get outside, see if you can get a line to your ship. I need to know what the ETA is on those engineers."

"I'll take him," the Preacher offered, sliding in beside me and shouldering more of Sahluk's weight than I possibly could.

I nodded, and managed to retrieve my empty rifle from the water, slinging it over my back. Thankfully, Justified guns were designed to fire wet, and our munitions were waterproof. "Take someone with you," Sahluk said, still leaning on the Preacher. "This place isn't clear yet; none of us should move alone."

"I'll go," Javier offered. "I could use some fresh air."

"I think we all could," Sahluk agreed. "Get moving. Like I said: we're not done yet."

CHAPTER 21

We went to work.

Javier and I rejoined the others as they emerged from the basement. The Reint who had survived our initial purge were either the sickly and the old—those who had remained hidden—or those injured in our attack. They didn't have much fight in them. We were merciless anyway. It would only take one left behind to decimate the engineering team, and we'd just been through a bloodbath. Violence makes sentient beings more violent.

Besides, what we were supposed to do, herd them all outside? They'd just run into the fences and the autoturrets. There were millions of lives in the balance, and these devolved Reint would never be able to return to a sapient state.

We killed them all, every living thing we found inside the facility. Then we swept again, looking to make sure we hadn't missed any. And again. And again.

By the time Scheherazade returned with the first team of engineers, Bravo emplacement was officially clear. The technicians had studied the videos we'd sent back, and had been poring over the plans for the facility besides; they had Schaz drop massive payloads from orbit, crates filled with tools and equipment and supplies. Getting the gun up and running—and keeping it up and running during the coming battle, even as its shielding was fighting off whatever damage the Pax could dish out, not to mention the thick radiation—would take a great deal of work.

Sahluk left half of his remaining team with them, to maintain the autoturrets and the fences and to cover the engineers just in case, and the rest of us climbed back up to Scheherazade. Time to clear Alpha gun.

First, though, we plotted a return course to Sanctum. We needed more equipment; at least half our number needed medical attention; most of all, we needed new soldiers. And we needed to return our dead to their home.

When we set down inside the hangar, Marus was waiting for us. He hadn't returned with the first set of engineers—had sent a message saying that he was assembling equipment for us back at Sanctum, that he'd be waiting. He was as good as his word. Sahluk had another dozen volunteers from his police force standing by, with fresh gear and charged exosuits, ready and willing to take on Alpha.

Sahluk let the new volunteers handle rearming the men and women he'd returned with and got himself to the medbay to get treatment for his damaged face. He should have stayed there, but he said that he'd rejoin us before we left, and I didn't try and stop him. It was his decision to make.

I'd spent most of the flight over in the shower, trying to warm up again and to wash the blood off of me. I popped a few caffeine pills and crammed down a quick meal in Sanctum's cafeteria as the others loaded up—Javier joined me, though we didn't talk much, both of us too busy thinking about how we were going to survive another action like the one we'd just made it through; worrying about our long shared history or how anything was going to play out other than the next day or so would have taken more energy than we had to spare.

With a hot meal and fresh ammunition, we were about ready to go again, regardless of the fact that I didn't *want* to be ready to go again. I didn't want to spend any more time fighting monsters in the dark. Truth be told, if you'd offered me a choice, right then and there—try and clear the Alpha gun, or have the Pax show up, a week earlier than we expected them, and start that fight right now, I would have taken the second option. Better to have it over and done with.

Criat swung by the cafeteria to thank me for the mission. He'd wanted those guns reclaimed for decades now, and taking Bravo was the closest he'd come to that goal since we'd settled in this system. I told him we likely couldn't hold them after the Pax assault was over, that the pulse radiation and the Reint were just too thick, that it would be too expensive. He dismissed my worries.

"If we have to abandon them after, we can do so," he replied. "You've proved that they can be retaken when we need them. We'll just do it again if necessary."

I fought the urge to throw something at him. He was my boss, after all.

Feeling marginally more human—but nowhere back to a hundred percent—Javi and I rejoined the others on Scheherazade, and we lifted off again.

One gun cleared; one to go.

CHAPTER 22

Compared to taking Bravo, Alpha was a goddamned breeze.

For one thing, the storm system that had plagued us before had moved on by the time we even reached the second facility, leaving the sky a crystalline blue, clear enough that once we'd set down—after Schaz had made her first circle, dropping the second round of turrets—we could actually see Sanctum hanging above us: not just the moon in the sky but Sanctum itself, lit up on the surface of the shores of the crystal sea above.

For another, the elevation helped tremendously: the second facility was high in the mountains, in inhospitable terrain—a pain in the ass for us, but overall a great benefit, since it meant that the Reint hadn't gathered in nearly the same numbers as they had at Bravo. Additionally, the mountains were at such great elevation that Schaz could provide almost constant cover; this high up, she could stay in the atmosphere for much longer, meaning we had air support the entire time we were setting up the fence. We simply moved around the perimeter, activating the turrets and picking off the few Reint who emerged from the facility itself.

Then it was time to enter and clear. We got lucky for a third time there: whatever in the blue fuck had been going on with the Reint at the first gun in terms of their deeply strange behavior, it wasn't happening here. These were acting much more like the lone predators they were, and most of those who *had* been inside had fucked right off when they'd seen what was going on with the fences. Even devolved Reint were smart enough to realize that a platoon of heavily armed soldiers murdering *other* Reint meant their chances for taking us on were slim at best.

We cleared the mountain facility without taking a single injury, much less a fatality. I sent Marus back with Schaz to pick up another round of engineers, and then I waited, sitting outside and staring up at that long stretch of blue sky. Above me, the giant gun pointed up into the sky; I wondered idly how long it had been since the damn thing was fired. Had it been used as the rest of the system was torn apart? Had its Reint operators—the ancestors of the creatures we'd just killed or driven off—been forced to watch, all their firepower useless against the merciless forces that had been unleashed in their skies against the other worlds?

Hopefully it would do more good for us, now that another enemy was about to come between the stars above and the gun below.

This emplacement wouldn't have as good an angle of attack as Bravo did, not on the Pax advance: Bravo would be able to pound away repeatedly at any dreadnaughts that made it into a position over Sanctum, whereas Alpha would only be able to deteriorate their shielding on approach. Still, no lives lost taking it, and even that small firing window could mean a big difference, given how many dreadnaughts the Pax were bringing to the party.

Taking the Bravo, in the city, had cost us nearly a dozen soldiers, with an equal number of casualties added to the injured list, those who likely wouldn't be able to rejoin the fight before the Pax arrived. Taking Alpha had cost us nothing, not even a bruise. Sometimes, that was just how war went.

Still, the losses we had taken earlier stung. I should have been able to view them as an easy price, for the good the guns would do us in the coming fight, but I couldn't. Not yet. I'd gotten used to . . . shifting my expectations as to what losses meant, in terms of tactics and combat. They had become dependent on the world I was on, the level of conflict, the level of breakdown in whatever societies had formed after the pulse. I'd fought in what the locals had called "wars"—usually as a pretext to get to whatever kid I needed to escort offworld—that had been nothing more than a few dozen men and women trying to kill each other in a field.

Of course, I'd also fought in the sect wars, *actual* goddamned wars, before the pulse, when the whole goddamned galaxy had been trying to kill each other. I'd learned to pilot in void—set battles just as full of dreadnaughts and frigates and fighters as this one was promising to be. For most of the Justified, this was going to be combat on a scale undreamt of; for me, it was like coming home.

It would be easy to say one level of violence was worse than the other, that a few dozen dead was far preferable to thousands, millions, more. After all, that was the argument we'd used when we first built the pulse. It was a lie. I knew that now, had realized it far too late. The mind can only process so much; watching someone die in front of you, whether on your side or in another uniform: it does its damage, regardless of how big the fighting raging around you is.

All you could do was try to carry it, to let it make its place in your soul, before moving on to the next fight, damaged and wounded inside, if not physically. This galaxy had always been defined by conflict, one way or another. I'd spent my life bouncing from violent action to violent action; I knew it was taking a toll. But at the end, it was all I knew how to do.

I lit a cigarette, and just stared out at the mountains. Eventually, Javier joined me.

"We can win this, you know," he told me, taking a seat at my side. It was the closest we'd been to each other since he came back. Everything else aside—all the violence, all the fear, all the desperation—the human body is the human body, and mine reacted to him being so close to me, to his physical presence, the weight of his form, to his smell. That's just . . . biology.

Javier and I had known each other very intimately before he'd made the decision that saw him exiled. It's not exactly that I thought we'd have a future with each other, or that he'd always be there—our work was dangerous, and took us to far-flung corners of the galaxy; we'd gone months without seeing each other sometimes—but physically, my body didn't care about any of that. It had been through trauma, and it wanted what it wanted.

Specifically, it wanted me to reach over and run my hands down his skin, to pull his body into contact with mine, to make me feel something other than the shame and weariness and fear that was overloading my nervous system. It could want that all it liked; I wouldn't do it.

"We can." I nodded, still smoking my cigarette, trying to shut down the stupid impulses of my sex drive. Trying to reclaim what we'd had, once, would just lead to a great deal of hurt down the line.

"It'll deal a great blow to the Pax," he continued. "Maybe even ruin them. That's not just good for Sanctum; that's good for everyone, everywhere in the galaxy, even if they don't know it. The Pax are a damned plague. We get to be the cure."

I shook my head, exhaling smoke. "Not so simple," I replied. "Even if we did that, hit them hard enough that they never recovered—and this, the fight here, this would just be the start of that; agents like Marus would have to be sent back to their conquered worlds, to make sure they didn't store the location of Sanctum or share it with anyone else—another sect would just rise up and take their place. A different group of would-be zealots or conquering assholes, sure that the pulse left them guns for a reason, and that reason was to use those guns to subjugate anyone else who doesn't agree with them."

Javier looked at me. I didn't look back. I knew the expression already. Like I said, I knew him well. "You're in a mood," he said. He was trying to be kind.

I shook my head, stubbed out my cigarette. "You weren't born when we decided to use the pulse," I reminded him. "It wasn't supposed to spread across the universe, and it wasn't *supposed* to spread unchecked, but I'd be lying if I said we didn't intend to use it again, over and over, on the assumption that taking away the worst tools from the worst aggressors would somehow make a better galaxy."

"So you would have taken the Pax's favorite toys away, if you'd managed to keep control," Javier shrugged. "So what? That wouldn't have been a bad thing."

"Not the point. The me who would have said that was a good thing, that would help—she would have been wrong. The last century has shown me that. I can't keep watching people die, Javi. I just can't do it. And there is *nothing* that can stop us from killing each other. Absolutely goddamned nothing. That was the mistake we made, designing the pulse."

He put an arm around me, and kissed me on the crown of my head. Absurdly enough, it did make me feel better, just a little; I kind of hated that it did. Again, biology. We're just not meant to be alone. "Let's survive this, first," he told me. "Then we can worry about fixing the rest of the universe."

I shook my head, and managed a smile for him. "Always the optimist," I told him.

"Always something," he shrugged. "By the way—I talked to Marus; he's back at the first gun, at Bravo. Says they found . . . a *thing*, buried in the sub-basement, where it was flooded."

"Yeah? What kind of a thing?"

"Damned if I know. Damned if *anybody* knows. Weird tech, weird materials, apparently been there since before this world cracked apart. One of the

Barious engineers swears it's forerunner design, but Barious say that about everything they don't understand; could have been something the Reint here were building on their own. Anyway. That's what was making them crazy. It was all tangled up with the fusion reactor, messing with the radiation it was putting out, doing weird shit to their . . ." He tapped the side of his head. "Screwing with their senses, with their pheromones, with their neurochemical balances."

"So it wasn't the pulse," I said.

"Just because *most* crazy shit in the galaxy has to do with the pulse doesn't mean *all* of it does. I think there's a saying about that. Some kind of platitude."

I frowned at him. "Do *not* start with the platitudes, Javier."

"I just said there *was* one, not that I was going to *say* it."

I sighed, shaking my head. "So we walked into a trap—we walked into a bloodbath—because some ancient relic, some fucking *thing* was making the Reint crazy. Crazier. All because it got left behind when the sect that used to live here . . ." I looked up, above the mountains, to the cracked sky of the system above. I wondered if the thing we'd stumbled upon in Bravo's basement—and had cost us lives—had anything to do with whatever weapon had ruined this system. I wondered if it had been what their enemies had been *looking* for.

"Pretty much, yeah," Javier agreed with my unfinished statement. "Somebody's always paying for someone else's sins. Even a hundred years after whatever those sins *bought* is long gone. That's the way the galaxy works, right?"

"I'm not the only one in a mood today," I told him, managing a slight smile.

"Ah, it's nothing," he said. "Just nerves. I never thought I'd be risking getting killed fighting the Pax, of all people."

"You're not going to get killed, Javier. I won't let you."

He shook his head at that, smiling despite himself. "I appreciate that. But I mean—come on. The Pax? Really? Of all the sects out there—of all the sects still *flying* out there—I think I'd rather get killed by almost *any* other one. Even the weird ones. Especially the weird ones. The Mahrielle, or the Argiscene, even the Dryatalia."

"Aren't the Dryatalia the ones who worship . . . like . . . forests? The ones on those worlds with flora that didn't come from any of the sentient species' home planets—they worship the wood itself. Like, the actual trees. The roots and everything."

"Yeah, that's them."

"Wasn't aware they went around killing too many people. I thought mostly they just stayed on their weird-ass worlds, and were only dangerous if you landed and looked like you were going to build yourself a lumber mill."

"Still. I'd *still* rather die at the hands of tree-worshipping nutcases than the Pax. They're thugs, and idiots."

"They're thugs and idiots who stumbled into an untouched fleet of ships, and somehow found their way to Sanctum. It's not the fact that the Pax are the Pax that brought them here, Javi. This could have been *any* sect who wanted power—and that's most of the sects out there. Give any of those what the Pax got—a fleet of dreadnaughts and Sanctum's location—and it'd be them knocking at our door, instead."

"Everybody wants someone to blame. Might as well be us."

I smiled at him. "Not your weight anymore, remember?"

"It'll always be my weight. It—" He stopped, then reached up with his hand to touch the side of his neck. He was getting a transmission on his implanted comm. He listened for a moment, then grinned, his black mood banished seemingly in an instant. "Just heard from Var," he told me. "He and Schaz are on their way in. Apparently he got tired of sitting around Sanctum and decided to help ferry engineers. He's playing it off like he wanted to help, but I think he was just bored: apparently all there was to do back at the docking bay was listen to a bunch of Reint engineers argue about whether or not they were allowed to service him, given that *technically* he was just as guilty as me for our desertion."

I shaded my eyes as well; I could just make out the two ships on approach. It wasn't like they were using stealth kits—the Reint on this world didn't exactly have the tech to pick them up on radar, or to take shots at them even if they did.

"We're back," Schaz said mildly into my ear. "We brought your engineers. And also . . . a surprise."

I sighed. "Schaz, today is not the day for surprises," I told her, standing anyway. "Actually, 'never' is the day for surprises. I hate surprises."

"I know," she said, but that was all she said.

The mountains were high enough that the ships could actually set down long enough that the engineers didn't have to try and descend rope lines to get down to the gun. As Schaz's ramp descended, they poured out, eager to get to work, to do their part for the upcoming fight.

Esa came out after them.

CHAPTER 23

What in the *hell*?" I wondered out loud. I'm not sure exactly what Javier heard in my voice, but he reached out and grabbed my elbow, shaking his head as he did.

"Hold on," he told me. "Let's see what she's trying to—"

"What she's trying to *do* is get herself killed!" I hissed. "I did not drag her off of that backwater planet and halfway across the goddamned galaxy—"

"It was, what, a hundred or so light years, at most?"

"I did not go through all the *shit* I went through in order to get her here just to have her wander into the middle of a soon-to-be-battlefield," I finished, fuming. "I repeat: what in the *hell*?"

Meanwhile, Esa had seen us, and waved cheerily as she approached. "Hi, guys," she said. "I got bored back on Sanctum, so I thought I'd come see what you were doing."

"You got bored," I said slowly, trying to parse this information. It was like she was suddenly speaking a foreign tongue, one I only knew a handful of words in. "Shouldn't you still be in orientation?"

"Yeah, they canceled that," she told me. "I guess they kind of figured if we're about to all be killed by Pax, it wouldn't really matter. If we're still alive at the end of the invasion, I guess they plan to do it after. I—"

I held up a hand for silence; raised Schaz again. "Schaz," I said. "Why is she here?"

"I am truly not sure, boss," Schaz replied.

"Then *why is she here*? If you're not sure, why did you fly her across the system; why did you even let her on board?"

"She boarded with all the engineers; I didn't even notice she was there until halfway through the flight, and what was I supposed to do then, turn around and take her back to Sanctum? You needed the engineers here, now, soon."

"Right." I turned back to Esa. "You're going back to Sanctum. Now."

"Actually, I'm not," she disagreed. "Like I said: they canceled orientation. I still got to meet a couple of the other kids, though, the ones like me. And they said something interesting—said they'd been told what was coming, and they'd been offered a chance to help with the war effort. Those with mechanical skills, for example, were supposed to—"

"You don't. Have. Mechanical skills." I ground out the words through gritted teeth.

"You don't know that," she returned, sounding a little hurt.

"Fine. But even if you *did*, they would have wanted the students with engineering skills working on restoring the frigates, not out here working on the guns. You do understand that as soon as this all starts, this position is going to be a primary target for the Pax, right?"

"Yeah, but it's not like Sanctum won't—"

I shook my head. "Not just for the Pax dreadnaughts; I mean everything else the Pax have got. Every ship in their armada that makes it through the minefields is going to try and take out this gun, because unless they do *that*, this thing will be picking their dreadnaughts apart. And if they can't do it with ships, I guarantee you, they *will* land ground troops. It isn't a question of 'if' the Pax overwhelm this gun, it's a question of how long into the battle it will take to fall."

"Oh." Apparently she hadn't put all that together.

"Still seem like a good idea for you to sneak on board Schaz?" I asked her.

She glared back, defiant. "Yeah. It did. If things are going to get as bad as all that, then you *need* me, even more than I thought."

"Esa, this won't be like escaping the settlement back on your homeworld, or even the observation tower. This will be war—"

"I know, war, the thing everyone keeps talking about, the thing your whole"—she sort of churned her hand uselessly in midair, giving me very little actual information—"*thing* was supposed to stop. It's big and it's scary and it will change me for good. But you know what else would change me? Dying. Dying, or being a Pax slave, being *brainwashed*. That's one thing I learned growing up on my homeworld, on a pulsed world: if you have the chance to fight, you fight. Don't wait, don't expect a better moment to arrive, don't think someone's going to come along and save you—if you need to fight, you fuck-ing *fight*, you start and you don't stop until you're done, one way or another."

She had actually thought about this. She'd applied typical teenage logic, convoluted and self-serving, but at least it hadn't been a spur-of-the-moment decision to hop on board Schaz and take a joyride to what would soon be the middle of a war zone. She glared up at me, having worked herself up into a fit of anger, like she was daring me to bundle her back on Schaz and send her back to her minders on Sanctum with a sign taped to her back: "Found wandering the warzone. Please be sure to latch her gate tighter from now on."

I sighed. I'd wondered often in the last century, especially in moments like this: of all the Justified agents Criat could have picked, why had he cho-sen *me* to mind teenagers? What about me said that was a good idea? "Ma-ternal" was never a word that had been used to describe me, ever.

Still, with Esa glaring up at me, simultaneously begging and daring me to send her away from the fight, I couldn't help but see something in the tilt of her chin, in the furious glint in her eyes: something very much like myself.

"Fine." I sighed. "But if you get yourself killed, you're not allowed to blame me."

CHAPTER 24

No," the Preacher said flatly. I hadn't even heard her approach; she was surprisingly stealthy for a person made entirely out of metal. "Esa, you need to get back to Sanctum. Now."

Esa shrugged, holding fast in the face of the Preacher's wrath. "Die here, die in Sanctum, become a slave to the Pax. One's much the same as the other, isn't it?"

"This isn't funny; this isn't a game, and you've been through too much to act this childish."

"Childish?" Esa's anger had returned, far stronger. "I'm about to die—everyone in this system is about to die—and you think wanting to fight to stop that is *childish?*"

"You can't help."

"I can, actually. She taught me how to work Scheherazade's gunnery station." She thrust a finger at me, dragging me back into the middle of this fight. "I can help plenty. Even on the ground, I've got my powers."

"That's not enough, and you—"

"Then what is? What the hell *is*, Preacher? Ever since the Pax attacked I've been dragged around by my ears into one shit situation after another. Is it so goddamned wrong for me to want some control over my own life? Just a little? The Pax want to kill me, the Pax want to make me a slave? Fine. Fucking fine. Just let them try. I'll rip their goddamned tits off when they do, and I'm not waiting for them to get close. I'm not cowering in some bunker back in Sanctum, not when I can fight back here, now, not when I can stop them before they get to those other kids, the ones who are too *scared* to fight." She was actually shuddering with the weight of her own labored breathing now that her shouted speech was out of her. I doubt, if someone had just asked her before that moment, if she could have even vocalized how she felt about some of that. Sometimes it takes pressure to show us how we really feel, who we really are.

I'd always had Esa's measure, from the moment I saw her saving children from a collapsing building; now she did too.

"I think that's settled, Preacher," I stepped in. "She says she wants to stay, she stays. She says she wants to fight—"

"You are in no condition to make decisions for her." The Preacher glared at me. "You've known her for all of, what, two weeks? Beyond that, you're injured, you're a zealot, and you're half-delirious from lack of sleep."

It had been two days since I'd slept; that was true enough. The rest I took a fair amount of offense to. "I'm twice the fighter injured than most people you've ever known," I replied, drawing myself up to my full height, which was not inconsiderable. "As far as my being a *zealot* is concerned, maybe I am— maybe believing that something *good* can come out of all the shit in the galaxy makes me one—but zealots are the ones standing between her and the Pax right now; zealots are the ones fighting to protect you, too. And as far as the other thing is concerned—"

"She's actually pretty right about that," Javier added mildly. "The sleep thing, I mean."

"Stay the fuck out of this," I growled at him.

"I'm not agreeing with her—if Esa wants to fight, she should fight; it's her decision—I'm just saying she's not wrong about the sleep bit."

"Thank you, Javier," Esa said quietly, not taking her eyes off the Preacher.

"No problem. I'm all about free will."

"You can't risk taking her into a battle in the void." The Preacher shook her head. "You won't. You know how much she means to the Justified, how rare her gift is. You know—"

"What the hell is this about?" I asked her, breaking into her argument. I wasn't trying to disrupt her; I was actually curious. Too many things were starting to line up not to make me wonder what the missing variable in the equation was. "You traveled halfway across the galaxy with her, with us, and it wasn't just to get off her homeworld—I have a feeling you could have done that any time you wanted. You faced down a death sentence from the Justified to stay close to her, agreed to come with me to clear the Reint. It all has to do with her, I'm guessing: it sure as hell wasn't for me. So what the hell is this *about*?"

"She's important."

"She's a person." Javier again.

"She's a child who can't be trusted with—"

"You were always there." Esa, watching the Preacher carefully now. "Watching over the orphanage, watching over me. The other kids—the older kids, the ones who were my age then when I was just little—said you hadn't always done that, that you just showed up one day, founded your church. Shortly after I was left at the orphanage. But you were always around, always—"

"Oh, fuck," I sighed. It came together with an almost audible "click" in my mind. "You dropped her off, didn't you? At the orphanage, hell, maybe even on that world. You've been trying to keep her safe, not just for the last couple weeks, but for the last decade and a half. You've been guarding her."

"That's not—"

"Did you know my parents?" The question was small, and tremulous, and heartbreaking. Esa just watched the Preacher, suddenly aware that answers to questions she'd had all her life might have been just a few streets down from the orphanage entrance doors, all that time. "Did you—"

"I did," the Preacher sighed, all the fight running out of her in the face of that one question. "I did."

CHAPTER 25

We all just stared at the Barious for a moment. In truth, it shouldn't have mattered much—the Pax were still coming, the guns still needed to be brought back online, and somewhere out beyond the edges of the galaxy, the pulse was preparing for its return, ready to render everything we did moot, to push every single world even further backward in time, a hunger that wouldn't be satisfied until we were all huddled in caves and desperately sharpening sticks to fend off our neighbors who wanted to kill us for having the temerity to be huddled in a better cave than they were. In that moment, though, it all felt very far away.

I'd felt bad for keeping secrets from Esa—who the Justified were, what my name was, what Sanctum really was—and I'd only known her for a few weeks. The Preacher had been around her entire life, had held the answers to the questions that helped define her, and had kept silent.

For a second, I thought Esa was going to charge the Barious, to flail at her with her fists. The pain that passed across her face was a desperate kind, almost a purity to it, it was so raw. As much anguish as anger. I knew what she was feeling, what she was thinking: that everyone betrayed her. That everyone lied.

"Tell me," she said, her voice little more than a whisper. "Tell me everything."

"It's not—"

"It *matters!*" the girl shouted, almost screamed, the words echoing in the clear mountain air as if someone had rung a bell. "It matters."

The Preacher sighed, and sat on a low rock wall, her back to the sweeping vista of the mountains, staring at Esa, yes, but also beyond her, staring into the past. "Your parents were scientists," she said. "They were . . . helping us. They were my friends. They—"

"Us?" Javier asked quietly.

"A Barious sect," I filled in, the pieces slowly coming together in my mind. "Studying the pulse. Doing the same work we've been doing, just without as many of the pieces. Trying to figure out how to reverse it, so that they—"

"You did this to us," the Preacher said to me. "Don't think I'll forget."

"Not important right now," Esa reminded her, her gaze still fixed on the Preacher, pinning her in place. "My parents. Talk."

"I never would have . . . I didn't know that your mother was pregnant," the Preacher told her, trying to explain, trying to make her side clear. "If I had . . . I was in charge of the facility, of the laboratory. Not a scientist myself, not really, but an . . . administrator. We were studying pulse radiation, trying to figure out how it did what it did, the selections it made—"

"And why it affected children in the womb," I added.

"And that," she agreed. "There was . . . an experiment proposed. By your parents. It doesn't . . . it's not important why, what they were trying to achieve. Something went wrong. The radiation multiplied exponentially. Swept through the facility, the lab, half of the station, in incredibly concentrated doses—passed through every safeguard we had like they weren't even there."

"You're saying it was their fault." Esa sounded like she was choking as she spoke.

"That's not—it could have been a thousand things that went wrong. Any thousand things. Believe me. I've been over that day . . . so many times. Reviewing it in my memory banks. Asking if there was something I could have done, if there was anything . . . anything anyone could have done, to change the outcome. In hindsight, there was, of course, a hundred different decisions, a thousand, that if anyone had acted just slightly differently, had known what was coming, could have prevented it."

"But you can't change the past," Javier said.

"No. You can't. You can only go forward." The Preacher looked at Esa—really looked at her, for the first time since starting her story. "Pulse radiation can be lethal. It's benign in smaller doses, when spread across entire worlds, but concentrated like that . . . the Barious in the facility were unaffected, of course. We always are. But the others, many of those who were helping us, those that . . . those like your parents."

"It killed them." Esa said the words flatly, her voice empty of anything.

"Not right away."

"She doesn't need to hear this," Javier warned the Preacher.

"I do." Esa turned to glare at him.

"You need to hear what happened." Javier shook his head. "You don't . . . there are some things you don't want to learn. Trust me."

The Preacher sighed, looking away again. "We found out that your mother was pregnant while we were treating her and your father for their exposure. She wasn't able . . . she begged us. To keep her alive, long enough to . . . long enough. She didn't manage to carry you to term, but she managed long enough that we could . . . that we . . ."

"Javier's right," I said. "We all understand what happened next. Move on." Esa didn't need to hear that she'd been cut out from her mother's dying body, kept alive by machines. Maybe she understood that much anyway, maybe she didn't, but she didn't need to hear it said.

"We knew she—you—would be affected by the radiation, just like all the other children conceived or carried when the radiation hit natural spikes. We theorized that, because the radiation had been so much more concentrated, she would . . ."

"That's why her gifts are so strong," I murmured, mostly to myself. "All the other children are exposed during flare-ups that happen naturally. She was at the heart of an artificial storm, a concentration a thousand times more than that which leads to other gifted children."

"Yes." The Preacher nodded.

"And then?" Esa asked, willing herself to hear all of it, now, right now, to understand that which had been kept from her for so long. "You . . . kept me alive. Why the orphanage? Why that world?"

"You must have had other facilities, other places you could take her to," Javier said. "Why not raise her there? You must have wanted to—"

"Because I *didn't* want to," the Preacher told him. "I didn't want her raised to be . . . I didn't want her to be a lab rat for her whole childhood, studied, tested. I know what I am, what the Barious are. Our programming is dictated first and foremost by logic. Regardless of the circumstances that made her . . . special, regardless of the guilt I felt for the accident that claimed her parents, if I allowed the other Barious in my group to choose the best possible action, they would choose one that would sentence her to a life as a . . . specimen, to be studied. I owed her more than that. I owed her parents more than that."

"So you took her. And you ran."

She nodded. "I did."

"Someplace you didn't think the other Barious would follow you," Javier continued. "A world they'd never consider looking twice at, because they'd never expect you to be willing to forego the tools and technology you'd had at your disposal at your own facility."

"The accident . . . changed me. Not the radiation, I mean, not that, but . . . my guilt. My grief. My culpability, in what had happened. For the other Barious in my . . . group—"

"Sect," I interrupted. "You can say it was a sect. They all are."

"We don't use that word." She glared at me.

I shrugged. "You can pretend you're better, but you're not," I replied. "That's what it was."

"They wouldn't have understood." She kept staring at me for a moment, even as she returned to her tale of Esa's childhood. "So, yes. I took her, as soon as she was old enough to . . . but still just an infant. I found a world that had been pushed far back enough on the technology tree that the rest of my . . . sect . . . wouldn't come looking, but was relatively peaceful, relatively secure."

"But why the orphanage?" Esa whispered.

"You weren't unhappy there," the Preacher said, less a statement, almost a question. "You weren't—"

"I was desperate to know the things you knew," Esa told her, the sadness in her voice like a living thing, a wounded animal locked in her breast like a cage. "I was desperate for a . . . family. Like other people had. You could have been my family. You could have been—"

"I couldn't." She shook her head. "Even if the people of that world wouldn't have thought it strange to see a Barious raising a human child, I couldn't . . ." She looked up again. "Every time I look in your face I see your mother's eyes. I see your father's smile. I am reminded of my great failure, of my . . . crimes."

"So you left her at the orphanage," I nodded, "and you kept an eye on her, from a distance. Close enough that you would know if she was in trouble, close enough that you would know when her powers manifested, but far enough away that you didn't have to suffer much yourself." I couldn't help it—a thread of contempt wound its way through my words.

The Preacher glared at me again. "Judge me all you like—"

"I am. Believe me—"

"I did all I could. Threw my old life away, made myself a . . . a street-corner preacher for the people of that world, all so I had an excuse to visit the orphanage. Charitable works." Something of a sneer in her own voice. "Assuaging my own guilt, yes. But also because I knew what I owed her."

"Which is why you invited yourself along when I turned up. You knew she wouldn't turn away a chance to get *off* that world, to see more of the galaxy, to find some meaning in the gifts she'd been given."

"She has her parents' curiosity," the Preacher said dully. "She always did."

"And you wanted to know what the Justified knew," Javier added. "Deep down, you were still a scientist. Still looking for answers."

"And that. Yes. Can you blame me? Can you really—"

"What were their names?" Esa didn't care about the Preacher's moral weight, about her guilt or her shame; she didn't care about the wrestling match between the metaphorical demons and angels in her core code. She cared about the parents she'd always known she had, parents she'd always thought had abandoned her. Now she learned that there had never been a choice, that her mother hadn't left her in a bundle on the orphanage steps, that she had been dead long before. I didn't know if that was better, or not.

"Janah," the Preacher whispered. "Janah and Paul."

Esa closed her eyes; I couldn't hear it, but I could see her lips move, her throat work, as she repeated the names to herself, several times over. Committing them to her memory, locking them away in her heart.

Then she reached out, and touched the Preacher. The Barious almost flinched away, but held still. I had a feeling that even if Esa had reached out with her gifts, used her prodigious talent to rip the Preacher's head from her shoulders, the Barious wouldn't have resisted.

"You changed the course of my life, several times over," Esa told her. "I don't know . . . I don't know if what you did was right, or wrong, good or bad. I don't know if I should hate you for it, or thank you, or try . . . try to forgive you. But you told me the truth, now, when I asked. So thank you. Thank you for that."

Then she turned, and walked away, as the rest of us pretended like we couldn't see the tears streaming down her face.

CHAPTER 26

I sighed, and rummaged through my pockets until I produced another cigarette. Staring out at the mountains, I lit it.

"You're still smoking those things?" Javier sighed. "Such a barbaric habit."

"Well, I'm a barbarian," I shrugged.

"You going after her?"

"I'll give her a moment."

"Someone needs to go after her, is what I'm saying."

"And I will, but I'm going to give her a fucking moment, Javi, come on.
She just had everything she knows about her life upended. She deserves a
moment." I needed sleep. I needed to be preparing for the Pax invasion. I
needed to be doing anything other than this. But Esa deserved a friend right
now, and maybe I was that and maybe I wasn't, but I was what she had.

"I'll talk to her," the Preacher said, starting forward.

I reached out to put a hand on her shoulder. "Yeah, I don't think you're
who she needs to talk to right now," I told her.

"And you are?" she asked, her voice still hollow, like the tale she'd told
had been taking up a space deep inside her that she now had nothing to fill
with. "You don't care about her—not really. She's just a tool to you."

I shook my head, took a drag from my smoke. "You don't know me," I
told her.

"I know enough."

"Apparently not."

"You're not her mother."

I looked at the Preacher, let her see how closely I was studying her, an
inversion of all the times she'd scanned my blood pressure and nervous system and whatever else just to answer her own curiosity "But you could have
been. And you chose not to. That was a decision *you* made. So you get to

live with it. I'll talk to her. You just . . . make yourself useful somewhere. Give her space."

The Preacher stared right back at me, her expression almost comically shocked—it likely would have hurt her less if I'd actually slapped her. Actually, with her metal skin, that probably would have hurt *me* more. But I was tired, and I was worn, and we had a lot of other problems to deal with; the Barious's emotional wounds could wait. Esa was who I was worried about now.

She deserved better than . . . all of this. Not just the Preacher's revelations. She deserved Sanctum to actually live up to its namesake, to be a sanctuary, a haven. Instead, she'd found yet another war, just another outbreak of the plague of violence and danger that had followed the pulse wherever it went.

"We destroyed the life she should have had," the Barious told me. "You and me, together. Before she was even born. She deserves better than either of us."

"Maybe." I nodded, exhaling smoke from my nostrils. Javier was probably right; it was a barbaric habit, but it helped calm me. "But we're what she's got, and you can't help her. Not right now. So go do something useful. I'll talk to Esa."

I wandered off in the general direction the girl had fled, before the Preacher could rally a response.

The engineering teams were swarming around the facility, all sorts of rigging and scaffolding and pulleys and lifts going up. High-tension lines were stretched all over the gun, construction materials were scattered everywhere, and bright blue sparks from welding torches scattered through the day. The work was going well, which meant it was loud, which meant Esa had gone elsewhere to think.

I found her out beyond the fence; she'd slipped out through the bars of electric light. Thankfully, she'd picked up a tag somewhere, or someone had the presence of mind to give one to her. I could barely fit through the hole myself, but I managed, cursing as I did. She was a nimble one, that girl.

She was sitting on a rock, staring out at the distant mountains, the gun rising behind her almost like a natural formation in and of itself. If we all died here, and if the Reint ever managed to overcome their predatory instincts to form an actual functioning society, maybe a hundred thousand years from now this gun, this facility, would be wonders of their primitive world, temples to gods unknown. For now, it was just a weapon, one we'd fire at our enemies, those who had come to destroy us. So I guess it was already a repository for plenty of prayers.

I sat beside Esa on the rock. Didn't say anything, just finished smoking my cigarette.

"There's another person," she said quietly, finally. "Someone else, the person I was supposed to be. If my parents hadn't died, if . . ."

"We're defined by things outside of our control," I said. "Where we're born, our circumstances, how we're raised. Who we are is something we don't actually have a great deal of say in. Until we do."

She turned to look at me. "What do you mean?" she asked.

I shrugged. "Before I joined the Justified, I was just a soldier," I told her. "I fought for a sect, the sect I was born in. I wanted to believe the things they taught us, the world they sold—I tried, I did. I just couldn't, not quite. Then I encountered the Justified, and I found a creed I *could*, one that made sense. One that I wanted to believe in. But I didn't have to follow them. I didn't have to leave everything I'd known behind. It would have been easier just to stay, pay lip service to the ideals I'd been raised with, and fight, and die, like I was supposed to."

"But you chose the unknown instead."

"I did. Even though it came with a cost. A great cost."

"Why?"

"Because it felt braver. Because it felt right."

"Was it?"

I was still just staring out at the mountains, aware that she was staring at me. "No idea," I said. "But if I hadn't, I'd be a different person now. Or I'd be dead; that one's much more likely. The choices I made—and the choices of others—they all led me here. To you. To this moment. The fight that's coming: it won't be the first time in my life I've fought to try and stave off something that felt inevitable. It won't be the first time I've fought to try and stop something I thought was wrong."

She smiled, just a little, despite the fact that she was still crying. "Hopefully it won't be the last," she added.

"Hopefully."

"What would you have done?"

"What would I have done when?"

"If you had been the Preacher. If you'd . . . if you could have raised me."

I shook my head. "That's not fair. She did what she thought she had to do."

"And I'm asking you what *you* would have thought you would have had to do. I don't know if that sentence makes sense; I'm sorry."

"No, I get it." I sighed. "You know about the choice I made, with Javi."

"You didn't make him lead those refugees to Sanctum."

"No, I didn't. But I could have followed him, when he ran. Could have tracked him. Could have forced him to come back with me, or to take me with him. At the time, the thought of living without him . . . it hurt. I won't say it was unbearable—there's surprisingly little in this galaxy that's that— but it hurt. A great deal."

"And instead you stayed. Because that's what you thought was right."

"It's where I thought I could do the most good."

"Even though it hurt."

"Even though."

"Do you still love him?"

I smiled, just a little. I wasn't even prepared to ask myself that question, let alone have Esa ask it. "Let's just get through the Pax assault," I told her. "Javier and I, our little . . . whatever this is . . . I don't know that it matters all that much, not if we'll both be dead in a few weeks' time."

"Isn't that when it should matter most?"

I was taken off guard by that; it hadn't been what I was expecting. I mean, she was probably right; that just wasn't the angle I ever would have come at it from. "Maybe so," I told her.

She nodded, like I had confirmed something she hadn't asked. "But you still haven't answered my question," she told me.

"I would have done what I thought was right," I told her. "I can't say what that would have been. It's easy to judge the Preacher for the call she made, but the truth is, we don't know if that was the right call or the wrong one. We just don't *know* what things would have been like if she'd taken another path. Maybe things would have wound up better for you. Maybe you wouldn't be here at all."

"And you think I should be. You think this . . ." She raised her face heavenward, toward the moon that held Sanctum, its seas of crystal glittering in the reflected light of the slowly rising binary stars. "You think *there* is where I belong."

"I think you're a fighter," I told her, and I meant it. "I know what that looks like when I see it, because I see it in the mirror, all the time. I think maybe you didn't know that about yourself, not until the time came to fight. You came out here, looking for us, even though you knew that meant you'd be putting yourself in danger. That says something."

She gave a little half-smile at that. "That I'm stupid and reckless?"

I nodded. "Those things, yeah. And also brave. And willing to fight. That's all we have to be, you know. Willing."

"That life I should have had, where my parents are still alive, where I was raised on a world not thrown so far backward in time. I'll never know what it would have been like, will I? I'll never know who that girl would have been."

I shook my head. "That's the thing about choices, those we make and those that are made for us—once a path is chosen, the other gets closed off, for good."

"So all I can do is . . . what? Knowing what I know now, that this isn't who I'm supposed to be—"

"You don't know that. You don't know that at all. I'm not going to tell you that things happen for a reason—I mean, yeah, they do, because of the decisions people make. But who you are, right now, the young woman sitting beside me: maybe that's *exactly* who you're supposed to be."

She was still looking up at the sky, but I felt her hand slide into mine. I squeezed her fingers, and held her hand right back. Let her know she wasn't alone. "We made it to Sanctum," she told me.

"Yeah, we did."

"Does that mean you're allowed to tell me your name now?"

I laughed. "You're going to be disappointed," I told her.

"Why? Is it a dumb name? Or scary or mean or something?"

"It's just a name. Doesn't really mean anything at all."

"But you *are* allowed to tell me."

"I am, sure." Actually I didn't know about that; after I dropped the kids off, I was never supposed to see them again. Their loyalties were meant to lie with Sanctum and the Justified, not me, and I was supposed to be off fetching other children, not worrying about the ones I'd left behind.

"Will you?" she asked.

I looked over at her; she was watching me.

"Jane," I told her. "My name is Jane."

ACT
FOUR

CHAPTER 1

I slept, finally. Then I got to work.

I only knew a little bit about electrical engineering—enough for me to brute force my way through sealed airlocks, and that was about it—and I knew even less about fusion reactors or even weapon calibrations on a gun that size, but I was a pair of hands, and every pair of hands was put to use. We didn't have much time.

The Preacher spent most of her time inside the facility, getting the systems up and running; Javier and I did odd jobs in and around the complex. Esa was actually the most useful of our little party—as she'd shown back on her homeworld, she was capable of lifting several tons' worth of equipment, and she swiftly became in high demand, differing groups of engineers clamoring for her attention.

The days passed in a blur of hard labor, snatched sleep, and worry. When we'd needed to clear the devolved Reint to secure the guns, I could focus on that, the first step; now that it was done, the only thing looming was the Pax armada that was on its way, that could arrive any day now. I'd spent the last hundred years working to keep Sanctum safe, to build it up, recruiting children from all across the galaxy into our—my—crusade. We were still well short of our goal—turning the pulse back around before it could sweep across the galaxy again—and it felt as close to collapse now as it had in the days and weeks and months just after the pulse. We hadn't faced a threat like this in a very long time.

I didn't know if we were going to be ready.

I got reports from Criat; the lunar guns above on the far side of Sanctum had been secured, were prepared. Chariot, Delta, and Echo positions, they would have firing solutions on the Pax as they arrived, but once the enemy moved to circle the moon and come into the orbit of the world beneath our feet, they'd be useless.

The repairs to Bravo emplacement, down in the city a thousand miles away, were coming along as well, and just like here, at Alpha, the engineers were working not just on the gun itself, but on defenses and shielding. The Pax would have to dig us out of these two positions before they could attack Sanctum proper—or at least, if they didn't, we'd be biting them in the ass the entire time they tried.

It was an odd thing, to know that all the work we were doing—and the blood we had shed, clearing the guns—was almost certainly going to be undone in the coming fight. Our entire strategy revolved around keeping the dreadnaughts off of Sanctum for as long as possible; I had no misconceptions that we would be able to do the same for the big cannons, either here in the mountains or in the city below. Eventually, the Pax would break through the defenses we were setting up, and pound both locations to dust.

We were repairing weapons that had lain dormant for well over a hundred years, and at the same time, we were planting charges to bring both facilities down, in case the Pax tried to seize the guns rather than destroy them. We couldn't let them be turned on Sanctum itself, and Bravo, at least, had a firing angle that would make that a real possibility.

Even if some minor miracle happened and the Pax were turned back before they could destroy these facilities, we'd still have to abandon them again. This was still a pulsed world, and it was still filled with devolved Reint; we couldn't keep the perimeters up and fight off the radiation indefinitely. Even now, the engineers were working to replace burnt-out parts and constantly reinforcing the shielding on the turrets; otherwise, the rads would have claimed them, rendered them inoperable hunks of metal.

The Reint still tested our defenses occasionally, but they didn't get through. Sheer animal cunning has its place, but, just like on every other world that had produced sentient species, big fuck-off guns and electrical fences were more than a match for predatory instincts.

I was pacing the perimeter one morning, roughly a week since we'd taken the guns; my shift hadn't started yet, and I was drinking coffee and checking how well the turrets were holding up when Schaz buzzed my comms. "You might want to step back inside," she said, her voice quiet for some reason. She was still on world; this high up in the mountains, she could remain in the pulsed atmosphere for quite some time, and we'd been sleeping on board, then letting Schaz return to orbit after. "Esa's . . . studying. She's accessed my databanks, looking for some very specific information. I think there might be a conversation you two need to have."

I nodded, and finished my coffee, heading back toward Scheherazade. I could have asked her more—it's not like she was broadcasting our conversation to Esa inside her living quarters—but I didn't have to. I had a pretty good idea what the girl was looking at.

Schaz's ramp was lowered; she was inside the perimeter of the guns, so we weren't worried about Reint creeping inside. She was due to take off in a bit, but Esa was using the time she had with Schaz's databanks, putting her access to good use. Or at least what she thought of as good use.

I moved quietly up the ramp and watched her from the airlock doorway; I don't think she saw me. She was too busy studying the holoprojection before her, one of the very first images I'd ever shown her on its glowing wireframe surface: the image of a Pax. A basic Pax infantry unit, specifically.

As I watched, she rotated the image; stripped off its armor, piece by piece. Its kinetic shielding, its bulky plating, its extraneous ammunition pouches and gear kits. The scan was very detailed, based on Pax units we'd captured or autopsied over the years. We knew what was inside that armor. Now, so did she.

She put the bulky figure back together, then took it apart again. For a moment, I wondered if she was looking for weak spots, trying to figure out where she should *hit* them, but: no. That's what *I* would have been doing, when I was her age. Esa wasn't me.

With the skeleton of the armor laid bare around the faceless, amorphous outline representing the soldier within, she reached inside the hologram, pulling out a single piece of machinery and expanding it to take up the entire projection. "This is it," she said quietly, at first I thought to herself until I realized that she'd known I was standing there, might have for a while. "This is the part I can't get past."

I nodded, moving past her very deliberately to pour myself another cup of coffee. I wasn't feigning disinterest, exactly, but if I acted concerned over her discovery, demanded she shut the projection down, that would only confirm her fears. "You know what it is, I suppose?" I asked her.

"I do," she nodded, still staring up at the glowing image. It was an autosyringe: specifically, a series of microsyringes, one of the few pieces of the basic Pax gear that changed based on what species was inside the armor. She was staring at the type designed for use on human soldiers, the kind that fit just at the top of the spinal column like a mechanical centipede with needles for legs. That positioning gave it access to the spine and the brain stem and the blood-brain barrier at once so that it could be remotely triggered, delivering its payloads directly into the nervous system of its subject like an insect administering a dose of venom.

She turned, finally, not glaring at me, exactly, but not happy, either. "You told me they were brainwashed," she said. "You told me that once the Pax were done with their . . . with their *subjects*, that they weren't people anymore. That they were just Pax."

"I did," I nodded. "And it's true."

"Then why . . ." She gestured helplessly to the ugly-looking needles, then stopped. Pulled up Schaz's vidscreen, instead, where she'd been doing the rest of her research. "Epinephrine," she read off from her list. "Dopamine. Methamphetamines. Benzodiazepine. A whole host of other narcotic cocktails that I can't even pronounce." She turned from the screen, back to me, her face still beseeching, more than demanding. "I looked them all up. Every single one. Different chemicals for different species, but all with the same goals; they're used to *control* behavior, to control aggression, to sedate or enrage. Jane, if they're so brainwashed that there's *no* going back, *why are they being drugged?*"

I took a drink of my coffee, said nothing. Let her work it out for herself. There was another question, one she hadn't asked me, one she was still working up to. I wanted her to get there on her own.

"If the Pax are controlling their soldiers remotely with these . . . these . . ."—she gestured at the remote syringes glowing on the hologram—"then they're *not* soldiers, are they? They're slaves."

"They were always slaves. And they're still soldiers."

"And that's who we're going to fight. That's who you're asking me . . ." She turned, looking at the projection again. Pulled out from the set of syringes, put them back in their place in the armor, then pulled the armor itself apart, until there was just what lay in the middle: that androgynous, species-ambiguous form, the Pax within. Still a person. "That's who I'm going to have to kill," she said, so softly I could barely hear it.

"Do you think you can?" I asked her, taking another sip of my coffee.

"Do you think I *should*?" She was almost angry now. Finally.

Without saying anything, I reached past her. Adjusted the wireframe again, until the electrical systems were exposed, including those linked to the autosyringes. "Take another look," I told her.

"I don't understand—"

"There's always more you don't see," I said, then nodded again at the hologram.

She turned, studied. Still didn't see it. "They're drugs—the soldiers that wear this armor, they're constantly being shot up with narcotics, filled with cocktails promoting aggression, tamping down independent thinking. If we could just—if there was a way to *break* the transmitter, or wherever the order to inject them is coming from—"

"And where is it coming from?" I asked her. "What's the trigger for the injection system wired to?"

She frowned, started looking again. At first she tried to trace it back to the comm system in the helmet, but that wasn't where the wiring led. After a moment, she found it—traced it back down, from the neck, across the shoulder, down the arm. To the wrist. Into the hand.

"Oh, god," she whispered. The hand in the projection went through a series of motions, an illustration. Ring finger to base of palm was one signal; index finger to base of thumb was another. At least a dozen, each different touch triggering the syringes in the armor to begin a different type of injection.

The narcotic deliveries weren't controlled by some Pax commander up on the dreadnaughts, or even by some sort of slave master in charge of each platoon. They were controlled by the individual soldiers on the battlefield. They were doing it to themselves.

"They are slaves," I told her. "You're right about that. They were made slaves the day they were broken. But there's no freeing them, Esa; there's no putting them back together. By the time they put on that armor"—I nodded to the hologram—"by the time they're given a gun, they're Pax, and nothing else. We can't save them. And yes. We will have to kill them. Do you think you can?"

"I don't know how," she almost whispered.

"You do." I hated myself for saying it, just a little bit. I said it anyway. She had the instincts for it, and she had the power. All that was required now was the will. If she looked at a Pax and saw a person, she'd hesitate, she'd freeze, and she'd get herself killed. She needed to see an enemy instead.

"You do it to survive," I told her. "You do it so that *you*, and the people you care about"—I nodded at the hologram—"will *never* become *that*."

"And it's that simple."

"It's always that simple," I told her.

She took a deep, shuddering breath. She'd been trying to find a way around it; a way to save them all, somehow. Still young enough to believe there might be some solution where a lot of people didn't have to die. We were well past that point. One way or another, blood was going to be shed.

Better theirs than ours.

"So what *do* I do?" she asked me.

I'd delivered a lot of children to Sanctum over the years. What happened to them next wasn't my responsibility. I wasn't a teacher; I wasn't a leader. I didn't know how to make her into what she needed to be, what the *galaxy* needed her to be.

But I could keep her alive. I could do that.

"The armor's weak here," I told her, circling a join under the arm, "and at the top of the neck, here, just under the jaw. They'll likely have antigrav gear and kinetic boosters, so they'll be faster than you think, but they can't *duck* very fast. Use that."

How to fight; how to stay alive. How to *win*.

It was all I had to teach.

CHAPTER 2

A few days later, still working myself into a bone-weary exhaustion every day then dropping into a dreamless sleep, my conversation with Esa about the nature of the Pax continued to echo through my thoughts. It didn't haunt me—I'd done the right thing. But it was good that the girl was prepared for what was coming, and I needed to make sure that I was just as ready. The fight was on its way.

After our discussion after the Preacher's revelations, and what I'd told her in Scheherazade's living quarters, Esa and I were good, so I didn't have to worry about that, or really Esa at all: she and the Preacher had reached a detente, wherein Esa would work with the Barious, and she could be civil, but the bond between them was damaged, maybe irreparably. Still, that wasn't my problem—if they both survived, their conflicting feelings toward each other could be ironed out later.

What I needed sorted was a great deal closer to home, and a great deal harder to face.

I found Javier down in the bowels of the gun, sorting through various detritus that had been pulled from the machinery, deciding what might still be of use here, what could be sent back to Sanctum to be repurposed, and what was simply scrap.

"Hey," I said to him. Even to my ears, it sounded weak.

He turned and looked at me. Raised his eyebrow. "Hey," he said back. "You need me for something?"

"Yeah." I took a breath. "We need to talk."

He laughed. "You've been avoiding talking to me ever since you pulled me off of Beyond Ending," he said. "Don't think I didn't notice."

"We've got a great deal of history between us." I shrugged. "Not all of it is good. I thought—"

He stood, and shrugged, stretching his arms over his head. I don't know if he did it on purpose, but he was definitely showing off the fact that life as a pirate-smuggler-whathaveyou had kept him in shape. "You thought, since there was a good chance we were about to both die anyway, why reopen old wounds?" He nodded. "Sure, I get that. But then you thought about it some *more*—because that's what you do, you're always thinking, always running scenarios in your head—and thought that, if we *did* die, and we *didn't* talk, we'd never get a chance to have that conversation, the one you were so keen not to have. This conversation."

"It's not *not* a possibility," I told him, a little annoyed, I wasn't *that* transparent.

"Of course it's a possibility." He nodded, turning to face me. "So's the third option: that only one of us dies, and the other has to go on wondering if things had been different, if we'd just—"

I kissed him, just to shut him up. Or, you know, partially.

He *had* kept in shape, and he had also remembered everything he'd learned when we'd been together. For the first time in over a week, I spent the next hour *not* thinking about the Pax, or violence, or my responsibility for what had happened to the galaxy. I didn't even feel guilty for taking a break from working on the gun. Javier was too busy not letting me feel anything but him.

Afterward, we lay entwined on the pile of bedding we'd managed to collapse into, shoved up against the wall. No, we hadn't even managed to make it *outside* of the gun before we sated our carnal desires. Both of us had a great deal of built-up need, that had become very clear, very quickly.

"Do we still have to talk?" he asked, stroking my hair.

I blinked against his chest, not looking at his face. "Do you hate me for not coming after you?" I asked him.

He shook his head, gently, careful not to dislodge me from my rest. "Do you hate me for betraying the Justified, for making things more difficult for you?" he asked.

Here, in his arms, it felt right, I felt safe, and good, and warm. It would have been impossible for me to hate him here, in this moment. Had I hated him, after he'd done what he'd done? At times, yes. We'd had something, and he'd abandoned it, and I'd been hurt by that, even though I understood that he'd only been doing what he thought was right, and he, like me, knew that sometimes doing the right thing entailed sacrifice.

I looked up at him then, my chin on his chest. "No," I said, and it was the truth.

He bent toward me—I could feel even that small movement, my body pressed against his, could feel the muscles move under his skin, and I'd forgotten how good it felt just to be this close to someone, to have someone hold you—and kissed me on the forehead. "Then do we pick up where we left off?" he asked. "Assuming the council doesn't decide to execute me after we're done. Can we do that?"

"I think we just did," I replied, kissing him on the chest.

He smiled, but didn't take his eyes off me. "There's more to us than this, and I don't know if that's patched yet. On either side. Can we fix that? Do you want to?"

I stretched out over him, so I could kiss him on the mouth. "I think we just did," I said again.

Then I showed him what I meant.

CHAPTER 3

I felt better, after that.

Javier and I had gone from dancing around each other, half-avoiding each other, half-seeking each other's presence, to behaving like moonstruck kids, finding excuses to be around one another. I'd almost forgotten how good it felt, to be with him, to know that he was mine, that anytime I wanted, I could grab him and steal a kiss, or more.

Of course, the change in our behavior didn't go unnoticed.

"Humans." Marus sighed, after watching me watch Javier during our lunch break. "Always ready to start mating season. It must be exhausting, being your kind." He'd rejoined us after ferrying engineers back and forth, but I pretty much only saw him during meals, which we took in the makeshift cafeteria in the facility; he was working with the crews digging out and rewiring the targeting systems, whereas I was mostly doing physical labor on the gun itself.

"What?" Esa looked up from stuffing her lunch into her mouth as fast as possible, first looking at Marus, then looking at me, then looking at Javi. As she realized the implications of Marus's observation, she screwed up her face, still half-full of sandwich. "Ew. I mean, great. I mean, ew. I mean, I'm happy for you two. But still . . . ew."

I threw a roll at her head. It bounced, and she grabbed it before it could hit the floor—even if she didn't have her gifts, she had the reflexes to make a damned fine Justified operative—then swallowed her sandwich in one massive gulp, and shoved the roll in after it. After all these years escorting teenagers, I was no longer surprised by just how much they ate.

"You know the shoot-to-kill order on you has only been frozen, right?" Marus asked Javi conversationally, like they were discussing the weather. "It hasn't been rescinded completely." His words were directed at Javier, but they were meant for me.

"I know," Javi replied, answering for both of us. "But given that our odds of surviving the coming fight are pretty slim anyway . . ." He shrugged, and reached for another helping of . . . protein. I really wasn't sure *what*, exactly, we were eating; I hadn't managed to snag one of the sandwiches Esa had grabbed. Sanctum itself usually had pretty good meals, but they were too busy readying for the fight to send us prepared food, and so we were making do with the emergency stuff that came along with the engineering supplies.

"What are you going to do if the council asks you to kill him?" Marus asked me, his tone still conversational.

"Not do that." I shrugged. "I've made up my mind about that one."

"Well, that's good to know," Javi responded dryly.

"Is this really the time to worry about this, Marus?" I asked.

"I am . . . quite fond of both of you," he told us. "I really don't want to see you survive the coming battle, only to wind up torn apart again over stupid Justified politics."

"God, Marus." Esa rolled her eyes. "Will you not let them, you know . . . just *be* for a while?"

The Preacher sat next to us. She didn't have to eat, but she was trying to be companionable—and trying to just be around Esa as much as possible, without forcing the issue. "Humans experience a spike in endorphins, oxytocin, and dopamine when first engaging in a sexual relationship," she put in.

"Ew," Esa said again, not quite directly to the Preacher, just to the world in general.

The Preacher pointed at Javier and me with a nearby fork. "Their decision-making abilities—especially when it comes to decisions about each other—are highly impaired at the moment," she continued. "It's entirely possible that they—"

An alarm started to sound.

"Oh, thank god." Javier sighed.

"Is it the Reint, trying for the walls again?" Marus asked, standing.

"No." I shook my head. "That's a different sound, and we'd hear the turrets, even in here. That's the old battle-stations alarm; I helped rig it up again a few days ago."

Esa looked up at me with wide eyes. "Does that mean—"

I nodded grimly. "It means we've heard from our scouts. The Pax are on their way."

CHAPTER 4

Everyone inside the makeshift cafeteria had stopped talking, fast, as soon as the alarms began to sound. A few vidscreens had been set up; Helliot was centered in all of them, giving a speech, the rest of the council sitting somberly beside her. Her prepared text was big on honor and duty and the importance of our work. I tuned it out. Instead, I watched Criat, seated behind her; I tried to read his expression. He was giving me nothing.

Helliot finally got to numbers. They weren't good. We didn't know how many spacecraft they had, because at least three of the dreadnaughts en route had their guts ripped out, been retrofitted into carriers. Just an unmodified dreadnaught—one with its big gun still intact—could carry upwards of two dozen fighters, ships roughly the size of Scheherazade. With all of that interior space converted to holds, that number would skyrocket.

We did have an estimate on frigates, the larger vessels that would screen the dreadnaughts from attack. Sixteen. That was bad. What was worse was the count of dreadnaughts themselves: twenty-two at a minimum, maybe more. The supercraft had still been arriving from various hyperspace vectors when our scouts had retreated. Wherever the hell the Pax had picked up their armada, it had left them one of the best-armed forces in the galaxy. They'd lost one of their supercraft over Esa's homeworld, and at least one more—maybe two—in the assault on Beyond Ending, using up the least of their dreadnaughts to clear the path to Sanctum.

We had *no* dreadnaughts. Only three of the four frigates in our possession had been restored to working order. Work on the fourth would continue, of course, and if things got desperate—which they would—it could be sent out, but not at full strength. All we had were the big guns: Chariot, Delta, Echo, the three bases on the far side of Sanctum's moon, and Alpha and Bravo, the two I'd helped reclaim from the Reint. There was also the cannon in Sanctum itself, but that one didn't get a codename: it was just Sanctum. If *that* one fell, the fight was over.

We could set up an anti-orbital bombardment with those six guns, and Justified operatives had spent the last few weeks seeding the entrance to the system with mines and other traps; I'd take our fighters over theirs, both in terms of the ships' design and construction, and in terms of our pilots' abilities. We could make them pay for attacking us.

But I didn't like our odds of surviving.

It felt like a last stand. It always had, true enough, but I had thought we'd have more of a fighting chance. This . . . it would take a miracle for us to survive this. Miracles had always been in short supply in this galaxy, even before the pulse.

After Helliot had finished her speech, I retreated with my makeshift crew—the Preacher, Marus, and Esa—to Scheherazade. Javier came with us, but he wouldn't be joining us when it came time to fight; he'd be in Bolivar instead.

We stood around Scheherazade's living quarters, just staring at each other. Javier was gripping the back of a chair with hands gone white around the knuckles; it seemed almost absurd that just a few hours ago those hands had been caressing me, had been tender, gentle, kind. Now they were tense and desperate.

Marus stood, his arms wrapped tight around himself, his fingers tapping out a rhythm against his arms. He'd almost died to get us this information, to buy us the time we'd had to prepare. I had to believe that it had been worth something, worth more than just us putting up a fight before the Pax swarmed us under.

The Preacher was looking at Esa. Usually I found Barious hard to read, and the Preacher harder than most, but at this moment her expression was crystal clear. She didn't know if she should have brought Esa here, and she didn't want to die with the girl still angry with her. She'd given up everything she'd known to try and protect her, and that series of decisions had led her to this, a desperate fight in a dead-end system with the Pax coming to avenge the pulse itself. Not to mention to claim all of the gifted children hiding in Sanctum.

The Pax could try and say they had come because of what we'd done to the galaxy, and maybe their rank and file troops even believed that, thanks to the brainwashing and the drugs and the idiot philosophizing of the Pax creed, but it was a lie. This was about resources, plain and simple, just like everything else the Pax did. The children were just another tool to add to their arsenal, to help speed their spread through the galaxy like a metastasizing cancer.

Of course, they hadn't been powerful enough to do that before the pulse, or, at least, they'd had enemies who could have stood up to them. So in a way, the Pax were our fault as well. That's the thing about changing the galaxy: everything that happens after the change is on you. For good or for ill.

Esa herself was watching me watch the others. "It's worse than you thought it would be," she said finally, the first thing any of us had said.

"Yeah." I nodded. "It is."

"Bad enough that we won't be able to win?"

"There's always a chance to win," Marus told her. "It may be slim, but it's there. We just have to hold strong, to defend the guns, and we can fight them off." He was more confident than I was, or, at least, he was doing a better job of *pretending* he was.

"Just so someone says it," Javier pointed out, looking up from his hands and straight at me. "We could run."

I shook my head. "We couldn't."

"We could, actually. Yes, there will be an entire battle between us and the exit from the system, but it will be chaos out there once the fighting starts. Once the dying starts. All we have to do is look for our moment."

I made him look me full in the eye. "You want to run?" I asked softly. He'd known me better than that, once. I thought I'd known him better.

He shook his head. "I don't want to," he said. "But if we have to, if things start going south and there's no way for the Justified to win, two ships aren't going to make a difference. They're just not." Harsh, but probably true; mostly true, maybe true. But not completely. Marus was right: there was always a chance to turn the tide.

"She won't run," Esa told him, still looking at me. "And you won't run while she's still here. So that's that."

"We fight here," the Preacher said. "They've come to kill us; we kill them back. It's that simple."

"Just like in the sect wars," I murmured. One way or another, this was the world I'd always lived in.

"Are we ready to do this?" Schaz asked through her comms.

I nodded. The time for introspection was over. There was nothing in front of us beyond the fight. If we lived through it, we could ask ourselves what we should have done differently, if there had been another possible outcome, other choices we could have made. If we died, all of that wouldn't matter. "Start up the engines, Schaz," I told her. "Get ready for war."

CHAPTER 5

I kissed Javier goodbye. I could see him try to think of something to say, then discard those thoughts; there was nothing good enough to be our last words to each other in person. I was doing the same thing. So we kissed, and he headed out, and no words were spoken. We'd watch for each other, in the fight above.

The Preacher went with him. I was surprised by that, but it was helpful. With Esa running the guns on board Scheherazade—and I'd had her running drills for days; she was an asset now, rather than just ballast—Marus could take the tail gun, which meant the Preacher wouldn't have had much to do here anyway. On board Bolivar, Javier would take the stick, which meant the Preacher could run the guns.

Criat had left a private message for me. I watched it as Schaz ran through her pre-flight check; I wondered if he'd left them for all of his operatives. If he'd recorded them as soon as we knew the Pax were on their way, or even earlier than that—if he'd had these in a drawer somewhere for years, knowing that this kind of fight would come to our doorstep someday. I wondered if he'd left one for Javier.

He told me to fight. He told me to survive. He told me he was proud of me. He referenced missions I'd survived that I probably shouldn't have; desperate situations that I'd escaped by the skin of my teeth. He even made a few jokes, which was rare for the boss. Mostly, though, he told me to fight. I'd oblige.

Schaz was ready to go. I strapped myself into the pilot's chair, made sure Esa was strapped in behind me. Then we lifted off, out of the atmosphere of the icy world, leaving the mountains behind for the vast canvas of stars above.

Sanctum, the Pax's eventual target, passed by above us. We could see the shimmer of the shielding, already in place as the big gun was extended.

The city was locked down. Inside the mountain, millions of Justified noncombatants—scientists, children, cooks and janitors and artists—were huddled together in the bomb shelters.

It would take some pounding for the Pax dreadnaughts to get through the big shield that spread over the entire city, and while they were pounding on that, we'd be hitting them with the cannons on the world below, and with the cannon inside Sanctum itself. The fight would come down to exactly that kind of attrition—how much damage each dreadnaught could do to the shield over Sanctum before we blew them out of the sky. Powered by a half-dozen fusion reactors, the massive web of energy could have held off a single dreadnaught indefinitely, maybe even two or three, but the Pax were going to make sure it was constantly under fire from far more than that.

The Pax's plan of attack would be simple: arrive in-system, make their way to the firing position on Sanctum, start their artillery barrage, possibly diverting some of their forces to blast apart our own gun emplacements on the way. We'd be hitting them the whole time, first from the guns on the moons, then from the two planetary weapons. They wouldn't turn their dreadnaughts to those targets—dreadnaughts were slow, cumbersome things, took a long time to move, a longer time to aim, and longer than that to fire. Instead, they'd try to knock out the guns with their fighters or their frigates, or even by landing ground troops.

That's where we'd come in—the Justified fighters would have to take as many of their ships down as possible, before they could even launch their attack runs against the guns. Every fighter we took out was one less fighter to blast away at the shielding over the cannon; every second longer the cannons were shielded was more time for them to attack the dreadnaughts; every second the dreadnaughts took fire was one second longer for us to try and blast them apart, before they could do the same to Sanctum.

It was complicated—massive battles like this always were—but at the end of the day, it came down to a simple concept: fight. Fight until you can't fight any more, and then fight anyway. During the sect wars, in all the fighting I'd done on the ground, it had often seemed like a single soldier in all that chaos wasn't making a difference, couldn't achieve anything, but that wasn't true. Every shot you fired—whether it hit an enemy or not—was another round pinning down an enemy position, or another round clearing the path for your side's assault. This was the same thing, just in a ballet of death in the void rather than in mud and blood on the ground.

The Justified vessels were all getting into position, scattering ourselves around the system, ready to hit the Pax from all sides. We wouldn't attack first; we'd let them come in, let them hit the mines, let them get close enough to take fire from the cannons on the moon. A trap's no good if you spring it early.

We didn't know if they knew that *we* knew they were coming or not. They might be expecting resistance; they might be expecting to take us by surprise. Either way, they'd brought along enough firepower to finish the job five times over. Or so they thought.

We were going to make them pay for trying.

CHAPTER 6

The Pax didn't make us wait for long.

The first ship came through, drawn down out of the stars. You never quite get used to seeing ships come out of hyperspace; they sort of . . . fade in, a little bit at a time, as if they were being painted on the light-speckled canvas of the cosmos. It was just a scout ship, a recon vessel. If it wanted to reconnoiter the system then return to the larger flotilla, we wouldn't let it, but we had time before it tried to run—it would have to wait for its hyperdrive to cool down.

It didn't make any moves to return to hyperspace, though. It didn't make any moves at all, just hung there, in the void, at the far edge of the system, between the spinning calderas of the black holes. Like it was waiting for something.

Every single Justified vessel was watching it. I guess that's what it was waiting for.

Scheherazade's comms crackled to life. "Justified." A single word. Not a question, not a query—a statement. The voice was masked behind the usual filters; all Pax sounded alike, very much on purpose. You couldn't tell species or gender or even tone, really; even inflection and pitch were taken out. It was the voice of the Pax, the voice of many forged into the will of one.

"We wanted to thank you," the Pax scout craft said. "You made this new galaxy what it is. Purposefully or not, you paved the way for our rise. Before the pulse, the Pax struggled. Too many were deaf to our call, too many already following blind paths of faith or weakness. You changed that. So many stars are now unclaimed, waiting just to hear the word of the Pax, that before were deaf to our call. Now, they will be made stronger. Now, they will make *us* grow stronger. For that, we thank you. For that, we give you a choice.

"Join. Give your ships, your guns, your arms over to the Pax, so that they might be used to claim this galaxy for our will. Give us your soldiers, your engineers, your intellectuals, so that they might further the Pax cause. Give us your children, so that they might revel in the glory of the Pax. Join us now, and together we will make this galaxy into what it was always meant to be—a bastion of peace, of prosperity, all people united under one will, toward one goal, with one aim.

"The Pax are peace through force. The Pax are prosperity through simplification. The Pax are the only path to the future. For centuries, even before the pulse, you have struggled to make your mark on this galaxy, to do things that you thought would make life better for others, whether they could see that was your aim or not. The Pax are the same, but the Pax are greater. *We* are greater. You prepared this galaxy for our rise. Now you can join us in that ascent.

"Become Pax. Become the peace this galaxy deserves.

"Or die."

The usual tin-pot dictator shit. I'd heard it before, on a hundred different worlds. Sometimes it was from a scout ship declaring the arrival of an armada; sometimes it was from a dozen hungry men standing at the gates of a township armed with spears where those inside only had stones. They promised peace, but only with capitulation. What they understood about the Justified made them think we were the same; they thought we both believed *force* was the only way to turn people to a cause, that merely possessing strength gave you the inalienable right to use that strength in whatever way you saw fit, made every action you took righteous so long as you were strong enough to take it. Accordingly, they still thought we'd triggered the pulse on purpose. Because that's what they would have done.

The Pax scout ship drifted forward, its engines firing slightly. Waiting on an answer.

One of us gave it. I wasn't sure who it was—not Scheherazade, and not Bolivar, that was all I knew. But one of the Justified gave the Pax the reply they were waiting for, in the form of a railgun blast that tore into the unprotected side of their craft. They didn't even have their shields raised—a sacrificial calf, exsanguinated on a battlefield for the frenzied joy of whatever god. The scout ship was torn in half.

The remnants of the Pax vessel drifted in the void. The avenue between the two black holes was narrow, and the attack had pushed the remains of the scout ship off course. We all watched as it was pulled into the cosmic riptide of the gravitational maw, dragged into the dense oblivion of the devouring star. I'm not sure what the rest of the Justified were thinking at that moment; we were a diverse bunch of people, as defined by our backgrounds and our history as by our shared creed. I'm also sure, however, that I wasn't alone in my thought:

One down.

The rest of the Pax fleet started to fade into existence, already in motion.

Hundreds to go.

CHAPTER 7

The battle was joined.

The black void, filled with starlight, absolutely glowed with the heat of the passage of rounds fired from the anti-orbital cannons on the approach side of Sanctum's moon. The lunar guns roared and roared again into the silence of the void; the first of the Pax dreadnaughts on approach was battered, twisted, already punctured on multiple decks before it could even move far enough into the system to allow more Pax vessels clearance to arrive.

Still, the Pax must have known something like that was coming, because that first ship was just another sacrificial lamb of a kind—it was one of the converted carriers, and from out of its splitting hull burst forth dozens of fighter craft, like a wasp nest cracked open and divulging its frenzied cargo. Despite the supercraft collapsing around them, the fighter pilots were still Pax, and Pax ingrained discipline; they taught that no matter what was happening, if you were Pax, you behaved as Pax. The wasp-like fighters formed into an attack wedge and headed straight for the moon, aiming for Delta cannon.

That was our cue.

I threw Scheherazade's throttle to full and we raced out of our hiding place, joined by the other Justified ships in-system. Schaz kept note of the Pax dreadnaught positions and highlighted the likely paths of the cannon-fire trajectories in my HUD; I weaved among them, dancing my nimble ship through the lines of high-velocity death. We hit the Pax ships from all sides, tearing their formation apart.

I had control of the forward guns and the missiles; Esa had the short-range omnidirectional lasers at her fingertips; Marus was in the rear turret. Together we cut down Pax craft everywhere we found them, and they were every-

where, trying to fight their way through the Justified counterattack, still sui-
cidally focused on the lunar cannons below. They wouldn't make it, of
course—this was just a ploy by the Pax generals, meant to draw us out of
hiding, so the next round of forces would know where we were and could
respond accordingly—but they were fighting like the outcome of the entire
battle rested on their success.

The dogfight took us through the debris field of the pulverized celestial
bodies, the ships drifting and jockeying for position among the shards of dead
planets. The void was full of tracer fire and explosions as we danced and
twisted through the sepulchral remnants of the brutalized worlds. There were
more of the Pax ships, but we had the advantage; this was our terrain, and
our traps had been laid well.

Most of them were down before they even reached the atmosphere of
the moon. A few made it all the way down to the surface, close enough to
train their guns on the shield over the cannon, only to be cut down by the
anti-aircraft batteries we'd installed below. The first wave of the Pax attack
was over, and listening in to the chatter on the comms, I don't think it had
cost us a single Justified ship, but the Pax had forced us out of position—
now our fighter craft were between the Pax fleet and the cannon, and it would
take us longer to engage the next wave of assault ships. We wouldn't be
able to hit them from all sides like we had this time. This would be a war of
attrition, and the Pax had the numbers for it. We didn't.

The enemy was still arriving, pulling out of hyperspace one at a time, their
path constrained by the spinning black holes. There were four dreadnaughts
in-system now, bulling their way through the cannon fire to try and orbit
the planet below. The first was almost entirely out of commission, explosions
rocking its structure; our gunnery crews had stopped targeting it entirely,
marking it down as no longer a threat.

But the time it had taken for the cannons to put that *first* dreadnaught out
of the fight meant that the others were clearing the black holes without taking nearly as much damage, and soon the second of the massive supercraft
would be clear of the lunar firing solutions entirely.

More fighters were arriving as well, first clustering in the protection of
the dreadnaughts' guns, then, when they'd reached some agreed-upon number, starting their attacks on the moon, on us. A frigate had joined them. A

second had tried, but had pushed the envelope of its trajectory too far, and was even now being pulled helplessly into the gravity well of the merciless black hole. Even that loss would teach the Pax—now they knew exactly the edges of their avenue of approach, the red lines of their vectors in-system, a few scout ships winking away to warn the others in their staging area.

I shifted Scheherazade's shields to full forward, and I may have shouted an obscenity as I pushed the throttles to full; I honestly wasn't sure. We were in it now, there was no turning back, these motherfuckers were here to destroy my home, my friends, everything I'd ever stood for, and all I had was Schaz and the guns fused to her belly and the missiles in her banks; all I had was her engines and her shields and her responsive flight stick, and I was going to make them pay for that.

This was what I *did*.

We hit the second wave of the Pax attack head-on, just at the shimmering edge of the lunar atmosphere, the fight taking place in high orbit with boiling seas of crystal below and the mass of their protective frigate angled shark-like above, just starting to enter the ring of debris surrounding the inner system. The battle was well and truly begun now, and there would be no turning back. Fight or die.

The Pax had thought we would join them, that any of us would join them. They thought they knew the Justified—thought what we had done made us who we were.

We would make them pay for that mistake.

CHAPTER 8

"Jane, you've got one trying to zero in for a distance shot; pull to port and let me angle in for an attack run." Javier's voice jolted me out of the almost reverie-like state I'd been pulled into by the focus of combat; I realized I'd barely been listening to the comms, so intent had I been on the Pax ships filling the sky.

"Roger," I confirmed, rolling Schaz away from my current target and firing off a single missile to continue ruining his day. Javi's warning came not a moment too soon; mere seconds later a rail-cannon blast sang past us, lighting up my screens. I marked Bolivar's position and swung even wider, coming around the edges of the fight.

"Got him," Javier said, pulling Bolivar free of the trailing smoke from the Pax craft's engines. "You're clear." The enemy ship he'd targeted was locked in a spiral down to the sea of molten crystal on the lunar surface below; even if the pilot survived the crash, I didn't envy him what came next.

"We're more than that." Our little evasive maneuver had pulled us out of the heat of the combat, and as a result, we'd somehow wound up closer to the Pax frigate than I'd expected, just outside of its firing envelope. For the most part, at least. I was still diving and juking around turret fire, but that particular ship was built for frontal assault, and we'd wound up in the debris field almost behind it. "Line up on me, Javi," I told him.

". . . Why?" He asked the question, but I was tracking Bolivar's movements; he was getting into position. "I only ask because you seem to be lining up for an attack run on that goddamned frigate."

"You always have been a sharp one, haven't you?" I replied. The frigate—shaped almost like a crescent, the forward guns lining the interior arc, and us facing the glow of the engines at its rear—was still trying to pull free of the debris field, which meant at the moment a great many of its defensive turrets were firing on the asteroids, trying to clear a path to get it closer to the fight.

That wouldn't last long; once it was clear of the field, the turrets would be free to attack all comers making for the turret itself. We'd only have one chance to pull this off, and it was now.

Ordinarily, a ship Scheherazade's size—or Bolivar's—could only be a nuisance to a frigate like that; if she was a mosquito up against a whale when compared to a dreadnaught, the frigate was at least a hefty terrestrial mammal, like a bear or an elk or something. This particular frigate, however, had already taken a battering from the mines and traps we'd left in the debris and the approach. We didn't have anything else coming to bear on her; left alone, her shields would recharge, and we'd lose the moment when both her defenses were battered and her turrets were otherwise occupied. Now or never.

"Is that smart?" Esa asked nervously, eyeballing the massive ship rising ever closer through the cockpit, the glare of a single one of its engines larger around than Schaz's entire chassis. "Is . . . should we be doing this?"

"No," Javier told her in no uncertain terms; I'd forgotten that Esa was patched into the comms as well. "But it appears we're doing it anyway, so get ready."

"We're doing what?" Marus asked from the tail turret. "What are we doing? Why am I facing the debris field? Will you people *please* remember that I'm back here—I can't see what's in front of us at all."

"Just get ready to shoot," I told him, pushing the throttle to full and shifting all of Schaz's shields forward.

"At *what?*"

We were well and truly inside the frigate's firing envelope before he could respond, and the turrets were already starting to target us fully, aware that we were more of a danger than the debris free to crash into its shielding. Still, I had us lined up on an approach at its engines, where the fewest turrets could fire on us, and Schaz's shielding was only *mostly* stripped away before I got us into range of the forward guns and opened up.

Bolivar was right there with us, and while he didn't have as much firepower to add, every little bit helped. We poured fire into the shields, cutting thrust and dancing and juking through the field of lasers trying to cut us out of the sky, matching the slow swing of the frigate as it tried to turn and bear down on us. They were pulling their shielding from the rest of the craft now in an attempt to repel our assault, but that only meant that the whirling debris was crashing into the structure of the ship itself, the very system the Pax's enemy.

A web of crimson heat began to spread through the gossamer shimmer of the frigate's shields, and then they cracked, and then we were through, pounding the engines mercilessly; my guns were approaching the red line, but we were *close*, goddammit, almost there, and finally the engines erupted into flame, first one, then the damage chaining to the others. I pulled us back, racing out of the firing envelope of the frigate, Schaz's own shields in tatters as Marus picked off the missiles on our tail; I'd pushed it close, maybe too close. But the frigate was badly damaged, incapable of keeping up with the roving firefight above the moon's surface, the ruin of its engines spreading chaos throughout the vessel.

We raced away, trying to give our ships' cores a moment to recharge our shields.

"A hell of an attack run, you two," John Henry came out of our comms, his voice admiring. "We'd been shifting our frigates into position to take that one on, but now we can continue to hold them until the Pax push closer into the system. Well done."

"How far have the dreadnaughts penetrated?" I asked him, scanning my screens even as I asked.

"They're pushing past the moon now, around the curve that will put them above the planet below, but we're making them pay for it. We've taken four entirely out of commission, and they've just now entered the firing solution of the planetary guns."

That was good, but hardly enough; it meant that as we were, at full strength, we still wouldn't be able to stop all of the dreadnaughts before they reached position over Sanctum. If things continued as they were we could take them out before they could do any lasting damage to the shield over the city, but that was *only* because we were at full strength, and I had no illusions that we'd be able to stay that way for long.

Even as that thought crossed my mind, I saw it; new contacts on my screen, closer than they should have been. The frigate knew it was mostly out of the fight, and it had launched everything it had as far as craft went. That included dropships.

The frigate hadn't been here to back up the fighters; it had been here as troop transport, no different than the dreadnaught the Pax had sacrificed over Esa's homeworld. They hadn't been able to take the lunar guns out with an airstrike, so now they were committed to getting boots on the ground.

The nature of the fight had just changed.

CHAPTER 9

"Schaz, mark those dropships," I snarled. "Send it out to the entire Justified fleet; I want everyone to know those are priority targets." As we'd spent the weeks before the assault building defenses around Alpha and Bravo, the anti-orbital guns on the planet's surface, similar crews would have been working to ring the lunar guns with turrets and defenses as well. They wouldn't stand up to a sustained ground assault—we just didn't have enough soldiers to spread them out across all five cannons, and most of the defenses would have been anti-air in nature. Plus, if the Pax were able to claim the lunar guns for themselves, turning Chariot and Delta and Echo against Justified ships, it would mean our frigates, at least, would be denied a large swath of the sky. It might take a while for the cannon to destroy a dreadnaught, but a frigate would go down in just one shot. The only reason we hadn't done the same was that we couldn't afford to divert the guns from their larger, more dangerous targets.

My transmission was sent and bounced back, the dropships highlighted in every Justified pilot's HUD, but the Pax knew what they were doing—assaulting defensive positions was what they did, after all; conquerors by nature focused more on assault than defense—and they'd timed the next wave of their offensive perfectly. One of the dreadnaughts that had just made it past the black holes split open, disgorging wave after wave of fighters—another carrier ship.

"Justified forces, fall back to the lunar atmosphere," John Henry ordered. "Get in range of the anti-aircraft guns around the three cannon emplacements. You can't weather this assault on your own. If you can, divide evenly between Chariot, Delta, and Echo—don't give the Pax a clear target to prioritize."

A good strategy, but if we were too busy trying to just survive this attack, it meant no one would be able to take out the dropships.

Still, I didn't see another move—not yet. I did as John Henry had bid us, dropping back into position with the other Justified forces, still fighting the second Pax wave. The whole dogfight was shifting into the atmosphere, ships racing and clawing at each other even as we fought the pull of the gravity well, littering the surface of the moon below with burning wreckage and no few blackened bodies.

Frustrated and stymied, I kept at least a sliver of my attention on the dropships, getting farther and farther out of the combat envelope, untouchable. I'd fallen back toward Echo gun, and it was like pressing on a bruise just to remind yourself it was there, watching the dropships move out of range so they could disgorge infantry to assault the very gun I was defending.

Perhaps if I'd hit the frigate just a little earlier, or done just a little more damage, they wouldn't have been able to launch in conjunction with the new wave of fighters. But I hadn't, and we didn't, and there was nothing we could do now as the dropships got clear of the fighting and set down, the soldiers starting their march across the moon's surface just beyond the temperature divide where the crystal froze out of the heat of the suns. There was nothing we could do—we were too busy just trying to stay alive as more and more Pax fighters flooded into the atmosphere.

Esa's hands were flying over her controls, and the blue laser fire she spat from the wing-mounted units was almost stuttering as she swapped targets on the fly; she was good at this, very good, knew when to pursue an enemy and when to let them escape, turning her attention to a closer foe. Marus was keeping them off our tail from the turret, which meant I was free to concentrate Schaz's flight path on offense, a relative rarity among the Justified pilots.

I swept us through the battle, identifying hard-pressed Justified ships and trying to at least buy them breathing room, but I couldn't be everywhere, and Scheherazade's shields still hadn't returned to full after our attack run on the frigate, which meant I had to be more careful than I would like.

We were fighting back, fighting hard, but we were losing ships, even after we came into the firing solution of the anti-aircraft batteries around Echo. Slowly but surely, we were losing the fight for control of the moon's atmosphere.

"All Justified fighters: break off," came John Henry's voice, heavy with loss. After all, he was an AI, powered by a massive complex of databanks deep in the heart of Sanctum, capable of being a hundred places at once and processing a million thoughts simultaneously. Every pilot who died was his friend;

every ship that flamed out was an AI he had helped raise. Still, he knew a losing fight when he saw one, and there was no clawing our way back from this. "We're moving the frigates into position to cover your retreat, just over the storm line," he continued. "Get back to Sanctum; repair, rearm."

"We can't give up the lunar guns yet!" I shouted back. I knew that the other pilots would be doing the same. We hadn't fought this hard, given so much, watched our friends flame out and die, just to surrender this ground. As I banked Scheherazade I could *see* Echo gun just over our wing, the cannon blasting at the enemy above. "There are still dreadnaughts coming through, we have to—"

"If you all fall here there will be none of you left to protect Sanctum itself," John Henry thundered, cutting through all the objections at once. "We *knew* these guns would fall. It was only a matter of time. We are at war; losses are inevitable."

He was right, and I knew he was right; this had been part of our plan all along, we'd just hoped it wouldn't happen so *fast*. I'd thought we might at least be able to evacuate the gun crews before it came to this. But the Pax had established aerial dominance, and it was only a matter of time before their siege troops reached the cannons as well. The turrets and the anti-aircraft batteries would protect the gun crews for a time, but they'd know what was coming, even as they kept fighting. They'd know they were finished.

The Pax didn't take prisoners. Not if a battle was still being fought.

I opened up a comm channel, wide to the whole Justified fleet, and to the gun crews as well. "This is Jane Kamali, of Scheherazade," I said, and my voice sounded dull and empty, even to my own ears. "To the gunnery positions on the surface: if we can come back for you, we *will come back for you*. Keep fucking fighting. Hold on for as long as you can. They'll try to take the guns intact; you can make them pay for that. Set traps, set ambushes, keep yourselves *alive*. Give them hell."

"You do the same, Kamali," one of the gunnery crews replied; whoever was on the comm. "You do the same."

My teeth clenched, my vision almost shaking with rage, I peeled off from the fight, moving into the protective screen of the frigates' fire and heading back for Sanctum. Beneath me, the storm that raged across the temperature divide on the surface of the moon spat and growled and screamed; I knew just how it felt.

CHAPTER 10

What's happening?" Esa asked. "Why are we retreating? Why—"

"We can't spend all our forces over the lunar guns, Esa," Marus told her through the comm. "If we did, there'd be no ships left to protect the planetary cannon, and those will be able to hold a firing solution on the Pax dreadnaughts for much longer."

"But there are still people down there, we just *heard* them!" Esa protested. "They—"

"They knew when they volunteered that this would happen," I told her. I didn't like it, not any more than she did, but it was the truth. "We were never going to be able to hold the lunar guns."

A few of the Pax fighters—the bravest, or at least the most zealous—were still trying to engage us, even under the screen of our frigates' firing solutions. As we rose above the storm below I painted as many of them as I could with targeting locks and released the few missiles we had left after our attack run on the frigate, catching the enemy between the razor-sharp rain of the storm front, the frigates' fire, and the missiles now homing in on them from our position. No sense in hoarding ordnance if we were heading back to Sanctum.

"But . . . but . . ." A teenager's favorite word spilled from Esa's lips like it was something she was fumbling in her hands.

"We were never going to get out of this without casualties, kid," I told her softly. As if to prove my point, one of the suicidal Pax ships managed to sweep through the frigates' fire and release a missile; it connected, short range, with a Justified fighter, and the craft broke up in a wave of flame, pieces scattering into the storm clouds below. Unbidden, my hand rose up from the stick, pressed against the cockpit window, as though I could feel the sear of the fires on my palm. All I actually felt was cold.

"Our scouts said there were at least three dreadnaughts modified into carriers," Marus reminded Esa. "We've only seen two so far. That means we've only faced two-thirds of their fighter groups, at best. If we fought to the last over the moon, that third carrier could jump in and release its waves of fighters to pound the planetary guns without us being able to do a damn thing to stop it."

"But they're still alive!" The words were almost a scream.

"They are," I agreed. "And we're not abandoning them. But we can't do them any good like this. Combat burns through fusion energy, fast—the constant firing of our weapons and the battering of our shields takes its toll. We need to get to Sanctum, recharge Schaz's core, resupply our missiles, let the engineers patch the damage she's taken."

"You've taken damage?" Esa asked Schaz softly. "You're hurt?"

"Just a few scratches, my dear," Scheherazade replied, her plummy aristocrat's voice as nonchalant as she could make it. "Nothing serious." She wasn't lying, but it was at the very least an optimistic view of the truth; we'd taken a battering assaulting the frigate, and again fighting off the Pax attack before our shields could recharge. Nothing critical was damaged, but the parts that *protected* the critical systems were.

As we retreated toward Sanctum, we could see the line of Pax dreadnaughts stretching through the system, hulking pieces of darkness against the spread of the cosmos and the spin of the ruined system beyond. The guns on the planet underneath had firing solutions now, and they were hammering the dreadnaughts with all they had, but at least a few of the enemy supercraft had changed their approach, were lining up shots on the planetary cannon instead. The scale of the Pax attack—the size of the dreadnaughts, the simple mass of them—made Schaz seem tiny in comparison, made even our protective frigate seem like a small boat on a deep sea where leviathans moved under the water.

"We can't just leave them," Esa said again, almost begging.

"We won't," I told her. I was watching the dreadnaughts trade fire with the cannons on the planet below, but my thoughts were still with the crews manning the guns on the moon, the shields around their compounds shuddering under Pax bombing runs, knowing that ground troops were moving toward their location, inexorable and relentless in their march.

"You have a plan?" Marus asked me.

"I don't know if it's a good one." I shrugged.

"Doesn't matter." Javier, on the comms; I'd almost forgotten that I'd patched Bolivar into Scheherazade's internal network, so he and the Preacher could hear anything Esa and I said to Marus. "We're in." Javier had never been the type to leave anyone behind. It was one of the things I loved about him.

"I was counting on that," I told him, almost managing a smile. "Let's get back to Sanctum, get resupplied. I'll fill you in on the way."

CHAPTER 11

We descended past the exchange of fire between the dreadnaughts and the anti-orbital cannons on the planet's surface; even the main gun at Sanctum herself had fully emerged now, rising up out of the mountain instead of being half-hidden in its silo, which meant there would soon be at least one dreadnaught in firing position over the city itself.

I ran a quick count, across Schaz's scans: we'd knocked out seven of the Pax dreadnaughts so far, and had battered three more enough that they'd retreated out of the cannons' targeting spread, all but conceding the use of their main guns, instead acting as protective shields for their fighters, the same way the frigates had shielded our retreat inside the envelope of their firing solutions. The Pax were still arriving in-system, however, dreadnaughts, fighters, and frigates popping into view on the scans—they had nineteen of the supercraft on course for orbit so far, weathering the pounding of the still-firing lunar guns on their way to rain death against the shields above Sanctum, Alpha, and Bravo.

We slipped through the envelope of Sanctum's shield, and touched down on one of the airfields jutting from the side of the mountain that had been cleared and set up for quick repairs. The rest of the Justified fighters were doing the same, our engineers absolutely swarming over them as soon as they landed, trying to get our fighters back into the fray as soon as possible.

"Get out, stretch your legs," I told Esa. "We'll be here ten minutes, at least."

"Don't leave me behind," she warned me, standing from her chair.

"Don't worry. I'm up for a little perambulation myself."

"What?"

"I'm going to do the same."

I did, heading out down Schaz's ramp to get some fresh air, but I also brought up Sanctum's internal communication network in my HUD. "John Henry, get me Seamus," I said around a cigarette. Better than fresh air any day.

Despite the fact that I'm sure he was just as swarmed-under with responsibilities as anyone else in the city, the chief of staff of the Justified came on the line in less than a minute. "You've got a plan to get our people out of the lunar guns," he said; it wasn't a question. Seamus had always been a quick thinker, and an observant one, as well. I wasn't one of *his* people, but he still made sure he knew all of the operatives of the Justified, knew how we thought.

"Bolivar and I have stealth systems," I said. "If we can reach the guns undetected—"

"You might be undetected *getting* there, but once you get close, they *will* spot you, and they will cut you down," he warned.

"I know. I'm counting on that. If we can *get* there safely, surprise them, we can do some real damage to the ground troops, then lead the fighters on a merry chase. They'll be resupplying at the moment as well—the Pax are stupid, but they're not that stupid. You've got gunships here on Sanctum; not many, but a few. Strip everything out of them, down to the chairs. Stick a single pilot in each one, send them the long way 'round, up over the pole. While we distract the Pax, you can get the gun crews out."

"They'll be on our tails as soon as my pilots dust off from the guns. If you and Bolivar can't return to cover our retreat, it'll be a slaughter, only it'll cost us gunships *and* the gunnery crews, not just the crews."

"I didn't say it wasn't a risk."

"No," he sighed. "You didn't. Criat?"

I hadn't realized he'd brought my boss onto the line as well. "Do it," the old Wulf said shortly, the words a low growl. "Get them out of there."

"Yes, sir," I acknowledged. "Let me know when the gunships are ready to launch."

"They'll be ready sooner than your Scheherazade is repaired," Seamus promised me. "Good luck, Kamali. You'll need it."

"Thank you." I looked to the side; Javier had joined me at the railing of the landing platform, but he wasn't looking at the vista of crystal mountains sweeping toward the horizon—a horizon where, far beyond the curve of the moon, desperate gun crews were fighting off a Pax assault, still firing on the dreadnaughts emerging from hyperspace. He was looking at me instead.

"I volunteered you for a suicide mission," I told him. "Sorry." I seemed to say that a good deal.

He grinned back. "Don't be. Life as a smuggler was never nearly exciting enough for me. Pirates and tyrants and tin-pot warlords on pulse-soaked worlds can't possibly compare to this. We're not—"

"There will be no need for dramatics." Great. Helliot was on my comm now, apparently she'd been informed of my little plan. I could almost feel her tentacles waving dismissively in my direction. "You won't be launching your operation, operative. You can rejoin the fight over the planetary guns as soon as your ship is ready."

"Why the hell not?" I tried to keep myself from shouting at her, but it didn't quite work.

"Very simply, it's a waste of resources," she replied. "Removing the gunnery crews will only let the Pax take those positions sooner, and after we win—and we *will* win—we'll have to risk more people clearing them out. Just because we destroy the dreadnaughts doesn't mean the Pax stuck in-system will just go away. The math simply doesn't work."

"Those are our people, Helliot—"

"Councillor Helliot—"

"Those are *Justified* up there. Fighting, dying, for this cause."

"As you will, as I will, if it comes to that. They knew what might happen when they agreed to operate those guns."

With a touch of the comm bud under my ear, I flagged Seamus and Criat back into the conversation, hoping they had still been listening in. "You don't have the authority to—"

"I do, actually. As a member of the council, I have exactly the authority I need to—"

"You *don't*, actually." Seamus, who apparently *was* still on the line. I wondered if he'd been expecting this. Like I'd said before: Seamus knew politics. "Those gunships, and their pilots, fall under *my* jurisdiction as head of security. You don't get a say in—"

"Then I'll call it to a vote," Helliot snapped. "I have Bathus's proxy—he's busy doing *actual* work on our defenses, not arguing over doomed romantic foolishness. He stands with me."

"As do I, unfortunately." Acheron, the Barious leader of the research initiative, had joined the conversation as well. Apparently most of the council was listening in; I would have felt honored, except, well, I didn't. "Helliot is right—the odds simply are not in our favor, either to succeed, or as a measure of risk. We need those guns to fire for as long as possible if any of us are going to survive."

"The gunnery crews can set them to auto-fire before they evacuate," I objected. "They won't be as accurate, but John Henry can still aim them, and he'll be aiming at dreadnaughts: pretty big damned targets. He won't miss."

"Every round counts," Acheron replied. "Sentient operatives fire more accurately, yes, but they also fire *faster* than slaved AI." Of course the Barious made a distinction between her own race, and the more recent inventions like John Henry. "We *cannot* cede the guns early. I'm sorry, I am, but it is the only way we will win."

"Acheron's right. But so is Seamus." Aoka, the head of Marus's faction, was the new speaker, the spymaster playing both sides again toward whatever outcome he viewed as best. "I cede the field to those who see a clear advantage to either side; I abstain my vote." Or not. I really should learn not to try and predict what that particular Vyriat would do in any given situation.

"Come on, boss!" Marus, now, joined in, begging Aoka to reverse his position. "We have to—"

"We have to do everything we can to survive," Aoka replied firmly. "It's a net loss either way. I abstain."

"Which means the tiebreaking vote falls to MelWill," Criat said. "She'll be joining us momentarily—"

"I'm here now," the Reint engineering leader—the legend in our midst according to most of the people at Sanctum, including myself, a genius in every sense of the word—broke into the conversation. She only carried one vote, but her *voice* meant more than that. "The men and women manning those guns are from my teams, my engineers. Kamali: get them out."

Helliot hissed, and cut communications. I closed my eyes and banged my head against a nearby wall. Yes, we'd gotten what we wanted, but it had still taken longer than it damn well *should* have. "I forgot how much I missed this place," Javier said cheerily. "Don't hurt yourself. At least we get to go." He paused, frowned. "Hooray," he added mildly, remembering what going would *entail*.

"We may need Helliot's support later, and Bathus, and especially Acheron." Marus sighed as he spoke. "We should not be divided at a time like this."

"Democracy, man." Javier just shook his head.

"We're going," I said, pushing thoughts of diabolical revenge on Helliot out of my mind. "The repairs to Bolivar and Schaz should be almost done. Everybody get ready." I frowned, scanning the platform. "Where's Esa?"

"Already back inside," Marus told me dryly. "Once she heard someone say the word 'suicide run,' I think she decided to strap herself into her chair rather than risk you trying to leave her behind."

Since that had been exactly what I was planning to do, I sighed. Fine, her choice. "Get back on board," I told them all. "I'll see you back here—and the gunnery crews as well."

CHAPTER 12

I was almost to Scheherazade's ramp when the whole world shook, and I meant that almost literally. A sonic reverberation strong enough to rattle my teeth swept across the landing platform, making the very mountains quake—I could see a landslide in the distance as crystals shattered and a bright bloom of light spread across the sky. I knew what it was, but I couldn't help myself: I looked up anyway.

It had been the cannon in the heart of the mountain, firing. There was a dreadnaught inside its firing solution, slowly maneuvering into place over Sanctum. It wasn't quite in position, high up, barely visible from down here, but the fact that I could see it at all meant that sooner rather than later—its return fire struck back at us, streaking down toward the city. The blast hit the shield high up in the atmosphere, at the apogee of the invisible barrier, spreading fire in waves through the sky. The Pax's attack on Sanctum itself had begun.

"That particular dreadnaught won't hold for much longer," Marus said, reading scans from his HUD. "It's still being targeted by both planetary guns." As we watched, there was another bloom of light, up where the dreadnaught hovered like a smaller moon; it wasn't from Sanctum's gun—that was still cooling—so it must have come from one of the planetary emplacements.

"Yeah, but if it made it this far, it means that others won't be far behind," I replied. "Come on. We need to—"

There was a tug at my elbow. I turned, surprised; JackDoes, the little Reint who had messed with Scheherazade's voice before we went out the last time, was standing behind me. "Hello," he said, grinning toothily at me.

I frowned at him. "Whatever this is, JackDoes, I don't have—"

He held up his scaly hands. "No prank, no joke. This is not the time for . . .

fun. I came to tell you that I have delivered a package, to Scheherazade. A . . . thank you. From MelWill. For going after the gunnery crews."

My eyes narrowed some more. "What package?" I asked.

"Specially designed code booster, experimental, very hard to produce, required . . . strange compounds, black-magic coding. MelWill has been saving it—says it came to her in a dream. Wanted me to give it to Scheherazade. Said it will . . . help. It has already been installed."

I sighed. "Fine. Thank you." Was now really the time for this? Granted, anything that might give us an edge in the upcoming fight would be useful, but anything that changed how Schaz reacted—or how I *thought* she would react—might be a net loss, even if it allowed her to process faster.

"Stay alive." JackDoes grinned at me. "I have plans for new improvements to Scheherazade. Think you will like."

I pointed at him. "Don't mess with my ship's voice again," I told him.

"All sorts of improvements. Think you will like." It was as though he didn't even listen. "Good luck. Stay safe. Rescue my friends."

I nodded, and headed up Schaz's ramp. Bolivar was already lifting off; I slid past Esa to take my seat in the cockpit. "We ready to go?" I asked Schaz.

"Oh, yeah, we're ready," she affirmed, something strange about her already-strange voice. "We're more than ready, we can take all of them . . . *all* of them on, I mean, we're good to *go*, let's *do* this."

"Schaz?" I asked, even as I lifted us off from the landing platform. "What exactly did MelWill give you?"

"Improvements to my pathways, clarification of my processes, overclock in cycles. It's bleeding into my personality matrix, ever so slightly." The words came tumbling out of her speakers like she'd forgotten when to pause during a sentence. "A human analog might be . . . a drug. A performance-enhancing drug."

"She gave you AI steroids."

". . . Possibly something closer to a stimulant. Don't worry—it should improve my combat capabilities by at least ten percent."

"And the effect on your personality matrix?"

"To continue the metaphor, I believe, if I was human, you might describe me as 'high as a motherfuckering kite.' I feel *great*."

". . . Terrific."

CHAPTER 13

I matched Scheherazade up with Bolivar in formation, and both ships activated their stealth drives. We'd be running close by the Pax forces, close enough that they might be able to spy us anyway, but now that the dreadnaughts were beginning to arrive over Sanctum the fighting had spread everywhere, a ribbon of conflict stretching between the moon and the planet below. Every ship Sanctum had was either scrambling toward the dogfights that stretched over both the moon and the planet below, or diving back to the city for repairs and to rearm. Hopefully there was enough going on that the Pax wouldn't have time to investigate what little scans they got off of two stealth-masked craft.

That also meant that we were unable to join the fighting, and just had to watch as we passed by the terrible ballet of dancing craft and twisting fire. The third Pax carrier had arrived, disgorging another massive wave of fighters, and their forces divided out, some to attack the Justified craft still in the sky, some to bombard the planetary guns, some to dive toward Sanctum itself.

The scale was almost overwhelming—the scrum of fighters, and beyond that, the heavier, slower exchanges between the frigates, trying to maneuver into positions where they could both defend the smaller craft on their side, and also exchange fire with their equally vast counterparts. And above even *that* hung the dreadnaughts, still weathering terrible blows from the antiorbital guns, and in turn raining fire down on both the planetary emplacements and Sanctum itself.

Everywhere we turned there was another exchange of fire, another explosion; debris was being tossed into the void to join the detritus of whatever fight had emptied this system centuries ago. I aimed us at the constant storm front of the razor rain that divided the habitable sliver of the moon from the boiling seas and frozen wastes beyond; if we hugged the tops of the crystal clouds, our stealth drives should keep us damned near completely invisible.

"Schaz?" I asked.

"Yep. I'm here. I am *so* here."

"How long can Sanctum's shield hold up against the current Pax assault?" Beneath us, the roiling storm was like a lake of fog, a fog through which I could barely make out the whirlwind of constantly spinning razors.

"With just one dreadnaught in place," Schaz replied, "the exchange of fire could go on for hours, maybe even over a day, even factoring in the bombing runs from the fighters. Every moment that passes, however, means more dreadnaughts maneuver into position over Sanctum. Add in *their* attacks, and the effect is more than an addition of forces, it's exponential, given that the cycling of Sanctum's shields means the more often it is struck, the less time it has to rejuvenate its power from the—"

"So we've got a few hours, at least."

"My calculations suggest that statement will remain correct until there are six dreadnaughts in orbit, firing in waves. At that point, we will have less than two. Hours, that is."

"How soon will that happen?"

"Difficult to calculate. Too many different factors, the added unreliability and virtuosity of the sentient species at the controls of the guns impossible to take into account. A few well-placed shots from our side could cripple the dreadnaught already in position, pushing the Pax's timetable back even further; a few poorly timed shots from our gunners could allow their supercraft to get into position faster than we—"

"Worst-case scenario."

"Sanctum has four hours to live."

"Got it."

I followed Bolivar; now that we were past the storms, Javier was keeping him low, hugging the surface of the boiling seas. We swept around the curvature of the world until we passed out of the sunlit zone and into the frozen wastes beyond, hopping over the second storm front and making for the besieged gunnery positions. I opened up the encrypted comm line. "Seamus," I asked. "How soon will your gunships be into position?"

"They're about halfway around the moon, taking the polar route to avoid the storms," he replied. "How far are you from hitting the Pax?"

"Five minutes, maybe less."

"That should work almost perfectly. Draw off as many of them as you can. Remember, there are three different emplacements for us to evacuate. We have enough gunships to reach them all, but they won't be able to approach until you've drawn off some of the assaulting Pax. That means you'll have to decide where to focus your fire, and *that* will mean—"

"I know." Whichever gun we approached first, it meant the Pax would realize what we were up to, and likely intensify their assault on the other two guns. The plan would almost certainly buy Seamus's gunships enough time to evacuate the first gun; after that, though, the second gun would be harder, and the third harder than that.

We would have to choose which crews to save.

"Javier," I opened up my comms to Bolivar. "You hit the enemy around Chariot first; it's the furthest out. We'll hit Echo, then meet you at Delta. Try to add as much chaos to the mix as we can."

"Got it," he replied, rolling Bolivar off our current trajectory, to speed over the frozen lunar landscape. "Stay safe."

"You too."

Then there was no more time—the battlefield appeared around the curve of the moon, hundreds of Pax troops, if not thousands, surging toward the shielded fortresses of the guns, the autoturrets and anti-aircraft emplacements roaring at their attackers, gunships and land-based assault craft returning fire.

"Target the gunships as much as you can," I told Esa and Marus. "They'll pose the greatest threat to our evacuation squad."

"Got it," Marus answered. I could hear Esa swallow, but she didn't say anything, though her hands tightened on her controls.

As we sped closer to the fighting, my finger hovered over the command to de-stealth. I'd have to pull us out of concealment before our weapons could fire. The timing would have to be precise.

Scheherazade shook with flak and turbulence from the rounds ripping through the atmosphere; none of it was *aimed* at us, it was just everywhere. "Here we go," I told them. "Stealth systems disengaging in three . . . two . . ."

CHAPTER 14

I pulled us out of stealth, and we opened fire.

I kept us as close to the surface as possible, under the angle of Echo's anti-aircraft guns, so we could hit the enemy ships trying to approach below the same defilade. We'd taken them by surprise: I'd had a more difficult time tracking and taking down targets in simulators. Esa dragged the lasers through the Pax contingent of ground forces charging at the gun; Marus fired at the tanks and troops transports as we passed, leaving a wave of explosions in our wake.

I banked hard as we approached the far edge of the Pax line, veering back toward the next mass of gunships beginning their attack run on the facility. They scattered like we were a predator among a flock of birds, and I targeted whoever I could find with the forward lasers, using Schaz's stronger engines to rocket through their ranks, and let Marus pick off those we passed.

Together he and I dropped an impressive number of them, sending them spinning or falling down to the surface and sowing more chaos among the ground troops; *that*, in turn, caused even more of the gunships to panic and run, trying to pull up to escape both us and the wild return fire the soldiers below were shooting off. Unfortunately for them, the only vector left for the gunships to use to try to escape the chaos took them directly into Echo's anti-aircraft targeting solutions instead.

Esa was still causing chaos in the ranks of the troops below; the moon itself offered little cover from the azure fire scything out of Scheherazade's laser batteries, and they hadn't really been prepared for an assault by a ship of Scheherazade's size. Everywhere the infantry turned there was either falling gunship debris or bright blue death cutting furrows through the lunar surface, and whatever else got in its way. I pulled us up into a hard loop; the Pax had started to recover from the surprise attack, and were beginning to muster return fire. They didn't have much that could really hurt us, but any depletion to our shields meant we'd have less time when the enemy fighters arrived.

Right on cue: "We've got incoming fighters," Schaz warned. "The ground troops have called for help."

"Good. That's the plan," I replied. "What's the angle?"

"Most of them were concentrated at Delta; they've split between coming after us and going after Bolivar at Chariot."

Perfect, exactly what we wanted. "One more pass, then we'll hit them head on," I said. I brought us back over the facility itself, the intensifying fire from Echo's autoturrets scorching across the moon's surface below us as the remaining Pax tried for a last charge at the big gun. We let loose with everything we had at whatever targets we could find, then I banked Scheherazade again, setting a course for Delta and the Pax craft on intercept.

We'd hardly escaped the envelope of the fighting around Echo when the massed flight of Pax fighters appeared over the horizon, nearly a dozen of them. More than we could take on at once. Beating them, however, wasn't the plan. "Schaz, shift everything to the engines and to the forward shields," I said. "We'll bull right through them. As soon as we pass through their ranks, shift everything back to the stealth drive."

"We won't lose them for long, not at that close range," she warned.

"I know, but it will confuse them long enough for us to adjust course. We *want* them to chase us, remember?"

"Ordinarily I'd complain about the damage you're about to incur to my systems and my paint job right about now," she said.

"You're not going to?"

"I could not give less of a shit. That programming spike MelWill whipped up for me is *super* exciting. Let's give them hell."

We raced right into the Pax's targeting solution, and the air around us became fire. I danced us through the maelstrom, not worried about picking targets for Esa or Marus or myself, just keeping us alive long enough to blast right through the mass of Pax ships.

Our guns dropped into silence as the stealth systems kicked on, and I immediately shifted course again, my attention flicking to the damage readouts on my HUD. Our shields had taken a beating, but very little actual damage had made it through, and Schaz was shifting power through her systems with remarkable efficiency, so fast I could barely follow: a side effect of the new temporary programming MelWill had granted her, no doubt.

"They're still right behind us," Marus warned from the turret. "I do not like staring at a mass of enemy ships and not being able to fire at them. Just so you know."

"Don't worry, they'll force us to drop the stealth drive right about—"

A shock vibrated through Schaz's systems as the Pax detonated an EMP torpedo somewhere in our vicinity, the time-tested method of shifting an enemy craft out of stealth. The EMP wave didn't make it through our shields, of course, but it did disrupt the stealth systems, and just like that we were visible again, both to radar and to the naked eye.

Marus opened fire, as did Esa, and I shifted our shields to our aft and put everything I had into the engines. We roared over the moon's surface, whipping past canyons and peaks of frozen crystal, heading toward Delta position, and the second gun there.

"Javier?" I opened a comm channel to Bolivar. "How you doing?"

"On course for Delta," he confirmed. "I've got a great many friends following me to the soiree, though."

"We picked up a similar group of pests. We'd love to introduce them to *our* pack of party-crashers."

"It's always nice for old friends to meet new friends. Dead-on course?"

"Sounds about right."

He sent me his approach vector; it scrolled across my HUD, and I shifted course to match. The second gun was approaching at speed; we'd be right above it when the two groups met.

The Pax forces assaulting the facility came into view just before the facility itself did, again, both sides trading fire over the desolate landscape. I sent a few loose shots toward the Pax ground forces, managing a truly impressive detonation when I landed a lucky shot on the fusion battery of a troop transport, but mainly I focused on keeping my course set, and then there was Bolivar, screaming toward us, the pack of Pax fighters on his tail nearly identical to the group on ours.

I shifted our approach just slightly, until we were pointed directly at Bolivar's nose. We screamed toward each other over the lunar landscape, racing across the surface and the conflict below. Javier opened fire; so did I, each of us targeting the enemy craft on the far side of the other, finding a rhythm—like a dance—as we each shifted our craft to let the other's forward fire sweep past us.

We both banked at the last moment, passing each other with only meters to spare, and hit the enemy craft racing toward us dead on. Even as Esa cut through their ranks with her lasers, I painted as many as I could and opened up the missile banks. The Pax were doing the same, of course, and I was dodging and weaving through their fire even as Marus kept attacking the ships behind us, picking them off as they scattered from Bolivar's frontal assault.

The fighter pilots were smarter than the gunships had been; they managed to avoid flying directly into the line of Delta's anti-aircraft fire. That meant their movements were more constrained than ours, however, and we were dropping them right and left. Their munitions and their shields were running dry; at least some of them hadn't been able to resupply since they'd arrived in-system, and even those that had managed to do so had spent most of their ordnance against the guns already. By contrast, we were fully loaded, and ready to kill.

Which isn't to say it was *easy*; we were still vastly outnumbered, substantially outgunned, and we were still trying to hit the targets on the ground and the enemy gunships assaulting the cannon, as well as dealing with the fighters. Javier and I wove our ships around each other, anticipating the other's movements, a kinetic dance of death and salvation, making sure one of us always had a straight line to the blind spots of the other. I'd forgotten how *good* it felt to fly combat missions with another pilot, one who was attuned to my proficiencies and adept at masking my weaknesses; I hadn't done anything like this since the sect wars, flying nighttime bombing runs into the siphoning fields of a local gas giant.

I'd missed it.

War is terrifying, and war is awful, and war is death and carnage and mayhem, but there's at least a little part of it that was exhilarating, too, that was thrilling in all the right horrible ways, and the very fact of our survival, of our success, sent my heart racing. We're terrible creatures, all of us, to get such joy out of so much death, but we are what we are.

I was *good* at this, and so was Javier, and being good at something felt *right*, even when it was something violent and bloody and *mean*.

Bolivar and Scheherazade danced among the inferior ships, fighting and clawing and spitting fire and tearing the enemy out of the sky, letting none come close; we were immortal in that moment, the best of the best, and nothing could touch us and nothing could bring us down. We had a mission and we were going to execute it and the Pax would pay for attacking our homes, would pay for raining fire down on our friends, would pay for every Justified they'd ever laid low. We were goddamned war incarnate, the living embodiment of death and carnage and vengeance and *wrath*, and as horrible as it might have made me, it felt like the best thing in the world.

CHAPTER 15

It couldn't last forever.

Even as fast as we were cutting them down, the Pax fighters still greatly outnumbered us, and our shields were draining in such sustained combat conditions. "We can't keep this up much longer," Javier warned, even as he dropped low, racing across the Pax battalions on the surface to let the Preacher cut them apart with Bolivar's lasers. "We've taken a real beating."

"And we've got more incoming," Schaz warned as well. "The Pax have seen what we're trying to do—they've diverted forces from the main combat, up by the frigates, to try and bring us down."

A part of me was still singing from the violence, still exulting in the terror and the chaos of it all; it wanted to charge the new assault as well, to make them pay just like we had all the others. I shut that part down, hard. "Then we run," I said simply. "Set a return course for Sanctum, over the pole of the moon. It'll be long, but we can't risk leading them to the gunships." Speaking of, I scanned my HUD; Seamus's extraction crews were indeed landing at the cannon sites, slipping through the shields to extract the remaining gun crews. We'd led the enemy fighters into the no-man's-land between the guns, and they were so busy worrying about *us* they hadn't even noticed the evacuating happening at the sites they were meant to be attacking.

The weapons at the facilities were still firing, of course, but John Henry was running them now. With as many different processes as he was managing, not even he could match the accuracy and the fire rate of sentient operatives, but he was doing the best he could, trying not to let the Pax know that we were evacuating the sentient beings that had been running the show.

"Can you take one last pass over the enemy positions on the ground?" I asked Javier. "The gunships have landed; we just need to buy them a little more time." At Chariot and Echo, the enemy would be regrouping, readying to push their attack again; there was nothing we could do about that. We hadn't had a free hand over the assault group pressing Delta, though, and they were still pushing forward, trying to claim the cannon. If they managed to get through with our gunship still on the ground, it would be a massacre.

"We're locked in on your run," Javier confirmed. "We'll follow you."

I cut Scheherazade in a tight loop, still firing at the airborne Pax forces, and then rolled over the assaulting troops, giving Esa one last shot with her lasers. She diced them apart as if she were wielding a knife on a cutting board, the light of the blue fire reflecting in the crystal sea around the Pax soldiers until the whole surface of the moon glowed with shining indigo flame.

My comm crackled to life as I pulled us away from the combat, peeling off across the moon's surface, the Pax fighters still on our tail. "This is Riot Tallgrass; I'm in command of the gunships from Sanctum," said the Justified on the other end of the line. "We've completed extraction at the lunar guns; we're headed home. Thanks for the diversion."

"Any time, Tallgrass," I replied. "Stay safe."

"You too. That was a hell of a——" His signal cut out in a burst of static. I frowned, and looked to my scans; at least a few enemy gunships had made it through our attack, and were harrying the Justified forces as they fled across the moon. I cursed, but there was nothing we could do about it now—trying to aid them would just lead the fighters behind us directly to the fleeing gunships.

"We've still got a great many fighters back here," Marus warned. I could hear the rail cannon in the turret chugging away over the comms. "Any plans to deal with them?"

"Just hold tight," I promised, shifting our throttle to full and pushing all the shielding we had left—which wasn't much—to the aft of Scheherazade. "We're on a course back to Sanctum; keep them from shooting us out of the sky, and we'll lead them right back into Sanctum's anti-aircraft solution."

"Easier said than done, you know."

"It's that or die above this moon."

"I didn't say I wouldn't *try*, just that I can only shoot at one of them at a time, and there's at least a dozen back there."

I keyed the comm over to Javier. "How are you two doing?" I asked him.

"We've taken some hits," he acknowledged. Bolivar wasn't the combat craft

Scheherazade was; it made sense that he would be worse off. "Could really use a resupply and a few minutes with friendly engineers right about now."

I read the scans of his ship; if anything, he was understating the damage. Bolivar was listing badly, barely able to keep up with the pace I was setting. The stick must have been shaking in Javier's hands as though he were trying to pilot through a hurricane. "Pull as close in front of me as you can without giving up your rear turret's solution," I told him. "Let us take the brunt of the—"

Again, my comms crackled to life. "This is John Henry, with a message to all Justified fighters active in the fight," the AI said. "Situation report follows: the Pax will shortly overwhelm the lunar cannon emplacements. They're refocusing their attacks on Alpha and Bravo sites, trying to bring down the planetary guns, including shifting two frigates to screen the approach from Sanctum. Anyone outside of that envelope—get into the skies above the guns, now. Once those frigates seal the Sanctum approach, the path between the moon and the world below will be cut off. You'll be on your own.

"The only good news I have to offer is that we believe their last dreadnaught has entered the system. They have ten fully functional dreadnaughts in theater, and there are at least three more that have been knocked out of firing position and are incapable of regaining it, but still have functional anti-aircraft guns: be wary of straying into their envelope.

"We *can* hold the line here; we *can* win this fight. But we must protect the planetary guns, or else all of the dreadnaughts will be able to focus their fire on Sanctum and we will lose two-thirds of our remaining offensive capabilities. I say again: any Justified craft capable of reaching planetary atmosphere, divert to the defense of Alpha or Bravo, now. Those guns *must hold.*"

I cursed again. "What does it mean?" Esa asked.

"Nothing good," I told her. What it *meant* was that if we returned to Sanctum, we'd be able to repair and resupply, but it also meant that once we did so, we'd be functionally cut off from the fighting planetside. Any attempt to reach Alpha or Bravo from Sanctum itself would see us flying through the gauntlet the Pax had set up with their frigates, not to mention getting past the dreadnaughts they already had in place over Sanctum. Not even our stealth kits were up to that.

Right now, however, we were clear; we could make it to the planet without getting anywhere near that kill zone. Of course, that would mean diving into the fight on the world below, where our positions were already beat half to hell, and it would mean doing so without a resupply.

"What do you think?" Javier asked me quietly. Both our ships were streaking across the lunar surface, fleeing the Pax ships at our backs, but in that moment, they didn't matter; what mattered was the choice laid out before us.

"You *can't* make it to the planet," I told him. "Even if you did, you wouldn't do any good."

"I can't," he agreed. "But I can draw these Pax bastards off of you, if you cut on your stealth drive."

"Without us drawing fire, it's no guarantee you'll even make it to Sanctum."

"That's the thing about combat: there are very few guarantees, anywhere. Are you going to go?"

Damn it. God *damn* it. I didn't want to have to make this choice. I didn't want to abandon Javier to nearly a dozen Pax fighters; I didn't want to take an already weakened Scheherazade directly from one firefight to the next. But the planetary guns had to stay up, had to stay firing. If they didn't, we had no chance of taking out the Pax dreadnaughts; none.

Somehow, through the silence I was broadcasting over the comms, Javier read my answer in the static. "Good luck," he said softly.

"Stay alive, you son of a bitch," I told him, and I might have been crying; I was so keyed up I honestly couldn't even tell. "Don't you *dare* die on me now, not after I just got you back."

I could actually hear him smiling over the comms. "I love you," he said.

I didn't even have a chance to say it in return; he rolled out of our protective envelope, and the Pax pounced, putting everything they had into one last desperate attempt to bring down the more damaged ship. I didn't know if I was crying, but I *do* know that I screamed as I pressed the button to activate the stealth systems, and then our guns went silent, and we could only watch as Bolivar streaked away across the moon on a different course, Pax fire chasing him over the surface, leading them away from us.

He was making for the razor rain dashing down from the constant storm front, and he wasn't planning to fly above: he was going to try to go *through* it. Even at full shielding, it would have been insane, but it was the only way he could tear the Pax off his six.

I didn't dare interrupt him, not when he was in the fight of his life, so I switched off the comm as I whispered into the void: "I love you, too."

CHAPTER 16

We pulled out of the atmosphere of the moon, leaving the Pax fighters behind. They disappeared over the curve of the world, chasing Bolivar, chasing the Preacher, chasing Javier. I told myself that he would make it. Bolivar was fast; Javi was a great pilot. He would make it through the storm. He had to.

"Will they get to Sanctum?" Esa asked me quietly. "Will they be okay?"

"I don't know," I told her. I could lie to myself. I couldn't lie to her; not anymore.

We reached the void. To one side, everything was chaos and light, the remaining Pax dreadnaughts highlighted in the halo of the suns as they rained fire down on the planet below, on Sanctum. They were surrounded by the crackle and fire of their shielding as it repulsed attacks from the guns both on the world's surface and on Sanctum itself. The frigates had also engaged, the Pax vessels forming a cordon around the dreadnaughts, our own trying to stay out of the firing solutions of the larger vessels while still doing what good they were able to do, picking at the Pax fighters on their approach. All of the space between was filled with fighters, intense dogfights that spun and twisted as the pilots went dashing and blasting their way across the stars.

Meanwhile, from the back of the dreadnaughts came a steady stream of gunships and troop carriers, headed toward Alpha and Bravo on the planet's surface. The trio of lunar guns were lost, or would be soon: now, the planetside pair, those we'd taken from the devolved Reint, were more important than ever.

I pulled Scheherazade in a wide arc, staying well clear of the battle itself. I'd cut the stealth drive as soon as we came out of the atmosphere, letting Schaz concentrate power on getting our shields back up. The fusion core was draining much faster than I would like, but at least we wouldn't be only half-shielded by the time we made it back into the fight.

"Jane, wait." I could hear the frown in Marus's voice.

"What do you see?" I asked him, knowing he was looking at his own screens, studying the Pax attack patterns.

"The trajectory of their troop carriers; it's odd. Those heading into the city, especially. If they continue on their current vector—and there's no rea- son they shouldn't, we don't have enough ships in the air past the dreadnaughts to force them to take evasive action—they'll be setting down at least a few miles out from the cannon, from Bravo gun."

"So? They want to stay well clear of the anti-aircraft batteries." In rebuild- ing the anti-orbital guns at the two planetary positions, we'd also reinforced their defense systems; both had a full shielding suite, and were fully capable of devastating surface-to-air fire. Nowhere near the defenses of Sanctum, but still, it would take some work to pound them apart from the sky.

"Yeah, they do," Marus agreed with my reasoning, "and that explains their route, but it doesn't make it *wise*. It means their ground forces—once they've unloaded—will have to march through the city itself."

I tried to follow his thought process; it was absurd, in retrospect, how long it took me to get there. After all, we'd bled to clear that facility, Bravo gun—fought, and lost people, to make it safe from the dangers lurking within the sepulchral metropolis surrounding it. "They don't know about the Reint," I breathed.

"I don't think they do."

I adjusted our approach. "New plan," I said. "We hit them from behind, try to make them shift even farther outside of their approach. Every step further back from the gun we can make them march is one more step they have to take through murderopolis down there."

"They'll still have tanks, gunships," Marus warned. "They will *absolutely* still be able to reach the cannon."

"Yeah, but the further back we push them, the more damage their infan- try will take. We can let the Reint do our murdering for us." Speaking of which; I swapped comm channels. "Sahluk," I called into the frequency the Justified were using on the planet below. "Sahluk, do you read me?"

"I'm here," he came back; I could hear gunfire on the line, the chatter of the autoturrets we'd set up. Whether they were firing at Pax troops or still holding off devolved Reint, I didn't know. "We're watching a line of Pax ships descend into the atmosphere. Tell me you have good news."

"Which cannon facility are you at?"

"The city; Bravo." The first gun we'd taken from the Reint. "It looks like that's the one they're going to hit the hardest." That made sense; the city gun had a wider range of fire, and was pounding the dreadnaughts hanging over Sanctum itself. Plus, they *thought* Bravo was the easier approach: taking Alpha would have required fighting their way up the mountainside.

"Disable the autoturrets," I told him. "Don't fire on the Reint; don't fire at *all* if you can help it. Keep the fences up and keep yourself safe, but don't give the Pax any sign you're already in combat."

A beat, as Sahluk thought through the implications of what I was saying. "Son of a bitch. You think they don't know about the Reint," he said, echoing my own reasoning.

"And every Reint you kill is one less to attack *them*. Most of those around the facility will have figured out we're too hard a target to mess with by now. They'll be frustrated, and desperate—"

"—and primed to take all that frustration out on the Pax," he chuckled. "That's absolutely evil, Kamali."

"We spilled blood taking those guns from the Reint. I figure it wouldn't be fair if the Pax didn't offer up a sacrifice of their own."

"Got it. Good luck."

"You too."

We were in the planet's atmosphere by now, heading directly toward the line of Pax gunships. They'd noticed us coming and were beginning to adjust course, fully aware that their troop carriers couldn't stand up to a sustained combat with a fighter; that was fine by me. I marked targets in my HUD, prioritizing the vessels carrying tanks into battle—those, the Reint wouldn't be able to do anything about.

We opened fire.

CHAPTER 17

We pushed the line of Pax troop carriers and gunships as far as we could, willing it to snap. It didn't *quite* get there, but a few links did fracture, ships that took too much damage or panicked, dropping early to the city below. That was fine—they'd be alone, relatively speaking, in prime Reint hunting grounds, and they'd either have to waste time trying to regroup with their main column or they'd move directly to assault the facility, which meant Sahluk and his teams would be dealing with a piecemeal assault rather than a full attack.

Every time they diverted their course because of our attack run, pushing further out from their initial landing zone, it felt like a thrilling victory. Behind me, Esa kept up a steady string of whispered curses, language blue enough that by the time I actually *got* her into the university back at Sanctum—please, whatever god, let me get her back to the university—her instructors might be taken aback by the vocabulary she'd picked up on her homeworld.

A well-placed laser sweep from Esa ripped open the bottom of a troop carrier; Pax soldiers started falling, still burning, from the sky. The cursing stopped suddenly, and Esa made a sound halfway between a cough and a retch. I imagine our conversation before the battle was coming back to her: it was easy to forget that the targets we were shooting down were full of living people, brainwashed and abused by the Pax, victims in their own way. Firing at specks on the ground during the fighting over the moon had been one thing; watching the soldiers fall screaming to their deaths was another entirely.

"No time for that," I told her. "We can shake our heads at the atrocities of war later. For now, every one of these bastards that dies is one less to attack the guns; every one that can't attack the guns is a minute longer the guns can keep firing; every minute the guns can keep firing is another minute Sanctum keeps standing. The math is that simple, kid."

"I know," she said weakly, returning to her firing position. "But I don't have to like it."

"You don't," I agreed, dropping Scheherazade into a dive so that I could unleash the forward cannons on a tank carrier.

"The Pax have noticed what we're up to," Schaz said crisply. "We've got fighters on the way."

"How many?"

"More than we can comfortably handle on our own."

I nodded; I'd expected that. Again, it worked to our advantage, on a larger, tactical scale—every fighter we could pull away from the battle over the skies of Sanctum was one less the other Justified would have to deal with, one less that could launch attacks on the shielding over the city itself. Grand for them, but it meant we were about to have a great deal of company.

I swept us past the line of Pax gunships for one more attack run, then changed course, diverting us back toward the cannon, and its defensive perimeter of anti-aircraft guns. We'd managed to push the Pax landing craft back a fair ways; that would buy Sahluk some time, at least.

It would also buy me time to prepare for what came next. I was not looking forward to it. "Marus, get up to the cockpit," I told him through the comms. "Schaz, ready supply drop Charlie three-oh-three."

"Why are we dropping more of my supplies to Sahluk?" Scheherazade asked, sounding vaguely nettled. "They have plenty of guns down there."

I swear, the things she got possessive about. "We're not," I told her. "We're—"

"What's up?" Marus asked, appearing at the cockpit door.

"Take the stick," I told him, standing from my chair. We were locked into our course; we had a few minutes before the Pax fighters reached us.

"We're in the middle of combat, Jane," he told me. "What, exactly, do you think you're doing?"

"Maximizing resources," I said. "You're a capable pilot, nearly as good as me."

"Thanks."

"You can take on these Pax assholes just as well as I can; just keep them in range of the anti-aircraft guns at Bravo and you'll be fine. You'll only have a little bit of time in atmosphere left, anyway; Schaz is going to need to get out of this radiation pretty soon. The elevation's too low here for her to stay much longer."

"You still haven't answered my question: while I'm doing *that*, where the hell will you be?"

"There's a skyscraper still standing in view of the cannon. I marked it when we were down there before. It'll have a perfect line of sight on the approaching Pax column."

Marus paused, staring at me. "You're fucking kidding me," he said finally.

I shook my head. "With the Reint crawling all over them, the same math applies—every second we can slow them down is another second they get torn apart by the poor bastards down in the city. I've got Schaz readying an anti-armor supply drop for me. I'll be able to hit their tanks before they can do any real damage to the shield at Bravo. The longer that shield holds, the longer Bravo can pound away at the dreadnaughts above."

"And when the tanks decide to hit *you*?"

I grinned at him. "I'll burn that bridge when I get to it," I told him.

"You don't have to do this, Jane," he said.

My grin dropped away. "Sit in the damned chair, Marus," I said. "This is our best shot, and you know it."

He stared at me for another beat, then sighed, slipping into the pilot's chair. "Don't get yourself killed," he told me. "If you do and Javier finds out that I didn't stop you, he will absolutely murder me. In my sleep. He's not the type to fight fair where that sort of vengeance is concerned."

"Thanks, Marus."

"Just keep yourself alive. I'll do the same for your ship."

Esa had unbuckled herself as well, and was starting to stand up; I put a hand on her shoulder and pushed her back down. "What the hell?" she asked, glaring up at me. "You'll need me down there! Crazy brain powers, remember? I bet I can crush a tank into a pretzel just by *looking* at it!"

"Maybe you can. Schaz can survive without a tail gunner; the same doesn't hold without someone at main gunnery controls. If I keep myself alive down there, I'll need you guys to do the same, if for no other reason than I'll need extraction. I *don't* want to spend the rest of this fight stuck on a goddamned rooftop. It's pretty cold up there."

"That's . . ." I knew what she wanted to say even before the words came out; that it wasn't fair, the last bastion of a child. The words died on her lips.

It was almost sad, watching that vestige of her childhood shear off and float away.

Finally she snorted, then nodded, turning back to her console. "Just don't die," she said, her voice thick with an emotion I couldn't quite place. "There's still a whole hell of a lot I need to learn from you."

"Good to know I still have my uses," I told her.

"Your supply drop is ready," Scheherazade said.

"You're not going to try and stop me?" I asked her.

"Would it do any good?"

"Nope."

"See? That's why they call AI 'learning machines.' We learn. Eventually."

"Also you're still, just, super high on MelWill's crazy programming spike."

"Also that."

"You see the building I marked?" I called to Marus, heading for the living quarters, then the airlock and the armory, and then the ramp down and a long, cold drop.

"I've got it!" he called back.

"Get us into position overhead. If I break my leg getting onto that roof-top, I won't do much fucking good, will I?"

"You can still shoot with a broken leg, kid," he shouted over the rush of incoming air as I opened up the airlock. "I *know* Mo taught you that."

Now I *knew* Marus was under a lot of stress. He rarely mentioned my former mentor at all, given the circumstances of his departure from our ranks, and it had been *decades* since he'd called me "kid."

CHAPTER 18

The airlock cycled open; the ramp lowered. Schaz unspooled a rope line, and I grabbed it, leaning out over the drop. At least it wasn't raining anymore. It was snowing instead, but only lightly. The ruined city spread beneath me, gray blanketed in white. Scheherazade was holding just above the remains of the former skyscraper—my firing position.

I stepped out into the void, and slid down.

Almost as soon as I'd dropped to the snow-covered concrete below, Marus was peeling off, Schaz reeling in the line as she disappeared into the white cloud banks of the storm. Maybe there were fighters incoming, or maybe Marus just didn't want to give away my position, but either way, I was well and truly alone again, for the first time since Schaz had left me on Esa's home-world. I took a breath, and stared out over the edge.

I could see the cannon from where I stood; you could probably see it from everywhere in the city. The electrified lines between the turrets still glowed, but the guns themselves were silent: Sahluk had taken my advice. I was on one of the taller buildings still standing, and the cannon still towered over-head, reaching toward the sky. It fired like clockwork, the big, booming recoil shaking off all the snow that had settled since the *last* time the gun went off. A tower of metal, spitting thunder up into the frozen atmosphere, aiming out at where our enemies hung between the stars: that was what I was here to pro-tect, our last line of defense against the dreadnaughts in the void above.

Even as I watched, return fire smashed down, making the shield visible for a moment before the enemy bombardment dissipated across the crack-ling electrical surface. It was like watching big, beefy pugilists trade heavy blows—they seemed to be weathering the storm, but you never knew ex-actly which shot would crack through the defenses, and one was all it would take.

I turned to face the other direction, where the Pax would come. Nothing but snow-choked avenues and rubble down that way; nothing moving, not even Reint. My HUD lit up, scanning the remains of the city, analyzing approaches and looking for the most likely route the enemy would take based on their prior heading.

There: a broad avenue through a central square, a few blocks away, the centerpiece a toppled statue of some forgotten hero, half-covered in snow. Here and there beyond that square, bright "pops" cut against the white: isolated pockets of gunfire where Pax troops, cut off from their main column, were defending themselves against the rush of the devolved Reint. The main force wasn't visible yet. I still had some time.

The supply drop was behind me, already covered in a faint dusting of frost from the winds. Schaz hadn't just sent the single crate I'd asked for; she'd given me four of them. Made sense, I guess—if we didn't use them now, it would be moot later.

I pried them open, one by one. The first and second were almost entirely loaded with combat drones. They wouldn't last too long, the tech in their guts too advanced for the level of radiation in the atmosphere, but every little bit helped. The third was the crate I had requested, full of anti-armor weapons—gauss rifles and single-fire RPGs and even more anti-infantry drones. The fourth was much of the same, with a few smart additions; apparently Scheherazade thought I'd be up here long enough that the pulse radiation in the atmosphere would be chewing through my weaponry almost faster than I could use it, and I'd need backups.

Hopefully, she wouldn't be wrong.

I activated my comms. "Sahluk, you still out there?" I asked, turning back toward the cannon as I said it. It was a fruitless gesture—it wasn't like he was going to be standing just inside the fence line, waving at me; he had better shit to do right now—but I did it anyway.

"I am," he replied. "We have more awfulness incoming?"

"No," I returned, looking down at my ambush spot, then further back, along their route. "I mean—yes, the main column of Pax troops are still on approach." Even as I said it, I could tell it was true; the first of their soldiers were visible, picking their way through the rubble, their guns out and ready as they watched for the next Reint ambush. They were looking low, determined not to be taken by surprise again, the same way they had been by the presence of the Reint. Too bad for them.

"That's not why I'm calling, though," I told Sahluk. "I decided to take a little vacation. I'm up on top of the tallest tower to the northeast of your position, with a fuck-ton of artillery."

Stunned silence filled the comm channel for a moment. "You really are one crazy human, you know that?" Sahluk came back finally. He almost sounded impressed.

"I have been told that," I agreed. "Just wanted to give you a heads-up what was happening when the Pax started firing on a random skyscraper for no apparent reason."

"That structure's a century old. All they'll have to do is pound it a couple of times with their big guns, and they won't need to target *you*—the entire building will come crumbling down."

"I know. I've got a plan for that." I hadn't, really, not when I'd stepped off the ramp and out into the snowfall, but apparently Schaz had—hence the surprise in the fourth crate. I didn't know whether to thank her, or MelWill's good programming drugs.

"Well. All right then." Sahluk paused again; apparently he just didn't really know what to say to all this. I couldn't blame him. "Good luck," he added finally.

"Yeah. You too." I switched off, and picked up a gauss rifle from the crate. I opened up its tripod and set it on the edge of the skyscraper, not looking through the scope quite yet.

Instead, I swept my HUD across the square below, looking for my moment. The Pax column was already in range of the rifle, and their tanks would be just behind, but that didn't mean it was time to fire yet—I'd need to wait for the precise instant at which I could do the most damage, and also which would keep the Pax from returning fire for the longest amount of time. That would be right before they reached the square, picking their way through the rubble that choked the mouth of the boulevard just before it opened up.

Enough buildings remained at least partially standing around that position that their tanks wouldn't be able to draw a direct line of fire on me until they'd entered the square proper, and if I could create a bottleneck at the end of the avenue, they'd stack up on top of each other, letting me do a great deal of damage before they managed to push through and blow the building I was currently standing on straight to hell.

It wasn't optimal, but it was the best I had. I set up the drones in waves, leaving them just waiting for an activating signal from my HUD, then I lay prone behind the rifle, peered through the scope, and waited.

CHAPTER 19

It was goddamned cold on that rooftop, especially lying prone in the snow. I mean, it wasn't *so* cold that I was looking forward to when the shooting started, but still. It wasn't warm.

The first tank crept into view, coming around the bend in the distant boulevard. Just like everything else the Pax had ever designed, it was an ugly fucking thing: all tanks tended toward a certain brutalist utilitarianism, but I think the Pax must have made theirs even uglier on purpose, all hard edges and chunky blocks of gun emplacement. Even if you didn't know what a goddamned tank was, you'd still hate the sight of it: from all the way up here, it looked almost exactly like some sort of steroidal roach, crawling along the avenue on wide, chewing treads, surrounded by the tinier fleas of the infantry.

Pax troops were all over the repulsive-looking tank, seated and standing and clinging to wherever they could, firing sporadically into the buildings around them at any sign of Reint movement. They'd shifted their combat posture—they thought they'd have a clear shot to the gun once they set down, but now they were dealing with a dangerous insurrection of local fauna that they hadn't seen coming, and they were trying to adapt.

Time to change their calculus yet again.

I centered the gauss rifle's scope squarely at the engine block of the tank, then used the information streaming across my HUD to factor in elevation, bullet drop, and wind. Breathed in, the icy air arctic in my lungs; breathed out. Breathed in, and as I exhaled, I fired.

It didn't really matter where I hit—the kinetic shields surrounding the vehicle dissipated the force of the hyper-accelerated round. As a matter of fact, it dissipated it right *through* all those troops clinging to the sides of the tank, outside of the shield's envelope. They died instantly, torn apart. I fired again, and again, even as I activated the first wave of drones, sending them swarming down toward the enemy.

Three shots from the gauss rifle and I was through the tank's shield; I launched the second wave of drones then, and kept right on firing. The fourth round I put right through the engine block, stalling the tank's forward momentum. The fifth landed where I thought it would fracture the stored fusion cells, but apparently I didn't have Pax engineering down as well as I thought I did—or basic roach anatomy—and it took a sixth shot to wrap the entire back half of the tank in a terrible expanding wreath of fire. The resulting shrapnel cut through the scattering Pax troops in a storm, and the snowy avenue was suddenly choked black with smoke and screams instead of just the moaning winter winds.

I was reloading then, even as the first anti-infantry drones reached their targets and started firing. None of them were that powerful alone—they had relatively long-range rifles attached, firing slugs that would take a few rounds to penetrate the soldiers' shielding, as well as a few grenades each that their rudimentary AI would fire at any cluster of troops that presented an opportunity—but there were quite a lot of them, and the Pax troops were still scattering, unsure where the attack was coming from, and of course the Reint in the surrounding buildings took the chaos as an opportunity to strike as well.

High up in the winds, I finished reloading the big rifle and started picking my targets, firing at any Pax soldier who seemed on the verge of getting their shit together and launching a counteroffensive. The longer I could keep them in chaos, the longer I could stall them from reaching the cannon, and the more damage both the Reint and I could do. I saw one Pax soldier hauled bodily right up the steel face of another ruined skyscraper, two Reint on either side of him, clutching his arms in their jaws. They almost had him to their nest within the shattered upper levels when a third stuck its head through a window and bit the soldier's face in half. One less Pax to kill.

A week ago I'd been doing my damnedest to kill the Reint in those buildings, and they'd been doing the same to me. Now I was using them to kill another enemy. The face of this city had been torn apart by whatever war had ripped through this system, and its populace had been abandoned to become the *things* that even now were feeding on stragglers from the Pax position. I should have felt bad about using them. Maybe later I would. Right now, every Pax they killed—and every bullet the Pax spent killing them—was one more I didn't have to worry about myself.

I was on my third magazine—the gauss rifle was starting to make bad hissing sounds as the pulse radiation corroded through it, but it wasn't done yet—when the next tank appeared, pushing its way through the burning ruin of the first. It made it just a little farther than its predecessor before I brought its shields down and took out its fusion cell, with just five shots this time: I learned from my mistakes.

We were off to the races now.

That was it for the gauss rifle; I dropped it over the edge of the building and scrambled back to the supply crates, snatching up another. In the few spare seconds that took me, the Pax infantry had made their way into the square proper, forming up in defensive positions and trying to figure out where I was firing from. That was *going* to happen, one way or another—I was stuck on this goddamned rooftop, couldn't even make it down into the building itself on account of the floors below me being nothing more than a caved-in shell—so since relocation wasn't an option anyway, I just kept firing, waiting for the next tank to come into view.

It did. At the same time as more Pax gunships arrived.

I dropped the rifle—it had been smoking and nearly done anyway—and rolled through the snow toward where I'd left the RPGs, lined up neatly in a row. Picked up the first: targeted, fired, tossed it aside, then snatched up another and did the same. I let loose with the third as well.

Two of the three missiles found their targets; the Pax pilots hadn't been expecting resistance this heavy, not this far from the cannon. The third managed to twist out of the way, but I'd activated a third drone swarm, sending them all toward the gunship with a thought, and almost as a mass they fired their grenades, the force of the blast physically shoving the aircraft through the side of a half-collapsed building. That brought the entire structure down, choking the square below with rubble and flaming gunship parts.

I dropped the last RPG, picked up another rifle, and swept the scope over the killing floor below. Found the tank again. Too late. Its barrel was raising up into firing position; I wouldn't be able to crack its shields before it got at least a few rounds off, and that was all it would take to bring *this* building down, just like the crashing gunship had collapsed the other.

I slung the heavy gauss rifle on my back and dashed away from the edge, just before the steel and concrete exploded from the first tank shell. The building shook and a geyser of rubble filled the air before it started raining down on my head and back, bouncing off my intention shields. Didn't matter; I just needed to stay upright, to *move*.

I was almost to the supply drop when the second shell hit, somewhere below me, the tank intent on bringing the whole building down.

I was thrown off my feet as the whole structure shook again from the force of the blast, and then it was tilting ominously. "Up" was no longer "up," not entirely. Still on my knees, I pulled my way to the crate, reaching in and grabbing Scheherazade's desperate measure, then scrambled to my feet in the snow.

Now or never—another shell would be on its way. The whole snow-slick surface was tilted at a terrible, uneven angle as the entire structure started to collapse under my boots; I ran anyway.

The tank fired again, and the building started to come apart in pieces, entire slabs of the roof cracking and giving way. I woke the last of the drone swarms even as I threw myself over the edge, slapping the activator on the antigravity rig Schaz had provided. For a sickening second I thought it wouldn't kick on, it was faulty or already eaten into by the rads, and I was just going to fall and hit hard on the streets below, and then with a silent push I went moving forward and upward instead, sailing out into the falling snow.

CHAPTER 20

The antigrav unit failed, chewed up by the pulse radiation, about ten feet from the nearest rooftop.

I was carried on by the forward momentum I'd built up, but instead of the perfect landing I'd been planning I hit hard, on my shoulder, hard enough that if I hadn't had my intention shields up I likely would have broken my arm in a dozen places. As it was, I slid through the drifts of snow and hit my head on a collapsed doorway instead.

Not my most graceful moment. Given that I'd just escaped a tank trying to kill me and a building collapse, however, I'd take it. Or I would, as soon as my head stopped ringing. I wavered in and out of consciousness for a moment, clinging to the concept of light and awareness as hard as I possibly could. I didn't quite escape that sucking black hole—I definitely lost a few moments—and when I came back to the world, everything was still vibrating slightly, and someone was shouting in my comms.

"Kamali! *Kamali!* Are you still alive?"

"Maybe," I croaked, managing to get to my knees, if not my feet.

"Oh. Shit." It was Sahluk; he actually sounded taken aback.

"Thanks," I told him. "Asshole."

"We saw the building go down, thought for sure you were done for."

"What can I say? I'm a durable bitch." I slapped ineffectually at the anti-grav unit strapped around my chest, now about as useful as a twenty-pound sack of rocks. Finally I hit the release and it slid off of me all at once, to flump undramatically into the snow. I'd managed to hold on to both of my usual weapons and the second gauss rifle, but other than that, I was empty-handed; all the rest of Schaz's supply drop was currently somewhere far, far below, mixed in with all the other rubble from the building that had just collapsed.

"That you are," Sahluk replied. "Do you know—"

I heard the hissing just in time, and rolled.

The Reint spat toxic steam at me; I kicked out, connecting with the side of its head, as the cloud of expectorant seared its way through the snow and concrete of the rooftop where I'd just been. My hand scrabbled for my pistol, but I stopped myself—a gunshot here would tell the Pax I was still alive, and that was the last thing that I wanted. Instead I activated both of the close-quarters implants in my wrists, and just in time, too.

The Reint recovered from the blow to the side of its face and leapt at me, claws extended. I hit it in the chest with an uppercut, my taser knuckles activating in a wash of blue light, making its whole body spasm. It still collapsed on top of me, snapping and clawing as an autonomic reflex, even with however many volts of electricity coursing through it. I rolled with it, hitting it again and again with the amplified force behind my other hand, until I felt several things snap in its chest cavity.

Panting, I climbed off of the dying creature, scrambling backward to put a little bit of distance between me and it. It had scored me with its talons, and more than once; I was bleeding from several gashes, including one in my face, but I didn't think any of them were too deep, not too dangerous. Then again, that might just be the shock, and the cold. The blood was already freezing my body armor to my skin.

The Reint hissed weakly, still trying to get to its knees. I shook my head, leaned in closer, and snapped its neck, letting its body fall back to the snow.

The building I was on wasn't nearly as tall as the one I'd just evacuated, but it was still a solid ten stories off the ground. I hadn't thought there would be Reint this high up. Maybe it had been sick, or wounded, hiding from its cannibalistic brethren; maybe not. Either way, I'd have to watch my back up here.

My breath still heaving from my chest in puffs of frost, I raised Sahluk on the comms again. "Okay," I told him. "Pretend I was in a fight to the death for the last few moments, and missed everything you just said after 'how the hell are you still alive.'"

"You've delayed their ground forces quite a bit," he told me, "and they've delayed *themselves* even further by bringing that building down—it landed right in front of them, blocking their clearest path to us. We're still getting pounded by the dreadnaughts in orbit and Pax fighters in the sky, though."

"Not much I can do about that," I told him. "Where are Marus and Schaz?"

"They're trying to engage the Pax fighters, but Scheherazade's only one ship, and she has to return to orbit periodically to keep from getting chewed up by the radiation. Plus they've been in combat for a long time; their core must be running on fumes. The Pax don't seem to give a fuck about the rads—their ships just keep attacking until they fall out of the goddamned sky."

Sounded about right. How in god's name had we managed to come under such great threat from an enemy that was *that* stupid? Even with all the ships they'd gained from wherever they'd dug up their extra materiel, they couldn't afford to waste *pilots* like that, not when the pilots would be ejecting into enemy territory filled with *very* aggressive wildlife. "How are *your* shields holding up?" I asked Sahluk.

"We're at about half-strength, and returning to slightly less after every hit," he told me. "If it wasn't for the fighters, we could sit here and trade shots with the dreadnaughts in orbit all day; they've only got one left that's firing on us, and so long as both planetary guns are firing back, they're taking too much damage themselves to really shut us down. But they've concentrated the fighters on our position, I think because they haven't managed to land ground units up in the mountains by the other gun."

"In other words, you're holding out right now, but if the army on the ground gets to you, you'll be getting hit by three different forces, and that will change the game real fast."

"That's pretty much it, yeah."

"Well, fuck, Sahluk, I don't know what you expect me—" There was a low roaring overhead, the unmistakable sound of atmospheric engines.

A Pax gunship was hunting me.

CHAPTER 21

It hadn't found me yet, but given that it had diverted from attacking the cannon to make sure I was still dead, I doubted it would give up that easily. It actually gave me a perverse sense of pride—I must have done a fair bit of damage to their ground forces for them to retask gunships to come after me, rather than keeping up the pressure on the cannon that was pounding their dreadnaughts in orbit.

Staying low on the rooftop, I crept to cover—that wouldn't do me a great deal of good, I'm sure they had all sorts of scanners in the gunship, but there wasn't a lot else I could do. Likewise, I unslung the gauss rifle, checking to make sure it was loaded. Again, it would take a great deal to bring down a gunship with just the rifle—if it had taken five shots to crack the shielding around a tank, the gunships would require nine or ten, and I doubted they'd hold still long enough for me to land those clean—but it was what I had.

I'd just faced down an entire column of Pax armor and infantry, not to mention all the other shit I'd been through over the last few weeks, *and* all the shit I'd been through the rest of my life. I was not about to go down to one prowling Pax gunship with a grudge.

Then again, very few of us are lucky enough to choose the day we die.

The gunship hovered into view; I raised my rifle up to my eye. I fired before they found me, then worked the bolt, fired again. And again. They jerked backward and soared up, out of range, as they tried to identify the location of the threat. Keep trying, you bastards. Just give me time to bring you down.

I tracked their movement in the scope, and fired again as they approached, and once more. That was that for the magazine in the gun; I replaced it without looking down, hours and days of training on board Schaz during long hyperspace jumps making the action automatic, thoughtless, and I had the rifle back to my eye in less time than it had taken me to fill my lungs. I fired again.

Their shield was starting to crack—it was glowing red now with every hit, as opposed to the usual pale blue—but I wasn't through yet, and they'd found my position, their big guns starting to spin up. They'd strafe the whole goddamned rooftop until I had more holes in me than flesh to connect them. Nothing for it—I fired one last time.

The gunship exploded in a ball of flame and metal.

That wasn't me. That *couldn't* have been me. Even if I had punched through their shielding, the entire goddamned gunship wouldn't have gone up, not even if I'd hit the fusion core directly. Besides, I'd only hit them seven times, barely enough to start cracking their shield, let alone penetrate it with a round.

"Getting lonely yet?" Javier asked on my comms.

Bolivar swept past me, close enough that I could feel the wash of his passage. He was headed for the Pax ground column, the speed of his flight making the snow falling around me swirl and dance in eddies. I shouted something—I am honestly not sure what, just kind of a wordless affirmation—as I raised my gun over my head in the wake of his passage.

Two Pax fighters were close on his tail, but then Schaz hit them from out of nowhere, dropping out of stealth and blindsiding them completely. Marus may not have been quite the pilot I was, but he was a strategic genius, and decades spent as an information specialist had given him a great breadth of tactical knowledge involving the stealth suite on board Scheherazade.

They were both here. They'd both come to watch over me.

There were more Pax fighters trying to intercept them, but they wouldn't get there in time: both vessels had already reached the heart of the city, where the Pax troops were presumably still trying to pick their way through the rubble they themselves had caused.

I could tell Schaz and Bolivar had found the infantry positions when lasers started stabbing from their bellies and wings in stuttering fire, Esa and the Preacher marking targets for the ships' guns to incinerate.

"You've got company headed your way," I warned Javier, marking the approaching fighters in my HUD and broadcasting the information to him and Marus both.

"No worries," Javier said blithely. "We brought a friend."

The shimmer of a dropping stealth drive filled the snowy sky above me—only now that I knew it was there did I see how the snowstorm had been warping around it, creating a dry area underneath its bulk—and suddenly there was an entire goddamned *frigate* there, blasting the Pax ships out of the storm, flames and wreckage burning bright amid the snow.

The nameplate *glowed* in the light of the lasers dancing from its undercarriage: "Poseidon," proclaimed the twenty-foot-tall letters of brass. The name was more than just a callsign—it was recognizable to every Justified operative who knew anything about our history, the ship an antique, older even than I was by centuries. It had been one of the first ships ever flown under Justified colors, permanently retired well before I'd ever joined the sect, and the originator of the conceit that all Justified craft were named for mythological or historical figures from distant legends.

It was the fourth frigate. MelWill's engineering team had gotten the mothballed fourth frigate up and running, and they'd somehow fitted it with stealth tech. That was how Javier had escorted it right under the nose of the firewall the Pax had created between Sanctum and the planetary guns. The long-forgotten relic of the Justified's glory days had been revived to fight for our very survival.

Son of a bitch.

Schaz and Bolivar were still chewing up the ground forces; the Poseidon was hauling its bulk over toward the cannon itself, engaging the fighters there, who had been thrown into a blind panic by the sudden appearance of a much, much larger vessel in the atmosphere. I could tell by the way the frigate was moving that the repairs to it hadn't been complete—it probably wouldn't be able to stand up to one of the Pax vessels of similar size, not even for a little bit—but right now, it didn't matter; the fighters were completely outclassed.

"How the hell . . ." I wondered into my comms.

"There's a whole . . . I'll tell you later," Javier said. "Right now all that matters is that it can cover the cannon. It can't stay in atmosphere for very long; it'll have to pull out in just a few minutes—but it can hover in orbit outside of the range of the other ships in the main body of the fighting, picking off fighters that try to descend to the guns. Unless the Pax want to task one of *their* frigates to chase after it, we've got control of the sky over the cannon."

"They'll do that," I warned.

"They might not." Even over the comm, I could hear the shrug in his voice. "Most of their frigates are tied up keeping *our* ships from their dreadnaughts. Either way, the ball's in Pax command's court now."

"This wouldn't have worked if you hadn't been down here to delay the Pax ground offensive, you know," Marus told me. He'd brought Schaz around, to hover above my head; as I looked up, the ramp extended, and there was Esa, unspooling a line for me and waving.

"Sahluk could have held them off." I shrugged, grabbing onto the rope and letting Schaz winch me back up toward her.

"Maybe so, maybe no, but either way, it blinded Pax intelligence. They were so busy trying to get extra troops on the ground—and sending extra fighters to protect them—that they weren't paying enough attention. Even stealthed, a ship the size of the Poseidon shouldn't be impossible to pick up; not if you're looking. They weren't looking, and that is most *definitely* because of you."

I grinned, even as I reached out and took Esa's hand. "I like to do my part," I said.

"You like to blow shit up," Marus retorted. "Now get up here and take the stick from me; Schaz complains *so much more* about my flying than Khonnerhohn used to."

"That's because your flying's terrible, and *you're* terrible, because you're not Jane," Scheherazade retorted, her tone somehow wistful and dreamy, despite the words.

"Still high, Schaz?" I sighed.

"Yup."

Marus ignored both of us. "We need to get back to Sanctum and resupply—we're running on nothing here. And after that, well . . . I'll let you look at the scans. We're not done with this fight yet."

ACT
FIVE

CHAPTER 1

Y ou're injured," Schaz said as I peeled off my various weapons, dropping them on the armory floor with a clatter. Ordinarily I wouldn't have done that—if nothing else, Scheherazade would object to the clutter—but I was damned tired.

"I'll be fine," I said. "They're just—"

"You're hurt?" Esa had stayed on the ramp to watch me as I ascended, and stayed right beside me in the airlock; now I winced as she grabbed my jaw and rotated my face so she could look at the gashes the Reint had carved into me. "You're hurt."

"I'll be *fine*. Just—"

"Marus!" Esa shouted back at the cockpit. "Where's the—that spray stuff?"

"Check the medbay!" he shouted back. "How badly is she hurt?"

"I'll be fine!" I shouted at him. "Just—"

"Shut up and sit down," Esa told me, pushing me toward a chair. She wasn't strong enough to actually move me, but I let her anyway; if she decided to use her telekinesis, I *would* move, and I wasn't sure how good her fine control was.

I dropped into the seat as Esa found the binding spray and proceeded to cover my face and arms with coagulating foam. She must have used about half the vial. "Do not do that again," she lectured me.

"Esa, it was—"

"Jane," she replied sternly, relishing in her ability to use my name, "I don't have many friends around here. I don't need one of them to get herself killed just because . . . just because of . . . just because. Do *not* do that again."

I smiled, even though it hurt, more than a little. "Roger," I said.

"Who the hell is Roger?"

"It means I got it. Are you going to let me stand up now?"

"Are you hurt anywhere else?"

Grudgingly, I lifted my arm so that she could coat the slash on my ribs with spray as well. When she was done, she finally let me stand, and I made my way back to the cockpit.

Marus laughed when he saw me. I scowled back, and then turned on my heel and stalked back into the living quarters until I could find a towel to wipe off the excess foam. "You look like a Vyriat with . . . with . . . what's the fungal rash they get?" he called after me. "The one where they grow mushrooms on their faces?"

"Shut it," I growled, brushing off flakes of the hardened gel.

"No, seriously, what's it called? I didn't know a human could *get* that. Have you been dallying with Helliot? Javier will be pissed."

"Shut. It." I tapped him on the shoulder; he relinquished the stick, still chuckling to himself.

"Oh, I needed that," he said, still laughing. "That may have felt better than watching Bolivar ride in like the cavalry earlier."

"Are you two done? Are we finished with the . . . with all the funny bits, now? Any more jokes? Any more, you know, whatever? Or can we get back to the—"

"We watched the building collapse," Esa told me as she took her seat at the gunnery station. I wasn't looking at her—I was too busy adjusting various settings on Schaz's boards, changing the shifts Marus had made—but I could hear the lingering fear in her voice. "We watched it come down around your head. We couldn't tell if you got clear or not. Schaz told us she'd left you an antigravity unit, but . . . we didn't know. It was awful."

"I'm sorry," I told her. "It had to be done."

"Well, yeah, obviously, otherwise the building would have fallen on your head, but—"

"No, I mean . . . all of it. I had to buy Sahluk the time."

"Do you really not care if you live or die?"

"I care," I told her quietly. I didn't tell her I just wasn't always sure which direction it went in.

"It wasn't your fault," Esa said.

"That's not—"

"The pulse. It wasn't your fault. I was mad earlier, before . . . I was mad, and the Preacher was mad, and we probably . . . I may have said some things that I . . . it wasn't your fault. You didn't do this. You didn't make the Pax."

"No, I didn't. I just made it so that the Pax didn't have any enemies that could put them in check."

"You didn't want all this to happen."

"That doesn't mean . . . this isn't the time for this, Esa. We've still got a fight to win." I'd pulled Scheherazade into a climb. Her radiation alarms were squawking; we'd spent too much time in the atmosphere already. I checked the scans: Bolivar was right behind us. Reaching down, I keyed on the comms.

"How's it looking down there?" I asked Sahluk.

"Survivable," he grunted back, though I could hear gunfire in the background—not just the rhythmic repetition of the autoturrets, either, but closer, louder. He may well have been firing himself. "With the frigate in a firing position above us, we can catch any incoming fighters in between its solution and the anti-aircraft guns. Ortega and Marus did a nice job denting the ground troops, too, so they're not hitting us as hard as they might. You don't necessarily have to tell Ortega I said that."

"I'll keep my teeth together," I promised him, even though I'd opened up the signal to Bolivar as well; Javier was likely listening in already. "What about the dreadnaught? How much longer can you stand up to its pounding?"

"Depends on how much damage the ground forces can do. With just the dreadnaught's fire wearing down the shield, we can recover almost as much energy between its shots as we lose from the attacks—we're only dropping about half a percent each hit. The engineering team did a good job with the fusion reactor. But that means we don't have either the time or the energy to—"

"I got it. You want me to swing back down once we shake some of this radiation, do another strafing run on the ground forces?"

"I think you may be needed more above. What we're reading from down here . . . it's not good."

I frowned, looking back to my scans. We were too far out from Sanctum to get a good read on their shields, but as soon as we broke atmosphere and got out of the sea of rads, I'd be able to get a clear view of the remaining Pax forces. Still, I didn't like what I heard in his tone, or his words. "I copy," I told him. "Keep yourself alive down there."

"You do the same. And Kamali?"

"Yeah?"

"Well done earlier. You find a way to hit them up top as hard as you did down here, maybe we'll survive this. Maybe."

"I'll do my best. Kamali out."

CHAPTER 2

We came soaring out of the snowy atmosphere, into the black of the void above. In between us and the spread of the stars lay the meat of the main fight. It was awesome, and terrifying, the sight of the seven remaining Pax dreadnaughts locked into an almost circular pattern, four pounding down on Sanctum, three firing at the anti-orbital gun we'd just left behind. They'd set themselves to rotating slowly, so that none of the cannons—either Bravo and Alpha on the planet's surface or the gun within the mountaintop at Sanctum—could concentrate fire on just one ship.

Around them, almost like moons in orbit, circled the frigates from both sides. They were trying to keep out of the firing solutions of both the dreadnaughts and each other, trying to pick off fighters instead. We had two operational to their four remaining, which meant our fighters were still at a serious disadvantage, but we at least were just using fighters as a defensive measure, keeping their own from dive-bombing Sanctum. If their own fighters wanted to engage the planetary guns, they had to break through the firing line of Poseidon, hanging over the planet just outside the solution of the dreadnaught group and merrily picking off the few craft suicidal enough to try.

The cosmos beyond was scattered with the wreckage from the rest of the fight. The Pax had entered the system with nearly thirty dreadnaughts all told. At least a dozen of them had been cracked open, destroyed completely, spreading ruin across the void in a path leading all the way back to the choke point leading into the system. There were more that had withdrawn from the planetary guns' firing solutions, limping back to defensive positions, including three that were blocking the system's exit. Their main guns were down, but they were still a force to be reckoned with.

They wanted to make sure we couldn't run, if it looked like we were losing.

I raised John Henry on the comms. "John," I asked him, watching the dreadnaughts trade fire with Sanctum. "I need the math. Can we survive the current rate of attrition on the shield?"

"No," he said simply. That one word sent absolute chills down my spine. "If it's any comfort, their dreadnaughts will not either; we'll bring down at least four of them before the inevitable ending, one of them any moment now. But 'the math,' as you say, is crystal clear at this point. My initial estimate was that once six dreadnaughts were firing on Sanctum at once, we would have slightly over an hour before the shield collapsed. We've done enough damage to their cannons' capabilities that I'd stretch that estimate out to two. If I was feeling optimistic."

"And are you?"

"No."

I swallowed, still staring out at the ballet of destruction through the cockpit window. The lashes of cannon fire rising from the planet below and the moon above struck the dreadnaughts' shields in blazing lines of light, but for every shot we got off, they managed at least two, if not three. It was a slow-motion stabbing, a simple brute force equation—they had more guns than we did, and could diffuse the damage we were inflicting upon them across seven different ships. We only had three locations to shield.

Even as I watched, one of the dreadnaughts took a direct hit, and its shields cracked apart. Explosions started rippling through its hull, and it drifted out of its position, trying to put as much space between itself and the other Pax ships before the inevitable. It was a bit like watching a watercraft sink beneath the waves. The Pax soldiers on board were my enemy, and the death of their ship meant that Sanctum would survive for at least a little longer. That didn't mean I would wish such a death on anyone—trapped on a vessel that was ripping itself apart, knowing at any moment the fusion reactors would go and you'd be vaporized and spread across the cosmos.

The Pax didn't even believe in escape pods. Thought they encouraged cowardice.

"I don't suppose that changes your math," I asked John Henry dully.

"No," he replied. "As I said: we knew that would happen momentarily. I factored its loss into my calculus. Two hours, at most."

A bright, shining line of light, almost indigo, spread through the enemy dreadnaught, and then it was gone, the massive explosion of its reactors going critical swallowed up by the very vastness of space around it.

"There has to be something we can do," I told the AI in Sanctum. It occurred to me that this whole fight—the dreadnaughts firing down at the city from orbit, us firing back from the mountaintop—must feel very much like a close-quarters brawl to him; the city was his body, after all, he had sensors everywhere. Every shot the shield took from the dreadnaughts above was the equivalent of being punched in the ribs. Every bit of energy the shields couldn't replace was like him trying to get air back into his lungs, and not quite getting enough before the next punch came.

"You're free to join the defense of Sanctum, of course," John Henry said politely, as though inviting us for tea. "Even considering the fact that Scheherazade, especially, is running low on core energy, both she and Bolivar are extremely capable—helping to keep the enemy fighters at bay might stretch out Sanctum's remaining time as much as twenty minutes longer. Alternately, you could attempt to flee, but I wouldn't advise it; the Pax have some of their dreadnaughts—"

"Guarding the path out, I know," I told him. "I wasn't thinking about running, John Henry."

"I know you weren't. If they didn't have their ships blockading the system exit, though, I would likely be suggesting you do just that. This is not a fight we can win."

"There must be something—"

"I have examined all the possibilities, Jane. Sanctum is lost."

CHAPTER 3

N o," I shook my head. "No. No." It was as though, if I kept repeating it, it would somehow come true; the situation would change somehow so long as I kept denying it. The act of a child, I know—I'd seen it enough in my charges—but I couldn't help it. We'd fought too hard, sacrificed too much, for us to lose now.

"Have they figured out a way to evacuate Sanctum yet?" Marus asked John Henry, his voice sober.

"Evacuation was never a serious consideration," John Henry replied. "If we were going to evacuate, we would have done it before the Pax even arrived in-system. We gambled; we lost. There are some countermeasures that are being taken—some of our data is being broadcast on coded frequencies, where hopefully it will be intercepted by agents that were unable to return to Sanctum in time to join its defense. But that—"

"We need another gun," Esa said suddenly.

"Well, yes, child," Marus told her. "But that's—"

"That's all we need, though, right? Another gun? That would change the . . . bad math, that would be enough to pound the dreadnaughts out of the sky before they can get through Sanctum's shield?"

"Yes, but there is no other gun, Esa," I sighed, trying to keep a handle on my temper; I didn't need to be dealing with this right now. "That's just—"

"Sure there are," she said. "Four or five of them, actually."

"The other cannon in-system won't work; even if they were operable, which they're *not*, they're not in firing positions where they could even *hit* the Pax dreadnaughts—"

"Not the anti-orbital cannons; the dreadnaughts themselves. I'm saying . . ." She unbuckled herself, came to stand at my shoulder, and pointed out the cockpit window. From the angle Schaz was drifting at, we could see three separate Pax dreadnaughts—not the circle of still-firing ships above Sanctum, or the grouping guarding the exit, but some of the others, those that had been so damaged during their path through the system that they'd withdrawn outside the cannons' envelope rather than risk being destroyed completely. "I'm saying *those* are guns, right?"

I just stared out the cockpit for a moment. It was insane. It was the reckless, impulsive, desperate act of a teenager—it was ridiculous to even suggest it, to think about it. Those dreadnaughts had been taken out of the long-range fight, but that didn't mean that they were drifting empty; they were still full of Pax, however many had survived the hits they'd taken when their shields were breached.

We were already fighting on three different fronts: the battle in the skies over Sanctum, the battle above the planetary guns, the battle in the void. Now she wanted us to open up a fourth assault, to try and take a Pax dreadnaught away from its crew, so we could aim its main gun at its former compatriots and hit them with a surprise attack.

"That's insane," I told Esa, after processing even the *idea* she was suggesting.

"Yeah, sure, whatever," she sighed, ignoring the actual *words* I was saying to stare at me intently. "But would it work?"

"You're asking . . . what you're suggesting, it would mean storming through a half-dozen fortified positions *inside* the dreadnaught, somehow sealing off—"

"I didn't ask 'can we do it?,' I asked 'would it work?' If we got to one of the enemy dreadnaughts, if we were able to commandeer its big gun—even if just for a shot or two—would *that* make the difference in the fight above Sanctum?"

"John Henry?" I asked, swallowing. No one said a word; we all just waited for the computer housed deep beneath Sanctum to finish his calculations—to see if Esa's insane idea meant there was a chance that he, and all of us, might survive.

"Yes," he said.

CHAPTER 4

F ind me a target," I told Scheherazade, my hands already running over the instrument panels, getting as many scans as I could before I folded us into stealth mode. "We need to know which of those dreadnaughts has taken the most damage *without* possibly ruining the shaft of their main cannon. We need to know which of them will require the least shifting to aim at *our* targets; we need to know which of them has functioning reactors on board still; we need to know—"

"Are we actually doing this?" Marus asked faintly.

"You just started moving," Javier called in over the comms. "Where are you going? What do you know that I don't know?"

"We're going to go storm a dreadnaught," I told him. "You were a pirate for a bit there; this should be right up your alley."

"I was never a—we're going to *what*?"

"Have Bolivar drop in behind Schaz. We're going to storm a dreadnaught." I actually grinned as I repeated myself; I couldn't help it. The very idea was ludicrous.

The Pax would never see it coming.

"*. . . Why?*"

"Because if we can get to the gunnery controls of one of those damaged vessels out there, if we can get to the gunnery controls and we can get just a *few* good shots off, we can break up the Pax firing pattern. Right now they're rotating their ships in and out of the firing solutions of our three cannons, giving their shields time to recharge. If we can hit one of them before that happens, we can shrink the circle, we can make it so that they—"

"I—okay, I get, you know, the plan, such as it is, but what in any god's name makes you think we can *do* any of that? Those dreadnaughts were taken out of the fight over Sanctum, sure, but they're not, you know, they're not exactly sitting empty. There have to be hundreds, maybe even thousands of Pax troops still on board—"

"We do nothing and Sanctum dies. It's that simple."

"That's fine, and I understand that, and believe me, I want to do something too, but I'm saying—you're not hearing what I'm saying. Whose idea was this, anyway? Yours? Marus's?"

"Esa's."

"Esa's. This was Esa's idea."

"Yes, it was."

"Does she—"

"I'm listening too, you know," Esa told him.

"Great, fine. Do you understand that we can't *do* this? I'm saying regardless of whether it will turn the tide of the battle, the five of us—"

"Twelve of us." That was a new signal; another ship was lifting off of the planet, joining our formation.

"Sahluk?" I asked. "Is that you? What the hell are you doing off of the ground?"

"The rest of my team can hold the cannon—you did a pretty good job ripping their ground forces apart," he told me. "John Henry filled me in on your plan, such as it is. There was another stealth ship, apparently, a prototype in the labs at Sanctum—he managed to get it—"

"He? Who the hell's he? Who's *piloting* that thing?"

"That would be me, Jane." It was Criat. What the hell was Criat doing behind the stick of a prototype stealth ship? He'd never been one to shy from a fight, but this was a different thing entirely.

"What the hell are you doing out here, boss?" I asked him. I couldn't even *remember* the last time Criat had been in a cockpit. That thing over Last Echelon; that had been half a century ago.

"Well, I *had* been coming to help you, but since you seem to have a plan to save all of us, I figured I'd pick you up some reinforcements." It was a tiny craft, a scouting ship—I could barely imagine Criat and Sahluk squeezing in there together, let alone with five other soldiers, Sahluk's best. Still, twelve was better than five—that was for damned sure.

"Great, wonderful," Javier said. "Can we circle back around to the part where this is a crazy plan that sprouted from the mind of a teenager who knows fuck-all about interplanetary combat?"

"Aren't you going to add 'no offense'?" Esa asked him.

"No! I'm not! You don't know what the hell you're doing! Even if we did manage to board one of their ships, and even if we did manage to seal off the gunnery controls and, you know, access them, even if we *did* all that, there are more Pax dreadnaughts out there, waiting out the fight. The instant they figure out what we're doing, they will blow us right out of the void. The Pax on board the ship we're trying to take will lower their own shields, and their brothers will blow us to hell and back before we can even—"

"Not if we take that one." I highlighted one of the enemy craft in my HUD and bounced the information along the comm channel to Bolivar and to Criat's craft.

"That one," Javier said slowly. "That's the one you want to hit."

"Yes."

"That's a Nemesis class dreadnaught, built by the Atellier sect during the wars. It's crewed by twenty-five hundred. It took less damage from the bombardment coming in than any of the others, there's still likely—"

"And that's exactly *why* it's our target. It had to pull out of the fight because we landed a lucky shot on its propulsion systems." I had been busy scanning the enemy dreadnaughts as Javier laid out his objections. "It still has full shielding."

"Which—yeah, which, again, the Pax inside will just drop the instant that—"

"Not on a Nemesis. Its shielding station is located right beside gunnery control. They're built to keep fighting, even after . . . you know, to keep fighting at the last minute. We're going to use that against them. We take gunnery control, we take shielding, and with its engines down it can't maneuver away from the angle it's already sitting at—an angle that already gives us a firing solution on the dreadnaughts attacking Sanctum. Javier, listen: *look* at it. What do you see?"

He paused for a moment, looking at the *ship*, not just the scans. "It's new," he said finally. "It's one of the ships from—from whatever forgotten depot they raided. Even after all the fighting today, it's still all shiny, barely touched."

"Exactly. That meant the Pax inside will barely know its layout; they'll be less familiar with its controls, we'll be able to lessen their advantage. It's *perfect* for this plan."

Javier sighed, long and hard. "We're really doing this, aren't we?" he asked.

"We don't have many other options," Criat reminded him. "It's die trying this, or die as the Pax round us all up after they obliterate Sanctum. One way or another—"

"Yeah. I get it. Fuck it. God hates a coward."

"So now you're on board with my plan?" Esa asked him.

"No, I think it's a terrible plan. But since I don't have a better one—fuck it," he said again. "Let's go storm a dreadnaught. What's the worst that could happen?"

We might just be about to find out.

CHAPTER 5

S o," Javier asked, "how do we actually *do* this?"

"I thought you were on board now," Criat asked him.

"I am; I'm saying—what's the actual *plan* here? We can't just fly up to the docking bay doors and ask politely if they'll let us in. We can't *fire* on them and blast *open* the docking bay doors; even if we had the ordnance to do so, which, by the way, all my missiles are spent, if anyone was asking—but even if we *did* have the ordnance, their shields are still up. We can approach, and we can *maybe* stay off their radar, assuming our stealth kits hold up and we're, you know, *very* lucky, but how do we actually breach the damn ship?"

Silence for a moment, both inside Scheherazade and on the comm channels. The dreadnaughts loomed ahead of us against the sweep of the stars; three massive ships, two of them heavily damaged, the third—our target—in the center of the pack. Unlike the others, which bristled with guns and towers, the Nemesis was a lean, long beast, more rounded edges and recessed guns than bulky protrusions—the product of an entirely different design sensibility than the Pax's homegrown dreadnaughts. The void around it shimmered slightly, visible only in erratic pulses as the debris that floated through the system deflected off its shield.

"Have we considered the idea that—it's a target, a very clear target," the Preacher put in. "Like you said"—she turned to me—"it's *perfect*. How do we know it's not a poisoned chalice?"

"A what?" Esa asked.

"How do we know it's not a trap?"

"Because nobody—not even the Pax—would be stupid enough to come up with an idea like this," Javier replied.

"Hey!" Esa objected.

"Did I say stupid? I meant brilliant. It's a brilliant plan, and we're all most assuredly not going to die, assuming we can even come up with a way to get on board."

"The damage to the engines," Marus said suddenly.

I pulled up Schaz's scans of the dreadnaught's superstructure. "We can't get a ship through that breach, if that's what you're suggesting," I told him. "Even if we did, we'd have nowhere to go; we'd be stuck behind the bulkheads."

"Not the ships," he said. "Just us. As long as the ships approach slowly enough, we can get through the shields; shielding only stops objects moving at dangerous velocities. We can—"

"Oh, no." The words escaped me in a kind of moan as I saw where he was going. I couldn't help it. I knew what he was planning, and I hated it. I hated it.

"We can reach the dreadnaught's hull directly," Marus bored onward with his terrible plan, "and climb into the breach ourselves. Make our way through the engines. There has to be some sort of maintenance access in there that will let us into the dreadnaught body proper."

"You want us to go EVA?" Even Javier sounded impressed by the insanity of the plan. "You want us to climb around on the *outside* of an enemy ship. Then climb *into* their engines—which, let's hope they're not currently doing repairs, on their, you know, broken ship that *requires exactly those*—and then from there, make our way into the ship itself."

"It's not far," Criat rumbled. "From the engineering sector of the ship to the gunnery controls, I mean. It's feasible. It's very feasible."

"So it's a good idea, then?" Esa asked him.

"I wouldn't go that far. It was Marus's idea, after all."

"I don't hear any other options," Marus sighed.

I tried like hell to think of one. I hated EVA—extravehicular activity, otherwise known as spacewalking. I hated it unreasonably. Something about being surrounded by all that nothing, with just one misstep sending you spiraling off into the void, doomed to slowly suffocate as the oxygen supplies in your suit drained down . . . I'd had nightmares about it all my life, ever since my original sect had put me through a terrifying training scenario in EVA combat. It had only been compounded by an incident shortly after I joined the Justified, an incident where . . .

I didn't even want to think about it.

"There's a problem, though," Criat added.

"Of course there is." I tried not to sound too thankful.

"We've crammed more people into my ship than it was meant to hold. We don't have enough suits or magboots for all of us to go EVA."

"So we split into two teams," the Preacher put in. "That's simple enough. Those of us on Bolivar and Scheherazade will go EVA, enter the engines and assault the gunnery controls. If we move quick enough, we can seal off that section of the ship. The Pax will still be trying to get in, but from there, we'll have access to docking systems."

"They'll be locked down, though," Marus reminded her.

"The Pax won't have an AI I can't hack," she replied confidently. "I'll bet my life on it."

"You will be. And the rest of ours in the bargain. If we don't get Criat's crew on board, they'll cut through the seals and butcher the rest of us where we stand."

"But if we do, they'll be able to dock and hit the Pax trying to get to us from behind. Not to mention holding us an exit route off the ship once we're done."

"That's optimistic," Javier told her. "You're still planning for some of us to get out of this alive."

"Of course I am," the Preacher told him, sounding almost shocked that he'd suggest otherwise. "No matter how unlikely it is, one should always plan for both a best- and worst-case scenario."

I laughed; she just sounded so prim when she said it. Also, I laughed because it took my mind off the insanity we were about to undertake. I hated EVA so, so much.

"So that's it?" Esa asked, nervous, now that everyone had actually agreed to her plan. I could tell by her voice—she was terrified, not of the idea of assaulting the dreadnaught itself, but because it had been *her* idea. If they were ready for us, if we failed, it would have been her plan that put us there.

"That's it," I told her, trying to banish the fear *I* felt from my voice; she didn't need me sounding afraid—that would only add to her own fear. I unbuckled myself from my chair. Stood and stretched, let the motion last for a moment, pretending a calm I sure as shit didn't feel. "Schaz, you've got a course set in, right?"

"I do indeed."

"And you're still keyed up on . . . whatever it was that MelWill gave you?"

"I most certainly *am*. It's lovely."

"Wait, what?" Javier asked. I'd forgotten I was still on comms.

"Don't worry about it," I told him. "We'll see you on the other side."

"Don't you hate EVA?" he asked me.

"Don't *worry* about it," I almost hissed at him. There went my cool. "We'll see you there." I switched off the comms, and turned to face Esa.

"Come on," I told her. "Let's get you suited up."

CHAPTER 6

The space suits I had on board Scheherazade actually weren't that far from my usual combat vestments: the same armored plating, the same intention shielding for firefights, the same comms systems and tactical gear. The only real difference was the helmet, the seals, and the magboots that would let us clamp onto the outside of the dreadnaught.

Fortunately, they were designed to be resized—all Justified equipment was, given the diversity of our members. A suit on board any given ship could go from being able to fit a Reint to being able to fit a Mahren with just a few tugs and pulls, then suction in tight with just a press. That meant that neither Marus nor Esa had trouble suiting up. Or rather, it meant that the suits I had on board would fit them—Esa had a little trouble getting one on, given that she'd never worn anything like this before.

Should I have tried to get her to stay behind, to stay on board Scheherazade? Probably. But we were so few, and we were so desperate, and this had been *her* plan; it would have felt cruel telling her she couldn't come. And we might need her abilities, once we were inside.

"We're in position," Schaz informed us as we crowded into the airlock.

"Open the ramp," I told her.

She did as she was bid. The ramp slid open, exposing us to nothing but void. Even through the heated suit I could feel the sudden cold, the warmth of Schaz's interior being pulled out past us with all the atmosphere in the airlock. Beyond us was nothing but the distant stars—we weren't even facing the battle, couldn't see the flash and flame of the exchange of cannon fire at the distant Pax firing position.

Beneath us was the hull of the Pax ship, a matte black alloy broken only by the occasional gun emplacement. If any of those noticed us, we were done.

The hull below was drifting past, slowly; Schaz had killed her engines to get here, not able to risk firing them so close. Her stealth systems were good, but it still would have been tempting fate.

I looked up the side of the Pax craft, trying to keep my breathing steady, trying not to think about all the nothing surrounding me. There was the breach, a jagged gash in the otherwise smooth metal of the dreadnaught's surface.

Esa reached out, with her gloved hand, and took my own. I nodded at her, then at Marus.

Then we jumped.

Fell through nothing. Fell into nothing, fell past nothing. I tried to keep the angle of my body ramrod straight, so that I'd hit the surface of the vessel below flat with the soles of my boots, give the magnets within their best chance at connecting with the metal. Otherwise I might bounce, and roll, and then I really would be gone, floating forever into the void—or not forever, if I managed to enter the orbit of one of the celestial bodies, or the pull of the black holes. Either way, I'd be dead long before then, having long since choked to death as my suit's oxygen supplies ran out.

Stop thinking about it.

My boots hit the surface. As always, there was a brief moment of horror as it seemed like they *wouldn't* connect, and then they did, and I was pulling Esa down beside me, into a crouch, until her boots connected as well. Marus landed picture-perfect beside us; thirty feet or so down the hull, Javier and the Preacher were doing the same.

Criat and Sahluk had elected to remain on board their craft until we could open the docking bay doors—they'd had enough suits that two of them might have joined us as well, but they didn't want to risk approaching so close to the dreadnaught, and then staying in that envelope long enough for us to open the doors for the others. Instead they were hanging just outside the Nemesis's sensor envelope, waiting for our signal to approach.

Which meant the five of us were it, at least for now.

I raised my arm slowly and unholstered my pistol. My rifle was strapped onto my back, but it had greater recoil, and I didn't want to risk the force pushing my boots out of their magnetic contact with the hull. I pointed toward the gash in the dreadnaught's surface—barely visible except for the fact that it blocked out some of the stars behind it—and we started in that direction, slowly.

We were actually doing this. We were trying to slip inside an enemy dreadnaught from a breach in their outer hull, so that we could take over their gunnery controls and fire back at the battle they'd limped away from. This was the *best* plan we had been able to come up with.

The desperation was a bitter taste in my mouth.

One foot in front of the other, slowly, we moved across the surface. It felt like it took forever, and I watched the gun emplacements the whole time, waiting for them to circle and casually blast us off the hull.

In actuality, it was less than five minutes. Javier went over the edge of the gash first, dropping down inside; he'd always been good at EVA, and never the slightest bit afraid. I sent Esa in after him. I had no idea toward *what*— from where I stood, I couldn't even see into the ship itself. But Javier had landed somewhere within, and he'd be able to catch her.

Marus thumped my arm with his fist. We were trying to stay off comms as much as possible; it wasn't *likely* that the Pax on board were idly scanning frequencies, but it wasn't impossible, either. I turned toward him, then followed the line of his raised gun.

There was a flood of light coming from a square on the dreadnaught's surface; an access hatch was opening. Technicians, engineers, coming to assess the damage, maybe? Or the Pax knew we were here, and they'd sent soldiers to pick us off.

I knelt against the dreadnaught's matte hull, raising up my pistol. The Preacher was up and over, down into the ship itself. I nodded at Marus; he started over as well. I watched that square of light like my life depended on it, which it very well might have. Watched for any shadow, any break in the illumination, but there was nothing. Whoever was in there, they were taking their own sweet time getting out.

Marus was over now. I had to choose—wait for the Pax to emerge, possibly blowing our position early, but giving me a clear shot at them? Or try to scramble into the breach and hope we could get far enough inside the engine that they wouldn't see us from the hole above, assuming they didn't emerge and shoot me from behind as I was climbing over?

I hated giving my back to the enemy. But I hated giving away our position more. I cursed under my breath, the word still sounding loud as anything inside of my helmet given that it was all I could hear, then I stood, and turned, and clambered over the damaged hull, careful not to slice my suit open on the jagged metal.

I didn't even have time to see what was below me. A glance back was enough to tell me that *someone* was about to emerge from the hatch. I could feel the slight tug of the dreadnaught's gravity below—all I had to do was let go.

I did, and I dropped.

CHAPTER 7

Marus caught me by the wrist.

It was a good thing he did, too—*he* was standing on a catwalk, torn up by the shot that had ripped through the dreadnaught; I was falling right past it, into the engine itself. He and Javier hauled me onto the metal as the Preacher crouched past them, aiming her rifle up at the hole in the bulkhead, waiting to see if whoever had come out onto the hull was about to peer down at us.

I tapped Marus on the thigh, twice. We needed to get moving.

We scarpered down the catwalk as fast as we could—making noise didn't matter, it wouldn't travel through the vacuum of space. At least there was lighting, emergency lighting, bathing the interior of the engine in crimson.

The damage that single cannon shot had done was severe, the great machinery around us pretty much destroyed by just one round. It really had been a lucky shot; just a few meters off, and it would have avoided most of the major components of the massive engine. Instead, it had hit most of them, managing to take the most damaging path through the engine possible, so much so that making repairs in the void would have been impractical at best. If that one shot hadn't managed to do almost catastrophic injury, this dread-naught would likely still be hanging in the skies over Sanctum, pounding away, and we would be that much closer to losing this fight, if we hadn't already.

Sometimes luck, more than anything, mattered in a war.

The hull breach vanished behind us as we made our way through the laby-rinthine passages of the interior of the engine. With every step we took I expected a platoon of Pax soldiers to materialize in front of us, or to start firing from behind, but there was nothing—they hadn't detected us yet. It was only a matter of time, but the further we could make it forward before the Pax knew we were here, the less time we'd have to spend fighting *through* them to get to our destination.

We arrived at another access door, this time leading to an airlock directly connecting to the interior of the ship. The Preacher touched the access panel, hacking through the Pax's computerized security, until the door popped open with a hiss, atmosphere escaping around its edges. We crowded through into the airlock, then sealed it behind us.

Someone was hammering on the other side. They'd noticed the airlock activating, wanted to know who the hell was messing about in the engine. You'd think that they would have been more wary—they were still at least adjacent to a battle, after all—but that's the thing about being in space, the one advantage we had: you don't expect to be hit like this. You just *don't*.

You're insulated by all that nothing—you think that if there is an enemy boarding party approaching, it will only be after a long, protracted fight in the void, and the enemy craft will latch on and bore a hole through your hull, replete with warning sirens and klaxons and security personnel running to and fro. You never expect the enemy to just *appear* at your door, already inside, with no warning. It just doesn't happen.

That element of surprise was what we were counting on.

The Preacher opened the airlock door.

The Pax on the other side were still wearing their full suits; they kept themselves cloaked like that as much for their own purposes as they did to intimidate their enemies, made it so that they all looked alike, regardless of what race they were underneath all the black leather and armor plating, so that they were all Pax first. We couldn't even read a reaction in their faces when we came boiling out of the airlock, because we couldn't *see* their faces—just expressionless black masks.

Still, they froze for just an instant when we were revealed, and that instant was all we needed. I took the Pax on the left with my knife—not likely a soldier, probably just a technician, about to go assess the damage to the engine—as the Preacher hit the one on the right and snapped her neck. We hid the bodies in the airlock, and sealed it again. They might be discovered in due time, especially if the crew that had entered into the breach after us decided to return through this airlock, but we'd be long gone by then, and likely discovered anyway.

We were inside. We'd gotten this far, at least.

I pulled up a map of the typical Nemesis layout on my HUD. We were two levels above the gunnery and shielding station we needed to reach, but it wasn't far. We just needed to find the nearest stairs. According to the old blueprints, there should be a stairwell down the corridor and to our right. We'd just have to hope that the Pax were still at battle stations, and there wouldn't be many of them prowling the halls.

I opened the door and crept out. There were three of them in sight. So much for luck.

We'd all attached suppressors to our rifles; they didn't make the gunshots quiet, just less loud. Javier took one, the Preacher another, and I took the last. Nothing we could do about the bodies—someone would be along to investigate the shots before we even found somewhere to hide them. Instead, we just made for the stairwell, as quick as we could. The time before the Pax realized they'd been breached was now measured in minutes, if not seconds.

We were down most of the second flight before the alarms started wailing.

CHAPTER 8

We ambushed a security detachment as they came pouring out of their armory. Again—even with the alarms sounding, they didn't really expect someone to already *be* on board, not really. They thought maybe a craft had made it through their firing solution, or they were being called to sort out an internal problem, not that the enemy was already among them.

We made a brief stop at the armory itself, to hook ourselves some extra gear, then to leave tripwired explosives behind—any Pax who tried to prepare themselves before assaulting us were in for a nasty surprise. The resulting explosions would both take them out and mangle the massed equipment here. It wasn't the only armory on board, of course, but it was the closest one, so maybe we'd just bought more time.

The doors to gunnery control had sealed shut when the alarm went off. Not the blast doors—they didn't know this was our target yet—just the regular airlocks. The Preacher knelt beside the access panel, hacking us in, as the rest of us watched the hallways, Javier and Marus taking one direction, Esa and I the other. The slowly curving corridors seemed to stretch on forever, bathed in the oscillating red light of the alarms; they were coming, and they were coming fast.

"Hurry," I said to the Preacher. No need to stay off the comms now—they knew we were here.

"I'm hurrying," she told me. "It's not like—"

Gunfire from behind me; Javier and Marus had made contact. It took everything I had not to spin around and fire on their threat—that would just mean this direction was unprotected. Instead, I had to trust that they could hold their side.

Something rolled into view around the curve of the corridor; an explosive. No, not that—a flashbang maybe? I wasn't sure until it snapped into activation, and a shield spread across the hallway. A portable barrier. The Pax began massing behind it, safe from any return fire.

I almost smiled. The shield kept them safe from my rifle rounds, yes. I *could* have poured fire into that shield until it cracked, but that would have taken several magazines, and would have been pointless—they'd be ready to come through before I'd really done any damage. Besides, I didn't need to. I had an even more potent weapon kneeling beside me, one that wouldn't be affected by shielding at all.

"Esa?" I invited her.

She didn't say anything, just laid her rifle on the ground, focused her will, and brought her hands together in front of her, like a clap. She didn't actually *need* to do that—to match the force of her gift with a physical motion—but I guess it helped her visualize what she wanted to happen, or something like that.

The results were impressive either way. The Pax massing behind the shield slammed into each other as if invisible walls had smashed them from either side. I'd guess that most of them were at least knocked unconscious, if not outright killed, though a few were still moving. With a motion almost like a shove, she sent the whole pile of Pax sailing backward down the corridor, as if they'd been caught by the blade of a plow.

"We're through," the Preacher said.

CHAPTER 9

We stormed into the gunnery control station, firing as we came.

There were a few armed security guards—we took those out first. The rest were technicians, engineers. Yes, we killed them anyway, and we did it without hesitation, even those running for the opposite exit. They were armed— Pax always were, wherever they went—and they were in our way.

Would I regret it, later? Would I have nightmares about it? Was I doing permanent damage to Esa, teaching her to view the world this way, that sudden, immediate violence was a tool at her disposal, one she should lean on? Yes, yes, and yes, to all of them. But the stakes were too high, and the risks too great.

If we tried to take them alive, if we spent time tying them up or setting a guard over them, that was time we couldn't spend on our objective, and our objective was all that mattered. There were millions of lives hanging in the balance, and those were just the inhabitants of Sanctum—if you considered the Justified's mission, preparing for the return of the pulse, then the fate of untold trillions was at stake.

Javier and Marus got to work sealing the airlock doors—not just locking them with the security panels, but physically welding them together. The Pax would be able to breach that eventually, but it would buy us more time. I made sure the room was clear; it was two stories, the second a catwalk above that could have held hidden threats. The Preacher started hacking into the controls themselves.

"Esa," I called down to her, my rifle still raised. "See if you can find the access for the docking bay doors. Let's invite Criat and the others to this little party."

"What will they look like?" she asked. She'd adapted so well to this new world I'd almost forgotten she'd never seen the interior of a starship until

Scheherazade had plucked her from her homeworld, scant weeks and what felt like forever ago.

"There should be a screen that says 'Maintenance control,'" I told her, praying that there was, in fact, a maintenance-access system inside the gunnery station. "Look for that. How's it coming, Preacher?"

"The Pax AI is fighting me," she said. If she'd been any other species, I would have said she was grinding her teeth.

"And?"

"And I'm winning. But it's going to take time."

There was a dull thump from behind the first set of doors Marus and Javier had welded shut; the Pax were trying to get *in*. They'd moved on to the doors on the opposite side of the room, but Marus cast a worried glance backward. "If they're willing to use explosives to get in here, we won't have as long as we thought," he warned me.

"They don't know what we're trying to do yet," I told him.

"They know we've locked ourselves in gunnery control. They're stupid, but they're not that stupid. They—"

An explosion tore through the door. Not all of it, not even a person-sized hole; the doors were thick, and hard to breach. But it was enough for the Pax to start firing through. A few of their shots bounced off of my intention shield, ricocheting around the room. I fired back, just putting rounds through the breach, as even more alarms began to sound.

That was when the automated security kicked in, and an even thicker blast door slammed shut over the entranceway.

I grinned over at Marus. They hadn't *known* how the Nemesis would react to someone trying to use explosives to force their way into its gunnery controls—it was too new, its interlocking systems still partially a mystery to the Pax. As a result, they'd just given us better armor than we could ever have hoped to weld in place. "No, I think they're exactly that stupid," I told him.

CHAPTER 10

Did they really just lock us *inside* their gunnery control station?" Javier was dumbfounded; he was staring literally slack-jawed, his mouth hanging halfway open as he tried to process what had just happened. "Is that . . . did that just happen?"

"It did," I confirmed as my shields slowly reached full capacity again. "Or rather, the ship itself did, and they hadn't done their homework to know that's *exactly* what it was going to do when they set off those charges. Seal the security doors, too; let's buy ourselves as much time as we can, huh?"

"On it." He headed to the door they'd almost breached; Marus was already on the other side, welding shut the heavier blast door.

"Preacher?" I asked.

"Do not ask me 'how are we doing,'" she said, her vocal modulation *still* giving the impression that she was speaking through gritted teeth, even though she had no teeth to grit. "I will tell you how we're doing when I'm through their firewalls. Until that time, please be so kind as to—" She stopped, jerking back from their system as though it had shocked her. "We're through their firewalls," she told me.

"How soon until we can fire this thing?"

"I just need to line up a shot."

"Then what the hell are you talking to me for? Esa? Any luck with the—"

"I've got . . . I'm at the docking bay controls, I think, and I think I know how to open them, but should I—"

"Yes. Go ahead." There weren't many guns on Criat's prototype ship, but it wasn't like it was unarmed; if he could land inside the Pax's own docking bay, he and his men would have their own base of fire. They'd be able to hold their position fairly easily, unless the Pax managed to get to some of the dormant tanks or heavy infantry weapons they doubtless had stored in the bay as well.

I raised Criat on the comms. "You're about to get an invitation to the party," I told him.

"About damned time," he growled. "I've been sitting here fixing my makeup and worrying about which dress to wear."

"Was that . . . were you just—"

"I was sticking with your metaphor, yeah. Just open the damn doors."

"Firing solution locked in," the Preacher reported. "Firing the main cannon . . . now."

Just like when we were on Sanctum, when the big cannon fired, you *knew* it. The massive gauss barrel ran the entire length of the dreadnaught—all the bulkheads and all the insulation and all the metal in the world couldn't keep that sound out. I rushed over to the monitors to see if she'd connected.

"What . . . what did you *do*?" I asked. One of the Pax dreadnaughts was already down, a hole blasted clean through its hull—one of the dreadnaughts on the *opposite* side of their formation from us. I wasn't even able to piece together *how* she'd achieved that result.

She hadn't had a clean shot on it, which was *why* she'd been able to do the damage she'd done; its shielding had been concentrated on its outward-facing starboard side, the side taking fire from Sanctum itself. She'd some-how hit it on the port hull instead, regardless of the fact that there were two other dreadnaughts in between her and her target.

"I banked it," she said, sounding smug. Deservedly so.

"You *what*?"

"She ricocheted the round off the shielding of one of their other dread-naughts." Marus sounded stunned; he had just finished welding shut the far door, and was staring at the screens as well. "She hit the shielding of the clos-est dreadnaught at just the right angle—not full on, that would mean all the force dissipated, but not oblique enough to send it howling off into the void—and she *banked* it inside their defensive circle. She just made a trick shot with a dreadnaught cannon across half a million miles. That's a thing that just hap-pened."

"Well done," Javier told her, a grin spreading across his face.

"Thank you. I played a great deal of—what's the human game, with the sticks and the little balls and the felt tables with the pockets?"

"Pool. You just fired a dreadnaught cannon like you were making a pool shot."

"Pool, yes, that's the one. It had something of a resurgence back on—"

"How soon can we fire again?" I asked her. We'd taken another dreadnaught out of their formation, but it wasn't going to be enough to save Sanctum, and the Preacher's clever trick wasn't going to work again. The other dreadnaughts were already reacting, shifting their rotation, closing ranks, already preventing her from doing the same thing twice.

"Two minutes," she replied.

"And the rest of the Pax . . . you know, they noticed that one of their ships just fired on *another* one of their ships," Marus reported.

"Yeah, I didn't think that was just going to slip by them."

"The other dreadnaughts close by are already firing on us. Not with their big cannons—they've got either damaged engines or damaged main guns, so they can't do that—but with everything else they've got."

"Take over at the shielding controls."

"I am already doing that."

My comm crackled to life. "Was that the main cannon firing just now?" Criat asked me. I could hear gunfire in the background of the channel; he must have set down almost immediately after the big cannon had fired. "I only ask because—"

"One Pax dreadnaught down," I told him, fighting the urge to crow. "It's working."

"Good. We're carving out a defensive perimeter in the hangar; we can act as a blockade for their forces forward from this position. You'll still have to deal with those trapped aft, but we should at least be able to cut off their reinforcements."

"Criat—stay alive."

"You too. One down, Kamali. Five to go."

And with us pounding the Pax dreadnaughts from their exposed side, the cannon at Sanctum as well as Alpha and Bravo would be able to do more damage as well; the Pax ships couldn't rotate out of a firing solution long enough to let their shields recharge before they'd rotated right into the next. For the first time since I'd seen the Pax circle of ships between the moon and the world below, I thought this might actually work.

"Five to go," I repeated into the comm, more to myself than to Criat.

CHAPTER 11

W e've got a problem," Javier reported. He was at another station; I couldn't tell which one.

"Of course we do," I said; there went my brief moment of optimism. I moved to stand beside him. "What are they—"

"The fusion reactor," he said. "We took control of the guns from them, and we took control of the shields, but we didn't—"

I cursed. "How did we not think of that?"

"We had a host of bad options—"

"We did, and this was the one we chose. *How* did we not think of that?" There were more muffled explosions coming from either side of the security doors; the Pax were trying to get through again. I didn't know how long we'd have, but it wouldn't be long enough. And now we had this to deal with.

"Because we didn't," Javier shrugged, surprisingly calm about the fact that the Pax were currently—at best—trying to shut down the flow of power to the cannon, and at worst trying to scuttle the whole damned ship. "We just didn't. Even if we had, I don't know what else we could have done."

"Preacher, can you—"

"Already on it. Javier, will you take over at gunnery controls for me?"

"My pleasure."

Javi and the Preacher switched stations, Javier prepping the dreadnaught's cannon to fire another round, the Preacher hacking into the power relay controls, trying to stop the Pax from shutting down their entire ship. I held my breath. Soldiers were still pounding on the doors outside—they'd be breaking in any minute. If the Preacher couldn't do something, then at least one of us would have to break *out*, and I knew which one it would be.

She shook her head, moving back to the gunnery controls. "They knew we'd try it," she said. "They've locked me out. They've locked *everyone* out;

shut off network access to the power grid entirely, probably by cutting the hardline."

I'd thought the Pax had been remarkably stupid so far, even for Pax, and they *had* been, but it looked like not everyone on board had lost all of their cognitive processing ability during the course of the Pax brainwashing. "So someone's got to go down there," I said.

"*What?*" Esa asked. "There have to be a *hundred* soldiers between us and that reactor—"

"At least," I nodded, checking my rifle.

"That's exactly what they'll expect us to do," she said. "That's—they'll be waiting for us, they'll be—"

"No 'us,' kid," I shook my head at her. "Not this time. You're the biggest gun we've got: you need to stay here and defend the Preacher and Marus. If I stop the Pax from shutting off our power, it won't do any good if they've retaken this position."

"Well, you're not going alone," Javier told me. "I can—"

"*You* can stay here with Esa. Two access points," I jerked my thumb at one door, then the other, "that means at least one person covering each one. At all times."

"Criat," Esa suggested desperately. "Criat and Sahluk. *They* can get to the reactor—"

"Actually, they can't. They're forward, in between us and the majority of the Pax forces on this ship, and the reactor is aft. There's only one way this plays out, and it's—"

"Firing again," the Preacher said quietly, and the sound of the gun going off overwhelmed any more arguments Esa may have made. If I didn't get to the reactor, that might be the last shot we managed to make.

I pointed at the aft security door. "When they crack that open," I said— and the bright blue line slowly carving up the quick and dirty welding job Marus had applied suggested they were about to do just that—"you're going to hit them as hard as you possibly can."

"Please, Jane—*please*—"

"You're going to hit them as hard as you can," I repeated, "and then you're going to hold this position as I go *through* them. If I can take out . . . who-ever's down there in the reactor, then I'll be able to hold it, at least for a little while. I can buy us the time we need to keep firing." I slung my gun for a moment, and put my hands on her shoulders. "We *can* save Sanctum, Esa, and this is how we do it."

"That's not—"

"Take it from me, kid. I've lived through a lot. It's not often the right thing to do is *also* the easiest choice to make. This time, it is. I need to get down to the reactor. You need to stay here and protect our friends. It's that simple."

She put her hand over mine, and gripped it, tightly. "Stay alive," she told me, her voice little more than a whisper.

"I'll try."

"Do fucking *better* than that. I want you to promise. I want your word."

I smiled at her slowly, even as I shook my head. "Sorry, kid. I don't make promises I don't know I can keep. Don't come after me."

"They're coming through!" Javier shouted, and then the door was breached.

CHAPTER 12

There was a bright flash, and then movement, and gunfire. Esa hit them hard; I could feel the push of her power as it swept past me. It slammed into the Pax fighting their way through the breached door, smashing them up against the walls, hard enough to break bones. I pulled a couple of grenades from Javier's belt and rolled them through the hole, then turned away from the blast.

In the short window before the grenades exploded, Javier grabbed me by the wrist, and he kissed me. I hadn't been expecting it, and just for a moment, I melted. He was here. After all we'd been through, after all that had separated us, he'd come back to me.

"Stay safe," he told me, even as he pulled away.

Then the blast thumped through the walls, and I was moving.

I slid through the ruin of the door, firing as I went. The Pax outside weren't expecting it—they had thought *they* were moving forward, not that the opposition would be coming to them. A few managed to get their guns up and start firing back, and my shield took several hard hits, but I was picking my targets fast, they were having trouble adjusting, and then Esa hit them again, standing in the breach as she sent them flying backward, down the hall.

"Go!" she shouted at me.

I picked myself up and started running.

I had a map of a Nemesis pulled up on my HUD, a single bright line pulsing along the floor, laying out the swiftest route to the fusion reactor. It helped, but not as much as it should; either the Pax or whoever had owned this vessel prior to its being mothballed had modified it extensively since it rolled off the production line, and I was constantly finding walls where there shouldn't have been walls, doors that had been sealed off, corridors that continued where my map told me they dead-ended.

And everywhere I went, of course, I found Pax.

Most of them had shields as well, but I'd toggled my rifle to fire four-round bursts—just enough to overwhelm a typical intention shield and punch through, assuming I connected with each round. Some of them I put down; some of them I just forced back into cover, into side rooms or other hallways, and I kept running. That meant they were still behind me, but there were *always* going to be Pax behind me. I'd shifted my shielding to my back, and every time I had a long run down a straight hallway, bullets sang past from the troops on my heels, and a few punched their way into my shield. I had to fight each time just to keep my footing.

The goddamned dreadnaught was like a maze.

I turned a corner and ran right into a platoon on their way to reinforcing the reactor itself; they hadn't been expecting me any more than I was expecting them. I dropped my rifle and went hand to hand, filling the corridor with the flash and sizzle of my stun knuckles and breaking bones right and left, using the close quarters against them, blocking their shots with the bodies of their allies. Somewhere in the middle of all that, the main cannon fired again, the roar and shake overwhelming us all for a moment—the fucking barrel of the gun must have been just on the other side of the bulkhead. I recovered first and finished wiping them out, then took off running again, moving as fast as I could through the strobing crimson-lit corridors before the Pax behind me could catch up.

I hadn't gotten away from the fight clean, though. I had at least two broken ribs, a grazing chemical burn along my scalp—my hair wouldn't grow back right for months, if ever—and they'd reopened at least a few of the wounds the Reint had carved into me back on the world. The ribs especially were slowing me down.

And the dreadnaught was *still* a goddamned maze.

According to my HUD, the reactor should be just on the other side of the wall ahead of me. According to my HUD, there also should have been a goddamned *door* on the wall just ahead of me. There wasn't. The corridor dead-ended in an intersection instead, breaking both right and left; I went left, on the basis of nothing but a coin flip in my head. Shut down the map in my HUD—it was useless. I just needed a door.

The hallway stretched forever to the left. I still had my intention shields raised over my back, and that was why I didn't die when a round hammered into what should have been the back of my skull. I dropped to the ground—that part was easy, given that my shields diffused the force of the bullet, but couldn't disperse it entirely—and rolled, so I was facing behind me.

There were two Pax, stalking down the hall, guns only half-raised; they thought I was dead. Just beyond them was their post—they'd been guarding a door. A door to the reactor. I should have chosen the right-hand path. If they hadn't fired on me, I never would have known I was headed in the wrong direction.

I brought my rifle up—they saw that I was still moving, were doing the same—and fired, two bursts, one at each. I killed the larger, but the second one had the sense to jerk away before her shields were entirely ripped down. I scrambled to my feet, trying to fire again, and of course my rifle clicked empty. My shields were stripped to nothing; if the Pax got her gun up, it was over.

She started raising it. I dropped my rifle and hauled at the pistol on my belt, firing from the hip nearly as soon as I got it clear of the holster. The first round punched through her shoulder, spattering the wall behind her with fuchsia blood—she must have been a Vyriat under all that leather and armor. The second round whined past her head, ricocheting off the wall, and she was *still* trying to raise her rifle, despite one of her arms not working properly anymore; her system must have been absolutely *flooded* with narcotics for her to even move it. I was almost on top of her when I fired again, directly into the faceplate of her armor. It was meant to deflect debris and grazing shots, not a large-caliber pistol round at point-blank range.

She slumped over, very dead. I'd survived. That fight, at least. There were still more Pax behind me. I picked up her rifle and headed to the door. It slid open—the bastards hadn't even sealed it yet. Maybe this actually *could* work.

The dreadnaught's big gun fired again; the Nemesis could fire *fast*. There was a long stretch of catwalks before me, hanging out over nothing—the fusion reactor took up about three stories, just like it had at Bravo facility on the planet. The main control station was on this level, suspended around the glowing centerpiece of the room—the reactor itself. Several engineers were working furiously at those consoles, trying to take the reactor offline.

Between me and them were three Pax in exosuits, guarding the catwalk approach. I was down to four rounds in my handgun and a stolen rifle, and my shields had yet to recover. I'd come too damned far to die here. I raised my rifle and started firing.

CHAPTER 13

My rounds pinged harmlessly off the shields of the exosuited Pax marines. The bullets weren't going to get through, but at least the sudden burst of fire kept them occupied long enough for me to slip inside and shut the door behind me, then smash the keypad—that would keep my pursuers out for long enough to . . . for long enough.

The first Pax recovered from my fusillade and raised her weapon: a flamethrower. Even *if* my shields hadn't been nearly offline, there wasn't much I could do about that. I fired off the last few rounds from my stolen rifle at the other two, then threw the empty weapon at the flamethrower itself. She triggered it just as the rifle hit, and a bloom of flame passed harmlessly through the metal of the catwalk to illuminate the piping and wiring below.

I leapt toward the Pax, trying to close the gap—the other two were trying to get their weapons up as well; one of them had a grenade launcher, the other some sort of massive rifle—and I passed over the still-billowing flames and punched the first Pax right in the battery pack of her exosuit. It hurt like a *motherfucker*—even with my stun knuckles activated, punching a large metal battery with a bare fist was still *punching a large metal battery with a bare fist*—but it worked. The battery exploded, peppering all of us with shrapnel and a hot lash of fusion energy, and the first Pax's exosuit went dead, trapping her inside the hulking frame.

I used my momentum to topple her backward, off the catwalk. She fell three stories below. I didn't know if she'd survive the fall, and I didn't much care; she was out of the fight. One down.

The other two were triggering their weapons.

The grenade launcher fired first. Here's the thing about being in combat for most of your life—whether that was on the ground, in dogfights in the void, or on board enemy ships like I was now—it's not that your reflexes get honed to a sharp edge, though they do. It's that you make decisions unconsciously, without even knowing that you are making them. I saw the grenade fire from the barrel of the weapon, less than three feet away from me, and I just reacted.

My force-multiplying knuckles still active, I backhanded the explosive out of the air, directly toward the other Pax.

I'm pretty sure it snapped my wrist when I hit it, but I could barely feel anything, I was so buzzed with adrenaline. The grenade itself hit the other Pax directly on the faceplate with an almost comically underwhelming metal "tink," and then dropped to the catwalk at her feet.

For a single moment, we all stared at it, spinning on the grating. Then we were trying to scramble away, the Pax somewhat slowly: exosuits make you stronger, but they *do* greatly limit your mobility, a definite downside when you're right next to, say, a primed explosive.

The grenade blew through the catwalk, and it took out the supporting suspension lines as well. The whole thing started slipping, too heavy now for the few lines that were left. I'd managed to hook an arm through one of the catwalk's rails, so I at least didn't plummet immediately—unlike the Pax who had fired the grenade, who went to join her friend down at the bottom of the room, likely crushed to death by the weight of her own suit—but I did slide *with* the catwalk, until I was hanging almost vertically from that lone railing.

Two down.

The other Pax had managed to scramble to safety as well, standing nearly back by the door where I'd come in. She took in the damage the grenade had done—took in me, hanging from the catwalk directly opposite her—and then, again, started to raise her fucking gun.

Still hanging, I drew my pistol.

We both fired at the same time.

Her clutch of bullets tore through what little bit of my shields had managed to regenerate, but her footing wasn't great on the shifting, dangling catwalk, and the recoil made her stumble backward; the rest of the rounds went high just as my shield sputtered and died. My own shot hit her shields square, deflected easily. She was bringing her rifle back to bear as I fired again, the recoil lifting my hand above my head. I fought to bring it back down, and fired one last time.

Her shields had been cracked by the earlier rounds. The third made it all the way through, and my aim was dead on, took her right between the eyes. She slumped in the suit, dead, and ever so slowly, the whole mass—Pax soldier and Pax exosuit—tilted and fell from the catwalk.

Three down.

I holstered my pistol, still hanging almost vertically above the drop. Gritted my teeth and hauled myself back onto the portion of the catwalk that wasn't broken or tilted, trying not to use the broken wrist on the arm still looped around the railing. For a moment, I simply sat there, trying to get my breath back, trying to believe that all of that had just *happened*, that I'd taken on three exosuited Pax at close quarters and *won*.

That was when something hit me from behind, hard, just beneath the ribs; a feeling I knew intimately.

I'd just been shot.

CHAPTER 14

I jerked forward from the force of the bullet—almost went over the edge. I barely put my hand out flat against the catwalk to stop myself falling off entirely, the impact making the broken bones in my wrist send shrieks of pain down my arm; it may have hurt more than the goddamned gunshot.

I turned, drawing my pistol as I did. One of the engineers. One of the goddamned engineers had a pistol out, a plume of smoke rising from the barrel of her gun—no Pax was ever unarmed, even those who weren't soldiers. I should have remembered that.

I reached down with my free hand, the broken one; felt blood, felt the wound with an almost electric shock of pain—before my hand touched the raw edges of my skin and muscle and came back slick with red, it was like I hadn't even been able to feel it.

The engineer who had shot me was just staring, her gaze going from the gun in her hand to me, like she couldn't quite believe what had happened. The Pax may have trained all of their people in combat, but it had likely been years since she'd fired a gun.

I shot her in the head.

That was the last round out of my pistol, but the other two engineers didn't know that. My teeth gritted around the rising tide of bile and blood climbing up from my throat—as if I needed confirmation that I was bleeding internally. I staggered to my feet, holding the empty pistol on the other two engineers. One of them raised her hands; the other just stood there, still working at the control panel.

"Hands up," I said. The words came with a mist of blood and spit that clung to my lips. The second engineer backed away slowly. I took a few trembling steps forward, off the catwalk and onto the decking of the main control station proper, then forced myself to kneel. It felt like my side was ripping open all over again, but I managed to holster my own pistol and pick up the weapon the dead engineer had dropped. It would have been easier—and faster, and safer—to do that in the opposite order, but I still didn't trust the shattered wrist to hold a gun.

For a moment, we just stared at each other, the two Pax engineers and I. I wondered if they knew I was dying. I wondered if *I* knew I was dying, really. I don't think that information had quite made it to my brain. My body was still just busy shouting *"hurt hurt* HURT" and getting shut down by my higher processes.

The cannon fired again. The draw from the weapon made the reactor flare bright; the first engineer thought that was her moment, and she charged me, not even going for the pistol at her side. She was wrong. I shot her through the chest, then turned, and shot the second engineer as well. She had been trying to run; I shot her in the back.

Just another crime I'd have to live with. Or not.

I staggered toward the control panels, fell, more than anything else, until I was half-leaning against the metal. What the fuck did I know about fusion reactors? Not much, but enough to see a lever had been drawn from "full" to "low." I cranked it all the way back up, then turned, and slid slowly down the panel itself, leaving a smear of blood behind me until I was finally sitting again, my back to the cool metal.

Sitting was good. Sitting was better. My side didn't hurt quite as much. It still hurt, it hurt a great *deal*, but it didn't feel like the rest of me was on fire. I could feel the nanotech swarming through my bloodstream, trying to patch the damage, being overwhelmed. Vaguely, I remembered that I had an emergency sealant canister on my belt. I fumbled it off, and gritted my teeth as I sprayed it on both wounds, entry and exit, filling each with cooling foam.

That would at least stop the external blood loss. As for the blood pooling inside my body, the sepsis from organs leaking fluid into each other, the damage to the organs themselves, and, of course, the simple shock—there was nothing I could do to stop that.

Like I said earlier: I was dying. That information was finally catching up to me.

I twitched my head, just a little bit; activated my comms.

"Marus, Preacher," I rasped. "Esa. Javi. The reactor's . . . back online. You should . . . should be able to . . . you're clear. Shoot the bastards out of the sky."

CHAPTER 15

Roger that," Javier's voice came back to me, clear and clean, sounding far-ther away than it should have, but also sounding like he was right there beside me. For a brief moment, I imagined that he *was;* that I was leaning, not against a cold control panel, but back into his chest, that his arms were wrapped around me, and I was warm, and I was safe, and I was somewhere other than here. "The guns at Sanctum and planetside are pounding holy hell out of them—we've taken another dreadnaught out of play. Jane, I think this is actually going to *work.*"

"Told you," I said, mustering a smile from somewhere, willing him to hear it down the line of the comm. I'd told him no such thing.

"Sahluk and Criat have cleared a path from the docking bay to the gun-nery station," the Preacher told me. "We've still got a few hostiles trying to hit us from your part of the ship, but I think mostly they went after you."

I looked up; I could see . . . *something,* some sort of color or motion back across the catwalk where I'd entered, but the distance made it impossible to focus. Something was going wrong with my eyes, behind my eyes. I blinked, tried to make sense of what I was seeing: sparks, falling from the sealed door. The Pax were trying to cut their way through.

It didn't matter much now. It took time to take the reactor offline, time the Pax could no longer afford. And even if they did—it wasn't like getting past me was going to be difficult, not given the state I was in—we'd taken another dreadnaught out of play, and were firing on the remaining super-craft.

The Justified had won. Sanctum was safe. The fighting might not be over yet, and wouldn't be over for quite a while—once we'd patched up the dam-age they'd done, we'd still have to clear the remaining dreadnaughts from the system, those, like the one I was currently sitting on, that had been knocked out of the fight but were still crewed by hundreds of Pax. But that was just mopping up. We'd won the war.

There was always a price. My life was just a part of that, a piece of the equation. I was surprisingly all right with the concept. I'd seen a great deal over the course of my long existence. There were worse things to die for.

"Do you want us to come for you?" Esa asked me. I could hear her swallow, trying to ask what she didn't want to know, what she wasn't *quite* sure she could hear in my voice. "Do you want—"

"Negative," I told her. "Stay where you are." The dreadnaught was shaking; the other Pax craft were still pounding holy hell out of her with their smaller guns, trying to cut off the damage we were doing. Dreadnaught shields were powerful things, but even they couldn't stand up to sustained fire from fixed positions coming from multiple sides. "When John Henry . . . when he gives you the all-clear, get to Sahluk and Criat. Get out of here."

Silence on the other side of the line, for a moment. "But . . . what about you?" the girl whispered.

"I'll find my own way back." I'd lied to her before, for worse reasons; I didn't feel bad, doing it again. "There are dozens of Pax soldiers between us. I'll find another way. If you can get clear, get clear."

The cutting on the reactor room door was going in earnest, now; they'd be through in minutes, maybe even less. I reloaded my own pistol—painstakingly, the barrel jammed between my knees, because I couldn't trust my broken wrist for the fine motor skills, or even just to hold the barrel. I'd set the stolen Pax handgun on the ground beside me. I wouldn't be able to put up much of a fight, but I'd be damned if I didn't put up any at all.

"Yeah," Javier said. "We're not doing that." I could hear gunfire, behind his voice; apparently I wasn't the only one who'd been playing down the amount of danger I was still in.

"Javi—"

"No, Jane."

"Javi, just—"

"*No*, Jane. If you can't—if you don't think you can get to us, then we're coming to get *you*. That's non-negotiable. You can shout about it all you like, but there's not a lot—"

"I'm dying, Javi." Finally, I managed to shut him up. "I took a stray round

CHAPTER 16

I don't remember much of anything about the trip back through the dreadnaught. The others assured me that it was absolutely hellish, and that they were all very brave. According to them I was conscious for parts of it—at one point I even managed to fire my weapon, though the one fact everyone seemed to agree on is that I didn't hit anything—so you'd think that I really *would* remember, but I just don't.

I *do* remember forcing Marus to help me into the cockpit as we returned to Sanctum. I remember looking out and watching as the final operating dreadnaught was picked apart by the twin cannons remaining; the Pax had finally brought down Alpha gun. I remember the way the flames spiraled out from the breaches in the giant ship's hull, following the path of the oxygen sucked out into the void; I remember the hazy purple afterimage, once the reactor went critical and the ship tore itself apart.

Why they'd stayed to fight, after the math shifted and they knew they couldn't break through Sanctum's shields, I have no idea. Maybe the Pax were just that stupid. Or maybe they just hated us that much.

It didn't matter now. The battle was won. We'd still have to mop up the Pax remaining on the damaged dreadnaughts, and that would be bloody, awful work, but it was the bloody awful work of another day. They weren't going anywhere, just floating through the system, their engines damaged, building their barricades and preparing their defenses for when we tried to take the ships.

An atmosphere of paranoia and oppression was standard practice on any Pax vessel—*knowing* their enemy was coming for them must have made things intolerably worse, especially once they started to burn through their supply of on-hand narcotics. I wouldn't be surprised to find that at least some of them had torn each other apart by the time we came on board to finish the job.

I don't remember descending into Sanctum; I don't remember joining the ranks of other injured soldiers filling the medical facility there. The next thing I *did* remember was lying in a hospital bed, wired up to all sorts of machines that were either doing the work some of my organs weren't currently capable of doing, or reinforcing the nanotech in my own bloodstream.

I have a synthetic liver now, pieces of synthetic intestine grafted onto my own, and a synthetic kidney, to join the *other* synthetic kidney I already had from a bad scrap fifty years ago. When I could finally talk I asked the Preacher if that made her like me any more, now that I was a little closer to being a synthetic life form than an organic one. She said no, that no matter how many organs I replaced I'd never be comparable to a Barious, but that I'd done all right, all things considered. For a bag of badly perforated meat.

Criat came by at some point, and said the council wanted to hang a medal on me. I told him where he could stuff his medal; he said that I wouldn't be able to do that even if I was hale and hearty, because as old as he was he was still a mean old bastard and tougher than me. Apparently they'd hung medals on everyone else: Criat, Sahluk, Marus, even Esa, so she'd have that to lord over her new peers at the university. Javier, too, who'd apparently been reinstated to his old position. Apparently, to overcome a charge of treason, you just have to save all of Sanctum from destruction. Good to know.

They counted the Preacher into their medal-handing-out ceremony as well. Apparently, they'd invited her to join the Justified, and she'd accepted, on the terms that she'd get to join Acheron's research initiative, a posting that her past made her eminently qualified for. That way, she'd get the answers about the pulse she was seeking—at least, those we could give her—and she'd get to keep an eye on Esa. Or so she thought.

Esa came by to see me after a while, to tell me that they'd offered her the same choice they offered all of the children the agents like me brought in: to study at the university and join the ranks of the Justified, or be sent back to the wider universe, never able to return. Most of the other children didn't know the full extent of what we'd done, of course, or how to reach Sanctum, so the risk was minimal—Esa was a special case. I was impressed they'd even offered her the option.

Apparently, she'd proposed a third choice. That's how she put it to me, anyway; Marus visited later and phrased it more along the lines of "she turned them down flat." She suggested that, since she was more powerful already than any of the other students they had (not precisely true, but comparing the different gifts of differing students wasn't necessarily a one-to-one comparison, so I let it lie) and since, unlike some of them, she'd grown up in a significantly more rough and tumble existence—and also since she'd, you know, saved Sanctum and all of its inhabitants—she be allowed to join the Justified, but not forced to join the university specifically.

I didn't learn exactly what she meant by that until I was finally well enough to move around on my own, and I went to visit Scheherazade.

By all reports, Schaz had been driving everyone, up to and including John Henry, absolutely crazy during my convalescence: trying to get information on me, trying to get information on Esa, threatening to hack Sanctum databanks—which she absolutely was not capable of doing—in order to get information on us both. That state of affairs wasn't exactly *helped* by the fact that it took her days to come down off the programming spike MelWill had given her; not even Javier could calm her down.

I went to see her mostly so she'd stop panicking the deck crews, but also because, well, Schaz was my friend. For long stretches of my life, she'd been my *only* friend, the only voice I had to talk to. I missed her too.

I noticed something was strange as soon as I walked—well, limped—up her ramp.

"Someone's moved my shit around," I said to Schaz, frowning. It was true in the armory, and it was true in the living area as well.

"Well . . . yes," Schaz admitted.

"You let someone come in here and touch our stuff? I'm surprised at you, Scheherazade."

"Take a seat; you look terrible."

"Thanks. Thanks for that." All the same, I made my way to the cockpit, and sat down. "I'm glad you finally got your old voice back, by the way." Out of habit, I started a diagnostic on her systems— it would be too much like JackDoes to have fixed her voice, only to have messed with some other trait in her databanks.

"I know! I'm so happy!"

"She does sound better." Esa dropped into the navigator's chair beside me. "More like herself."

"I'm worried that our relationship will always be colored by that awful, awful voice I had when we met," Schaz told her. "We're going to be working together for hopefully a long time now, and—"

"It's already forgotten, Schaz," Esa told her. "You sound like you were always supposed to."

I was frowning, at both Esa and the interior of Scheherazade. "Wait," I said. "Is it the drugs, or did one of you just say something important?"

"Did I not mention that to you earlier?" Esa batted her eyelashes at me.

"Stop that. Mention what?"

"I told Acheron—and the council—that I wanted to join the Justified, but I didn't feel like I would do the most good at the university. I mean, when the time comes for—whatever, to stop the pulse, to, you know, all of that stuff— of course I'll help. But that could be in a *century* or more. In the meantime? I feel like I can do a great deal more good than just sitting around in a school."

"Yes. We covered this. What does that—"

"Specifically, I asked Acheron to ask the council to ask *Criat* to assign me to you. I'm your new partner." She grinned at me.

I just stared back; it didn't make her grin falter one bit as she shrugged and said, "Well, your 'trainee,' anyway. I already know how to shoot the guns on Schaz, though, so I figure I've got a head start on ditching the 'trainee' part. All you have to do now is teach me how to fly her, and I can be your partner for *real*. We're gonna have so much fun!"

I stared at her for a beat, then closed my eyes, sinking back in my chair. She thought she was so clever, dropping this news on me while I was still convalescing. Time to remind her that I was sharper than she thought.

"So Criat says you're ready for that, huh?" I asked, keeping my voice mild.

"He does," she said, sounding suspicious—she knew I was up to something, but not quite what. "I mean, I have to stay here for more 'orientation,' whatever that means, but that's only another month or two, and you'll still be convalescing through all that anyway. I can take university courses while we're in hyperspace; Schaz has already loaded up on textbooks and whatnot."

"Well, that works out, then. I've been thinking about retiring anyway," I said. "Maybe it's time—"

"Don't! Don't you *dare!*"

"What? I thought you were all grown up, ready to join the workforce?"

"I mean—I am, but—"

"Esa?"

"Yeah?"

"I'm joking." I smiled, slowly, without opening my eyes.

She huffed. "I'd hit you right now, but I'm afraid I'd pop your stitches. Your many, many stitches."

"Why?" I asked her.

"Why would I hit you?"

"Why ask Criat to join me? If you wanted to be an agent—even if you wanted to focus on finding other kids like you, the work I do—there are dozens of others you could learn from, train with. Most of them are easier to get along with, too. Why me?"

She sighed, and I could *hear* her rolling her eyes, because I'd spent that much time with teenagers. "I love you too, Jane," she said.

"Yeah," I told her. "I know."

Together, my new partner and I sat in the cockpit, and stared up at the spread of the stars in the sky above Sanctum. She was right, of course: there *was* more still to do. Not just clearing out the Pax who remained in their craft, though that would take some doing, but also making sure they hadn't transmitted our location to anyone else; finding where, exactly, they'd acquired their armory; learning how, exactly, they'd found out Esa's location.

And past the Pax specifically, there was the work: gifted children to pull from rad-soaked worlds, an entire galaxy still reeling from the pulse even a hundred years later, threats to Sanctum—threats to the Justified—that we wouldn't be able to see coming, but that we'd have to be able to meet anyway.

And beyond *all* of that: the return of the pulse. It was still out there. Waiting.

But for now, I sat in the cockpit, with my new "trainee"—I'd never had one of those before; Criat hadn't thought I'd had the personality for it, and until now, I'd agreed with him—and we watched the skies above Sanctum, for the moment, at peace.

The ring of debris flashed in the reflected light of the suns, a ribbon of winking silver wending across the night sky. The black holes pulled at the edges of the horizon. Between them, and past them, were all the unclaimed stars, all the worlds thrown into chaos by the pulse, made into new frontiers, new conflicts, new missions. And down among those were all the children we'd have to find, to bring back to Sanctum, to save.

If even just a few of them turned out like Esa, I thought we'd do all right.

ACKNOWLEDGMENTS

Man, this acknowledgments business is hard work, huh? Like, way harder than the actual writing of the novel you just read—that happened pretty easily; it's all the work that goes in after that requires, just, a whole lot of help. (Also, hey, there's my first acknowledgment: to you, the reader who made it all the way to the end! Thank you! Consider this the fanfare that you should be hearing in your head right about now, something with trumpets and drumrolls.)

So I guess the easiest thing to do is start at the beginning, with Robert and Nancy Williams, without whom this book wouldn't exist, and not just because I wouldn't exist, but because they nurtured and shared a love of storytelling all throughout my childhood, and never thought twice about exposing me to all sorts of stuff that probably warped my young mind into the strange shape that gave rise to the novel you just read. In the same vein, endless thanks to the various far-flung members of the Williams and Barnacastle clans, with special thanks reserved for Daniel and Janna Barnacastle: to Daniel for keeping me sane, and to Janna for doing the same for him.

After that—still moving chronologically—I have to thank Paul and Dianne Seitz, for hiring a sixteen-year-old kid off the street even though he had no references, holes in his jeans, and all the social graces of a deeply introverted teenager (otherwise known as exactly the social graces of some kind of member of the lizard family, like a salamander or an alligator). Thanks, too, to all my coworkers at the Little Professor over the years, who, whether they knew it or not, probably found their way into my writing in one way or another, because writers are inveterate thieves, helping themselves to jokes or moments or silverware in equal measure.

Now we get into the meat of the thing: the people who knowingly and with presumably malice aforethought aided and abetted this book coming into being, none more so than Chris Kepner of the Kepner Agency, who took a chance on a blind query from an unpublished, unconnected writer whose initial correspondence probably reeked right through the computer screen of equal parts desperation and deep-seated confusion. I couldn't have asked for a better guide through the jungles of this industry, Chris, so from the bottom of my heart: thank you.

Of course, thanking Chris takes us directly to Devi Pillai—six-gunned editor extraordinaire—and her indefatigable assistant, Rachel Bass (hey, Rachel? Can you make sure "indefatigable" means what I think it means?), without whom you would be holding a much lesser novel in your hands today, one poorly structured and full of run-on sentences and just in general kind of a misery. The same goes for everyone else at Tor who in one way or another shaped this novel and helped prepare it as best they could for the cruel vicissitudes of the wilds, whether that was by copy editing, designing an awesome cover, or just making sure that Devi and Rachel had the resources they needed to turn a clunker into a beast.

All of the preceding paragraph holds true as well for Anne Perry and her team at Simon & Schuster UK, but in a more restrained, dignified manner, because they're mostly British (or adopted Brits, like Anne) and strong emotion makes them uncomfortable in an almost existential sense.

Now, I'm sure there are plenty of people I've forgotten, because I'm a terrible, self-centered person (holy shit, I really am a writer) so if you're reading this and you were hoping I was going to thank you: you definitely deserve it, so thank you. Thank you so much.

Oh, one more, so intuitive that it barely needs to be said (and since it's right there in the dedication), but: thank you, Sara. You were the first person who read this, or anything else I'd written in the past ten years, and in the decade I've known you you've been a constant source of inspiration, resolve, and grace. So thank you.

All right, that's it, book's done: put it back on the shelf (or power down whatever device you were using) and turn the metaphorical lights off on your way out—this world will still be here if you ever decide to come back, just waiting for you to crack the spine again. Because that's the thing about books, right? They're not just books: they're doorways, doorways and mirrors at the same time, doors that open onto new worlds, mirrors that reflect who we are in ways we never would have imagined otherwise.

So one last thank-you: to all the artists and writers who ever opened a doorway for me. Thank you.

—Drew Williams
November 9, 2017

Turn the page for an excerpt from
Drew Williams' next novel

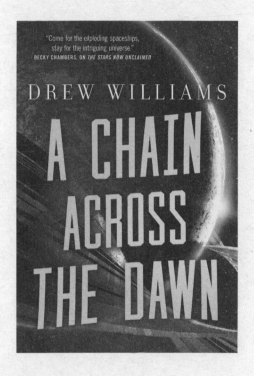

"Come for the exploding spaceships,
stay for the intriguing universe."
BECKY CHAMBERS, ON *THE STARS NOW UNCLAIMED*

DREW WILLIAMS

A CHAIN
ACROSS
THE DAWN

Available May 2019 from Tor Books

CHAPTER 1

The air-raid sirens were still screaming, echoing out across the golden sky of Kandriad like some sort of terrifying lament, hollow and vast and *loud* as all hell. The sound bounced off the concrete and the steel of the long-abandoned factory city around us, rolling out over the plains of metal toward the distant horizon still tinged with the faintest blue hints of the dawn.

There *shouldn't* have been air-raid sirens on Kandriad. Not because the pulse had repressed the technology for sirens, but because it had repressed the ability for anyone to conduct air raids at all: flight was supposed to be impossible in an atmosphere this choked with pulse radiation.

Except it wasn't. Jane and I had seen the shadows of the warplanes hurtling over the factory city as we approached by the bridge, dropping bombs and executing amateurish evasive maneuvers to wheel away from the strafing gunfire of the defenders' anti-aircraft weaponry. The planes hadn't exactly been modern spec—prop-driven, combustion-engine relics cobbled together from spare parts—but that didn't change the fact that they *shouldn't* have been able to get into the air at all. Something weird was happening on Kandriad.

Something weird *always* seemed to happen to Jane and me, but this was weirder than most.

"So we . . . knock?" I asked, shifting my weight from side to side, staring up at the massive barred door that was the one and only entrance to the factory city from the south. We hadn't seen a single native as we made our way down the abandoned railway line toward the factory—they were all hunkered down inside their converted city, being dive-bombed by impossible airplanes. The sect wars might have been forgotten by most of the galaxy post-pulse, but on Kandriad they'd never *stopped*, the locals locked in the same stupid conflicts that had led to the pulse in the first place. "Or . . . like . . ." I winced as the sirens came around again; I winced every time. I always *thought* they were finally going to stop as they dopplered away across the distance, and then . . . nope. Still going.

"We should probably wait until they're not having the shit bombed out of them," Jane said mildly, leaning against the railing of the dilapidated bridge and smoking one of her awful cigarettes. *Jane* wasn't fidgety. Jane never *got* fidgety. Taller, leaner, and in significantly better shape than I was, I'd seen her be more collected under sustained gunfire than I usually was making breakfast.

"Do you think that's likely to happen soon, or . . ." I winced as one of the bombers overshot its target, its payload coming down instead on the empty urban district beside the bridge—otherwise known as beside *us*. I was holding a telekinetic shield in place over both Jane and myself, and the feeling of the shrapnel from the blast smashing itself to pieces against what was basically a psychic manifestation of my own will was . . . not overly pleasant. Still, the shield held, and even if it hadn't, our intention shields—hardwired into our nervous systems—would have protected us. Hopefully.

I didn't particularly want to die on a bombed-out hellhole like Kandriad.

Jane waved her hand—and her cigarette—in front of her face, not so much dispelling the cloud of dust that had risen in the wake of the blast as adding to it with her cigarette smoke. "Doesn't seem that way," she said.

"So can we talk about *how* there are warplanes flying and dropping bombs in a pulse-choked atmosphere?" I asked instead. Since we appeared to be stuck out here, *underneath* the falling bombs, that seemed a topic of particularly hefty import.

Jane frowned at that. "I don't know," she said shortly. I almost grinned—despite the nearly-being-blown-apart thing—just because Jane *hated* to admit when she didn't know something, and a part of me was always a little bit thrilled when circumstances forced her to do so anyway.

Still would have traded it for "not huddled just outside a factory door, hoping not to get bombed," though.

"But how—"

"Still don't know, Esa," she sighed, dropping her cigarette butt to the bridge and grinding it out with her boot heel—though it wasn't like there was anything out here to catch on fire. "And either way, we're not likely to find answers standing out here. Go ahead and knock—we've got a gifted kid to find."

"I thought you said we should wait until they *weren't* getting bombed." As if cued by my statement, the air-raid sirens finally cut off, the last hollow howl echoing out over the horizon until it faded into the golden light of the day.

I looked at Jane. She was grinning. I glared at her; that just made her grin some more. She opened her mouth to say something, and I simply held out my hand, forestalling whatever smartassery was about to emerge. "Don't," I told her flatly. "Just . . ." I sighed, and reached for the heavy knocker welded to the riveted steel of the door. "I got this."

I knocked.

CHAPTER 2

In relatively short order, we got a response to our banging. That response was, of course, half a dozen rifles pointed at us from murder holes carved out of the sides of the high wall, but it was a response nonetheless. "Travelers," Jane said, spreading her hands wide to show that she was unarmed—well, to show that she wasn't *holding* a weapon, at least. On a world like Kandriad, nobody went *anywhere* unarmed, and the rifle butt sticking up from behind Jane's shoulder would have just seemed like an everyday necessity to the locals, no different than a farmer carrying a hoe would have been on my homeworld. "Seeking shelter."

"This city is at war, traveler," a voice said from one of the murder holes—sounded like a Wulf, which made sense, since the vaguely canid species had made up about a third of this world's population, before the pulse. "There's very little shelter to be had here."

"Very little to be had out there, either." Jane jerked her thumb behind us, indicating the smoking craters the poorly aimed bombs had blown in the urban "countryside" of what had once been a factory planet.

"How do we know you're not enemy spies?" the Wulf growled. I mean, Wulf almost *always* growl, the sound was just what their muzzles were built for, but I detected a distinct note of aggression in the low-pitched rumble of this one's voice.

"Esa," Jane prompted me, and I reached into my jacket—slowly, as the rifles were still following my every move—to produce a tightly rolled-up scroll. The parchment was as close to what local conditions would have allowed the natives to create as Schaz had been able to make it; hopefully they wouldn't ask too many questions about its provenance beyond that, questions we wouldn't be able to answer given that we'd actually printed it on board a spaceship in orbit, a concept that had receded mostly into myth for the people on Kandriad.

I held the scroll up, where they could see. "Reconnaissance," Jane told them simply. "Aerial photography of the enemy assaulting your walls from the north. Troop positions, fortifications, artillery emplacements—enough intelligence to turn the tide of the fight." Neither Jane nor I really gave a damn who won this particular battle, or even this particular war—whatever conflict it had spun off from, the fighting on Kandriad had long since ceased to matter to the galaxy at large, let alone to the doings of the Justified. What we *did* care about was getting access to the city, and to the gifted child hidden somewhere inside.

"You have planes? Like they do?" The guns were still holding . . . pretty tightly on us.

"Kites," Jane said simply. "And mirrors." *That* was a flat-out lie, but "we took images from our spaceship in low orbit, then smudged them up to *look* like low-tech aerial reconnaissance" wouldn't have gone over nearly as well.

A low sound from the Wulf, not that dissimilar to his growl from before; thankfully, our boss back on Sanctum was also a Wulf, and I recognized the sound of a Wulven chuckle when I heard one. "Kites," the unseen sentry said to himself, almost in wonder. Then: "Open the gate!"

The big metal gates rumbled open; Jane and I stepped along the train tracks, into the interior of the city, where the sentries—Wulf to a one, their rifles still held tightly, though at least not aimed directly at us anymore— watched us closely. Jane handed over the map to their leader, the one who'd spoken. He unrolled it, studied its contents for a moment, then without a word handed it off to one of his subordinates, who promptly took off, presumably for the factory city's command. "It's valid, and it's recent," the lieutenant acknowledged to us, his ice-blue predator's eyes still watching us closely, not as friendly as his words. "I recognize shelling from just a few days ago. Intelligence like that will buy you more than just entry here, strangers. Name your price."

"We're looking for some intelligence of our own," Jane replied. "Looking for one of your citizens, actually. A child, younger than my associate here." She nodded her head toward me; I didn't know how well the local Wulf population would be at gauging a human's age, but at seventeen, I guess I did still have a slightly "unfinished" look, as compared to Jane, at least.

"And why do you seek this child?" the lieutenant asked—not a no. Progress.

"He or she will have . . . gifts. Abilities. We seek children with such gifts, and we train them." All true, for its part. It was simply a question of scale that Jane left out.

"Train them to do what?"

"Whatever is necessary." *That* part wasn't exactly an official piece of the Sanctum syllabus.

The Wulf nodded his head, once. "I know the child you're looking for," he said.

Finally, something going our way for once.

CHAPTER 3

The lieutenant led the way, at least for a little bit, guiding us through the fortifications and the armories and the aid stations and the endless walls—the factory had been remade from a place where things were fabricated to a place entirely structured around war, and it looked like it had seen plenty of the latter.

Beyond the final checkpoint, he took his leave of us with instructions to head toward the "lower wards" and ask around: apparently the maintenance tunnels built beneath the complex, underground, where most of the civilian population lived, safe from the constant artillery attacks and bombing raids. Jane thanked him, and shook his hand—that curiously human gesture, for whatever reason, had spread through almost every alien culture during the Golden Age—and then we went our separate ways, the Wulf sentry back to his post, Jane and I toward the elevators.

We packed onto the massive lifting platform with a group of civilian volunteers covered in dust and stained with smoke, returning from work at the front. The elevator was operated by a clever mechanism of counterweights and interlinked chains: it's always impressive, what people can come up with when they don't have access to the levels of tech that actually *built* the world around them.

As the platform shook to life and began its descent, I looked around me, finding spots in the crowded elevator where I could peek in between the various civilians and out the chain-link cage that surrounded the descending platform. There are various advantages to being short; seeing above the heads of a crowd of people is not one of them. Still, I could make out some of the city passing us by, levels and levels of retrofitted factory turned into districts and facilities and homes. "Is this what it was like?" I asked Jane curiously, not really apropos of anything in particular.

"What *what* was like?" she asked, her gaze still set forward, staring out the cage around the elevator as we were lowered through the factory floors, the spaces once meant for building . . . who knows what, ball bearings or spaceship engines or anti-grav frictionless coagulant, and now retrofitted into armories and schools and churches.

"The sect wars. Your sect wars."

She shrugged, one hand linked into the chain, her fingers tight against the wire. "There were as many different wars as there were sects, kid."

"I know. I get that. I'm asking you if *yours* was anything like *this*."

"Some parts were. Other parts weren't."

"You don't like to talk about it, do you?"

"It was a long time ago."

"But you were—"

She sighed, finally turning and looking at me. "Esa, if you're asking me if I was born in a city under siege, a city like this, the answer is yes. If you're asking me if there was still . . . life, and people trying to *live* their lives, even under those conditions, people trying to normalize the aggressively abnormal until it was . . . just the way things were, then yes. It was like this. If you're asking me if I grew up in a massive factory complex retrofitted into a city retrofitted into the forward operating base of a theater of war, then no. No, I didn't. Okay?"

We were both silent for a moment; around us, the elevator still groaned as it descended, and the civilians sharing the space with us still spoke quietly, though none of them seemed inclined toward raising their voices, either, having just come from the destruction of the front. Finally, I spoke again. "I get that in your hundred and ninety-three years—"

"I'm not a hundred and ninety-three years old, Esa."

"Fine. I get that in your hundred and ninety-*two* years in this universe, you've seen a great deal, and not a great deal of it pretty. I came from a world that I'm not in any rush to remember either, yeah? So I get that. But a home's a home, Jane. It still . . . where we come from still *matters*. You don't get to just . . . turn that part of you off, make it into something else. Your life didn't just . . . restart itself, after you joined the Justified. Or after . . . after the pulse." I'd almost said "after *you* detonated the pulse," which would have been true, but also unfair. Not to mention a *stupid, stupid* thing to say when we were surrounded by strangers, even if we were conversing almost sub-aurally, thanks to our implanted commlinks. "You're still who you were, then. At least a part of you is."

"I'm really, really not, kid." She shook her head again. "Maybe you'll understand when you're older."

I gave a small smile at that. "When I'm a hundred and ninety-one, you mean?"

"Also not a hundred and ninety-one, Esa. We're here." The elevator shivered to a stop; the chain gates slid open, the maintenance tunnels before us as cramped and claustrophobic and silent as the factory floors above had been open and alive. Apparently almost everyone who lived down here was above, either heading to or from the front, or working in the various other areas of the city.

The locals shuffled out, still muted, making their way toward various side passages and the closets and storage rooms they now called living quarters. I mean, I get it, I was used to cramped quarters—Scheherazade's interior was not exactly palatial—but still: it was a tight fit, even to me. Jane stopped one of them, a female Wulf who hadn't shrugged off the armband marked with three diagonal blue lines—the universal symbol for "medic." "We're looking for a child," Jane told her. The medic stared at her face, her bone-deep exhaustion warring with open curiosity at the human asking her questions. "One with . . . talents. We were told to ask down here."

The Wulf nodded, then sighed. "I know the child you mean," she said. "I've . . . tried to help. He lives with his mother, in the subway line apartments. Find the ladders; go as far down as you can; ask around again. Everyone knows who they are. All the way at the edges."

"Do you—can you tell me what the child can do?"

The Wulf stared at Jane for another moment, then shook her head. "It's not my place to say," she answered. "Not my story to tell. Whatever it is you expect, though, prepare yourself for disappointment. It's a sad story. Like so many in this city."

Jane nodded, taking a step backward. "Thank you for your help," she said.

"Of course. Good luck. I hope you *can* help them. They deserve it." With that, she faded into the rest of the shuffling crowd, off to catch some well-deserved rest.

Jane looked at me; I looked back, then shrugged. "At least we know we're looking for a male," I said. "That's something, at least."

"True. 'Prepare yourselves for disappointment,' on the other hand, is . . . less than promising. And the boy still has his mother. That might be . . . tricky."

For whatever reason—most likely the activating trauma that most of the children we were seeking out went through—a substantial percentage of the kids we took back to Sanctum were orphans, more than half, at least. As an orphan myself, I kind of recoiled at the notion that it was a "good" thing, but the truth was it *did* make it easier to convince a child to leave their homeworld—usually the only world they'd ever known—if they wouldn't have to leave parents behind as well. Jane and I had managed it a couple times in the three years we'd been working together, but she was right: it did make things more complicated.

We couldn't offer to take his mother with us, either. That wasn't in our mandate. I gathered it had been tried before, in the early days of Sanctum, with . . . less than ideal results. It wasn't something operatives in our line talked about much—but it had been made very clear to me in my training that, of the things we *were* allowed to promise the kids to secure their co-operation, a place for their parents wasn't among them.

Still, a way off of a world like this one, most parents would want that for their child. That was usually our opening bargaining chip, and as chips went, it was not half bad, especially given the state of siege they were living in now.

We started forward, into the tunnels, looking for a ladder down.

ABOUT THE AUTHOR

DREW WILLIAMS has been a bookseller in Birmingham, Alabama, since he was sixteen years old, when he got the job because he came in looking for work on a day when someone else had just quit. Outside of arguing with his co-workers about whether *Moby-Dick* is brilliant (nope) or terrible (that one), his favorite part of the job is discovering new authors and sharing them with his customers.

Twitter: @DrewWilliamsIRL